My fingers searched the back of the drawer and felt something glossy. I pulled, and saw in my hand a colored photograph of a woman who looked to be about the age I was now. She had hair the color of fallen leaves. Only the woman's shoulders were visible below the head, she was wearing a scarf of blue and green, which reflected the color of her laughing eyes. In the background was the blurred green of a field. I flicked the photo over. The penciled initials *N.B.* were the only notation.

A cold prickle ran down my back as I stared at it.

I tucked the photo into my pocket. How peculiar was it to find this woman's image stuffed in the back of a drawer? Daddy had gone to pains to hide the picture.

In one hand, I lifted the plastic bags of trash, picked up the passport in the other, and went to find Tilda.

"Would you mind if I went home and rested?" I asked. "I feel a headache coming on."

"Yes, of course. What did you find in there? Oh, good, Daddy's passport. I'd like to keep that. How thoughtful of you. Anything else of interest?"

I turned so Tilda couldn't see and fingered the pocketed photo. The letters *N.B.* intrigued me. Was this just the acronym to remind our father of something important? Or did it mean something else?

Praise for Margaret Ann Spence

Margaret Ann Spence was a First Place Winner in the First Coast Romance Writers 2015 Beacon Contest, and a Finalist in the 2016 Author U Draft to Dream Book Competition.

~*~

"This bittersweet romance serves up tantalizing treats, as Camilla, a Boston caterer, finds herself up to her elbows in pastry flour, family secrets, and the big question—is she worthy of love?"

~Marylee MacDonald, author of Montpelier Tomorrow

Lipstick
on the Strawberry

by

Margaret Ann Spence

Lipstick on the Strawberry

Cover Art by *Debbie Taylor*

The Wild Rose Press, Inc.
PO Box 708
Adams Basin, NY 14410-0708
Visit us at www.thewildrosepress.com

Publishing History
First Champagne Rose Edition, 2017
Print ISBN 978-1-5092-1531-7
Digital ISBN 978-1-5092-1532-4

Published in the United States of America

Dedication

To John,
who introduced me to the beautiful city of Cambridge,
and whose love and support have been invaluable.

Acknowledgements

It's one thing to want to tell a story. It's another thing entirely to write a first draft, then beat it into submission so that the story tells itself. For their good humor and perceptive criticism, I owe thanks to my fabulous writing group, especially my beta readers, Marylee MacDonald and Deb Bauer, and to Judith Starkston for her practical advice. At The Wild Rose Press, the astute and patient Sherri Good guided the manuscript to its final version. Thank you.

Chapter One

They say if you can't take the heat, get out of the kitchen. But actually, when I heard the news, I wanted to crawl back and put my head in the oven.

Not really, of course. Figure of speech. But still. Everything stopped then and the world divided into before and after.

The first time Tilda phoned, flour dusted my hands. Mindy, scowling at the sliced apples, said, "If they really want something, they'll call back."

The caller ID had my sister's number on it, but I could call Tilda back after work. Pies took precedence. Orders were flowing in at Camilla's Creative Catering as the fall season began. I wrapped the pastry-filled pan in plastic and put it in the refrigerator, took off my apron, and went to my desk. On the computer, I created a custom menu for a prospect, hit send, and then hurried to the shower.

How clever I'd been to rent a space with a bathroom so I could change from spattered chef to smooth business owner. Dried off and dressed, my skirt slightly askew but with no runs in my pantyhose, thank goodness, I headed for the door with my hair still wet.

The phone rang a second time.

"Get that, Mindy, would you?"

My assistant held up her hands, covered in apples, sugar, and flour. The phone stopped.

"Why don't people text or e-mail?" Mindy slid her upper arm across her forehead.

"Check who called. I have to go."

"It's an art opening, Camilla. You could have just taken the order over the phone." Mindy's hair stood in tight curls and perspiration gleamed on her coppery skin.

I pressed the elevator button. "You know the personal touch is our trademark. I told the gallery owner I'd like to get a handle on the color schemes by seeing the artist's work."

Mindy was always second-guessing me. Let her get the clients then! My attention to detail brought the business. And to be truthful, the Anglophiles in Boston loved my accent. It must be the rounded vowels, the perfect English grammar. I had the tones of Downton Abbey's Upstairs, while providing the services of Downstairs, at least in the cooking department.

I waved to Mindy and descended to the street.

Under the blue sky of a clear New England September afternoon, seagulls circled. I inhaled the scent of the sea mingled with the gasoline stench of snarled traffic on the expressway and the pungent smell of Chinese food from the restaurants that bordered it. I took the car to a rundown part of town, near where the ships docked. Weeds sprouted at the curbside, while scraps of paper and cigarette butts mixed in with the gravel and brown grass of the abandoned lots in between industrial buildings.

A gray metal door stood flush to the street and opened to my touch. In the foyer, bicycles leaned against a grimy wall. I looked for an elevator and saw only a rickety stairway.

As I clambered up to the fourth floor of the old warehouse, I scrolled the phone and saw another message from Tilda. No time to talk to her now! I pushed a doorbell and heard it jangle. Footsteps sounded from across what must be a large and echoing room. A tall man in a streaked t-shirt and dirty jeans came to the door. He had dark eyes and a fashionably shaved head. He might have been handsome if he hadn't greeted me with a frown.

"You've got twenty minutes," he said.

"I know you're busy. Jake?" I repeated his name, but he did not put out his hand to shake mine.

"I told the gallery owner I always need to see the venue, and in your case, the art, before I plan the event."

He gestured with a sweep of his hand to a jumble of canvases piled in one corner, brushes in coffee cans, shelves bowing under the weight of supplies, a paint-spattered bench, and diagonal to a large window, a huge half-finished painting. The sharp, piney smell of turpentine flavored the air.

"If you let me see what's going in the show, I'll get out of your hair," I said.

Jake walked me into an adjoining room, a storage area without windows. He switched on a light. A dozen canvases stood neatly lined up against the walls. About six feet tall and almost as wide, they glowed with hidden color. The impression was of many sunsets, though an actual landscape or skyscape was just suggested.

I heard myself gasp. "How do you get such translucence?"

He beamed. "Yes, that's the effect I wanted. It's

actually metallic paint underneath the surface of another color, repeated over and over. Here, I'll show you."

He led me back into the studio and picked up a palette knife. He swiped it across a portion of the work I'd interrupted. A band of gold appeared underneath the red. He repeated this in several places, stood back, and observed his work.

"Now I'll let that dry for a while, and have another stab at it later." He moved about the studio, pulled out another big canvas that had been prepped in a blue wash, and removed a colored sketch from a battered file drawer. He studied the sketch for a moment and began to paint.

"I won't take any more of your time." I stood transfixed.

He muttered something and turned to his painting, and I took his lack of a goodbye as an invitation to stay. The muscles of his torso rippled under his shirt as he transferred the paint from can to canvas, deliberate as an athlete.

"Painting's much more hard work than I remembered," I said. "Not that I've painted since school." A sense of kinship bloomed. My work was hard labor, too.

He arched his back in a stretch. Perhaps he'd ask me for a drink. But he said nothing.

"Well, thanks for showing me your work." I stepped toward the door. "It's been helpful to know your style. I'll be back in touch with some ideas for the gallery opening."

I started slowly down the stairs and paused at a landing with a window. I had been amazed, transported to an inner space, a centered calm, by watching Jake paint, seeing how surely he translated what was in his head to strokes on the canvas. I could see the ships at rest in the harbor. It was a still day, so still that for a second the harbor below looked like a painting by Canaletto, the passers-by little figures marching across the composition, not quite like a camera's image but placed just so by the artist's sense of rightness. Then the feeling was gone, and I heard the noise of the city, muted by the water, pulling me back to the everyday world.

I planned the art show opening as I drove home. When I opened the door to my apartment it felt stifled and hot. The sun was lowering, losing its power to illuminate the dust on the wood floor and the sparse furniture.

The landline rang. I leapt for it, almost tripping on the coffee table. The sun had slanted across the wooden floor, making a yellow strip across the mellow oak loom up to my face as, lunging for the phone, I found myself sprawled across the sofa, my head toward the ground. The blood rushed downward, and I pushed myself up with my free hand. Sitting down, my head spun.

"I tried to reach you three times today," Tilda said. "Didn't you think I might have something important to tell you?"

"Sorry?"

"Daddy died."

****

When had he actually slipped this world? Had I been wielding the rolling pin, planning the menu for a wedding, or curled up in my husband-less bed?

Whenever it was, I had been absent. I should have tried to reconcile with him. Now I never could.

I should have seen it coming, should have realized after I moved across the ocean that I'd be away when important things happened in the family. But of course, you can't sit around waiting for milestones to happen. Perhaps, I mused now, sitting on the plane flying toward the sunrise—I'd had to shell out a fortune for the last minute British Air ticket to go to the funeral— I'd been so eager to throw myself into becoming the best caterer in Boston because it gave me an excuse not to go home.

Tilda and Geoffrey didn't communicate much. We were English after all. Someone described English expressions of emotion as "oblique." No one ever used the phrase, "I love you," in our family. That would be regarded as too cheap, too saccharine. My sister and brother kept their phone calls and even e-mails to Christmas and birthdays. I did the same. Not even birthdays, sometimes. Not that I wanted to remember mine. I'd be coming up on thirty-five this March, divorced and without the child Vincent and I said we wanted but never got around to having. One of my many regrets.

I pushed the button on the airplane seat to make it recline, but that gave little relief to the pain that was spreading from my head to my neck and on to my shoulders. The overnight flight was always difficult, but even if I had been home tonight, I would not have been able to sleep. I'd had to leave Mindy in charge for a week, and I had my doubts about her abilities. But it was more than that. With Vincent gone, Daddy gone, I had to wonder—it was a complicated kind of grief—I had to wonder why I was staying in Boston. Vincent had been the pull, originally, and Daddy had been the push. Love withdrawn from both of them had made me into the caterer I'd become. I worked to stifle loss by feeding strangers. But maybe, just maybe, all the love I really wanted had been at home, all along, if I could just unearth it.

Unearthing it was the thing, though. Love buried itself under duty in my family. And then, if the person you really love is first welcomed, then treated like the worst smell, what are you supposed to think?

"Anything to drink?" It was the flight attendant hauling the cart. A gin and tonic with a sliver of lime would be nice. In fact, it would be very delicious, and its taste would be worth the sink of depression that followed. Because I was sad at the moment, and I deserved the release of a good cry. But being English and stuck in the middle seat in the economy section of the aircraft on its way to Heathrow, all I could do was smile, and settle the glass gently on a paper napkin, then lift it to my lips with hands that shook. The drink sent shivers of pleasure through my palate. Maybe I'd order another, though I usually restricted myself to wine. One glass. Got to keep the figure.

I tried once more to adjust the headrest. Would Billy come to the funeral? He might. He just might want to say a final goodbye to the man who'd ruined his life. But then, maybe that was all in my head. Perhaps it had been for the best, really. It was an amazing coincidence, it occurred to me now. I was rolling pastry when I met my first lover, and I was rolling pastry when my father died. Not that anyone could anticipate that bashing a piece of dough with a

7

wooden cylinder would change your life. You trudge or hurtle through the days, depending on your mood, and you can't possibly know what ordinary actions signify until much later, when the pie is baked and the four and twenty blackbirds fly up to the sky.

Chapter Two

The sun streamed through the stained glass windows as we stood for the hymn. Outside, the college playing fields stretched away toward the river, wavy bits of green beckoning through the glass. As I surveyed the familiar pews, I remembered long ago Sundays when I ached to be outside and heard the soaring sound of the choir in my head again. Here, in England, in Cambridge, my early memories of this serene, ancient, beautiful town mingled with memories of what I'd tried to escape. I pulled my sleeves over my wrists.

The church was packed. Of course it would be. All Frederick Fetherwell's university and medical colleagues were here, and some of the neighbors, along with a few relatives. All dark suits and feathered hats. Could any of them be counted as my father's real friends? He had no hobbies. He was too busy, of course, with his work taking all his time. All those people at the memorial service, saluting a life of achievement, would any of those people truly mourn his death?

I shifted in my seat. Tilda sat to my right with Rupert, straight as a rod, and their two small daughters. Geoffrey stretched his long legs out at the end of the front row, alone, for he had never married. Frederick Fetherwell's children lined the pew in order of birth, and naturally, I was squeezed in the middle.

I hugged myself in my wool coat, although the day was not cold. "We're orphans, now, Geoffo," I whispered. "Isn't that the weirdest thought?"

Geoffrey squeezed my hand. "Dust to dust, Mille."

"Shh!" Tilda hissed.

From the corner of my eye I stole a look at my sister. Wasn't she the slightest bit unnerved? Now that our father was about to join Mother in the grave, we siblings, Geoffrey and Tilda and I, all in our thirties and still young, seemed closer to our own deaths than we'd been the week before. It was as if a barrier had been removed from the truth.

"I should have had the end seat," muttered Tilda. Her tight skirt hampered her as she tried to exit the row to give part of the eulogy. She stumbled and almost fell over my feet. Rose giggled. I turned to my niece with a finger to my lips and repressed my own smile. Squabbling over the best seat was something my sister and I had always done. Tilda seemed never to have recovered from the trauma of being displaced, a three-year-old when I arrived. Geoffrey, as the only son, would speak next. I had not been asked. I could have had something to say, but perhaps it was for the best.

Finally, the service ended, and the congregation spilled out into the afternoon. At the graveside, I reeled as the loamy clods of earth hit the casket. As the polished wooden box disappeared under earth and rock, all the emotion I spent over the years in conflict with Frederick Fetherwell mixed with grief and eddied somewhere in my psyche like a muddy stream. I raised my face to the sky, and as if sending a message, the clouds congealed in a dark mass and rain started to splatter on the mourners.

People milled, shook our hands, and kissed our cheeks. Then we siblings led the way to the college refectory, where tea and sandwiches waited. Murmurs pooled in the room. I heard many a "So sorry, such a fine man, a great loss," and smiled weakly in response. Within ten minutes, noise rose to the rafters as the congregation, released, relished the fact that they all still stood upright and most importantly, could eat. I could not help casting a critical professional eye over the catered spread. Not bad, not bad at all. In addition to tea, champagne was circulating on the trays, along with quite good canapés.

Still, I felt somewhat sidelined. Tilda and Geoffrey had picked out the polished mahogany for the casket, the music, and the eulogies. Tilda had made the arrangements with the college's housekeeping and catering department, and I was impressed with this show of support for the family. I imagined the money to pay for it all came out of the estate, or perhaps the college itself had put it on. I thought to ask Tilda, but she would tell me this was a crass question, not the right time to ask it, even if catering and event planning were what I did for a living. I took a glass of champagne and listened to the toasts, made by various members of the college community, praising my father.

Someone had placed a black-and-white photograph of Frederick Fetherwell beside the vase of white lilies next to the condolence book. Gazing at it, I was reminded that Daddy had been a fairly handsome man, with a strong jaw and a full head of hair. Over time that hair had faded to match his gray eyes. Without the photograph to jog my memory I couldn't really remember what he looked like. I thought of him in bits and pieces, like a mosaic; the way his steel-framed reading glasses slid down his long nose to rest just below his cheekbones, the warm, dry feel of his hand. Not that Daddy had taken my hand since I was a very small child. He'd been a man of moderate height, moderate girth, and he always wore a suit.

I turned away and saw the beaming face of my oldest friend coming toward me. Lucy! She was a little fuller around the middle than I remembered. Her green eyes now had tiny lines around them, but the warmth in her voice was unmistakably hers. I fell against her breast, and she held me tight.

"I can't stay," she said. "But please, please, come up to London and see me before you go back. So much to catch up on. Years."

I promised I would. I sipped a cup of tea. The heady steam of that full-bodied, strong-scented British beverage, served with milk and a touch of sugar, comforted me. England wasn't so bad, after all.

A woman with smoke-gray hair and a kind, lined face, came over. She kept her coat buttoned, as if she were on the verge of leaving.

"I'm so sorry, dear," said the woman. "Your father was a fine doctor. I worked for him for many years."

A distant memory flooded back. "Barbara? Daddy's nurse at the practice? It's so good of you to come."

"Yes, yes, of course. I'm retired now, as was your father. I understand you live in America nowadays."

"Yes." I didn't feel like explaining.

But Barbara was all smiles.

"I'd love you to come and see me some time. How

long are you here?"

"Not long, not long at all. Does Tilda have your number?"

"Yes, dear, of course she does. But here." She produced a small card from a handbag. "Do give me a ring. Come for tea."

Barbara drifted off, and I searched the room for another familiar face. They all looked prosperous, if aged, and I knew I should remember them. But the names drifted away.

A sensation floated by my ear. A warm, tenor voice. "Hello, Camilla. Need a shoulder?"

I turned and saw him.

Billy! He had grown, not old—he was a few months younger than I was—but up. I felt my knees go soft. No longer a scrawny kid, he looked, well, astonishingly attractive. He wore a blue suit with an open-necked shirt and a two-day growth of beard, the au courant style that mixed fashion with the just-got-out-of-bed look. His eyes were gray-blue and his light brown hair, worn as a teenager with a duck tail so it looked like tawny feathers, now stood short and spiky. He was taller than I remembered and not so much slender as fit. I noticed the ready smile, the dimple that had not disappeared beneath the stubble.

"My God, Billy. It's you. Amazing. How fantastic to see you! It's been years." I put my hands in his and squeezed. Their warmth jolted me.

"Your parents were good to me." Billy's voice was formal, as if he had rehearsed this speech. "Staying in England long?"

That question again. It always made me uncomfortable, exposing myself to my muddled life.

13

"Not really. A few days. Have to get back to Boston. Work, of course."

"Big success, I hear."

Hardly. I'd had quite the year, hadn't I, being dumped by my husband, and now I struggled to make a living. I turned away. Self-pity pricked my eyes. Recovering, I said, "Thanks for coming over. Tell me, what are you doing now, Billy?"

"I came up from London. I'm a software developer. It's William, now, by the way. I go by my real name now."

"Oh. Do you keep in touch with Geoffrey? He works in a museum in London."

"Yes. I know. We see each other now and then. But Camilla," Billy lowered his head and whispered, "I'd really like to be more in touch with you."

His breath warmed my cheek. I felt that jolt of electricity again, making me both magnetized and wary.

I heard my voice take on a flirtatious tone. "It does sound rather like you've been keeping tabs."

He nodded. He smiled. "I came to your mother's funeral, don't you remember?"

"Oh, yes. Of course. Thank you."

In fact, I didn't remember. He must have hidden amidst the crowd on that sad occasion, four years ago. There were many mourners for my mother, Helen Fetherwell, killed by an impatient driver as she motored absentmindedly across an intersection. Her students loved her, her friends were loyal, her children stunned by grief. Of course, I had been married then, not open to the current I now felt emanating from Billy. His smell was as I remembered it, the pheromones arousing me as he stood next to me in his suit. He was so

14

subversive. My heart mutinied.

"What are you doing now?" he said.

"What do you mean? I'm here with the family, being a hostess—I mean the grieved daughter." Of course I was. My eyes sought his, questioning.

"Have a drink?"

"Yes, if you don't mind." I gestured in the direction of a waiter carrying a tray of glasses.

"I mean, afterward. You and me. A pub. Lots to catch up on."

I felt that familiar warmth grip my thighs. I grabbed a corner of the white tablecloth and leaned onto the serving table, threatening to dislodge the enormous tea urn. "Well, all right, then. Just for a little while. I'll tell Tilda. Hang around till the guests leave and we can go out for an hour or so."

I felt a small hand seek mine and bent to pat the plaited hair of Rose, my seven-year-old niece. The child was tall for her age, serious and pale-faced, with big, round blue eyes. She looked a lot like her father, Rupert.

"How are you doing, sweetie?" I knelt to the child's level. Over her head, I saw Billy drift off into the crowd.

All this family. All these friendships of long, long standing. Although I had just told myself that my father was a man people admired rather than liked, and most of these funeral attendees were colleagues, still, they were connected to him by a long chain of proximity. Whereas I had cut myself off from the past. Well, it didn't do any good to dwell on it. I must get on.

Rose nuzzled my waist. "I'm glad you're staying with us, Aunt Camilla," the child said. "Can you tell me about America? Why do you live there?"

I brushed a pale strand of hair from her forehead. "I'm glad to be back here, Rosie. Especially to see you and Lily." I stroked her cheek. "Such wonderful little nieces I have. I live in America so you can have somewhere exciting to visit on your holidays when you get a bit older."

"Really?" Rose reached for a cucumber sandwich from a passing tray and skipped away.

Less than an hour later Billy found me and led me out into the cooling twilight.

"Where?" I said.

He grinned. "Somewhere they won't pester us."

My insides started to flutter just like they had when I was a teenager.

"There's this great pub near here. You'd like the food. Let's have a little more than those bits and pieces they shoved at us."

"Yes. All right, then. I should get back soon, though. Tilda will worry."

"You told her you were going with me, didn't you? Why should she worry about that?"

"Oh, I don't know. You know Tilda. She'll be in full mourning mode."

"It's just a drink and a meal, for God's sake."

I relaxed a little when we entered the warm buzz of the pub. I so missed pubs in the United States. At bars there, the patrons jiggled elbows aggressively and the point seemed to be to hook up with a stranger in the time it took to quaff two or three of those drinks with preposterous names. So different from the low-key friendliness of English pubs, especially ones that welcomed like an old-fashioned living room, with tables and chairs placed near the warmth of a fire.

After we'd ordered, Billy leaned across the small round table and smiled. Billy. I couldn't take my eyes off his. Here he was. After all those years of wondering what had happened.

"I want to hear everything," I said. "After you left us, where did you go?"

"You know."

"No. Not, actually."

"I managed, somehow." Billy picked a peanut out of a bowl and set it spinning. He did not look at me.

My heart was already hurting with the memory of his departure, guilt at my own good fortune and his bad luck. I heard my voice rise in a forced upbeat. "You seem to be doing all right now."

"I am. Thank you."

"Didn't you go to college or something?"

"Charmed my way into it, let's say. I could say that's what I did at your place, too."

"Oh yes. You did. My father had a way, didn't he, of picking up kids who needed help."

Why did I say that? Billy was no kid in trouble. Quite the opposite. He had been uncannily good at first, so anxious to please.

"I'm sorry, Billy—William," I apologized. "That was a terrible thing to say. I understand now about being an orphan, even though it's nothing like losing your parents when you're a kid."

"Let's not talk about that. Tell me about your life in America. How do you happen to be living there?"

"I met my husband, Vincent, looking at a Madonna."

"Ladies' man, eh?"

17

"Always, as it turns out. But I didn't know that then. Anyway, it was a painting, not the singer. I was in a museum in Perugia, and he was visiting Italy as well. You know how when you're abroad and you meet another English speaker, it's as if you're next door neighbors."

Billy looked blank.

"I'm sorry. That was tactless." I lowered my eyes to my drink. "I was studying at the Cordon Bleu in Paris at the time. Mummy insisted I get some formal training, even if it was nonacademic. Thrilled of course, to learn that Vincent was an assistant professor. He took me away from England."

A salad appeared in front of me, and I smiled my thanks to the waiter.

"Oh. And where is Vincent now?" Billy raised his fork, eyeing me expectantly over his steaming pub special.

I blinked. "We divorced a year or so ago. Our interests diverged, I guess you could say. And there was the baby issue."

"Did babies issue?"

I bit my lip and looked at the plate so Billy could not see my sadness. "No."

I glanced up to see him waiting for me to go on. "I suppose we were both too focused on our careers." I took a sip of water.

Billy sat back in his chair. He looked relieved.

"Do I smell of onions?" I said.

He sniffed the air. "You smell of perfume, overlaid with a little bit of vinegar and a good juicy dollop of olive oil."

I patted my chin with a napkin. "Vincent said I

smelled of onions. I probably did. He much preferred the halls of academe. One of his graduate students. It's an old story."

"I'm sorry to hear that." Billy's expression turned serious. "So now? Is there anyone else?"

He drew his hand across the table toward mine. I didn't withdraw my own but tapped my fingers on the tablecloth. "No. Oh, Billy. Stop that. You and me. We were teenagers then. I live in the United States now."

"I know."

"You? After you learned about computers, what do they call it, coding? What then?"

"Got a job in London. Making a life."

"With anyone?"

"Not at the moment. No."

Billy's shepherd's pie wafted deliciously. The scent emboldened me.

"May I?" I raised my fork and gestured toward his plate. He smiled. I pushed the fork into the delicious squidgy mass of the ground meat and mashed potato and bringing it to my mouth, rolled it around on my tongue. I stopped with a start when I noticed him watching. I had just melted back into the past as if all the years between had never happened. He leaned across the table and gripped my fingers.

"Camilla," he said, very softly. He reached with his other hand and brushed a thread of hair away from my forehead. "You're as beautiful as ever. More beautiful."

"You too. But we can't go through all that again." My voice was as soft as his.

"Your father's gone now, and we are adults. We can do what we want."

"This is not the time. It's too soon. You, here, out

19

of the blue, after all these years. I had to get over you because Daddy—" I stopped, and then said lamely, "I promised Rosie a story tonight." I dug my fingers into my hand. No. I was no longer a teenager. I had almost twenty years of experience, a divorce, and it would be really foolish to get into this again.

"Of course," he murmured and motioned a waiter for the bill. "I've got to go back to London tonight, but maybe you could come up in the next few days?"

"I really must get back to Boston. My business is pretty hands-on. And if I don't work, there's no one to pay the bills."

A mask descended over Billy's eyes. I recognized it. It was the mask he wore when I first met him, a defensive mechanism to hide his hurt. I put out a hand to touch his, but he was reaching into his wallet. How I wanted him. Guilt fought that instinct deep in my breast and collided with a wave of grief at all the loss, all the wasted years for Billy, my father and me. A sudden pain tore into my ribs. My eyes filled.

"Here's my number if you can get away." He handed me a card. "Text or call or just keep in touch by e-mail. Or maybe one day I'll come to New York."

They all say that. Say you're from Boston and people tell you they love New York. "I think I'm closer to London." I dabbed at my eyes with my hand.

He looked up and his eyes changed when he saw my face. He took his napkin and gently pressed it against my cheek under my lower eyelashes, blotting the spilling tears.

He smiled, and we both knew I would make any excuse to come.

Chapter Three

Rose and Lily scrunched up next to me on the chintz sofa and shoved a picture book into my hands. Lily was quick to interrupt if I made the slightest mistake as I read, but my mind kept wandering back to Billy.

"Excuse me, darlings, but I have to make some calls," I said as the story came to an end. "I'll read you another soon."

"Tomorrow night, Aunt Camilla?"

"Not sure, sweetheart. I may have to go to London, but I'll be back."

I climbed the stairs to the guest bedroom. The room smelled of furniture polish gone stale. On a pine chest of drawers crammed up close to the narrow bed a motley collection of evaporating perfume bottles collected dust. A window high on the wall gave a view of the neighbor's red-tiled roof and the top of a spindly crabapple tree. In the lingering light the clouds hovered, a mottled gray, pregnant with rain. I pulled a chair over to the wall and stood on it to crank open the window to let in some fresh air. A bird flew by, and suddenly I wanted to be that bird, flying over the narrow streets and the cramped houses.

To London. I wanted to fly to Billy. His eyes had begged me to come. His hand had brushed my tears. Surely, after her long day of receiving condolence calls,

Tilda wouldn't mind if I took off for a day or two? I'd tell her I was going to see my old school friend. The habit of subterfuge came naturally between my sister and me, but of course, I did want to see Lucy. There was bound to be a good art exhibition, too. Lucy and I could see it together.

God, Jake's exhibition! I saw him standing there in front of his canvas, brush in hand, racing to finish the work for his exhibition. How had Mindy handled the menu for the opening? I'd had a few ideas, but had just e-mailed the artist that I had a family emergency and would get back to him soon. Thank goodness the opening was not for another six weeks, but in the meantime, we had other functions to plan. After I'd found out about Daddy's death there had been a flurry. I called an emergency meeting of the staff, wrote lists and schedules and post-it notes, and saw Mindy's face looking both anxious and excited.

"You mean I have to manage this place on my own for a whole week?" she'd said. Ah, Mindy. The girl was competent, up to a point. Not so great at dealing with the kitchen staff.

I stepped off the chair, pushed it aside, reached for my phone, almost tripping over my suitcase, and collapsed on the patterned bedspread. Taking a long breath, I called my assistant in Boston.

"Hi! The funeral, did you get through it? Must have been sad, huh? Things are really, really busy here." Mindy rushed on, not waiting for a reply. "You caught me at a good time, though, taking a breather just after the lunch for the partners at the law firm."

I held the phone away from my ear. "Great, Mindy! You deserve a raise for bringing that gig in. Catering the partners' monthly lunch. Steady work. Love it."

"Thanks, Camilla, you've saved me an awkward conversation."

"What? Oh, the raise." My hand thudded on the bedspread. How could I afford to up her salary? "I was going to ask, Mindy, if you and Paige and Manuela are okay without me for another week. Family matters to attend to."

"Yes, of course. We're fine."

"You're the best."

Now I'd committed myself. I'd have to go see Billy tomorrow.

"That painter. Jake. He came in yesterday. Looking for you."

"Really? Why? I told him I'd e-mail him the menu and flower selections."

"I guess he wants input."

"Hmm. Unusual. In a man, anyway. What did you tell him?"

"I said you were at a funeral, of course. That you'd put me in charge and any details of the reception he could discuss with me, thank you very much."

"Oh. Good." Good? Why was it good Mindy sounded so assertive? I drew a breath. "Keep it low budget, would you, that's what the gallery wants."

"We're taking orders like crazy."

My stomach tensed. "There's that wedding we need to plan, and the bar mitzvah in early December, and those two fiftieth birthday parties. Then there are the Christmas parties. You'll be getting calls on those pretty soon. And I need to blog for the website." I pinched my fingers into my hand. "I'll be back soon as I can. Truly."

I ended the call and went downstairs, holding the banister carefully. I found Tilda and Rupert in their sitting room watching the news on a small-screened television.

"Would you mind, Tilda, if I went up to London for a couple of days? I want to see Lucy—may as well if I am here in England anyway, and I know you're busy."

I looked about the room to avoid Tilda's eyes. Despite its tall ceilings embellished with plaster roses and its white stone fireplace, the room seemed closed in with heavy dark wood furniture and floor-length curtains drawn across the windows against peering passers-by.

"Yes, yes, of course, Camilla, that's perfectly all right. I quite understand. One does need the comfort of friends at a time like this. Tea?" Tilda pointed to the pot and the flower-sprigged cups and saucers. The remains of a cake lay on a plate on the tray. "We just had nibbles for supper. Feeling a bit tired, aren't we, Rupert? Mourning's quite hard work, I find."

I poured a cup of tea, added milk to it, and succumbed to a cube of sugar. I sank into an armchair. The television screen flickered with images of terror and mayhem in other parts of the world, but here in Rupert and Tilda's house, time had stopped. I couldn't think of anything to say.

Tilda said, in a voice too loud, competing with the television, "Did you have a good catch-up with William?"

"Yes, yes, of course. It was lovely to see him. That pub is terrific too, very good shepherd's pie. I mean it looked good—Billy was really tucking into it." I scanned the room, searching for another topic. The mantel clock ticked loudly. "I'll give Lucy a ring in the morning, just to confirm."

"Will you stay the night at Geoffrey's?"

"Well, I hadn't thought of that. I was going to ask Lucy, actually. Didn't have time for much of a catch-up at the funeral. Anyway, I thought Geoffo might feel a little constrained, with his small place and his new partner."

Tilda raised her eyebrows. "I didn't know you had qualms about people like Geoffrey," she said.

"I don't. I just don't want to intrude on his new relationship. He told me about it after Daddy's burial service."

Rupert clanged his cup on its saucer. "Well, it's a new world, no one cares anymore and quite frankly I would like to have seen Malcolm at the church, show a bit of support for Geoffrey."

Tilda sipped her tea. "I suppose Geoffo was just trying to be the son his father always wanted, till the funeral was over, so there would be no whisperings."

"My dearest Tilda, you're being quite naïve," said Rupert, emphasizing the quite. "Don't you realize what half your father's university colleagues were up to? All the old codgers who live in college all their lives, never marrying, just like the old days when they weren't allowed to marry at all. But celibacy, my dear? Not on your life! Not then, not now." He turned up the sound on the television.

"Lucy will be happy to see you, I'm sure. I hope you won't stay there long, though." Tilda scooted her chair toward mine. "We do have to sort out Daddy's house when you get back from London."

"Sort out? Already?"

"Papers, financial records, that kind of thing. For taxes and so on," Rupert said.

"I see." Though I didn't see why it had to be done right at this very moment. I put my cup back on the tray and cleared my throat. "It's been lovely to get to know the girls a little."

Tilda smiled and Rupert too turned his attention from the news and beamed. "It's good for them to see you, too, Camilla," he said. "I think, before, the idea of you living so far away made it seem to them like you were some kind of exotic animal."

I smiled back at him weakly and thought again how Rupert, well-meaning as he might be, had a peculiar, not to say tactless, way of expressing himself. Good thing his work as a solicitor kept him in an office; he would be dangerous in front of a judge and so Tilda was lucky he had not tried his chances at the Bar. Rupert would have been a dreadful barrister, not attuned at all to the feelings of others. And at that I felt suddenly cheerful, confident that the subterfuge of staying at Lucy's would work.

Tilda hesitated, then said softly, "Poor Geoffo. Had to keep it all under wraps while Daddy was alive, but he's come out now. Pleased as punch to be able to. He says now he wished he'd done it sooner. He's been so surprised by all the congratulations he's been getting."

"I'm glad he's happy." I leaned over the side of Tilda's armchair to give my sister a hug. Tilda's shoulder was bony, and I wondered how she had become so thin. When we were younger, Tilda and I did look alike. We shared a perky nose, a thin face, blue eyes, and long legs that excelled in field hockey. We both had hair the color of tea. Mine was a darker English Breakfast while Tilda's reminded me of Orange Pekoe. I wore my mane longish, but this was because I barely had time to think about styling. I always felt a bit louche to Tilda's perfection, her classic clothes, and her sleek tresses that ended in a kind of slice just at the level of her chin. Tilda was more neatly put together in every way. But Tilda was way too skinny, and I—well you could tell I cook for a living.

Tilda patted my hand tentatively.

"Have you ever wondered, Tilda, how Daddy kept it all straight in his head? I mean, he was a doctor. He must have seen everything under the sun. Then he was a pastor as well. Those roles might have conflicted, sometimes."

Tilda looked impassive. "Faith and science. Two different worlds. People compartmentalize to deal with these kind of conflicts. You shouldn't take everything so literally."

Ouch. I stood up and spun around to the door. "I'll just get packed for Lucy's." I closed the door gently behind me, glad that Tilda could not see my blush rising at the lie.

Chapter Four

I ferreted through my suitcase for clothes. A coat would absorb the grubbiness of the train. Underneath—a skirt and tight-fitting blouse under a long cardigan. Boots. I hunted deeper through the luggage. No sexy underwear! I stopped and wondered what I was doing. Especially just after Daddy's funeral. Wanting to dress up for Billy, with whom I'd shared a bathroom and a breakfast table all those years ago.

A frisson of wickedness, delicious in its adolescent sense of daring, flushed through me. Billy. My first love. My only love? Maybe. The truth was, I had scarcely dated since the divorce. I was at first shocked and angry when I found out about my twenty-three-year-old rival for Vincent's affections. Then, when it was all said and done, and Vincent and I split our meager savings and possessions—no alimony, the judge ordered, since I was so young and employable and there were no children—I had to get to work to pay off my legal bills as well as to set up a household of one. For the past year, I had spent my days in a commercial kitchen, hair pinned up in a cap, apron festooned with spills, or dressed up in sensible clothes to meet with clients. For the funeral, I had brought my black, but I needed something more compelling for Billy. I ran a hand over my body, now curved at breast and hip, a result of endless tastings. Of course, I could go shopping in London. I rummaged through my elderly bras and plain panties and shoved them in the guest room's chest of drawers. No, I couldn't wait for that. I'd stop at one of those special lingerie stores on the way to the train.

****

The shops ran between two medieval churches and over a cobbled street that had guided traffic since Roman times. In the center, a new three-story structure housed chain clothing stores. At first, the din of shoppers and the tawdriness of most of the windows stunned me. I wanted things to remain fixed, as a kind of reference point.

The new shops, catering to students, sold clothes that seemed far too young and flimsy, but I picked out a skimpy black lace panties and bra set. I shoved my purchases inside my small wheeled suitcase and threw out the shopping bag, embarrassed by its label. Outside, across the market square, I faced the tall sandstone walls of an ancient college, where privileged young men had studied since the thirteenth century. A cacophony of voices rose as tourists, students, and shoppers thronged and browsed stalls that sold flowers and vegetables, cheese and bread. A fishmonger shouted his wares. His halibut and sole lay across melting ice cubes, exposed to the breath of customers. I wondered how he could keep it fresh all day, but he did a brisk business. A cobblestone loosened under my feet, and I teetered. Did Billy really have room in his life for me? Perhaps if I'd lived here the whole time the memory of Billy would have become part of my mental furniture. But he'd been banished from my sight so suddenly it was if part of my mind were a locked room,

29

labeled "Do not enter." The door had opened. Billy had looked at me with longing, and I couldn't resist. I steadied my footing on the uneven stones. A couple walked by, their arms around each other's waists. The young man was kissing his girlfriend's ear, burying his nose in her scarf. Encouraged, I hoisted my bag and walked to the train.

After the Oxbridge tones of my family, the polyglot voices of the people on the train startled me. Here on the train people spoke English in a variety of accents, some of which were very difficult to understand and a few spoke no English at all. No one smiled casually or said good morning the way they did back in the USA. I took refuge in the newspaper and did the crossword for the hour's journey into London.

Noise swirled in the King's Cross Station, where, just across the street at St. Pancras, the Eurostar spilled travelers from Europe. It was a bit too early to go to Lucy's, she'd be working her part-time job, so I bought a cappuccino and stood, sipping while I leaned against the counter, hoping I would not be shoved aside. This station really needed more places for people to sit. I spied an overcoat rising from a bench. My coffee trembled in its cup as I raced for the seat and claimed possession just as the occupant walked away. I shuddered. In the years since I was a child, the population had grown by millions, a global village that was not a village but an anthill.

I blew a little foam off the cappuccino and looked about. Near the huge electronic monitors that announced the trains arriving and leaving, people milled, their eyes searching upward to the screens, looking for their platforms, ignoring the signs warning about suspicious objects. England had been attacked on home ground time and again, my childhood marked by bombings by the Irish Republican Army. How had it been for Billy and his mother to arrive in England from Belfast, jostled and pushed at one of these huge, confusing, public train stations? They'd sought refuge, fleeing The Troubles—and his father—Billy told me, though he couldn't remember much about that. Knowing not a soul in England, they settled in the university town on the river. Billy's mother must have wanted the intellectual atmosphere to rub off on her son, eight years old at the time. She got a job as a secretary, and she and Billy made a life in Cambridge. A quiet life, a very different life from the one our family lived. I would never have known Billy if his mother had not become my father's patient. Nor would I have known him if my father had been content to be a physician. No. My father wanted his goodness to be visible.

I stirred the coffee, and the milky foam sank.

Frederick was first a doctor, and then, in middle age, decided to take Holy Orders. Ordained, he became a chaplain at the college. The audacity of it, really. To take on two demanding jobs, both of which involved people looking to him for answers. Maybe he needed answers himself. Or perhaps it gave him a way to express his sense of the divine without it taking over his life.

I took a noisy slurp of coffee. The foam adorned my lip and I stuck my tongue out to lick it. Daddy had always been very big on table manners; slurping coffee would have merited one of those pointed looks down the dining table. Not that Mummy was any more

31

lenient, but she didn't seem to notice a lot of the time. She was a classic example of what used to be called a bluestocking. Oh now, that was unfair. I finished the coffee and crumpled the cup in my hand, looking about for a bin to deposit it. How I missed my mother! My domestically challenged, brainy, plainly dressed mother. Remembering Helen, a warm ache flooded my heart. I wondered if it would be soothed by a pastry, and was about to get up and order one, when I thought of the lingerie tucked in my bag, and how I'd looked at my image so critically while trying on the lacy bra in the store. I was not the slender creature I'd been at sixteen. Would Billy care? There! I was thinking about him again.

Unable to find a receptacle anywhere else, I dumped the cardboard coffee cup in the Ladies' Room. Now I had to hunt for the Underground train that would take me to Lucy's. The plan was that I would "stay" at Lucy's. Then I had arranged to have dinner with Billy and would see how things developed. I hoped Lucy would understand.

Had she changed? I supposed she would be like everything else around here, the same yet slightly different from how I remembered it. Emerging from the Underground, I walked around several corners, dropped my carry-on to the sidewalk, and took a deep breath in relief when I saw the door. Lucy's tall white house, with its bold cornflower blue front door, signaled my friend's slightly offbeat taste.

"Darling!" Lucy's hug crushed my lungs. She led me into a hallway whose space seemed expanded with mirrors and ended in cream-carpeted stairs which beckoned the eye upward. I could smell something spicy. We went into a kitchen bright with pictures of Spain on the walls and a bowl of red apples on the counter.

"Come in!" Lucy said. "We've got a couple of delicious hours before I have to pick up Archie and Isabel."

The fragrance of allspice and saffron wafted from a pot bubbling on the stove and drew me to it.

"What are you cooking?"

"One of our favorites—I know you love Lebanese food." Lucy's eyes sparkled.

Automatically, I picked up a spoon from a drawer next to the stove and tasted, approved. But I could not help a spurt of envy as Lucy showed me to the guest room, its thick palest-yellow carpet and well-polished furniture reminding me of my friend's well established married life in contrast to the shambles of my own.

"Shame I can't stay," I said and then told Lucy about my plan.

Her eyes widened. She grinned.

"I can see you like a bit of intrigue. Adds a bit of spice, doesn't it?" I burst out laughing. "You know, isn't it funny, you and I haven't seen each other for years, since Mummy's funeral, anyway, and yet it's like we were still at school."

"We pick up as if you had just left yesterday!" Lucy switched on the electric jug and started making tea. She paused. "Something stronger?"

"Later. Thank you. It'll give me courage for when I meet Billy. But now I want to hear all about your life, Isabel and Archie, Hugo, everything!"

For the next hour and a half, we gossiped till Lucy said she would be late picking up the children. "Now remember, if it doesn't go well with Billy tonight, just get on the Tube and come back here. I won't say anything to Hugo, no need, unless you actually arrive." She winked. "The guest room's made up for you. If you want to come back tomorrow night, or whenever, we're ready."

"You are a darling. I'll just get on my way. And we're meeting tomorrow, aren't we? At the Royal Academy? We'll see the exhibition."

Thank goodness for mobile phones. I would never have found Billy in the tangled thread of London streets without his directing me to a small restaurant down a lane. In the warm September evening, window boxes of late annuals ruffled their petals, thriving in the carbon dioxide breathed out by the thousands who tramped by the buildings each day. The street was cobbled, the buildings eighteenth century, built flush to the pavement, and most were painted white. I felt a wave of homesickness. An English city street. Unlike anything I've seen anywhere else. Beautiful. Civilized.

But we were not to eat at any place so conventional. Billy had suggested I meet him at a restaurant attached to a fish market. When I got there, the smell from the sea-water tanks rose like the voices that echoed off the stone floor. Diners selected their own fish from the tanks and it was taken away to be broiled, baked, or fried. It was a nice trick—almost fast food because it was standardized, and the menu never changed—but the fish could not be fresher. The restaurant certainly wasn't up-market however, and I wondered at Billy's choice. The place was too casual for wooing, and I felt a bit silly about the care with which I had picked out my wardrobe. I could not regret the new black underwear I'd put on in Lucy's bathroom. I just wanted to make my attempts at sexiness seem less purposeful. I scuffed my boots on the cobbled floor, pulled my skirt down toward my knees, and mussed my hair.

But here was Billy, a little bit late, a little bit agitated because he was late. His chest heaved as if he had been running.

"You're hot. Your face is red. But I mean hot in more ways than one. You look wonderful." He smiled and kissed my cheek. "I can't quite believe all this. Us meeting up again. I've been thinking about it all day."

He squeezed my hand and longing overcame me. I squeezed back as a waiter led us into a cool corner, to a checkered cloth-covered table where two small squat candles offered barely enough light to read the menu. Billy's face was half in shadow. Our table was cornered by floor-to-ceiling plastic tent walls shielding the sidewalk tables from the outside. I thought them ugly and utilitarian, but now they gave the impression that Billy and I were alone in a soap bubble, the candle's glow sending back a rosy reflection. I touched my hair, glad I hadn't completely ruined it. Billy looked eager, his eyes laughing, with his tie-less shirt open to reveal the Adam's apple I had always found so attractive. He took my hand from the menu and gripped it in his over the tablecloth. I was for a moment too overwhelmed to speak. The evening was over before it began in a sense because we both knew how it would end.

"You came," Billy said. "Wasn't sure you would. But here we are."

"Yes."

"Any trouble with Tilda?"

"Not at all. She's very sad about Daddy. She told me about Geoffrey."

"That he's gay? You knew that, didn't you?" Billy laughed.

"I guessed. But no one ever discussed things like that in the family. I mean Mother always said loyalty was the highest virtue, and we mustn't gossip about each other. So I didn't."

Billy frowned. "Gossip just shows people care about each other. If you don't talk about others, then it's as if they're forgotten." He looked at the menu.

God, Billy, I never forgot you. But I wasn't allowed to remember.

"What's it like in America?"

"Different, faster. People there have a lot of things. Everyone has a car. Apartments and houses are larger—you should see some of the places I cater."

"Wine? Red or white?" He motioned a waiter to the table.

"You choose." I guessed that the wine list would be deplorable. But actually, when it came, the Portuguese white that Billy chose was light and lively and smelled of apples. The alcohol loosened our tongues, and for a while we chatted and laughed, recalling some of our friends from childhood. Billy was a mimic, and he imitated the ponderous tones of one or two of my parents' more pompous friends. I giggled so much I almost knocked my glass over. Then I stopped suddenly and looked down at my plate.

"They're all gone now," I said. "Probably our children will think of our ways as funny and old-fashioned."

Billy took a long sip of wine and looked at me

through the glass. "Don't you miss England?"

"I do, and I don't, if you know what I mean."

"No."

"It's harder in some ways. After Vincent and I split up, I had—have—no family there."

"I understand that. Never had a family after Mum died. Well, your family of course. Very kind to me." He held my gaze for such a long time I started to feel uncomfortable. "If you've never had a real family, then you always feel left out. Never understood how you could walk away from yours. Your family is here, Camilla, to state the bleeding obvious."

I stiffened and refolded the dinner napkin in my lap. What right did he have to question my choices? My desperate need to prove myself? I pushed my plate away. The restaurant was becoming noisier and hotter. Twilight descended and the lights came on. The smell of the sea-water tanks and the fish mingled with the swaying of the long plastic tent-flaps. It was if we were on a boat. Suddenly I felt seasick.

I pushed my napkin to my mouth, held it there, then raised it to my eyes and dabbed them. I resisted blowing my nose on the white cloth, but my throat clogged.

Here was Billy, lost for so many years, now found. But he was a stranger, too. How could that be? It was not as if I did not know him. We'd told each other our deepest thoughts, back then. But now? I didn't want to open up old wounds. Perhaps I should not have come.

"Maybe I should go, Billy. Or should I say, William." I lifted my knife, ran the blade over my fingers, feeling its sharp edge.

"Don't be like that," Billy murmured. "I know you

must feel displaced—coming back and expecting things to be the same—and things have moved on. It's the same everywhere." He picked up my hand, took the knife gently from my tense fingers, and ran his own finger up and down my upturned wrist. "I know how that is," he whispered. "To feel foreign, everything and everyone different from what you're used to."

How could I have been so insensitive? Billy, too, had been displaced. "Don't you want to tell me how you got on after you left us?" I said.

"No." He dropped my hand onto the table. "But I was lucky. I was old enough to have a sense of myself, if you know what I mean. To have some good memories."

"Are you bitter? You don't seem to be bitter, Billy. You seem to have coped with life pretty well."

"I'm like a tortoise," he said. "Hard-shelled. Kind of slow, too." His lips turned up in a smile, and his eyes danced invitingly. "Let me make this formal," he said, drawing out the word. "Lady Camilla, may I have the pleasure of your company, the pleasure of you, this evening?"

I leaned over the table, smeared a whitish dill sauce on my black top, crushed a dinner roll, and then kissed him long and hard. Suddenly the table between us seemed a quite unreasonable blockade.

****

Billy's flat wasn't grand by any means. A one bedroom in an unprepossessing high rise. Giggling, we climbed two sets of stairs, then he keyed the door, and pulled me in. He pushed the door shut with his foot as he enveloped me in his arms, his mouth on mine, our hearts speeding. His smell, the taste of his tongue, just as I remembered it. His breath, our breath, running shorter and sharper, as we murmured between kisses. I fumbled with his shirt buttons. He ran his hands over my arms, over my hips, and crushed me closer. His hands pressed against my buttocks, so my own hands were stalled at the level of his chest. I wanted to move them lower, to unzip his jeans. In the part of my brain that was still thinking, I couldn't believe the actuality of him, the strength of him, his muscles taut under the shirt I was trying to take off. He stripped off my cardigan and unzipped my slinky skirt. It fell down my thighs and rested on top of my boots, unable to slide past the leather encircling my calves.

"They'll have to come off from a prone position," Billy said, grinning, as he bent to kiss the top of my breasts. He expertly unhooked my bra and for a second I wondered why I'd bothered with those expensive lacy underthings. Billy wasn't in the mood for gazing at my lingerie. His mouth was caressing my breast and heading for a nipple as I unhooked his belt. Skirt around my knees, I couldn't move, but an urgent sensation was rising and I started to moan. Billy stopped for a second to kick off his pants and then picked me up and carried me to his wide bed.

We fell back onto it half naked. Not naked enough. Billy paused for a moment as I lay on the bed in my tights, panties, and boots, and then sat up and pulled off the left boot and let it fall to the floor. I giggled. Billy's fingers ran up my left leg, my left thigh, over my panties, and then did the same on my right leg. The right boot discarded, Billy turned his attention to my last remaining articles of clothing, and what was underneath. I arched my back.

Billy the man, not the boy. Stronger yet more tender, hands assured rather than fumbling, he brought me to the pitch. The moment. Such a moment, I wished it would never stop, circle upon circle of pleasure, rising to a peak. A huge jolt of pure joy ran through me, and my brain seemed to explode, to burst its bounds of emotional restraint. Billy and I, grown up now, able to do what we wanted, with no one to answer to. The thought that he must have had many lovers between then and now I pushed away joyously, with triumph. I was reclaiming him. I cooed and planted kisses along the side of his perspiring body as he twisted toward the nightstand and opened a drawer, pulling out a packet.

"Let me do that," I whispered and put the condom on him. We rocked together in the most ancient of embraces, thrusting and rising and falling in instinctive rhythm till we peaked and fell together tangled and sweaty on the sheets.

Afterward, Billy started to laugh, a big deep laugh of relief. He hugged me closer, and we laughed and laughed, like kids again.

"You'll stay?" he said.

"Tonight, or do you mean in England?"

"Both, I guess. But let's take tonight for a start."

"Mmm." I kissed him again, so I didn't have to answer.

In the night, Billy woke and went to the bathroom. I heard him and reached over for my purse, which lay on the floor with my clothes. Quickly, I texted Lucy that we'd meet tomorrow at the Royal Academy, and Lucy confirmed the arrangement.

As I snuggled into Billy's back I thought how he had changed, grown, but was still the boy in the way he laughed. The sex was different, that was for sure, better now. But he was Billy. It was not that I loved him still. I did not know that. But the itch had been scratched. It had been pure pleasure.

As the sun rose his lips brushed mine and I turned sleepily. For a moment I thought he was Vincent, but I opened an eye and saw his slim back as he sat on the bed, head bowed as if willing himself to get up.

"Umm?"

"I have to go," he said. "We could meet later—after work."

"I—I have to get back to Tilda."

"Why?"

"Just that I told her I'd only be in London a day."

As I said this, I had no idea what to do. But here he was, pulling me toward him like a magnet. I was surprised to hear myself say, "All right, then. I'll text her and say I'm staying on for a catch-up with Lucy—she'll organize a lunch with some other friends who live in London. Tilda will understand."

"She might be relieved to know you're able to enjoy yourself with your old friends."

"Or maybe relieved I'm not staying with her the whole time."

He laughed. "Guests are like fish, eh?" He edged himself over the bed and stood. "But it's never been like that with us."

"I always felt closer to you than to Tilda. I used to think it was weird then, but it's just part of growing up, finding out what you're really like."

"What we're like." Hope shone in his eyes.

"One more night, then." I lay back down amongst the pillows while his shower ran. I saw myself coming back to the flat tonight and cooking up a curry for him—and yes, it would be nice if Lucy and I could set up a lunch for our old school friends. I could stay with Billy a few days, see how it went.

But what would this signal to Billy? That we would be an item again, adult lovers this time, out in the open, not hidden and hurried? I needed time to think that through. My business needed a hands-on owner. People depended on me.

He stood beside the bed now, a towel around this waist. "You'll stay?" he said.

"I'll see what I can arrange," I said and lifted my face for his kiss.

He smelled clean, of aftershave and fresh laundry. I pulled him down and kissed him again. Eventually, he gripped my forearms and pushed himself up.

"I'll be late for my meeting. Call me. There's an extra key on the hall table." As he turned toward me at the door, I saw the disbelief in his eyes.

Nevertheless, not quite believing I was doing it, I started tidying up. I looked in the refrigerator for ingredients for tonight. Not much in there. A dozen eggs, which I sniffed and found acceptable. Bread. A carton of milk, a block of cheddar cheese, some pickles. A half-empty bottle of white wine. Not a vegetable or fruit in sight. The same simplicity in the living room, two chairs, an uncomfortable retro Danish Modern sofa. Over the sofa a framed photograph of Billy, kicking a soccer ball, surrounded by laughing young boys. I knew I shouldn't be nosy, but I looked through his closet, saw how he'd lined up his suits and casual clothes, organized by color. Billy was always neat, in contrast to myself. He would like it if I made the bed. I took a shower and looked at the time. It was still only eight thirty, and I had no idea what to do next.

There was no point in calling Mindy in Boston, it was three thirty in the morning there. I waited a few minutes and rang Lucy, who was in the car, having just deposited the children at school.

"Can you come earlier to the Royal Academy? We'll have a coffee first."

"Everything all right, Camilla? How did it go last night?"

"Great. But can we talk? I'll meet you in the café as soon as you can get there."

I walked on jumbled clouds as I made my way to Piccadilly. I shouldn't take Billy seriously. I had to go home. Although where home was kept slipping my mind.

I felt at home with Billy like no one else. That was the problem. At home was where I met him, of course.

****

That day, twenty years ago, when Billy had come to the door, I had trouble opening it because my hands were sticky with dough. It had been a day like any other, a dark afternoon when I trudged home bent under my backpack and felt under the secret rock for the key. I entered the house and the locked-in smell assaulted me before I found the hall light switch. Hunger always attacked me at four o'clock, and I rummaged in the refrigerator. I retrieved a carton of milk, butter and jam for toast, and peering farther in, I spied a couple of sad-looking courgettes, an old lemon, and some elderly apples and placed them on the counter. It was not my responsibility to be the kitchen's keeper but I had taken on the role because Mummy was always working or distracted, and Tilda had no interest, and anyway, this year she'd gone away to university. In the pantry, I pulled out a can of salmon, two onions, and rice. I could make a nice risotto, even a kedgeree. It wasn't much to feed the family, so I decided I could make those apples more appealing if they were cooked in a pie. An hour later, I was covered in a sticky mass of dough. It ran from my fingers and threaded through my hair. Mummy would not be happy that my school uniform, only partially covered by an apron, was striped with pale smears of flour. The doorbell rang. A boy stood there with a satchel over his shoulder. His hair reminded me of sodden fallen autumn leaves, his eyes were blue with flecks of green, and he seemed to be about my age. A slight mustache furred his upper lip, and his voice started deep and ended in a squeak as he asked for "Mrs. Fetherwell, please."

"I'm sorry. She's not here. I'm Camilla." I let him stand there on the stoop.

"My name's Blanchard. William. Billy. Dr. Fetherwell, he's been looking after Mum and well, she's sick, and so last night when he saw her he said she had to go into the hospital and that I should come here after school."

I put my hand on my hip in a slightly defiant position before this stranger. My father had done this before. Waved a hand, so to speak, in his role as what— savior?—to young people in need of a temporary home.

"Is it all right?" The boy sounded anxious. A hint of an Irish lilt lifted his voice. Geoffrey could deal with him. The girls of the family—not that Tilda was around much anymore—would be off the hook.

"Come in," I said, begrudgingly. And so he came

to stay.

****

"I hope I'm going to hear something really juicy," Lucy's voice tinkled as she took our tray of coffee and scones to a table in the clanging cafeteria of the Royal Academy. "Because I had to make up a little fib to get away from work. Told them I had to pick up Isabel for a dentist's appointment. What happened?"

"Oh, Lucy. It was wonderful. Just wonderful. He's so…amazing."

"You're blushing."

"Am I? I feel like I'm gushing. Like a teenager."

"I take it the sex was good."

"Of course. Aren't you happy for me?"

Lucy forked a scone, scattering it into crumbles. "I don't want you to get hurt, Camilla. This seems to mean so much to you, but do you know what it means to Billy?"

"That thread between us, it's like it was slack on the ground all these years, and now—boom! It's pulled taut again. After last night, Lucy, I swear it's the same for him." I gripped my cup.

Lucy's face remained impassive. "First love's as much about discovering yourself as it is about the other person. You both must have changed after all this time."

"I suppose." I looked down at my coffee. A slight puddle had formed on the saucer where the spoon rested.

Lucy put her hand on my wrist. "It's just when we meet people after a long absence, we go back to how we were then, the experiences we have in common. In everyday life, we behave differently. You've grown up,

45

Camilla."

"Have I? Yes. Of course."

Lucy's green eyes held mine. "Maybe in your case it's more than nostalgia. Maybe you're just homesick. We've all missed you. Why not come home?"

Near the cash registers, clots of gallery visitors heaved their laden trays and hovered, looking for a seat. The sight of the scones and the cakes, the pressure of the waiting people, made me push my own plate away. "Mmm. I need time to think. Time to go back and get working and sort out if I can still make a life there."

"Has it been good, America?"

"Yes. But it's been a challenge, too. I mean, moving to another country permanently is a really hard thing to do. Much harder than I thought it would be."

"I can't imagine."

"George Bernard Shaw said that the English and the Americans are divided by a common language."

Lucy laughed.

I looked into the distance. "So there's that. On the other hand, moving countries ups your game, too. I do really like it there. I feel different in America. It's bouncy."

"Bouncy?"

"Everything seems possible there. I just need to work harder."

"So. It's much more complicated than I thought." Lucy sat back and drummed her fingers on the tabletop. "Maybe you should take some time to consider. They say that when someone dies the mourners should take a year before making a major change."

"You're right. As always." I pushed my cup away. "Let's see the exhibition, shall we?"

We went into the crowded halls. Lucy rented an audio guide.

"I used to want to be an artist, once," I said. "Now I cook."

Lucy snapped the recording off. "You are an artist in a way. But if you truly hanker to paint, why don't you take some lessons when you get back?"

"No time! I have no time to do anything but work!" I stepped up my stride down the row of paintings. We came to the end of the exhibition, and Lucy said she had to go.

We hugged. I went out into the autumn morning, onto crowded Piccadilly. I wandered, window shopping along Regent Street. Yes, I'd go back to Billy's tonight. First, I'd find a quiet café from which to call Mindy in an hour or two. Then I'd buy ingredients for dinner, cook for Billy, and see how we got on in a more ordinary situation than last night.

The warmth of the sun sank into my shoulders. It was almost one o'clock, but the coffee and pastry I'd shared with Lucy kept hunger pangs at bay, and I wandered farther from the gallery, into Mayfair. My walk brought on a wave of nostalgia for London, its depth, its density, its millions of lives being lived intensely and simultaneously so the city vibrated at all hours of the day and night.

Nevertheless, after an hour or so, my tummy started rumbling, and I found myself looking in windows of cafés, appraising the menus posted on the windows next to the entrance. Here was one that looked like a possibility, small and unpretentious.

Peering into the interior with its red-checked tablecloths, I saw a pretty woman who looked vaguely familiar. Shoulder-length hair the color of autumn, eyes focused on the person across the table. She was talking to a man whose back was turned to the window.

I realized in the time it takes for a heart to beat, that the woman looked much like I did, long ago. I stared at the girl. Noticing my stare, the young woman said something to her companion, who turned to the window. I saw, before he recognized me, that it was Billy.

The blood drained from my face. I fled.

Chapter Five

"There's so much to do with Daddy's estate. I do appreciate your coming back early so we can attend to it. How understanding of Lucy."

Tilda topped a cup with a tea-strainer. Last night she'd glanced at my face without comment as I walked in the door after my journey. I rushed upstairs to run a washcloth over my pudgy eyelids. Then I helped bathe the children and read them a story while Tilda made dinner. It was overcooked, and I had to force it down.

Tilda couldn't have guessed my stupid fantasy about rekindling my relationship with Billy. What a ridiculous idea! Billy had wanted reunion sex, I wanted reunion sex. That was it. Done and dusted. The whole scene was too familiar. In that other Cambridge, in Massachusetts, I'd peeked in a restaurant window and seen Vincent canoodling with another woman. Rage and shock had shredded me. Yesterday was not quite like that, of course. All I'd seen was a girl sitting with Billy. And I had no claim on him. After an absence of eighteen years, I couldn't expect things to be the same as they were.

"What?" I raised my eyes to meet my sister's, but Tilda was concentrating on pouring the tea. My prim, do-the-right-thing older sibling didn't even know, about the history Billy and I shared, let alone about the candle we'd held for each other, did she?

"I'd like to get a start on the old house, today, if you don't mind." She handed me the cup. "At least just take a look. It must be sold to settle the estate, Rupert says."

"You've already spoken to an agent?"

"Rupert had a word. But he says all Daddy's assets must be accounted for, first. Then the house can be sold."

I laid my cup carefully on its saucer. Ah, Rupert. "All right. I can only stay a couple more days. But I'll help. It will be good to do something constructive."

"Yes. Stops us moping around." Tilda said. "You must be feeling sad about Daddy. I do miss him." My sister's hand trembled as she took a piece of toast. "As soon as you have finished your tea, let's get on with it, shall we?" she said. "We could get a couple of hours in."

When we'd washed up the breakfast things, Tilda almost pushed me to the front hall, grabbed her coat from the tree, and urged me to get in the car.

The old house. A double-fronted late Victorian on a side street. Bay windows bulged on each side of a black front door. The heavy metal knocker needed a good cleaning. A pot of purple pansies, crumpled and wilting, stood on the encaustic tiled steps.

"I haven't seen the old house in quite a while," I said.

"Quite a while."

"Not since Mummy's funeral. I wonder if it has changed at all."

"Ta-da." Tilda opened the front door, and a stale smell escaped. "We should get rid of these flowers. It's too hard to come over all the time and water them. But the estate agent says that fresh flowers will go a long way to selling the house."

Sold. A final chapter in my long letting go of the past. I scrabbled my feet on the encaustic tile. "Maybe a general tidy-up is more important," I said.

"Let's get started then, shall we?" Tilda snapped off a dead leaf and led the way inside.

I'd forgotten how cramped it was. I had an impression of being hemmed in by the narrow hall's pattern-upon-pattern wallpaper and carpeted stairs that rose steeply to the upper floors in a busy design of lozenges in green and pink. The threads were tattered. "Maybe we should pull up the stair runner," I said. "It's making me dizzy."

The kitchen was exactly as I remembered it. Neither Frederick nor Helen Fetherwell had the slightest interest in redecoration, or decoration of any kind, for that matter. The refrigerator nestled under a countertop. No wonder I'd had to scrounge in the pantry for staples as a teenager. I'd learned to cook in this kitchen. I leaned against the worn wooden countertops and looked through the kitchen to the back hall where boots and coats hung amid ropes of garlic and string bags of onions and potatoes in wooden crates. Swiveling, my eyes took in the smudged windows, the old wooden table, and its slatted back chairs. The blue and white striped mugs still dangled from hooks above the worn pine sideboard, whose lower shelves sagged with Staffordshire china in varying patterns. I examined the stove, which always seemed to need a more thorough cleaning. I reached for a cloth and started rubbing its smeared backsplash.

"We don't have time to do a big clean today."

Tilda sounded weary.

"Yes, but I can't help myself. Seems as though the housekeeper hasn't been here lately." I looked about, cloth in hand.

"She was due to come. But then Daddy had the aneurysm and boom! He was gone. The housekeeper called me when she found him collapsed upstairs." Tilda's hand gripped the newel post, her face pale.

I put my arm around her and again felt the boniness of her shoulder.

Tilda freed herself from my arm, walked over and picked up a flower-patterned plate from the dresser. "The china—do you want it?" she said.

The plate looked like those we had been using at her house. Clearly, she'd had no compunction about already taking what she liked. A sudden wave of impatience mixed with exhaustion came over me. "No. No, you have it, Tilda. I like plainer-looking things, like the Denby china. It's that soft green color I like. I love the old pine Welsh dresser, though."

"I can't fit it in our kitchen. But you—how will you ship it all the way back to the States? Maybe Geoffrey will want it."

"Yes, our Geoffo has quite the eye for antiques. Isn't he the success, bagging that job at that museum in London." I opened a cupboard and started pulling out old cans and bottles of mustard and pickles and putting them in a cardboard box. "You'll be wanting these won't you, Tilda? Waste not want not."

"I don't know what he does there, do you?" Tilda considered the cereal boxes. She sniffed an opened box and made a face. "Ugh. Throw that out!"

"Digital preservation, I think he said. Keeping

computer records of all the items in the collections. Being an archivist nowadays has morphed into being a computer expert."

"The modern world. Not sure I can keep up."

"Me neither. Though this house seems like it has barely made it out of the nineteenth century."

Tilda looked pained. She swept the cereal boxes and opened jars of instant coffee and canisters of tea into another trash bag. "These must have been here for ages."

"You could have started without me, Tilda." How hard would it have been to get the old food out of here? That would have helped with the smell of the place.

"Ah. I did clean out the fridge. That was a mess." Tilda sounded defensive. "I just didn't see why I should do it. Just because you and Geoffrey had your careers to attend to. After all, I was the one who looked in on Daddy almost every day."

Yes, I'd avoided that.

Tilda sighed. "Today we have to get all the papers, books, records. All the investments have to be valued on the date of death. Later, we can go through the furniture. It's a process, Rupert says. Can take some months. I'll just pop upstairs." Tilda was already at the door, her hand on the knob.

"All right."

"I'll go through Mummy's desk and office. It shouldn't take long."

My usual efficiency deserted me as I watched Tilda's thin back ascending the stairs. Within minutes she was down again, holding a plastic box.

"Can you open this? It's jammed."

I took the box from her and tried its snap-on lock.

It seemed to be glued. A kitchen knife stood in a block before me, I lifted it, and swiped the plastic lock. It snapped back like a jack-in-the-box, but no little toy man leapt up. Inside the box, a stack of floppy disks layered themselves in a diagonal pile. I flipped through the plastic squares in their little white paper sleeves.

"People store the oddest things in their cupboards." Tilda peered at the box.

"They may be important. Who knows? Let's ask Geoffrey to have a look at them. At work, he must have access to all that ancient technology. It makes you think, doesn't it, that paper storage is probably the best way to keep records."

"Yes. These can't be more than twenty years old and they've already become a mystery." Tilda slapped a post-it note on the box and marked it "Give to Geoffrey."

"I'll tackle Daddy's library," I said.

Frederick Fetherwell's study looked like Sherlock Holmes' receiving rooms. A fireplace dominated one wall, with brimming bookshelves on either side. Two mahogany chairs covered in green velvet sat in front of a cluttered desk, and a chaise longue took up the length of the wall under the window. Underneath, a floral pattern meandered on a faded carpet under the desk and ended in front of the fireplace fender.

I scanned the books quickly, and finding none of the slightest interest, tackled the desk, plastic bag in hand. Bills, tax records, files, I scraped up and put them in the bag. I found a writing pad and a pen and wrote, *For Rupert, estate materials*, slapped the page onto the bag with sticky tape and tied it shut.

I pulled open a drawer. Another jumble, pens,

rubber bands, stamps. Frederick Fetherwell's passport, which was about to expire. I put that aside. Tilda might want it. The drawer's companion on the other side of the desk held much the same miscellanea. I felt my armpits getting hot with impatience. How could such an accomplished person leave such a disorganized mess, yet leave so little impression of his personality?

My fingers searched the back of the drawer and felt something glossy. I pulled, and saw in my hand a colored photograph of a woman who looked to be about the age I was now. She had hair the color of fallen leaves. Only the woman's shoulders were visible below the head. Her blue and green scarf reflected the color of her laughing eyes. In the background was the blurred green of a field. I flicked the photo over. The penciled initials *N.B.* were the only notation.

A cold prickle ran down my back as I stared at it.

I tucked the photo into my pocket. How peculiar was it to find this woman's image stuffed in the back of a drawer? Daddy had gone to pains to hide the picture.

In one hand, I lifted the plastic bags of trash, picked up the passport in the other, and went to find Tilda.

"Would you mind if I went home and rested?" I asked. "I feel a headache coming on."

"Yes, of course. What did you find in there? Oh, good, Daddy's passport. I'd like to keep that. How thoughtful of you. Anything else of interest?"

I turned so Tilda couldn't see and fingered the pocketed photo. The letters *N.B.* intrigued me. Was this just the acronym to remind our father of something important? Or did it mean something else?

"No," I said and hurried toward the door.

Chapter Six

The photograph was a peel away. That would date it to the era before digital photography. I was just a kid then.

I remembered Daddy taking instant shots on holidays. I'd watched, fascinated, as the finished photo reeled out of the camera seconds after I'd posed in front of the Christmas tree. A shot of jealousy surged. Inside my father's desk, on top of it, or on the study walls, there was not a single one of those family instant shots or any photos of the family at all. No portraits of Frederick's parents, no family shots, no individual portraits of us children, certainly no picture of Helen.

After we called it a day at the house, Tilda seemed subdued, feeling its imminent loss, no doubt. As we drove home, I tried to get my sister to talk.

"What was Daddy like, Tilda?"

"What do you mean?"

"What did he like, what were his pastimes? What preoccupied him toward the end?"

"No idea. Maybe he missed working?"

"Do you remember seeing any photographs in the house?"

Tilda brightened. "Yes—Mummy had some on her desk. Daddy gave them to us after she died. Rupert and I have them somewhere. Geoffrey has a couple."

"You didn't offer any to me?" I banged my

knuckles on the glovebox.

"You weren't here. Go through them at home and choose one or two if you'd like."

"I'd like that. What about photographs of friends? Find any?"

"Not really, no. They weren't those kind of people, were they? God knows what they would have thought of networking, all that waving in the virtual air, look at me, look at me." Tilda giggled.

"No diaries or journals? You didn't find any?"

"Really, Camilla, what's got into you? You know our parents were always reading and learning. They kept stacks of notes. I did save our school reports, you know."

"I'd like to read mine."

"They're at home. Somewhere. Not that I had time to read yours." Tilda turned away.

She was lying.

"You could have. You know I was the black sheep academically."

"Don't be silly."

"You were the clever one," I said. "And of course Mummy and Daddy valued brains above everything."

"Oh, do stop." Tilda gripped the steering wheel. "Our parents didn't play favorites at all."

They certainly did. Of course, Tilda would not see this. But my chip on the shoulder was long-standing. I know I should not complain, but I could not get over a sense of neglect. My mother was of the generation, which, marrying young, was caught up in the first wave of feminism of the nineteen seventies. Girls only a few years younger, the baby boomers, I am told, seemed to take charge of the women's agenda, giving their older sisters the impression that they were wasting their time in child-rearing. They should be out smashing glass ceilings if not burning bras. And so my mother, my sweet, gentle mother, rebelled. Quietly. She started her Ph.D soon after I was born and finished it when Geoffrey was in nappies. Then she started lecturing in history.

A succession of au pair girls, rather than well-paid nannies, looked after us while our mother was studying, then while she worked. Helen's head was in her books. At first, I think our father was proud of her ambition. It was when he announced he was studying for Holy Orders in addition to his medical practice that things became sticky. He undertook a long regime of part-time study when we children were still quite young. Things got more difficult when Frederick decided to expand his goodness. He must have somehow felt that being a doctor and a vicar was still not virtuous enough. Perhaps his very power as an authority in both physical and spiritual matters set off an alternate response in his mind—that he needed to prove himself to God. So he suggested to our mother that they take in children who needed temporary care. Why my mother didn't object more forcefully I don't know. She had little enough time for children as it was. I suppose she thought her husband just needed to get the urge out of his system. Perhaps she saw it as a blessed alternative to having more children of her own. Our father had been an only child and always said he wanted a big family. The problem was he had little time for the family he already had.

Katerina Petrovsky had been the worst of his fostering projects. A girl whose parents had gone back to Russia for a visit and had been detained there, she'd stayed for months. She and Tilda and I had simmered with mutual resentment. Sharing a room with Tilda first, then me, Katerina had flung clothes on the floor, made a mess of the bathroom, and managed to make us Fetherwell girls feel guilty that we didn't all live in a cramped apartment like Russians did. Finally, Daddy had the attic painted and a bed set up in it, and Katerina had stayed up there, turning the room into a hurricane, till her parents returned. By that stage, even Frederick seemed relieved to see her go.

There were other kids in need who lived with us, their names now forgotten. Except for Billy, who had stayed the longest, and been the last.

Now, with this photo I'd discovered, I began to wonder if Daddy flagged his goodness in order to hide something else. A secret, not so virtuous life.

Chills swept through me. Why was I still here? I had my own life to live now, away from all this. Tilda and Geoffrey could go through the house without me.

Later, when we got home, I tucked the photograph under the lining paper in the chest of drawers in Tilda's guest room. Let it lie buried there to be forgotten.

Easier said than done. That night, just knowing the photo was across the room from me made me toss and turn. I wanted to know my father, not as his child, but as an equal. Who could tell me? Someone he worked with? Barbara. Daddy's medical practice nurse. At the funeral, she'd invited me to visit. If I didn't do it now I'd never find the time.

I fished in my purse, scrabbling around the usual jumble. Lipsticks and creams in tiny bottles crammed in a small plastic baggie to satisfy the TSA, tickets and passport, a hairbrush with shreds of hair clinging to the bristles, my phone, and poking out of a side pocket, a small card. I rang her in the morning.

Barbara sounded delighted to hear my voice. "Can you come to tea, dear?"

"This afternoon? That would be lovely."

It was easy enough to catch a bus to Cherry Hinton. On the way to the bus stop in the town center, I bought a bunch of dahlias in vibrant reds and pinks from a street vendor. Their cheery colors improved my mood slightly as I approached Barbara's small white house with its tiny front yard. Within my purse, inside an envelope, I had tucked the photo I'd found the day before. I felt it burn through the paper, the bag lining, and its leather. Disloyal my father may have been, but that was only a suspicion, and my own disloyalty in trying to pry it out of his former colleague made my heart bang with trepidation.

I rang a brass bell, heard its chime, and Barbara, smartly dressed in charcoal slacks and a crimson sweater, greeted me. She was a little stooped, her skin papery, but her eyes, wrinkled at the edges, were lively and intelligent. When she smiled she gave a general impression of competence.

"How lovely. Dahlias!" she said. "One of my favorite flowers. Thank you—come through."

I followed Barbara to the back of the house, where a picture window overlooked a larger garden, in which flowers, thousands of them it seemed, flapped their heads in an exuberant breeze.

Barbara gestured to a chair by the table, and after fussing in a cupboard under the counter, fetched out a tall vase, and arranged the flowers. On the wooden counter oranges nestled in a blue and white Portuguese pottery bowl, and a matching vase held tall branches of hydrangeas in a paler blue.

"I see you have lots of flowers." I brushed my hair from my face, wishing I'd brought something more exotic.

"I love it. Gardening. It's my main hobby nowadays. Getting ready to put in the winter veggies, spinach, chard, lettuce. Now, some tea?"

"Thank you, I'd like that very much."

"How have you found everything?" Barbara asked as we settled with our tea cups perched on little tables. She offered finger sandwiches and slices of pound cake from a tiered cake stand.

I took a proffered sandwich. "It's sad, of course, with Daddy gone, and Mummy too, but you know, maybe it's hardest on Tilda." I stirred my tea. "She saw them every week, if not every day. For Geoffrey, living in London, it was less often and of course, I was in America." My tongue burned as I sipped my tea, and I put down the cup. "When our parents were still alive, I felt there was a future, always. If things didn't work out in the new country, I could return. But then, things happen, and suddenly you realize you can't, not so easily anyway."

"I understand," said Barbara gently. "Losing both parents, one realizes one's own time on earth is short, even for someone as young as you."

"You worked for Daddy a long time, didn't you, Barbara?"

"Let's see. At least twenty years. I enjoyed it. Your father—he was an inspiration." Barbara poured another cup of tea. "Cake?" she said.

"Just the sandwich, thank you. It's delicious." The cake looked pale and insipid. It had to be slightly stale and oversweet.

"You see, your father did so much more than most doctors. Took a real interest in his patients as human beings." Barbara took a defiant bite of cake as if to prove its edibility.

To make my avoidance of the cake less obvious, I bent down to pat a cat which was smoothing itself against my legs. The animal's body was warm and flexible as a yo-yo, and the cat purred as I stroked it.

"That's Petunia. She's not shy. Do you have a cat? No? I imagine you're too busy."

"Being a nurse must have been a busy life, too. Do you miss working?"

"Yes, one misses feeling useful, of course. Getting up in the morning with a purpose. Tell me about what you do in America."

I told her about the catering business, gushing in relief to talk about it. "It's just what I always wanted to do. I suppose I never felt I was good at anything else, really."

Barbara looked at me. "What do you want, dear?"

"What?"

"Something's on your mind. Something's worrying you, isn't it?"

I looked at my plate. "I'm trying…trying to learn about my father. Who he was, really. He was so distant, so busy with his work. Now he's gone, and I'll never get to the root of it. I thought, maybe you could shed some light on his personality."

"What do you mean, exactly?"

"He was such an authority figure to me. I was a bit

afraid of him. I was a child, always a child in his eyes, and the real world operated way above me, in his head."

Now or never. I opened my bag, and fished out the envelope, opened the flap and placed the photograph on the coffee table. "Do you have any idea who the person in this photo might be?" I asked.

Barbara glanced at the picture, then looked away. She put her cup down. She regarded her sideboard, its mahogany doors carved with a pattern of leaves, for what seemed like a full minute. Finally, she handed the photo back to me.

"Your father was a good man," she said. "He did help people in a very active way. That boy he took in. Son of a patient of ours. Blanchard, was it? Didn't he live with you?"

"Yes." I stared at her. "Billy? Yes. He did."

"I remember." Barbara stood up. "And I felt responsible. For Billy."

My insides started to flutter. "Why?"

"Let's go outside. Get some fresh air."

We put on our coats to go into the garden. A brisk breeze swooped through, ruffling the roses. Barbara picked the dying petals off the flowers as we walked. I waited for her to speak. My father's life was something I'd wanted to learn about, and Barbara had suddenly switched the subject to Billy. Why? I couldn't see the connection between him and the photo I'd just shoved back into my bag.

I quickened my step and nearly tripped on a stone in the path. I didn't want to miss a word. This—this was what I had really come for, to hear the beloved name spoken aloud, to hear everything about the boy, now a man, with whom I'd spent the other night.

"Well my dear, they were both, Billy and his mother, patients of ours. And she was dying. And Billy had nowhere to go. I suppose I could have offered to take him in rather than send him to Social Services, but I was selfish. I liked my single freedom. And your father had a family life to offer Billy. He was a clergyman, too, felt an obligation."

"It wasn't the first time he'd taken in a child in trouble."

"No. It wasn't. So I heard. Thought it his duty, I suppose."

Barbara stooped to raise a fallen hollyhock. She pulled a piece of string out of her pocket, tied it to a long twig she found on the ground, and pushed it into the dirt.

"I always wondered what happened to that boy. Such a sweet kid. Did he stay with you for a long time?"

My feet rooted themselves to the ground. I couldn't move. My throat caught as I said, "He stayed with us a couple of years. Then we lost touch."

Barbara turned toward the house. "I just thought—I saw him at the funeral and I assumed you two were still good friends."

I felt my shoulders tighten. "I think I should be getting along," I said. "Tilda will be expecting me."

"Yes, of course." Barbara ushered me inside, and I put on my coat. At the front door, I turned on the stoop, looking beyond Barbara through the hall to a tall mirror.

"A lovely woman she was," Barbara said. "I always felt so sorry for Billy, that he lost her so early."

"Yes, must have been awful."

"And he never really knew," Barbara said, her voice soft.

I could see the back of Barbara's gray cropped head in the mirror, and my own face, anxious and pale. "Knew her, you mean? He didn't have a chance to know his mother as an adult?" I clutched my purse tightly. I had to stop talking about him or I'd blurt out all the pain.

"She was braver than he ever knew. She sacrificed—"

"As a matter of fact, I am no longer really in touch with Billy." I heard my voice rise. "With me living in America and all."

"Oh, I see."

I stepped out the door. "I'll miss the next bus. It was lovely to see you, Barbara. I'll keep in touch. Thank you so much for the tea."

I pulled my hat over my head against the rising wind. Rain dampened my face, and I raced through the splattering drops to the bus stop.

Chapter Seven

Tilda gave me a long hug as I left the next morning and made my way via two long train rides to Heathrow. I knew I was lying when I promised I'd be back soon. Maybe I shouldn't come back at all. The funeral was upsetting. I'd reconnected with Billy, but he'd only been playing a game. To tell the truth, Billy's behavior had not been the worst of it. That photo surely took the cake. I'd sat down at my father's desk and stared at it, a hand over my heart to still its wild beating. A strange woman stared back through the glossy finish, a beautiful woman at that. Even after talking to Barbara, I had learned little to put my flawed memories of my father to rest. Barbara had avoided answering my question about the photo. Either she didn't know or she'd changed the subject deliberately. Then I got so flustered when she started to talk about Billy and his mother I couldn't press her on the photo. Too bad. I'd left the unsettling picture in Tilda's guest room bureau. Whatever it meant to my father was wild supposition on my part. I should just forget it.

Thank goodness I had the window seat on the plane to Boston. I closed my eyes and tried to sleep.

Of course, that was pointless; my foot cramped and my neck arched into the headrest. I tried to read my Kindle, then the newspaper. Useless. Images of Billy kept popping into my head. Billy in bed, Billy naked,

Billy naked in bed with another woman.

Last night, as I was about to drowse off, I'd glanced at the phone. I'd been so busy that I hadn't heard it ring all day. I pressed voice mail.

"Camilla." Billy's voice sounded husky. "You left me holding the bag. Literally. What should I do with that carry-on you left at my flat?"

Hah! Unsaid was Billy's fanatical neatness. The bag would have sat there taunting him until he had permission to throw it out. Let him throw it out or let him not. The message was so curt. He never said, "Why didn't you come back? I missed you!"

What did I expect? I had indulged in a fantasy we could be together again. But Billy and I—we just had sex. Sex with an old boyfriend. Means nothing, never means anything. Let it be.

But of course, it meant something. But was the meaning in Billy, or in the familiarity of the homeland? From my seat, I saw the buildings grow smaller, tiny, and then disappear under the clouds. Was that island my home anymore?

I twisted my head on the seat's backrest, waved away the flight attendant's offer of a drink, and tried to distract myself by reading. The cramped quarters of the airline's economy section made international relations cozy, but not comfortable. I flapped the newspaper, narrowly avoiding hitting my middle-seated neighbor with the tabloid. I sighed, turned to smile at my companions in flight, and shoved the newspaper into the netted receptacle on the seatback in front of me. I was glad to be coming back to the U.S. of A. Without much of a past in Boston, life was simpler.

Chapter Eight

Mindy's dark curly hair frizzed rebelliously from under its pins and scrunchies, disobeying any attempt at control. Even with the window wide open to the warm September air, the stress and heat of the kitchen palpated when I walked in.

"I need you to keep up," Mindy shouted at Manuela, the Brazilian woman who did dishes and prep work. Pots simmered on the stove, and a warm aroma of tomato sauce hovered in the air.

"I work hard as I can," Manuela replied, her Portuguese-accented voice rising, then falling as she saw me come in. She paused, chopping knife in hand over the board, then resumed, and zucchini thunked into thin slices under her practiced hand.

I directed Mindy into an office. She collapsed onto a chair in front of a computer and fired it up.

"So much is going on," she said. "I've been doing the planning and marketing, as well as trying to direct Manuela and Paige—and that's a full-time job in itself!" She tossed her head, and her almond-shaped brown eyes looked fierce. What genetic quirk had given Mindy such beauty and such a bad temper? I forced myself, through a fog of tiredness, to listen to her rant.

"The phone's been ringing off the hook," she said. "Christmas parties are coming—have you thought of hiring another person?" She lowered her voice. "Paige is all right, but she's a bit slow."

As Mindy quickly scanned our list of gigs I sensed that she had enjoyed her brief time as boss. Why did she complain? Was she overworked? I have a bit of a blind spot there; do I even know what that means? The four of us, Mindy and I, Manuela, and Paige had been able to handle the work so far, with serving help from freelance waiters.

I started to stack the scattered papers on the desk, putting aside the bills, and saw that the bill pile was higher than the rest. "You've been great while I've been away. Fantastic, really, Mindy. But right now I'm just so jetlagged."

"Yeah, but that wedding is late October. There'll be a hundred and twenty-five people!" Mindy's voice rose, panicky. "We'll need four hors d'oeuvres per person, that's five hundred pieces, a hundred and twenty-five entrees, and the cake! Plus all the flowers. They want that French china line, too."

"We'll get it done. What did the bride tell you about the entrée selections? Are they back yet?"

"Late, as usual."

"We'll probably have to hire some temporary help. Give me a few days."

Amazing what only a week away did to any sense of organization. It exposed how much of my time was filled with marketing. Still, work was what I needed now; clients, to pay the bills, and busyness to numb my mind. I tried not to think of Billy. Best to forget the photograph, too, no point in speculating. I took a deep breath. I should do meditation or something. Well, work would do the trick.

I did feel a comforting sense of calm as I brought

up lists of previous clients, sent them a greeting, and invited them to call for their Christmas and New Year's parties. I contacted the Consulate, The English School, the art galleries, the private schools nearby. I hoped for referrals. I rang everyone back, e-mailed recipe selections, and visited reception sites to look at the kitchen facilities. I set Manuela and Paige to mincing and chopping and freezing and Mindy to sourcing ingredients. At night, if there were no gigs, I lost myself in cookbooks, matching flavors in my head, calculating costs of incorporating new dishes into the repertoire.

"We need more help, Camilla," Mindy said.

"I know. Maybe for the holidays. Part-timers."

"Well, ask Paige to do more hours! Me and Manuela, we can't handle all this."

Manuela was the epitome of diligence. But we had to keep on top of Paige. Paige's memory lapses had let many a simmering pot roar to a boil, but with her huge blue eyes and her endearing apologies, she melted my heart.

"I'll look at the books tonight, and see what we can afford." I grew warm under my shirt at Mindy's infectious anxiety. If Mindy was itching to take over the business, it was clear that she could not handle it, at least not yet.

Under the furious work pace as the staff prepared for the October wedding, Manuela's temper grew increasingly short. Mindy's hair curled like steel wool and sweat appeared on her pale brown brow. Amazingly, we winged it through the wedding with only minor mishaps invisible to the clients. Every day was a mad scramble, from six in the morning till late at night.

"My shoes are wearing out! I need a haircut and I don't have time," I complained to Mindy. "Look at this!" I pulled a stringy tress and examined it.

"I told you, we need more help."

I tried to do the numbers. Despite our popularity, Camilla's Creative Catering always felt on the edge of financial catastrophe. Maybe it was my management skills or lack thereof. If I had more trust in Mindy, I'd feel more relaxed. Her attitude was both pushy and lackadaisical. I was doing the books when the crash of a pan clattering on the floor sent me running to the kitchen. I heard Mindy swearing as Manuela strained to lift a pot of water that had fallen. Puddles slopped on the floor.

"Sorry. But it not boil yet. I'm okay."

"What's the matter, Manuela?"

"Nothing. Just clumsy. Actually, Miss Camilla, I worry. I'm pregnant. Feel sick. Have to slow."

I turned aside so Manuela could not see my distress. Yet another person able to conceive. How fair was that? In the middle of the Christmas rush, too. I sighed. We'd just have to hire some more helpers, give Manuela more time off. But for now, I should sound enthusiastic!

I hugged Manuela. "That's lovely news for you and your husband. Do you want to take a little break? Work sitting down?"

"All right, for a few minutes. Eat crackers." Manuela pulled a chair from a corner and some crackers from a sleeve she kept in her purse. She sat, put her feet out in front of her, and ate hungrily.

How long could Manuela keep up the pace as her pregnancy progressed? Even if she worked to her due date, she couldn't be on her feet all day. Someone had to replace her, at least part-time.

I patted Manuela on the shoulder. "Rest, for fifteen minutes. Then let Mindy lift the heavy pots." I waved a hand in Mindy's direction, toward the office.

"We do need more help," I said, closing the door. Mindy did a high five.

It did not take long for the help-wanted advertisement to yield results. Many candidates looked unpromising, but one day a girl with pink and green hair, dripping with metal in her ears and nose, showed up.

"I'm Hannah," she said. "I'm an art student, do photography. I want to be a food stylist." She ran a hand through her hair, showing a tattooed wrist, from which dangled heavy bracelets.

"Can you cook? Most food stylists have culinary training," I said. "We're caterers, not in advertising."

"Yeah. It's hard to get a foot in the door in advertising. I need a part-time job now. I've waitressed, and I've worked in a bakery. A patisserie, actually."

"I ask my staff to cover their hair and take off their jewelry while they're cooking. Health regulations." I fingered my own hair, which could do with a cut. I wondered how anyone had time to color it so adventurously. I shook my head and tried to focus on the extraordinary girl who stood before me with a camera and a portfolio.

"I've looked at your website," Hannah was saying. "Maybe I could help it with my photos."

"Oh?"

"It's not that there's anything wrong with it, but it just doesn't zing. There are things you can do to food to make it look luscious."

"My food is luscious."

"I'm sure. I'm just talking about what it looks like in a photo."

"Let's see what you've done, then."

Hannah opened her portfolio, and I gasped. The food looked so good it was almost sexy. Tomatoes red and so ripe that little beads of liquid balanced on their rounded shoulders. Meat seared just so, leathery on the outside, pink tending to crimson inside, nestled on top of a glistening bed of arugula.

"You're so young to be so good," I said, almost under my breath. "Here." I gave Hannah a plate, glasses, a place setting. "What can you do with that?"

Hannah shook her multi-colored hair, and said, "What about that cake? That looks good."

"You want a piece?"

"Yes, to shoot it." She grabbed the cake, set it on the plate, then dug into her satchel and brought out a can of hairspray.

"What do you think you are doing?" I put my hand out to snatch the plate away.

Splurt. The girl had spritzed the cake slice with hair spray. "That will make it look fresher," she said.

A sheen enveloped the cake, making its icing look more delectable, its chocolate color deeper.

"What else can you do?"

Hannah picked up a couple of strawberries from a carton on the counter. They were almost out of season, but I had found a strawberry farmer in northern Maine who grew the Quinault variety, a godsend for cantankerous clients who insisted on fruits not seasonally available.

Hannah, however, seemed pleased at the slightly unripe strawberry. Turning one over, she ran a finger over a green part on its side. She fished a lipstick out of a plastic baggie and wiped it over the fruit. It shone.

"Amazing! I could use your help," I told her. A spurt of worry made me add, "On a temporary basis of course. See how it goes."

I asked her to take pictures of cakes, just to start. Then, some of our place settings. Camilla's Creative Catering rented out its own line of French-inspired dishes and linens. I bought them wholesale, but I also collected my own. I loved wine goblets, the weight and heft of them, delicate yet strong. A goblet and a plate could take many moods. If a bride wanted a wedding in a barn, we improvised by wrapping straw around the napkin as a holder, or if the society matron held a dinner, a thin slip of silver would do the job. Hannah's photographs of crystal and flowers, of a bride and groom dancing in the distance, the veil swirling in the dusk, as well as cakes, pastries, and steaming pies, made something new of these everyday things.

The pictures went on Camilla's Creative Catering website. And orders flowed in. I hired Hannah as a permanent, part-time employee.

Chapter Nine

All October I worked, trying not to think of Billy, not really succeeding. On weekends, after the gigs were over, I sat with my laptop and a cup of tea and fired up the social media sites. I stalked Billy. Trying to get a glimpse of his face, a mention of his private life. I found nothing but the strictest professionalism. Billy, a web developer, of all people, would not be so stupid as to leave a potentially damaging electronic trail. The silence left a hollow in my stomach. I wondered if I should contact him. Should I lie, tell him that a work emergency made me return without saying goodbye? Should I send him a tart note, implying that I knew he'd just wanted a one-night stand? Pretend that I, too, only had that in mind? I had wanted that, I believed then, but now I wanted more. Sometimes I had to bite my nails to stop myself sending him a message. Time, I told myself. In time I will get over the stupid fantasy that Billy and I could be together again. I should really move on.

And then the calendar rounded into November, the end of the year was in sight, and Jake's party loomed.

A gallery opening is usually a fairly small affair. I calculated and said to Mindy, "We'll just do wine, more white than red, and keep the hors d'oeuvres simple. You don't want them to be squashed against the paintings in the throng of people."

The exhibition was to be held at a fancy art gallery on Newbury Street, and I wanted to make the opening reception memorable, even though I barely knew Jake. I remembered the thrill I'd felt when I saw his work at his cluttered studio. Then, later that afternoon, the phone call had come telling of Daddy's death. So perhaps that day had a meaning for me that I only imagined it had for Jake.

The evening came. A Friday, cold but with the faintly warmer hint of snow in the air. As an early dark started to settle on the city, the metallic odor of coming precipitation infused the air. I hustled the wait staff to bring in the baskets and trays of food through the back door of the gallery kitchenette. I kept a waiter roster, mostly students and others who needed extra cash. Especially around the holidays there was no shortage of people who wanted to work, women with families, real estate agents, artists, musicians, and teachers, mostly. I hired men to handle the bar, because it was heavy work and because every now and then a guest could get out of hand.

The gallery owner, a thin woman dressed in black from head to toe, with a single, bright, patterned scarf to break the monotony, an outfit chosen, I guessed, to be both unobtrusive and singular, greeted us crisply and directed the workers to set the food out on long black-clothed tables at the back of the gallery space.

Jake, clean-shaven, in a white shirt open at the collar, a subtly patterned single-buttoned jacket, and pale tapered pants, appeared. He looked slightly uncomfortable in the dress-up clothes, but a grin spread over his face when he saw me, and he came over.

It might have been my imagination, but it seemed

his gaze fell to my ring-less left hand as he came near.

"Spread looks great. Thank you," he said and shook my hand.

I smiled. I was indeed proud of the antipasto platters, the sweet potatoes baked into rounds and topped with a miso and tahini filling, the hard cheeses, the crispy crackers, the hors d'oeuvres nestled in little caches of kale, tucked between spears of spring onion.

"Am I imagining it"—Jake picked up a celery stick and placed it next to a leaf of kale, whose color curled from mauve to a pale raspberry red—"or did you try to pick up the colors in the paintings?"

"Only you would notice that!" I laughed. "But I have to run. Be back to clean up. And you've got to go sell these paintings!"

He had noticed my extra care. And he seemed happy and much more pleasant than when we'd first met. I strode to the front of the gallery, giving the walls a quick survey. He followed me. A shiver of pleasure shimmied up my spine. Jake's luminous canvases beckoned the viewer into their depths in an extraordinary communion with their creator.

"It's wonderful," I breathed.

He leaned toward me and said, "Hey, wish me luck. I'll be here when you get back."

"I'm so sorry I have to rush off. We're so short-staffed." I regretted I'd taken on another job this evening. "I'll come back as quickly as I can. I want to see how it all goes. You know I love your work."

As I drove to the next appointment it started to sleet. The pelting ice hurtled itself almost sideways at the home-hurrying pedestrians, turning faces pink, smashing into inadequate coats. Would the guests invited to Jake's opening actually come? It was a night to be home in front of a fire. I hoped people would brave the weather. Not only for Jake's sake but for mine. I usually got a couple of referrals from public events such as these.

I imagined the guests bursting through the gallery doors. They'd thrust hastily folded umbrellas into tall cylinders, hang their dripping coats on a portable rack, and enter the soaring space of the white-walled art gallery, surrounded by the roar of chatter and clattering boots. Would the harried art-lovers respond to Jake's paintings as I had?

Now I had to stop at my own catering kitchen, pick up Mindy and more food, and the sleet had made me late. When I arrived, running through the freezing ice-rain to the kitchen, Mindy was there, waiting with the filled trays and baskets, and we bundled it all into the van. In Brookline, we set up a cocktail buffet in a huge, showy house. By the time we settled the food containers on the granite counters, set pots on the restaurant-style stove so spanky clean it looked seldom used, and resolved a mini-crisis when the icemaker shut down, it was seven o'clock. I needed to get back to the gallery in the city to supervise clean up there by seven-thirty.

My hands were damp with sweat as I tried to park in the alley behind Newbury Street. I almost knocked down some trash cans as I backed and filled into the parking space, my vision obscured by the driving sleet. As I entered the back of the gallery I heard a low hum of voices. Guests were still here! I hurried in and found Jake talking animatedly with an expensively dressed couple. The gallery owner hovered around, looking pleased.

Over by the bar, the tenders were piling bottles into cartons and glasses into crates. On the smeared black tablecloths the cheese was a matted mess, the sweet potato cakes were reduced to crumbs, and half a dozen meat pies littered the table. I made a few notes on the phone—as always I noted what was popular, what was left uneaten. I looked up to see Jake standing there with a grin on his face.

"Did it go well?" I asked.

"I think so. Very well. Sold four paintings tonight."

"That's amazing. At least I think it is. I'm not sure how these things work."

"Your food. Incredible. Looked incredible anyway. Not that I had any, I was too busy talking, but people said. Come to think of it, I'm starving. Can we have dinner?"

"You mean now? Tonight?" I gestured helplessly at the mess on the tables and flapped open a big black trash bag. I waved to one of my freelancers who was collecting glasses and pointed at the bag. "I do have another gig in Brookline. I'll have to take the van to collect those folks and all the trash about ten."

"So? We have a couple hours."

"All right. Let's get this stuff packed up and we'll get these people back home. You have a car?"

"Left it at home and came on the T. Hoped I might be doing a little celebratory drinking, actually."

"All right, come with me in the van."

"Deal. I'll just finish up here while you're doing that."

I noticed Jake's tall and confident posture as he strode back to the patrons and talked some more. It looked as though he was making another sale.

All of a sudden a clatter sounded at the front door. It opened, and two people tumbled in, obviously not very sober, and very, very wet.

"Sorry we're late for your opening, Jake," the man said. "Can we take you to dinner to make up?"

Jake looked discomfited. "Guys, the opening was two hours ago." Then he brightened, turned to me, introduced his friends and said, "We could all go to dinner if you like."

"No, you go ahead, really. I'm really in the middle of two jobs tonight," I said. For a brief moment I wondered if I should put pleasure above work but crushed the wish. "Some other time, I hope," I said, looking at the floor.

Jake's shoulders slumped. "Okay. Whatever," he said. He turned away.

"Wait!" I said. What was I doing, turning down the invitation of a perfectly attractive man? "If you come in the van with me till I get everyone back, then we could go out. What do you feel like? I know this Irish pub, Sullivan's Bar? How about that?"

"Sure." He grinned. "David, Melanie, meet you there, at Sullivan's. Go ahead and eat. We'll be along a bit later."

I pointed my workers in the direction of the van.

Jake helped us unpack. Lifting, sorting, it all flowed naturally from his years of physical work at his huge canvases, I guessed. I could see his pleasure in it; it must have released the tension of wondering if his paintings would sell. We ran a dishwasher load, then went together to pick up Mindy at the other party.

Mindy raised her eyebrows at me when she saw

Jake. She squeezed in next to him beside the pots and baskets and crates. Was I imagining it from my view in the driver's mirror, or did she push against his trim body in the crowded back seat? I couldn't see properly, had to concentrate on the slick road. But I heard her. She chatted like a sparrow; the cocktail party had gone well. Jake seemed to enjoy every minute of the ride back and the second round of clearing up of the kitchen. He was adept at unloading the washer and reaching into the high cabinets. He ran a finger down the stainless steel counter and smiled.

"I'd like one of these in my studio," he said, and I felt flattered; he seemed to imply I was an artist like him.

Mindy kept tidying, delayed putting on her coat, seemingly reluctant to leave. I told her we had another busy day tomorrow, and she left the building, glancing behind her, mouth in a slight pout.

Finally, Jake and I arrived at Sullivan's Bar.

The bar echoed with noise amplified by the brick walls and metal bar. My head started to throb, but I tried not to let it destroy the evening. We sat at wooden tables and ate hamburgers washed down with pints of beer, and Melanie and David talked nonsense over the roar. I didn't learn much about Jake that night, just sat there, tired and enjoying the happy camaraderie.

"So sorry, I just have to go," I said, close to one o'clock in the morning. Jake rose and took my arm. I must have looked done in because a look of concern crossed his face.

"Do you want me to come with you?" he said gently. I demurred, exhausted. "Let me walk you to the van at least," he said.

As he opened my car door for me I hesitated, unsteady, and unsure of his intentions. He just stood there, and then pulled me forward against his chest. His mouth brushed my hair, and he breathed it in. He withdrew, gently.

"Don't be a stranger," I said. "You know where I hang out most days."

With that, I was off with a warm glow around my shoulders where he had hugged me.

Chapter Ten

The next morning, I found myself scrambling. I had slept in, and scarcely left myself time to shower and pull on warm clothes to face the bitter November air before heading out to the catering kitchen. As was my habit, though, I checked e-mail and nearly choked on my coffee as I read Tilda's message.

Dear Camilla,

I trust you arrived safely back in Boston. Since we haven't heard from you, we assume you are swamped with work. How good for you to be such a success. (Not to speak of your waving the flag for old Blighty when you dish up your plum puddings and mince pies at Christmas parties.)

Speaking of Christmas, Rupert and I do hope that you can join us for that.

It's been years since we had the holiday together. The girls keep asking after you, too.

Please tell us you can come.

Love,

Tilda

That was a first. In all the years Tilda and Rupert had hosted Christmas, I had not been invited. Of course, that was of my own making. I lived across the ocean, after all.

When we'd been married, I'd enjoyed Christmases with my husband's family. After several generations in

83

America, they still called themselves "Italian," though none of them spoke the language. Much of their heritage resided in the food cooked by Vincent's mother.

Vincent and I had connected through food. The day we'd met in Italy he asked me for a drink, then dinner. His longish hair was dark and wavy, he looked at me with such eager interest, and told me he was staying in a hotel—a cheap hotel, but still, a hotel—and I packed up and left the youth hostel. Vincent and I had backpacked around Europe after we'd met in Perugia. Then he'd proposed.

His family's warmth seemed a refuge from the intellectualism of my own family, the bright star of Vincent bringing together his family's sense of generosity with his academic brilliance and a promising future. Or so it had seemed then.

I suppose I offered the opposite to him. I came from a family of some achievement yet offered an earthier lifestyle. Until, of course, he found I smelled of onions.

Remembering Vincent's words made me gag over my English muffin. I rose and slammed the muffin down the disposal, grinding and grinding to drown out that disdainful voice in my head. I threw the rest of the coffee in the sink and ran the water, rinsing the cup over and over.

Of course, I smelled of onions. Billy probably thought I did, too. I'd seen him with another woman the day after we'd spent a glorious night together. The humiliation of it.

A burning sensation rose from my toes to my chest. I tapped out a reply to Tilda.

Dear Tilda,

Thank you so much for the invitation. Of course, I would like to come.

Christmas, however, is our busiest season.

Perhaps I can come over in January. It's a bit of a dead season in the business.

Love,

Camilla

I looked at what I'd written. It was not exactly a "no," to her invitation. Maybe I did want to go back. But I'd go on my own terms and my own timetable.

It was midmorning in England. Tilda must be at her computer—what did she do all day?—because a reply zipped through the ether almost immediately.

Dear Camilla,

I am so sorry about Christmas.

The thing is, the house must be put on the market in the New Year, according to the solicitors.

It is your family home, too. I don't feel comfortable about rooting through everything without your help.

xx

So that was it. She really wanted me to do the heavy lifting. Just as she had always done. Her message had been less about a family Christmas than about getting our parents' house cleared out. She seemed to think I had nothing better to do than to be her little helper. I wrote:

Dear Tilda,

Can't Geoffrey help?

C.

I put on my coat, pulled on boots, and wrapped a scarf around my neck. I was already regretting my response. Maybe next time I should wait before replying so rudely. As I rode the subway the few stops to the catering kitchen I glanced at my phone. Tilda had sent a new message.

Dear Camilla,

Yes. Geoffrey and Malcolm are coming for Christmas, and we will make a start on the house. I would very much appreciate it if you could find time to come over here to assist.

We miss you.

Your sister,
Tilda

I'd take my time to think of an answer. In the meantime, the workday had begun, and because I'd overslept and wasted time on e-mails, I was late. Mindy raised her eyebrows as I walked in. Manuela finished scrubbing a counter and got out her tools. It would be the usual scramble today, and Thanksgiving was around the corner. I could not possibly contemplate going to England.

But then, that evening, another e-mail came, this time from Geoffrey.

I did miss my brother. So when I opened his e-mail, a gleam of warmth, as well as a little flip of curiosity, made my evening sparkle.

Mille,

Working on those floppies you and T. found in Dad's house. Should have them soon. Come over before too long. We miss you. And I want you to meet Malcolm.

Xxx your brother,
G.

Dearest Geoffo,

I will. Come over. Soon as I can arrange it. And

can't wait to meet your man.
                    Much love,
                        C.

Chapter Eleven

It was easier said than done, however, to get out of my duties. The Christmas season is the bane and the blessing for all in the catering business. Tilda and Geoffrey had no idea of the added pressure Americans felt in November. Wonderful and wearying, Thanksgiving was perhaps at its most traditional in New England. Only a month before Christmas, sometimes even only three weeks before, pumpkins, squash, and corn scrunched up against the mistletoe and the holly. Camilla's Creative Catering had to pull out all the stops to make the last two months of the year its most profitable.

It did not help that despite Geoffrey's letter, which piqued my interest about my father's hidden life, I had fallen into a funk.

After the first snow fell early in November, the forecasters predicted a long, cold winter. Despite the buzz of the season, I found it hard to concentrate; I stared out the window when I should have been directing the staff. As the city grayed into winter, the storefront decorations and the looming turning of the year made me sad. In the spring I would turn thirty-five. Vincent and I could have had children by now.

Would a baby have mended our marriage? Scotch-taped it up only temporarily, probably. We'd had such divergent goals. I had been too busy then, most days, to think of the flaws in our relationship. How Vincent was rarely home for dinner, even though I could cook whatever he fancied, could put on a restaurant meal for two in a flash. Not that I felt like eating much. I'd be happy to have cheese on toast and a cup of tea at the end of a day when the vegetables I'd bought at the wholesale market at sunrise had been chopped and steamed or sautéed into servings for one hundred, to accompany *steak au poivre* or boned and filleted lamb or pork, or transformed into soups, or pies or quiches, and the peelings and ends of the carrots and celery scooped up and simmered into stocks. I'd found it hard to focus on him.

Now I needed to forget him. Totally.

It was difficult to do that at this season, though. The shocking day Vincent left me had been just before Thanksgiving, two years ago. He'd said I'd made my choice that he was secondary to my ambition, and he'd made a choice too. It still made me quiver with anger. Perhaps I'd let him go too easily. Hadn't fought the divorce, out of stupid pride, and it was all done in the quickest possible time. If he didn't want me, why try to force it? Still, for months afterward I'd go home after a hard day's work and have a bath, and rising from the steam, stare at myself in the mirror and wonder what my husband had seen in the skinny student that he couldn't see in the more experienced body of his wife and the memory of our years of coupling. That was over now, and I'd felt unwanted. Until I'd met Billy again. I'd had the pleasure of being desired and it had been sweet, so sweet. So terribly short. Even for a fling, so short.

But Vincent had been my family, and I had ignored

my own. Should I accept Tilda's invitation to go back for Christmas?

Of course not. Orders were abundant, I needed to be here. I needed more income. In the tiny office behind the commissary, I started a spreadsheet of expenses and revenue. I was trying to get a grip on it when the phone rang just as Mindy walked by.

"Can you take it, Mindy?" I said. "I'm in the middle of a calculation here. See what the caller wants, find out the place and the date they have in mind, ask their budget. If they say they want to know what it costs before they give you a budget, then give them a per-person range."

"I know." She made a groaning noise as if I were treating her like an idiot.

"Just get that phone, please."

But it had already gone to answer mode. A familiar voice was leaving a message.

"Just wanted to thank you, Camilla, for the spread you put on for the opening at the gallery the other night. Give me a call."

Mindy smiled. "Told you his interest was not just professional. Jake," she repeated when I did not respond.

"Well, that's nice." I kept my voice neutral. "Let's see what we have lined up for the Christmas parties. Can we bake ahead and freeze? Let's do some chutneys. We'll get a start on the fruit cakes too."

"Yeah, right. You're on your own there."

I looked at the Christmas orders, the New Year's Eve parties. I reviewed the cakes I needed to bake and the trifles. In the cold of a Boston Christmas, I had developed a line of British specialties. English cooking is not famously good, but in certain things, it excels. I specialized in mince pies and deep dark cakes studded with dried fruits and citrus peels. I started the fruit cakes and froze any slightly imperfect sponge cakes to use for the trifles. My trifles were fabulous, cut up sponge or pound cake, soaked with sherry, topped with egg custard, whipped cream, and berries.

It had been a gamble when I invested in making the Christmas cakes. Americans hate fruitcakes. But there were British expatriates here who craved their richness and depth. They were expensive, they had to be started before Thanksgiving, to welter in their soakings of brandy and rum, coated with marzipan thick as an animal's pelt, and then iced again with fondant. Oh, I loved making these. They were sold out by mid-December. I learned to make *buches de Noel*, as well, those French chocolate-covered logs. At Camilla's Creative Catering we were nothing if not ecumenical.

"Here's a request for a full Thanksgiving dinner," Mindy said, pulling up her notes on the tablet.

"That's only two weeks away! Why didn't you sync it with the master computer?"

"Forgot, I guess. It's been busy lately."

"Yes, it has. Well, you'd better get back to them and get it settled, get the deposit. You didn't send them a contract? I hope they still want our services."

"I'll do that now. I was hoping to have Thanksgiving off, actually. We usually don't work on the day, it's sort of sacred in this country."

I drummed my fingers on the desk. "It's not sacred to me. But I suppose if we do as much as possible ahead, you can take the day off." I knew my voice sounded reluctant.

"Actually, I was hoping for a few days, Camilla. Maybe the long weekend?"

"Come on, Mindy! This is really our busiest time."

"I know. I'll work extra hard before and after. Let's get the pies started now, just as soon as I get these people signed up." Mindy sidled out the door.

"Please be available Christmas Eve, Mindy, and New Year's. I really can't do them without you. And I'm giving up my holiday with my family in England." I squared my shoulders self-righteously.

Mindy raised her eyebrows. "You were just there, and I didn't think you got on that well with them."

"I do have to go back and help settle my father's estate. But I'll do that later. Right now we just have to get through the holidays."

My fingers dug into my palm. Of course, it was unreasonable to expect Mindy not to take Thanksgiving off. It was only my own lack of a social life that made me accept a gig for the Americans' most hallowed day of the year. I should call Jake back. I would. He was attractive. Lovely dark eyes. I wondered what drove him to give up a regular job, a job with benefits, to paint all day. I supposed he couldn't bear to do anything else. That was something we had in common. I rang him back. I left a message, but he didn't respond. A day or two later, I thought about following up with an e-mail, but told myself maybe that was pushy. He'd get back to me if he wanted.

He didn't.

Chapter Twelve

Thanksgiving morning at five a.m., my alarm was about to go off when the phone rang.

A muffled, stuffy-nosed Hannah said, "I'm sorry, Camilla, I'm so sick. I can't come in."

"Yes, I can hear. Is it just a cold?"

"No. I'm throwing up too. You can't take the risk."

No. The last thing we needed was a health department citation. Mindy had taken the long weekend off—damn her! And Manuela was spending the holiday with her family. Paige and I would have to wing it together. Paige was not the sharpest tack in the box, but with supervision, it should be all right.

I staggered out of bed into the shower and then into my sweats. Then I packed a bag with a skirt, black top, plain black flats and tights, and as a gesture to the season, a bright orange scarf. If I had time, I'd have another shower and wash my hair before setting off to the client's house.

The first thing I did at the catering kitchen was pull the turkey out of the refrigerator. It would need an hour or so to thaw. I wondered about the hostess who had hired us. The woman had insisted on one large twenty-five-pound turkey for her eighteen guests.

"You know, if you get two smaller turkeys, say thirteen pounds each, they'll cook faster and make a pretty presentation, one at each end of the table," I told her.

"I want the full traditional effect," Mrs. Reilly said.

I doubted this stockbroker's wife had ever cooked a meal for a crowd, and carving at the table really didn't work. It took too long. The guests next to the carver could get sprayed with grease and bits of parsley, and the stuffing started to fall out of the bird.

"Camilla?" Paige said. "What are we doing for vegetables?"

"Start alphabetically." I handed her a piece of paper. "Here's the list. Top and tail the beans. Pull the Brussels sprouts off the stalk and slice them down the middle."

Paige began. I interrupted. "Slice them vertically, so they look like little trees inside. There you go!"

Paige methodically went through her list, preparing butternut squash after the beans and the Brussels sprouts. She retrieved the cranberry relish from the pantry, then frowned over a big gap in the alphabet till she came to potatoes and sweet potatoes.

"Where are the pies?"

"Out of the freezer. They'll thaw. We'll heat them slowly in the oven while the guests eat the turkey. Now let's make the sauce for the oysters."

"Oysters?"

"Yes, they are a treat, but it's an 'er' month, so they're in season. And this hostess can afford them."

"Will I have to open them?"

Alarm bells rang, silently. Paige was quite squeamish. With oysters, she was likely to cut herself. But someone had to shuck the oysters and it had to be last minute.

"I can do it," I said. "Just make sure the insulated

bags are packed with the oysters on ice and the knife. Make sure you separate the items that need to stay cold from the ones that need to stay warm."

"Yes, ma'am." Paige's blue eyes shot angry darts. "I'm not that stupid."

"No, of course not. I'm sorry."

We worked together, and by noon the turkey was cooked, requiring only an hour more in the oven to re-heat. We loaded the van with the food in its insulated carriers. It was a quiet half-hour journey to Wellesley through almost empty streets to a winding elm-lined avenue lined with mansions that looked like palaces. I parked in a wide driveway and knocked on the back door. Of all the sometimes difficult things I did in this business, this was one of the most galling. The idea that I, a professor's daughter, a doctor's daughter, now had to go to the tradesman's entrance. Even though this was America, where catering was quite a respectable profession.

An attractive woman, in her mid-forties, I guessed, came to the door. She wore a chocolate-brown silk dress and diamond earrings. Her hands were manicured and her heels made her totter slightly.

"Oh, good," she said, bringing a bejeweled hand to her right ear and pulling on it. "I was wondering when you'd get here. You see, some of the people have come early. Do you have any nibbles? I've set them to watch the football game."

"You told me the dinner was to be served at two p.m."

"Did I? Oh dear. Anyway, come in, do come in. Is it just the two of you?" she peered over to the van, where Paige was unloading pots and bags onto the driveway.

"We'll be fine. Thanksgiving really is not a complicated meal. Here, Paige, let me help you in with these."

We hauled the bags into a bright white kitchen, pristine and shiny. A stainless steel range with gas burners—thank goodness for that—a large refrigerator, a microwave. Everything looked in order.

"May I take a peek at the Thanksgiving table?"

"Oh, yes," Mrs. Reilly beamed. "I always love to set a holiday table. Mother's porcelain was brought out for the occasion." She directed us into a formal dining room where a very long table was set with a lace cloth, sparkling silver, and pretty china. I noticed several sizes of glasses in front of each plate.

"You're doing the wine?"

"Yes, Archer is in charge of that. He's got a very good vintage out. Actually," the hostess lowered her voice to a whisper, "I think he's got a bit of a head start. Maybe you can hurry up the dinner?"

Loud laughter boomed from another room. Several male voices shouted over the television. From another room came the lighter sound of women talking and giggling, and from upstairs, thumping as if someone was getting dressed.

"Well, everything looks under control," I said. "Let's get started, shall we?"

I went into the kitchen and turned on the oven. A light went on satisfactorily, and I pulled the turkey out of its carrier and into a metal pan. I just glanced at the oven after turning it on, and looking at my watch, started bustling. It's all about the timing, I always told my staff, and now Mrs. Reilly's pressure to get the meal on the table earlier than I'd planned had set our plans askew.

"Paige, can you prepare a bed of ice for the oysters and slice this lemon and rim the tray with parsley?"

I put the pies on the counter, pecan, blueberry, apple, and pumpkin. I checked the oven temperature. Lukewarm. My heart started to race. Surely it would heat up soon. I hoisted the heavy pan to slide it in the oven. The bird's breastbone stuck halfway in. I pulled out the bottom rack and moved down the middle rack as far as it would go. The turkey still would not fit.

My blood pressure rose. Mindy had come to visit the client. This order had come in while I was away. Surely this was the most basic information she should have noted. Small oven. Will not fit twenty-five-pound turkey!

Mrs. Reilly poked her head around the door. "Are we nearly ready?"

"We're getting there." No point in blaming the client for this lapse. It was the caterer's responsibility to make sure all the bits and pieces were in place.

"We'll serve the oysters first, of course. Would you mind if we plate the main course from the kitchen?"

"I really wanted to serve it family style. Sort of you know, like I cooked it."

"Uh-huh." I hated this type of client, the sort who pretended they made the food that someone else had slaved over. "Well, we could bring the turkey in on its platter and everyone can have a good look. But really, Mrs. Reilly, the turkey is difficult to carve at the table and it is easier and more elegant to serve everything on its plate from here. Paige can bring the plates out," I said. I lifted a pot, exaggerating its heaviness. "Very few Thanksgiving tables, I find, are large enough to carry eighteen place settings and the serving dishes. Let us serve from here, please."

"I'll have to bring the china into the kitchen." Mrs. Reilly's brown bodice heaved. "The table won't look so pretty!" With a huff, she left the kitchen.

"God." Paige looked terrified.

"Don't worry. Just start shucking the oysters now. Sorry, I know I said I'd do it, but I have to manage this disaster with the turkey."

"How are we going to give them turkey that's not cooked through? They'll get salmonella."

"Nonsense! It is cooked, but it's not hot. We can fix that. First, we'll show off the turkey like she wants, then carve it in here. Heat up some broth, then we'll put in a bay leaf and some thyme, and simmer the cut slices and the legs so they get nice and juicy and warm." I opened a can of chicken broth as I talked. "We'll pop the potatoes and squash and stuffing in the microwave, cook the beans on the stove top, and toss the Brussels sprouts in their sauce on top of the stove. All you have to do is—oh Lord!"

Paige had dropped the oyster tray on the floor. Pinky gray crustaceans slid over the wooden floor. Ice formed puddles around them and parsley skidded under the sink.

"I didn't see that. Quick!" I ran cold water in the sink and pulled open a cabinet to get a colander. "The three-second rule. They should be okay. Just rinse and rinse again. And again." I bent and picked up the few that had landed on their tummies, so to speak. "I think these would be fine, see how the shell's curve stopped the actual oyster from contacting with the floor."

For a moment, I stood there, hatred of wastage battling with my reputation.

"No. Throw those ones out. We'll just use the others. Put extra parsley on the plate so we can put fewer oysters on each one."

While Paige mopped the floor, I cut up more parsley, and the refrigerator's icemaker ground out another pound of cubes. I nestled them around the oysters. "Now. Let's get the sauce on the side of each plate, put three of these babies on each one, and you take them in, nice and easy. Look calm. Don't say a word."

I stopped with a parsley stalk in hand. The compulsively honest Paige would likely apologize publicly to the hostess. I grabbed the platter. "No. I'll do it. Let's get the gravy going, then take it off the stove. Line all the veggie dishes up so we can microwave and cook everything in order. Remember the order—potatoes and squash and stuffing in the microwave, heat the water for the beans, get the simmer broth on for the turkey which I'll carve just as soon as we've shown it to the owner—God, it's not brown enough!"

Deep breaths. "I wish Hannah were here—she'd put shoe polish on it or something! Just joking. What can we use? Can you look in the pantry—there might be some soy sauce in there? Maybe some molasses or honey?"

"Soy sauce?"

"Yes, it gives a nice brown sheen. Probably adds a nice taste to the turkey, too."

Paige frowned doubtfully as she sidled into the pantry. In a minute or two, she emerged brandishing a bottle of soy sauce.

"While I'm doing the oysters, could you run out to the car and grab my hair dryer—I've got an idea." I picked up the oyster plates and laid them across my arm.

A babble of voices rose from the dining room, Laughter tinkled and glasses clinked as I walked in. Mr. Reilly went from diner to diner pouring wine. His voice was loud, and he seemed a little unsteady on his feet. By the time I finished serving the oysters, he was back at his place, wine bottle in hand, and sliding into his seat, almost lost his balance. He caught me by the waist to steady himself and said, "Ah, oysters, food of the gods. Served by a goddess."

I felt one beefy hand squeezing my middle while the other reached under the table, under my skirt, to caress my thigh. His hand was warm and aggressive, rising higher. I recoiled. No one appeared to notice, except Mrs. Reilly. She glared across the table with furious dark eyes.

"I hope you enjoy the oysters," I said and pulled away. The tablecloth in front of Archer Reilly started to pull with me. The Coalport china and the Georg Jensen silverware teetered. I pushed my assailant on the shoulder, trying to get my own balance, and his red face veered dangerously close to the table. The hand fell away from my leg. I flicked his wobbling glass upright and with as much dignity as I could, walked back to the kitchen.

Trembling, I stood at the sink, pushed my hair back away from my face, and took a long glass of water. The groping made me feel utterly humiliated. Archer Reilly had treated me like a *thing*. A maid, a sexual object.

Not that men hadn't tried it with me when I was younger. But this was in public, in front of his wife, and I was not a lowly employee. I was a business owner, the daughter of people who took it for granted that they, too, would be waited on at the table, the ex-wife—here I bowed my head into the sink—of a Harvard professor!

I sensed Paige's alarm. Turning, I saw the hair dryer in my assistant's hands. I took it from her and placed it next to the turkey.

"How are the veggies coming along? Is the oven behaving itself yet?" My voice quavered. I opened the oven door and waved a hand inside. Still lukewarm.

The pies sat thawing on the counter, little beads of moisture twinkling on their surface. They were not ready to serve at all.

"We'll just have to put them in this pathetic oven and have them heat up slowly. They might be all right. If we microwave them, they'll get soggy crusts. At the end of the day, that might not matter. Judging by how these people are going with the wine, they probably wouldn't notice."

"Maybe you should go in there again and serve more wine!"

"I think Mr. Reilly's doing that. They didn't ask for bar help or a wine server. We've got enough to do in this kitchen. These dishes are all going to have to be hand-washed; the best china and all, too valuable for the dishwasher."

"I can wash the oyster dishes while they eat the main course."

"Good girl. Now, we're on a schedule here. Give me the hair dryer."

"You wouldn't."

"I would. I am." I plugged in the hair dryer and blew hot air over the turkey, sealing the soy sauce, which I had mixed with honey, onto it. We lifted the bird onto its platter, sprinkled parsley around it, and carried it into the dining room. The guests clapped, and Mrs. Reilly, not looking at her husband, raised a toast. I whisked the bird back into the kitchen.

When I carved I saw that the bird was pink deep inside. I lowered each slice into heated broth and let it simmer till the pieces were plump and white while Paige went around the table collecting the plates. The sounds of laughter and clinking glasses in the dining room assured us that we could take our time to assemble the plates in the kitchen and carry them to the inebriated guests.

Somehow, we got through the afternoon. Mr. Reilly kept his hands to himself as we served the main course. After surveying the guests patting their bellies and pushing their dishes away after they'd eaten, I decided to serve the pies in their room temperature state. The guests didn't notice. They all had the obligatory "little piece of each, please," and I gave myself a self-congratulatory hug. It had been a hard day, but we'd weathered the crises.

After we'd hand washed all the dishes and china and glassware, packed up the van, and been paid, it was after seven o'clock. I paid Paige extra, giving her the tip Mrs. Reilly had neglected to add.

Paige and I loaded up the van and headed back through the quiet, dark streets. It started to sleet again, needles of ice on the windscreen. I thought I was driving slowly enough, but on Beacon Street, where the shops disappear and the car picks up speed as the wide expanses of the lawns of the mansions of Chestnut Hill line the roads, I saw suddenly, out of the corner of my eye, a car hurtle out of a side street to my right. I tried to brake and skidded. With terror, I realized the brakes were not holding, and I forgot what you were supposed to do when that happened, and only too late remembered it was to pump the foot brake, not to press on it. I heard that sickeningly loud crunch of metal on metal as my bumper made contact with the side of another vehicle, just in front of the driver's door. I jolted in my seatbelt.

"God. Are you all right, Paige?"

"Yeah. That guy, he wasn't looking."

"I know. Stay here, don't worry." I patted her knee.

I got out. The sleet had eased to a dense mist, and I peered into the dark. The other driver seemed to struggle to open the door, and one leg appeared, then another, and a bent head. A man stood and scowled, then startled. I looked into the angry eyes of Vincent.

I had hit my ex-husband's car.

"What the hell happened?" he said. "Don't you look where you're going?"

"Black ice. It was icy, and I skidded. I'm sorry about the dent." I went around to the side of his car and inspected it. I didn't want to look at Vincent. As I raised my head from assessing the damage the passenger door opened. A woman emerged. A very pregnant woman by the looks of it; a young, pretty face, long hair under a hat. I recognized Vincent's girlfriend. She looked disdainfully at me, came around to the driver's side and laid her left hand on Vincent's. An enormous diamond sparkled in the dark.

I felt sick. Vincent and I had failed to conceive.

Perhaps we didn't try long enough. Infertility was obviously not his problem. I turned my head aside.

"Vanessa," Vincent said. He could have introduced us, but he turned to her. "Get back in the car," he said more forcefully. "I'll deal with this."

"Are you hurt?" the woman said to him, still not looking at me.

"I said, get back in the car. I can handle it." Vincent swayed slightly as he reached for the driver's door.

"Let's just exchange insurance information and we can go our separate ways," I said, emphasizing the "separate," though that had not been my intention. "I have to get Paige home."

"You were working Thanksgiving?" Vincent looked at me carefully for the first time. I drew my coat tighter around me so he could not see my stained skirt.

"Yes. You?"

"At Vanessa's parents. Let's just get on with this, shall we?"

He signaled to Vanessa, who had reinserted her pregnant self in the car, to retrieve the insurance papers from the glove box. I went back to my car to find something to write on and could find only the copy of the bill I had given Mrs. Reilly. I tore it in half and Vincent filled out his information on the back of one half, and I on the other. There was something so ironic in the whole situation that for a moment I almost laughed. The bill, the tearing in half, the broken car, symbolized the wreckage of our marriage. Vincent's hand wobbled as he wrote.

"When is she due?" I asked.

"Any day now," Vincent said. He leaned closer to

hand over the paper to me, and I smelled his breath. It reeked of alcohol.

Bastard. The child had been conceived when we were separated but not yet divorced. And he was drunk.

I turned away.

My only consolation was that I had damaged his car much more than my own.

Chapter Thirteen

That little car accident did it for me, really. Vincent was no longer of any interest at all.

Still, I was lost. I had lost Vincent, then had reached out to Billy and reacted like I'd been scalded when I saw him with a woman. Had I overreacted? Quite possibly. But then again, ours was such a tentative connection. Despite what I'd bragged to Lucy about the tension between Billy and me tightening again after so many years, we had really spent only one night together. So that was over, too. I just needed to stop thinking about him.

*****

I hung up the phone after placing a fish order at the wholesalers. Lobsters, clams, scallops, and shrimp were big sellers for the day before Christmas. As in the past couple of years, we were scheduled to cater a big Christmas Eve party out in the suburbs. The parties held loneliness at a bearable distance, at least until the stroke of midnight. The last two Christmases I had spent in misery. Ashamed to acknowledge Vincent's abandonment, for a while I refused to tell my family, let alone fly home to their muted sympathy. I'd licked my wounds in private. This year, too, an empty holiday stretched before me.

Mindy offered, her voice syrupy with sympathy. "Come with me, Camilla. My mother always puts on a spread for the family. It's kinda chaotic—my sister has twin toddlers—and there are cousins and aunts and uncles, but it's fun. You'd be welcome."

I turned my head aside so Mindy could not see my face. I did not feel welcome. Someone else's family. I had my own. I had escaped them. A headache tightened my brow.

"Thank you, Mindy. That's very kind of you. Actually, my sister has invited me," I said. "But I haven't yet committed."

Mindy sat back in her chair. She looked relieved.

I must reply to Tilda's e-mail. January was always quiet. I could leave Mindy in charge, then.

"I'm thinking I won't go just yet. It would mean foisting all these parties on you by yourself." I tapped my fingers on the desk. "But I do have to go soon after. My sister has more or less insisted that I come back and help her clear out the old house."

I could see Mindy tense, waiting to pounce.

"You're asking me to take over the business again while you're away?"

"I don't mean to be difficult. We're all pulling together here, Mindy."

"It must be nice to be able to afford to go back and forth over the ocean like it's no big deal."

I straightened my shoulders, stood up, and put the notepad deliberately, carefully, on the desk. Mindy was being nothing short of insolent. The pencil fell and rattled on the floor. "Not that January is a great month to travel, you understand," I said. "It's as miserable in England as it is here." I pulled my cardigan over my shoulders.

Mindy stood and crossed her arms, her toned

muscles visible through her long-sleeved shirt. "Well, you're the boss. But I think I've proved I deserve a bit more. With Christmas and all, I hate to max out my credit card."

Isn't that the truth, I would not be getting presents for the family this year. Nor for myself. Still, Camilla's Creative Catering had more jobs than it could handle. Picking up another pencil, I started to doodle. I must figure out a way to make more money or control costs without working everyone into an early grave.

"We needed more help. Hannah came, gives us that extra hand. But it means a tighter profit margin for a while. That's the way the business works, Mindy."

Mindy paced, then stood behind a chair, gripping its back. "What do you want to do with this business, Camilla? Do you want it to grow bigger?"

"Sure. Let's look through the orders, sit down and do the numbers, and we can figure that out better."

Could Mindy do the arithmetic? She could figure it out, surely. But Mindy was not the one who took the risks, rented the kitchen, got the permits, or paid back the small business loan. My heart tensed, remembering the bill payments automatically deducted and the pressure to refill the bank balance each month. I bent to retrieve the fallen pencil.

"Okay. Show me, I'd like to learn." Mindy sounded eager. "I think I'm ready for more responsibility."

As I straightened, I could see Mindy trying to mask her anticipation, her face bland as the tension flowing to her fingers made indentations on the blue fabric back of the office chair.

My fingers drummed. "I know. I appreciate what

you do."

"It's hard when you expect me to manage one day and chop veggies the next."

"We all do that."

"What about when you come back?" Mindy's voice rose.

"Don't be like that. Please. I know it's hard right now, but I am offering you an opportunity. You do well while I'm away, and we'll talk again about a promotion."

Was she capable of that? "At least a raise. I'll make sure you get a holiday bonus."

Mindy gave a half-smile.

I pulled up the schedule on the computer. "Let's see who is on the calendar for this Christmas. Will you promise to sell the clients on some of my British specialties?" I launched into the menu of mince pies, plum pudding, and Christmas cakes.

Mindy laughed. "Mince pies okay. Plum pudding, nada."

"Oyster stew then. I'll keep the puddings for the expats." My mind was already past Christmas, through the New Year, to January. Going to England would be an excuse to see Billy again, to have it out with him. To figure out if my father was the hypocrite I now suspected him to be.

The phone rang. I leapt for it, knocking the notepad off the desk.

"How have you been, Camilla?"

My insides started to waver as I recognized Jake's tenor. "Fine, thanks. Were you pleased with the exhibition? Don't tell me you're planning another—you must be a speed demon, to get all that painting done."

"No. Takes a while to get a painting finished the way I want it. I meant to thank you earlier for all the great food, by the way."

"Why, thank you, too. I know you called earlier, and I rang back. We've been…"

"Playing the old phone tag. I know. But that's not why I'm calling. Actually, Camilla, I want to ask you about New Year's Eve."

New Year's Eve? My heart lifted. Was he asking me for a date?

My heart sank. I had no time for a date on the busiest night of the year. When would I ever have time to date?

"I have two functions that night, Jake. I'm so sorry. New Year's Eve is a work night for me."

"Uh-huh."

Perhaps I had misinterpreted the call. Embarrassing. "Are you calling to ask us to cater a New Year's Eve party? We're doing two—I guess we could handle another. I'll check with Mindy." I could hear my tone brighten artificially.

"I thought you were the boss."

"Yes, but Mindy's been taking the orders." It was not entirely true. I was just trying to keep him on the phone.

I swallowed. Sweat tickled against my shirt. Why bring Mindy into it? "Do you have another party you want us to cater?"

I heard his soft laugh. Suddenly I wanted more than anything to see him.

"Actually, Camilla, I'm calling about something else entirely. I'm a starving artist, remember? Art sales are sporadic. I wondered if you could use a bartender over the New Year rush. Even after that."

I laughed. I could hear it—a weird-sounding laugh of relief. Jake—a bartender? Actually, he would be a good one. Arms and chest strong enough from years of wielding a paintbrush on huge canvases to lift the crates of glasses, artistic enough to arrange them prettily on white cloths. I had an image of the way he would arrange the liquor—by color and size, maybe. Perhaps he was just creating an excuse to get to know me. Good. That would work two ways.

"You know, we could really use the help. I usually hire students over the holidays. I assume you have some experience—not that it's all that hard to learn." My voice ran on and on.

Mindy was looking at me oddly. I picked up the notepad and scribbled furiously, hoping Mindy would not notice my agitation.

"Jake—this will work out well. We could certainly use a bartender for New Year's Eve. It means giving up your own chance for a get-together with friends, of course."

"That's okay. I need the money more." He lowered his voice. "And of course, your company, Camilla."

Warmth rose, all the way to my forehead. "That's good. What about your Christmas Day? Will you spend the holidays with your family?"

"My dad, yes." There was a silence. "What are you doing for Christmas?"

"Me? Ah," I moved the phone out of earshot of Mindy. Unsure of how to answer Jake's question, I walked into the kitchen. A big cauldron sat on the stove, and in the momentary silence, I heard it rumble to a boil. Holding the phone to my ear with one hand, I lowered the heat with the other. "Do you have a big family?"

"Not really. Just me and my dad. He's a handful."

"Oh? Tell me." I scrambled for something to say. "I'm making soup. Prepping for one of our New Year's parties. Do you cook for the holiday?"

"No. Not much good in the kitchen. I'd like to take my dad to one of those fancy hotel dinners you see advertised for Christmas, but well, his memory isn't what it was."

"Forgetful? Maybe a nice dinner out is just what he needs." How I would love to be taken out for a beautiful Christmas dinner with all the trimmings. I picked up a spoon.

"More than forgetful, I'm afraid. Anyway, it will be quiet. What about you?"

"Well…" I stirred, stalling again, hoping he would ask me out for a drink, at least. "I might volunteer. At a homeless shelter. They're always short-staffed on holidays."

I tasted the soup and turned down the flame, knocked the tasting spoon into the sink and picked up another. "You know, we might have some extra mince pies here or a trifle. I could drop them over, make your father's day special."

"We're good. Thanks anyway."

The spoon clattered to the counter. I hoped the noise would cover my embarrassment. Had I been pushy? I felt like an idiot.

"I'll see you New Year's Eve," he said.

"Look forward to it." My voice caught. "Merry Christmas, Jake."

As I turned away from the stove I saw Mindy

looking at me. "What?" she said. "That artist guy? He wants to work here? Isn't that a bit weird?"

"He says he needs the money. And you've just spent half an hour telling me we need more hires. So, a little gratitude, please."

"Oh, I am. Grateful." Mindy tried to suppress a smirk. "I'll look forward to working with Jake while you are away. We really need the help."

I walked to the refrigerator, pulled out a bowl of bread dough, which had been resting, washed my hands, dusted the counter with flour, and pounded the dough with vigor. I pushed it with the heel of my hand, patted it, and slammed it on the counter. So Mindy liked Jake, did she? I stared at Mindy's slender back, her ebony curls peeking out of her cap, and skin the color of cappuccino under its foam. She'd tempt any man. I kneaded the dough till my arm ached. I had to make myself stop, in case the dough became overworked.

Chapter Fourteen

Christmas was unspeakable, really. I'll gloss over how I woke up and saw frost and clumps of snow whitening the windowsill. No filled stocking or pillowcase tempted me to get up. I hugged my arms around my knees, wriggled my lonely toes under the blanket, and forced myself to rise.

I spent my Christmas at the Elm Street Homeless Shelter. In the end, I enjoyed it, up to a point. It was something I knew how to do. As a teenager, I had persuaded my father to set up a soup kitchen in the college chapel's basement. I'd begun cooking under the direction of the college's chef, who seeing me hang around the kitchen, invited me in, acknowledging I couldn't do much damage to a carrot. I'd started making soup and started the Sunday Soup Kitchen. That act of charity led to my career.

So, on this Christmas Day, I helped supervise the food servers though it did take a willful effort not to interfere with the kitchen's professional workers. I smiled till I thought the skin around my mouth would break. After the long day of dishing up plate after plate of mashed potatoes, turkey, gravy, and peas, I brought out my present for the other volunteers.

"Anyone care for a Cornish Fairing?" I asked.

"Cornish what?"

I lifted from my carry-all a zip-locked bag of huge

cookies, which I arranged on a plate. "Here." I pressed the plate toward my fellow workers. "These taste like gingerbread, so they're sort of seasonal, but they're more like a ginger snap. They used to be sold at fairs in Cornwall."

As the workers bit into the cookies, I saw the pleasure in their eyes. These eggless cookies were so easy to make and so richly satisfying, especially with my own tweak on the traditional recipe, which swapped ginger syrup for the hard-to-find British golden syrup.

I sought out the shelter's director. I found Meghan Blainey in an office at the end of a corridor decorated with tinsel and paper streamers, recognizing her from the blue metal name tag she wore on one breast of a red cardigan adorned with stitched reindeer. The stocky, gray-haired woman smiled wearily as I entered. She offered me a chocolate from a tired-looking box on her desk, and I countered by presenting her my Cornish Fairings.

"One of my English specialties," I said and launched into my mission before Ms. Blainey could finish her cookie. "It seems to me I could be useful here," I said. "You see, I'm a caterer, and I could use more help. Maybe I could teach shelter residents how to work in a commercial kitchen? Maybe we could work out a deal where I train some of your clients at my business. I get the help, and they get the skills they need for employment. Maybe we create a little co-operative, with your clients making something easy like these cookies and selling them."

"Hmm," Meghan Blainey said and dabbed her mouth with a tissue. "Job training is key, of course, to keeping people off the streets. But homelessness is not necessarily a matter of a person not having skills. Often there are mental health issues that make sticking to a schedule next to impossible. But sure, let's talk. You're welcome to volunteer anytime."

Dismissed, I thanked her, packed up my things, and left.

Driving home through the sleet, I shuddered to see people heading toward the subway. Some of them would stay there the night, out of the elements. Whatever the Elm Street Shelter could offer, there were simply not enough beds for all who needed them. How did one become homeless? It could be bad luck, a job loss, a difficulty in grasping society's rules, or simply the lack of family. Could it have been me? Women were most vulnerable. I pulled into the underground garage, grateful for its marginal warmth. Despite its shelter, I felt exposed. I had to do better than this. Living in that lonely apartment, dependent on no one yet with no one dependent on me, I needed a sense of purpose. But even a sense of purpose wouldn't save me if I became injured or sick. Here, in this country, without a husband or family, I lacked deep connections.

It suddenly dawned on me. I'd made myself into what Billy had become the day he'd been forced out of our home. He was, though he'd lived in England half his life, a foreigner. He had no family to support him. He'd had to use all his wits and inner resources to survive.

He had courage, and I needed it. I needed to do what he had been forced to do, as a kind of atonement. To know what it was like.

Exiting the car, I crushed the crumbling bag of cookies to my side and went upstairs. Like Billy, like all the lost people who'd lined up today at the shelter, I must make myself used to my loneliness.

Chapter Fifteen

Martyrdom is not attractive. Nor is it usually warranted. While I was wallowing in self-pity and remorse, Tilda sent a chatty note about her Christmas Day. Once again I was wrong about Billy. He didn't seem to be lonely at all.

Dear Camilla,

Christmas passed off with the usual cracker pulling, too much mulled wine and loud squeals from the children as they opened their presents. We missed Daddy of course, very much, and we always miss Mummy. Rupert's brother Henry came over with his family for the Christmas Lunch. What with Geoffrey, Malcolm, and William at table together with the children we were a very merry group indeed. Except it seems nothing could save the goose. It was tough and stringy though people were too polite to comment. (Well, Rupert couldn't help himself, I'm afraid.) I wish I had your culinary skills. We did raise a toast to you, Camilla, in absentia, and hope we will see you soon.

Love,

Tilda

P.S. William says he has some important news, which he wants to share with you. I am as intrigued as you must be about this. Do you have a clue?

I started to breathe heavily and reached for a tissue. I typed:

Dear Tilda,

What, do you mean that Billy is announcing his engagement or something?

He could tell you that himself.

C.

Dear Camilla,

No, I don't think William's news was of that nature. I don't know what it is.

You seemed to get along with him, after all these years, when you saw him in September. Why not just drop him a line?

You know perfectly well that he and Geoffrey are quite good friends, by the way; they reconnected some years ago and since they both live in London see each other occasionally. I will refrain from pointing out that you are the one who has been out of touch.

In the meantime, we want to begin cleaning out Daddy's house. Is there anything in the house you would like for yourself?

Love,

Tilda

Tilda certainly knew how to twist the knife. Reminding me once again of my intentional absence. As if it were my fault. A little over-politeness, that British game of conveying meaning in words that said the opposite, was in order. I wrote:

Dear Tilda,

Living so far away now, I can't think how I would transport anything over here from the old house. There were some nice rugs, a couple of lovely old polished tables. You take those, Tilda, you and Geoffrey divide those things between you. He'd like the good silver, I'm sure. You take the good china. I wouldn't mind the old

Denby crockery, though. And I think there are some books in Daddy's study I'd like to go through. Maybe look through the stuff in Mummy's desk. Could you keep that till last, please? I'm working my way clear to come over in January.

Will keep you posted on that.

Xxxx

Chapter Sixteen

New Year's Eve. A frosty night, a full van. Three parties. An order had come in at the last minute, and I could not refuse.

Mindy always supervised the newcomers, and that included Jake and two other casual bartenders at the largest party. As I dropped them off at the host's back door, I noticed how Jake leapt easily from the back of the crowded van and held his arm out for Mindy. She helped unload, as Jake heaved great plastic crates of glasses onto tables and organized all the alcohol.

Jake, in his late thirties to the other bartenders' early twenties, took instant charge. The authority seemed to stem not just from his tall, fit body, but from a commanding presence that flowed from him. I wondered if he had ever been in the military, he led others so naturally without ever barking an order. As I left, he waved. I was sorry to have to leave his side and take my employees to the other gigs. I hoped to get a chance to talk to him at the end of the evening, have a drink or something.

Hannah, Paige, bartenders, and more waiters staffed the next party, while I supervised the third, with help from Manuela. Thank goodness full sit-down meals were not required. Hors d'oeuvres, hot and cold, gently lifted out of metal trays and placed onto doily-covered, parsley-decorated serving platters were ordered at one of the houses. A huge ham studded with cloves, mustards and my famous chutneys, rye breads, and scalloped potatoes, mince pies, and trifles graced the groaning tables at another. While at the third, thankfully, the hostess had sent out an invitation to come for soup. That was simple. Three soups in huge cauldrons, breads and salads. And copious servings of wine.

At evening's end, I packed up the van and did the rounds to pick up the others. First, I dropped Manuela off at the catering kitchen to start the first load of dishwashing. Then I took Hannah and Paige and their trash back and sent them home. Getting into the van to pick up Jake and Mindy, I figured we could do one more dishwasher run, and then leave what remained to soak. New Year's Day would be a holiday for the entire staff of Camilla's Creative Catering.

I found Mindy and Jake good-naturedly joshing as they loaded up the plastic crates and the trays of dirty dishes. I noticed Mindy knock Jake's wrist with her own as she turned to me with a big grin and said, "Jake and I might drive up to the North Shore tomorrow. Walk on the beach as the big waves come in."

"Oh? Isn't there a storm predicted? You wouldn't want to be out in that."

"Not really. Just some high winds. Not too cold. Jake wants to take some photos and do some sketches of the waves—he has an idea for a new painting series, he says."

I turned away so Mindy could not see my face. Stupid. I had not given Jake any encouragement. Here he was openly hitting on Mindy. What did I expect? I swept a fist across the dirty tablecloth, knocked the remains of a cheese platter into a plastic bag and stood there gripping it tightly. I could feel myself pout. I sensed Jake looking at me and raised my eyes to his. He had such long eyelashes. A smile lifted his face. Jake had not said the trip to the ocean would be a twosome. Maybe he'd included me, unspoken. But I would not humiliate myself by asking him outright.

I ripped the soiled cloth off the table so hard I hurt my knuckles on the aluminum hinge. I said, "I'm so tired I'm going to crash tomorrow. But on your way back from the North Shore, why don't you come to my apartment for dinner? I'll make you some cullen skink."

Jake raised his eyebrows. "Cullen what? Stink?"

I laughed. "Skink. I don't know where the name came from but it's a kind of Scottish chowder with smoked haddock."

"I thought we sourced only locally-grown foods." Mindy sounded peevish.

"I have a vendor in Maine," I said. "Come, I think you'll enjoy it."

"I'm game," said Jake. "Thanks, Camilla, that would be great."

"Hmphh." Mindy turned on her heel.

I helped them load the last of the glasses and their crates into the van, took them back to the catering kitchen, and helped Manuela load the dishwasher again. I hugged her as I paid her, and Manuela's swelling belly bumped against my belt.

As she left, I pushed the door shut and leaned my back against it, taking ten deep breaths.

"Mindy, here's your paycheck, end of the month."

"Wow! Thank you, Camilla, nice bonus!" Mindy waved the check in the air. I smiled. It was silly to get all childishly jealous at Jake's attentions to the younger woman. Mindy was all right, really. "Yes, it's something to celebrate, but it's been a long day. Why don't we call it a night?" I said.

"Sure. But I'm hungry, haven't eaten a thing. Want to get a bite, Jake?" Mindy turned to Jake, her eyes shining.

My smile faded, and an ache started in my throat. Take the high road. Mindy had clearly taken Jake's affections. "You two go ahead if you like. I'm beat." I wiped a water spill from the counter and stole a look at Jake from under my eyelashes.

Jake gazed at me with his dark eyes and gave a slight nod. "Me, too. It's been a long night. Mindy, I'll pick you up at around noon to go to the North Shore. Camilla, we'll see you later tomorrow." Before either of us could utter a word, he'd backed out of the room, and we heard his feet clatter down the fire escape.

I pulled some Brie and a spray of green grapes from the fridge. "Here." I handed Mindy a hunk of French bread. "Happy New Year." I found two glasses and poured two modest portions of white wine. I raised them in a toast. "Help me lock up here, Mindy, and let's get some rest."

****

Now, on New Year's Day, I slept late. Slept the sleep of the deeply weary. About one o'clock I rose and went for a run. The city streets were almost empty. Strong gusts of wind blew newspapers, coffee lids, and other detritus into the snowbanks on the side of the roads. I slowed a bit to look in shop windows and realized there was little I wanted to buy. Not that I could afford even to think about new clothes; I'd had to buy my ticket for England. Good thing it was the low season. I'd never have been able to afford to go at the height of summer.

After I'd showered and changed, I walked the several blocks to the catering kitchen, where Manuela was finishing up the last of the dishwashing. The girl's face was drawn with tiredness.

"Manuela! You didn't need to come in to do this. Enjoy the rest of your day."

Manuela beamed, and she wiped her hands on her apron.

"Thank you, Miss Camilla. But I wanted to finish clean." She hung up her apron and pulled on a sweater. "New Year so cold here in Boston. I miss summer New Year at beach."

"I suppose you must. So go home now and put your feet up. You've got something to look forward to this summer here in New England."

The dark-haired girl strained to fasten the buttons on her coat. She must be farther along than she claimed. How would we cope without her? I must make a New Year's resolution about that. But for now, it was enough to think of tonight.

Inside the huge stainless steel fridge, I found what I'd been looking for, Finnan haddie. I'd been craving this treat of my childhood, and just before Christmas had ordered the expensive smoked fish, meaning to experiment with the traditional cullen skink. It was traditionally served thick and mushy, which did not appeal. This afternoon, I'd make it like a chowder.

I cradled the precious packet against my coat as I battled a strong wind on my walk home. Upstairs in the apartment I always found cramped in summer but cozy in the depths of winter, I started to make the soup. I had rolls in the freezer, thank goodness; I wasn't going to make bread for Mindy! A spritz of annoyance shot through me. Still, I was going to make a party, a little celebration for friends. I wasn't quite sure if Mindy was a friend, and Jake was a new acquaintance, but yes, I wanted very much to be his friend. I wiped the counter and then took out my tools.

A sliced onion, a sachet of rosemary, thyme, bay leaf, and sage, and a piece of the cold-smoked haddock all went into a big pot. Bringing it to a boil, I skimmed off the scum, covered the saucepan and reduced the heat. A lovely aroma warmed the tiny galley kitchen. I hovered, lifted the fish out as it started to flake, and removed the skin and bones. I refrigerated the fish and while the skin and bones simmered, peeled and quartered the potatoes. When the stock was done, I strained it, returned it to the pot with the potatoes, and set the pot to simmer once more.

As I opened the windows to let out the fishy smell, a fresh cold wind blew in, fluttering the newspaper I'd left on the coffee table. I needed a speedy clean up! I fluffed the pillows, hoovered the wooden floor and the faded rug.

The timer pinged. Putting away the vacuum and dust cloth, I had to laugh. I could spend hours cooking and only twenty minutes on cleaning! Stepping into the kitchen, I removed the potatoes from the saucepan and put them on a plate. The addition of milk turned the soup creamy, and just before it boiled, I put the potatoes and the fish back into the white fish stock and added some chives. Voila! The soup was done. I made a salad, set the table with vintage china and two mismatched candlesticks, put on some soft music, and waited for the doorbell to ring.

There was something unnerving about the sound of two sets of feet thumping up the stairs to the apartment. What kind of a day had it been for Jake and Mindy? They tumbled in the door, faces flushed, hair wild. Mindy's eyes challenged, a look of smugness in them as she hung her coat in the closet by the door. I hugged them both and felt the cold fuzz of Jake's cheek. Jake bent to tug his boots off, and his dark eyes caught mine, unreadable. "It's a real nor'easter out there," he said. "Huge waves."

"It was sort of fun on the beach, till it got scary," Mindy said. "Then we couldn't find any shelter. Finally, we found a coffee shop open and sat there for hours till the owner kicked us out."

"Umm." I wondered what Mindy and Jake had talked about. Actually, I couldn't imagine what they'd have to talk about. Mindy was so brainless, really. No, that was unfair. Mindy was very pretty, quite opinionated, and intensely practical, but Jake, he had an air of mystery about him. I said, "Did you find what you were looking for, Jake, in those waves?" I gave him a glass of whiskey. "This will warm you up."

I pointed him to the sofa, a lumpy outcast I'd found at an estate sale. I'd hidden its stains with an assortment of velvet tasseled pillows and a throw rug and saw how Jake, tall and muscular, settled in there slightly uncomfortably, hemmed in by cushions.

"I didn't know you did seascapes." The next instant I hung my head, regretting the comment. Jake's art was original, luminous, pulsing with feeling.

"Thanks." He took the whiskey and gulped it.

"Seascapes? No. I'm more of an abstract expressionist. I'm trying to capture atmospherics, going to start a series on climate change."

"That's political! That sort of spoils it for me." Mindy raised a glass of red wine to her lips. She stood beside the dining table, fingering one of my crisply pressed cutwork napkins. "I think artists should stay out of politics."

"Why?" Jake jiggled his drink.

"Because it makes the work look dated in a few years. Anyway, people get annoyed if they're being preached to."

"I don't mean to preach," Jake said softly. His eyes were on the amber liquid in his drink. "Anyway, some things are larger than politics. I don't want to paint pretty pictures just so they look nice on a wall." He put his glass on the floor next to the sofa and stood up, knocking pillows aside. He strode into the kitchen. I followed him.

"Do you paint political works?" I said. "I did see the review of your exhibition."

"And?" Jake frowned.

"The reviewer praised the paintings. He said you had emotional depth."

"Yeah. In the next review, right next to mine, he had accolades for a guy whose work features skulls, bones, eyes, and cameras spying on people. Some critics think art should be a social commentary on the nastiness of modern society."

"But most people—and Mindy—think it should be the opposite."

"Look, I don't believe any artist worth anything just puts paint on the canvas to make a pretty scene. But

Mindy's right. Artists whose work is about the politics of the day date themselves quickly. Politics is always about conflict. Artists can get beyond that, can't they? They can express wonder and try to get at it—what beauty is—in their work too."

"Yes, of course. I didn't mean to irritate you." Perhaps he hated talking about emotional things. I stood with my hand on the sink, facing him. He looked agitated.

"I'm better with paint than words. Still, not always getting it right. That's frustrating." He picked up a fork and held it to the light.

"It must take a lot of energy and give you a work-out every day, at least. Better for you than sitting in front of a computer." I couldn't believe I'd said those words, looking blatantly at his toned abdomen, his strong arms.

He didn't seem to notice my gaze. He paced the kitchen and gestured toward the window, which reflected our faces. "Light. It's white, right? But it has all the colors of the rainbow in it. The sea, it looks blue, or green, or gray, like today, but water's clear, too, transparent." He looked at me intently. "Things look one way, but they're really something else altogether." His hands flopped to his sides.

"Maybe art is more like science than people realize. Like trying to get at what's behind everything. Is that what you're saying?"

"Kind of." His brow knotted as if he were trying to assess if I understood.

I turned off the stove and pulled a ladle from the drawer. "Sounds more like philosophy to me." I'd never thought of art that way.

I called into the next room. "Mindy? Could you toss the salad, please? Oil and vinegar are on the table."

Jake went over to the window, flung it open, and took a deep breath of the cold night air. It whooshed through the kitchen, ruffling the tea towel hanging on the stove handle.

"Not politics or sociology, whatever that is. Skulls and spies," he said. "I've seen enough of that."

"Want to tell me?"

He looked at me strangely, his eyes far away. Then he banged the window shut. He held his hands out, offering to help. "Not really. Let's eat. I'm starving! What do you have here?"

"Help me bring this to the table." I filled a basket with crusty rolls and ladled the soup into a large tureen. It was one of my finds from Brimfield Antique Fair, a Victorian-style covered pot, in pristine white, with a scalloped lid and a curve so graceful and full it reminded me of a pregnant belly. Whoa! Where did that thought come from?

My eyes met Jake's in that instant, and I recognized that he, too, felt the jolt of tension between us. I handed him the bowl, touching his hands for a second longer than I needed to. He lifted a finger over mine in response. We paused. I said, "I'm going to England next week. Have to help settle my father's estate, clear out the house. But I'll be back soon as I can."

"Mindy told me," he said. "There's a couple of gigs she said I could work."

"Right. That's good. Mindy will be in charge." I gave a tight smile. Over dinner, I tried to keep the conversation light, poured wine for everyone. Even

Mindy praised the smoky chowder, and I gave her the largest slice of apple crumble with a huge dollop of ice cream on top. Mindy's eyes grew wide as I placed it before her, questioning. Whether the enormous helping was to reward her or punish her I was not quite sure.

Chapter Seventeen

The cloud was the blue-gray of a great whale as the plane flew under it to arrive at Heathrow. I felt cradled yet confined in familiarity as it landed. I caught the Piccadilly line to King's Cross and finally came out into the brisk early morning air of East Anglia. The air was cool, but not as bone-chilling as Boston's in mid-January. In fact, as I made my way to Tilda and Rupert's house, I noticed pansies brightening doorsteps. The taxi motored by the Cam and I was pleased to see the swans gliding sedately by as they had since the time of the Tudors. Along the banks, snowdrops poked up their white heads. On the other side of the road, pink viburnum blossoms peeked over brick garden walls and through metal gates the grass twinkled green under a frosty cover, releasing its dew.

Tilda must have heard the taxi's door slam. She opened the door, pulling on a cardigan. "You came!" She sounded a bit put out. "Why didn't you tell me what time? I would have picked you up."

Tilda always wanted to be seen to do the right thing. But I needed that little pause between arriving in town and coming to my sister's house. The taxi ride along the river had revived me. Still, apologies were in order. "I sent an e-mail—I thought I did, anyway. But maybe I didn't say exactly when I was coming—hated to bother you. What with customs and trying to catch a train, it's always difficult to get an exact ETA."

"Anyway, you're here now—the children will be delighted." Tilda led the way into the house. "You know your way to the guest room, don't you? Go up and I'll make some coffee for us."

"I'd love that. And I'm so glad to be able to see the girls, too. Not that I have presents! Could I sneak in a day of shopping?"

Tilda raised her eyebrows. "Shops will be packed. January sales."

"All the better for bargains." I resisted slapping my own wrist. How could I not have taken the time to buy presents? "You can help me choose, Tilda. I haven't a clue what little girls want these days." I started to climb the stairs.

"We don't have a great deal of time, do we?" Tilda called after me. "Could you do your shopping later? Please, let's tackle the house. It simply must be sold. We've had it valued, now we have to clear it all out."

I didn't answer. I had to concentrate on holding on to the handrail on the narrow stairs while hauling up my bag. I thumped the suitcase on the floor of the bedroom, sat on the bed and wiggled my toes. I looked around. Dust still covered the old dresser. Since my last visit Tilda had added a white Victorian washing bowl and a large jug filled with water. I recognized it. My sister had already selected things from the family home without waiting for me. Why had I bothered to come then? It wasn't worth an argument. I was kidding myself if I believed I came just to help Tilda clear out the house. Who was in that photo from my father's desk? Maybe I could find a clue here, now that I had a little time. I poured water into the bowl and washed my face with the towel hanging on a narrow wooden rod. I went downstairs gingerly, bones aching with weariness from the overnight flight.

Tilda was waiting in a room off the back of the kitchen. Winter sunlight bounced off the glass of the coffee carafe and onto flower-sprigged plates, on which sat some squat rounded scones. I accepted one and poked at a protruding raisin with a finger.

"I should have come back more often. You know Daddy and I didn't get along and I—well, it was hard." I kept my eyes on the scone.

"We all sensed that. But we didn't understand why. Rupert and I, and probably Geoffo. But you're here now, that's all that matters."

I worried the scone, crumbling it on the plate. "I feel I didn't really know Daddy. He seemed to operate way above my head. I could never really talk to him without feeling he was giving me a lecture. Four years between Mummy's funeral and Daddy's, and I didn't come once to see him. I know it's a long time. But I was busy." I pushed at my plate. "You see, Vincent got a tenured job offer at Harvard and then I needed to set my business up in Boston, and well, it's been rather hectic since then."

"I never did say how sorry I was that you and Vincent…" Tilda lowered her eyes to the coffee plunger, giving it a strong push to settle the grounds.

I held out a cup. "Yes. Well, very painful at the time, Tilda. But I'm all right now."

Tilda gazed at me as if looking at me for the first time. "The more fool him! You're pretty, you know. You always were the beauty of the family. I was jealous."

I raised my eyes from the scone. Tilda, the perfect daughter, Tilda the university graduate who had married successfully. Tilda, jealous! Imagine that. Maybe our parents' death had removed the pretense we'd lived under.

She was suddenly all business. "You know, let's leave the present shopping till later. What's one more day for a delayed Christmas gift?"

I winced. "Sorry about that," I said. "Things have been so frantic at work I had to hire a new person full time, then add another bartender, and well, let's just say the cash flow has been tight. I'll get through it."

Tilda looked at me with sudden sympathy. "That was thoughtless of me, I know. Here I was imagining you free as a bird, with just yourself to worry about, while I have the children and Rupert to manage."

Was Tilda being ironic? I looked about at the light-filled breakfast room, pictured the furniture-clotted sitting and dining rooms beyond it, the cluttered bedrooms, and tamped down a little spurt of resentment. Rupert had paid for all of it. Tilda had not worked a day since Rose was born.

"You know, I think William wants to see you," she said.

My coffee sloshed as my hand shook. The nerve of him. My heart went pit-a-pat.

"Do ring him, will you? He was quite full of it at Christmas, some news he wants to impart. Not that he thought we were important enough to give it to. I must say, Rupert got a little terse with him. Told him to spit it out. He reminded me to tell you before he left this morning."

"I see."

"Well, I don't. It's a great mystery. William asks about you every now and again, wanted to know why you went back to America so early after Daddy's funeral."

Did he now? "You told him it was because my firm was swamped with work, I hope, and I just had to get back?"

"Yes, yes, of course. I did get the impression he wanted to see you, Camilla. I mean you only saw him the day of the memorial service, and you hardly saw Geoffrey either. And Geoffo, after all, is your real brother."

I said nothing. I swigged the coffee and reached for another scone.

Tilda emptied a vase of its dying jonquils, rinsed it, and put it away in a cupboard. "I have an idea. We could have a dinner. Geoffrey and Malcolm, of course, and some other of your friends, if you like, and we'll invite William. How would that be?"

Acutely embarrassing. I ran a hand through my hair.

"I might make a hair appointment," I said. "I just haven't had time in Boston. Can I ask your hairdresser to fit me in?"

Tilda patted her own new hairdo. A recent new fluffy cut made her look slightly like a bantam hen, highlighted tresses feathering around her narrow pale face and her small straight nose. It suited her personality. Rupert tended to crow and strut, and Tilda fussed alongside him, often appearing put out as if she'd just been denied a chicken-coop crumb.

My sister said, "I take it that is not an absolute 'no' about a dinner party? You want to look your best."

"You could say that." The scone crumbled in my mouth, and I ran a hand down the side of my sweater, feeling the curve of my waist.

Trapped. I'd walked into it willingly, even hopefully. I could not refuse a get together with my brother and his partner and Billy, our former foster brother, if Tilda put it like that. Maybe Lucy and Hugo could come. Lucy would give moral support.

"London's a long train ride for an evening. Let's make it Sunday lunch."

Tilda came to the chair and rubbed my shoulders. "Yes, Rupert would like that. He always loves a good Sunday roast."

"Can he get some bottles of a good red? We'll make it really special."

"Good girl. This is excellent, Camilla. Let's arrange it for next Sunday, shall we?"

"All right."

"I was thinking we could use the lovely silver Mummy had and her good china."

"I thought Geoffrey put dibs on that."

"He did. He has such good taste. This will be one last time we use it as a family."

"What's the plan today?" I said.

"Sort and clean. Go through the books and so forth. Decide what each of us wants to take." Tilda's face looked pained, and she took a long sip of coffee. "The agent said something about lengthening the line of sight—makes the house look bigger."

"He means decluttering, I think."

"Probably. These sales people really do talk doublespeak, don't they? Shall we get started?" Tilda whipped the cups and saucers off the table, installed

137

them in the dishwasher, snapped its door shut, and then went to get her coat.

I followed, bringing a big box of garbage bags, a bucket, and a broom. Inside Tilda's small car the broom, shoved into the back seat, kept hitting my ear so I had to hold onto it tightly.

Hauling the cleaning equipment into our parents' house, I noticed the pots by the front door had been emptied. Inside, I smelled the same stale air and again had the feeling of being assaulted by the patterned wallpaper and the clashing carpet.

As I moved furniture and packed books at our father's house, I told myself how ridiculous I was being about Billy. Why did he tell the family he wanted to see me? Was this the big announcement about his engagement to that girl I'd seen him with? No, of course not. He would not hurt me that way, humiliate me in front of the family. That was not the gentle Billy I'd fallen in love with all those years ago. In this house. But what had I been thinking? That Billy and I would actually make it a real relationship? It was a waste of time to think that. I should think of him as an old friend, that was all. In any case, I should just chill about having Billy over with my brother and his partner. Be brave. Be strong. It would be better, just for now, if Lucy, who knew everything, was not there to hover and over-interpret every word. Just the extended family.

"Would you do the inviting, then, Tilda? Ring Geoffo and Malcolm? Just the family, this Sunday." I picked up a cardboard box, took it into the dining room and started packing the old silverware from the sideboard drawers. The cutlery was an old Georgian pattern, not quite a complete set, modern pieces amidst the old. Geoffrey would enjoy sorting it out. Newspaper rustled as I worked. I called to Tilda in the next room, "Of course, if Billy would like to come I have no objection."

****

The glint of Sunday morning's winter light woke me. Looking out the guest room window I saw the bare-leaved crabapple tree glisten with the remains of snow that had fallen in the night. A glob of it loosened itself from a branch and fell silently. By lunchtime, it would be melted. Again, I thought of the contrast between England's milder climate and Massachusetts, stuck in the grip of winter till early April. There the lilacs didn't surge till the first week of May, but here lemon-scented honeysuckle blossomed openly as if daring the winter to defeat it. Perhaps that was the attitude I should take. Be undefeated. The shower thrummed my skin. Thank goodness Rupert and Tilda had modernized the bath to include a hand-held shower attachment. I hated those wallowing baths the English indulged in because they had no shower-heads. Nothing like a good hot shower to make one ready to face the world!

I picked out clothes from my small suitcase. A charcoal skirt and black tights. A sleeveless pullover and matching cardigan with the top buttons left suggestively undone. Makeup? I opened my bag of cosmetics and peering into the mirror above the dresser, experimented with a little gray eyeshadow and lipstick in a more vibrant red than I usually wore. I moved the chair from its place beside the desk in the cramped room and placed it in front of the dresser, then clambered up on it and teetered in front of the mirror, checking my full-length reflection, relieved that the skirt still fit. Yesterday, Tilda's hairdresser had given me a fashionable trim. My hair looked better than it had in months. I tossed my head so the light brown waves flared and then climbed off the chair.

Sitting on the bed, smoothing my tights from the ankle to above the knee, I rang Lucy. I'd have to make time to see her somehow on this trip, once again rip away from Tilda and the task of putting the best face on our father's house. I needed the wisdom of my friend.

"Oh, how lovely to hear! Will you be here long? No? Well, I do want to see you!" Lucy's chatter was reassuring. She was well, all was well.

I bent my face to the phone, aware that I was almost whispering, though there was no one else in the room. I imagined what Lucy must be thinking. I was acting like a dorky teenager, massaging every word and unspoken gesture from the beloved, trying to decipher a hidden meaning.

"Tilda's asked Billy to lunch! He told her he wanted to see me. Isn't it odd, Lucy? Why didn't he ask me himself?"

"Didn't you leave rather abruptly last September?"

"True. But—"

Lucy sighed. "Oh, Camilla, he's probably embarrassed. Maybe he thinks you think he didn't perform well or has bad breath or something."

"Lucy!"

"I recommend a strong glass of something before lunch. Then let him drink all he wants at lunch and just watch and see where the wind blows."

"Brilliant as always."

"Good. Now let's make that lunch date. Would Thursday work?"

****

Tilda always deferred to me in the matter of the menu. Very wise, that was. I planned a simple meal, meat, vegetables, and a baked dessert. Several things that could cook together at the same temperature, for Tilda liked economy, didn't want to waste energy heating up the oven for a single dish. But some things I insisted upon. I hated Yorkshire pudding. My roast beef would be on the rare side. Several times in the late morning I had to banish Rupert from the kitchen when he grumbled that the meat was not yet on. I sent him off with a piece of cheese, and he'd gone to pick up the visitors at the railway station.

Now there was a scatter and a scramble at the door as Lily rushed toward the doorbell and her uncle Geoffrey. I followed and saw my brother look up as he bent to pick up the little girl and pull her into his arms. He grinned, then his face was obscured by Lily's wisps of hair. He handed Lily to Malcolm, who gave the child a big squeeze, and came toward me for a long hug.

"It's been an age—seems such a long time since the funeral. I don't think you've ever met Malcolm, have you?" Geoffrey brought his partner forward by the hand.

Malcolm was a burly chap with curly brown hair. He looked like he had played football at school and now strained a little at his shirt. His face was kind and intelligent.

"Delighted!" He pumped my hand. "You live in Boston, I understand. I spent a little time there some years ago. Beacon Hill. The most English-looking of all American cities, isn't it?"

"We must talk about all that," I said, looking past

him to Rupert, who was locking the car. With him was Billy.

I lingered in the hall and the men pushed through. Billy came up the steps last. I looked into his eyes and saw happiness, a slight resentment, and that deep knowledge we shared mingling in their blue depths. I caught my breath. He wore a leather jacket and jeans—lightly dressed for the weather. I wanted to hug him and to pummel him at the same time.

"Camilla." He came forward and held my hands for a moment in his in a gesture of friendliness but formality.

My insides tumbled. All I wanted to do at that moment was to run away with him, away from the chattering family, down to the back of the garden, off to the pub, up to the attic bedroom. It was like a river between us, the current of attraction.

"You left. Without a word," he said in a low voice.

"I did. I think you know why."

"Do I?"

His eyes changed as if he'd hooded their inner depths, and I lost the connection between us. My shoulders tensed. "You'd better come in, then. Tilda wanted to do the full Sunday lunch, sort of a post-Yule celebration. I understand you spent Christmas Day here."

"Yes. I do that—have done that—quite often. Depending on what's going on. *Tu casa es mi casa* and so on."

"I think it's the other way around. My house is your house, but yes, our family was your family for some time. It's good you keep in touch."

"And you, Camilla, how have you been?" Billy

now turned his hips sideways to me, a slightly defiant pose, as he opened a closet in the hall, removed his jacket and hung it, as if he knew the place well.

"I've been absolutely snowed under. And of course it does snow in Boston a lot, but I meant in terms of work." I crossed my arms in front of my chest. "I really did have to get back to Boston in September, you know. My assistant almost had a nervous breakdown while I was away."

"Yes, you are indispensable." Billy's voice held a hint of sarcasm. "And now, what will happen while you are here?"

"I have more staff now, and January is our quietest month, apart from August. So I was able to get away. I couldn't come for Christmas, as I'm sure Tilda explained."

"Well come on, come in and get warm." Rupert approached, rubbing his hands. "Sherry?"

"I'll just get back to turn the potatoes," I said.

"Come on, old girl, we can't have you stuck in the kitchen. Turn the oven on low and come in and join us for a drink."

"In a sec." I excused myself and went back into the kitchen. I straightened my skirt, smoothed my hair, and drank a glass of water. Despite Lucy's advice, it wouldn't help if my tongue was loosened under the influence of alcohol. The scent of roasting meat rose as I opened the oven and turned the potatoes and parsnips with a fork. They were browning nicely.

Rose appeared, a tray in her small hands. "Mummy said could I bring in something to start with—the men are starving!" She giggled.

"Oh, they'll just have to wait, won't they! But let's

see, what can we find?"

I looked in the pantry cupboard. "Here. Let's open this jar of olives. Here are some nuts. That will do." I brought down two little Chinese bowls from an upper cabinet, untwisted the jar of olives and spooned them in. "Here, Rosie, you pour the nuts in this other bowl. You are a helper." I smiled encouragingly as Rose walked out of the room carefully holding the tray in front of her. "Tell Mummy it will be ready in a few minutes—Daddy can get ready to carve."

I was hiding in the kitchen. How ridiculous. Here I was in my own sister's home, and I was acting like the caterer, not engaging with the guests but tending to the food. Even if the guests were my own brother and my former lover.

Let it burn. Or let it grow cold. I hung up the apron and followed Rose into the sitting room. Tilda could be seen through the open doors of the dining room fussing with the table, moving little vases of winter jasmine to make room for another set of glasses.

"You're on, Rupert," I said. "Whenever you're ready to carve."

"Right oh," said Rupert. "Come on, Geoffrey, let's get this show on the road."

"Absolutely. Just a word with Mille for a second."

He took me aside as he fished in his pocket for an envelope. "I had these printed from that trove of floppies you and Tilda found," he said.

"Oh? Thank you. And? Anything interesting?"

"Not really. Some papers, sermons, a photo of some kind of publicity event—ribbon cutting it looks like. Nothing to write home about."

"All right. Best just to put them in Rupert and

Tilda's study. Rupert might need them for the estate."

"Will do. Now, kitchen duty. You relax."

I meandered back to the others, took the proffered sherry from Billy, avoiding his eyes as I did so, and focused attention on Malcolm. He was only too happy, as he scooped mouthfuls of peanuts, to chat about his visits to Boston for his work with a bio-tech company. Ignoring Billy completely, I asked Malcolm about what the company did, my head spinning slightly as he tried to explain genomics.

Billy seemed faintly amused at my forced focus. I sensed the smile at the corner of his mouth as Malcolm talked about the potential pharmacological use of genes.

"Interesting, it must be such interesting work," I said to Malcolm, realizing that I had not the faintest idea what he was talking about.

"Lunch is served," boomed Rupert. He carried into the dining room a platter of thin-carved roast beef. Rose followed with a rounded dish of potatoes and parsnips, shiny with the fat they'd roasted in, aromatic with rosemary. Geoffrey brought in the mixed green vegetables, while Tilda wrestled Lily into a chair. She was past the booster seat stage but needed a little padding to bring her waist to the table top, so Billy offered a cushion from one of the kitchen chairs, thoughtfully covered with a tea towel. I watched it all, sherry still in hand. Amazing to see a meal being served without my doing the work. It was a pleasure, really.

Billy now took my elbow and led me to my seat. Rupert and Tilda presided over each end of the table next to a daughter, to attend to the cutting of her meat in Lily's case, and her table manners, in Rose's. Geoffrey and Malcolm sat opposite me, and I sat to

Rupert's right. The only place, the natural place, for Billy, then, was next to me. No one else seemed to think it contrived.

I felt a tingling along my right side, a subterranean message from Billy. But he kept the conversation general and the topics light, even sometimes amusing, till the plates were cleared and Tilda carried in the rhubarb crumble and whipped cream.

"Where's the custard?" Rupert glared at me.

"Camilla's trying not to kill us with cholesterol," said Tilda. "You know what's in custard, Rupert? Besides the cream we have here, there are egg yolks, sugar, and cornflour."

"It's so yummy. I want custard!" Rose banged her spoon on the plate.

"Stop that or you'll be sent from the table!" Tilda shot Rose a sharp look.

"I want custard too!" Lily chimed in, thumping her spoon on her plastic plate. Bits of rhubarb splattered on the tablecloth.

"I'll make you some custard later," I whispered across the table to Rose. "You can have it for your supper."

"Can I? I don't like rhubarb. It's too bitter."

"That's enough!" said Tilda. "Children, you may be excused."

"Should I make some coffee?" I started to get up from the table, but Billy held me back. His palm dug into the bones on the back of my hand.

"Not yet," he said. "I have something I wanted to tell you. Tell all of you, who were my family when I was a kid."

All eyes looked at him. My heart thumped.

"It's the most amazing thing." He stopped. He swallowed visibly, his Adam's apple bobbing.

"Yes?" Rupert said. The sound of the girls playing at the back of the house could be heard as the table silenced.

"I've discovered I've got a sister."

No one said anything for a minute. As I looked at the faces of my brother and sister I saw they remembered as I did the lonely boy who had come to live with our family all those years ago, fatherless, with a dying mother and no one else to care for him.

"Really? That must be wonderful for you, William," Tilda said at last. Her face had gone pale. "Is it an Irish sister, one who was somehow left behind when you and your mother left?"

"Not at all," Billy looked a bit confused by this question as if it had never occurred to him. He released my hand.

"Not a love child your mother had as a teenager?" Geoffrey chimed in. "I've heard that long-lost daughters and sons try and find their parents when they're older and then they find their siblings as well."

"Well, you're on the right track, Geoff," Billy said.

"How old's the girl?"

"Nineteen."

"So you were a teenager when she was born. Old enough to be a father yourself." Geoffrey stood. "Excuse me a minute. Nature calls. But do go on, Will. Fascinating story." He left the room and all eyes followed him. Silence fell.

Billy said, deliberately, drawing out the words, "It turns out my mother did have a baby. She had my sister just before she died. I had no idea she was pregnant."

"That's odd, how did that happen?" Rupert interrupted.

I started to fold my napkin, in half, then in quarters, then in eighths. Rupert had no manners whatsoever.

"Well, Rupert, I supposed it happened in the normal way." Billy picked up his glass. "Is there any more of that wine?"

Rupert passed the bottle down the table and Billy poured the entire remainder into his glass and took a long sip.

Tilda started fussing with the plates. Rupert put his hand up, and she silenced as Billy spoke.

"You know my mother died when I was fifteen. She had cancer. I came to live with your family when she was so sick and Mum didn't have any relatives or anything to stick me with. Your father was my mother's doctor, actually."

"Yes, we realized that. That's what he told us when you came to live with us." Tilda frowned at Billy. "Go on."

"Yes, well, what I didn't realize, what no one in your family was told, was that my mother was pregnant. It's the weirdest thing. She had a cancer that got worse when she got pregnant. She was hospitalized most of the time, and I just didn't see her much before she died. She had a baby and since she was so sick, she had it adopted out." He took a deep drink. "No one told me."

"Who should have told you?" Rupert asked. "What good would it have done?"

Billy turned to me and reached for my hand under the table. "I didn't know she had a lover," he said. He sounded desolate.

"That's something single parents often keep from children." I squeezed his hand. No one else seemed to notice the warmth rising to my face.

"Yes, I suppose you're right. Of course, you're right." Billy bowed his head.

"Well, who is this sister? How did she get in touch with you?" Rupert asked.

"She found me through the adoption records, somehow. She found her mother, then she traced me."

"What about the father?"

"She says the records said, father unknown."

Silence hung in the room. The family knew nothing of Billy's mother beyond what Billy had told us when he was a teenager. It was Rupert who broke the silence.

"Cheer up, old chap. That doesn't necessarily mean your mother was a trollop."

"Rupert!" Tilda sounded shocked.

"I just meant that if a woman is unmarried, she doesn't have to put the father's name on the birth record. In fact, only if the father signs a statutory declaration saying he is the father should his name be recorded. The mother has every right, if she so chooses, not to name the father."

Geoffrey came back into the room. "Must have missed something," he said, "But I heard this girl has no father? Why wouldn't a woman want to name the father of her child? Wouldn't she want to claim child support?"

"Not necessarily. If the child was to be adopted it wouldn't need financial support from the parents. Anyway, perhaps a woman might like to be independent and not be beholden to a man!" Tilda pushed her plate away from her so forcefully it banged into a glass, which in turn threatened to knock over one of the little jars of jasmine. Everyone turned to look at her. Tilda gave Rupert a hard stare. I shifted uncomfortably in my seat.

Rupert pushed himself away from the table, as if about to end a conversation he found distasteful. He said, "Under the circumstances, considering Will's mother was not married at the time, we have to assume she was trying to protect someone. Probably a lover who was married to someone else."

"All right, that's enough." Tilda wiped her lips with a napkin. "All of that's in the past. The important point is that William's found that he has family—apart from us, his foster family. That must feel good. Doesn't it, William?"

Billy looked up from his glass and smiled at Tilda. "Yes. After I got over the shock it did feel good. Strange, but good. I wanted to tell you together. Maybe you'd like to meet her, sometime. She seems very eager to know all about us."

Malcolm broke in. "I do understand that, Will. For you, it must have been a link with your mother, whom you lost as a boy, and for her, an amazing discovery. Of course, she'd want to know about any genetic diseases you carry and so on. That's the main reason adopted people try to trace their birth parents."

"Come on, Malc. I'm sure there are sentimental reasons also." Geoffrey, too, pushed his seat back. "Thanks for telling us. Now, Malcolm, let's clear these things and get them washed up, shall we? Then, what about a bracing stroll before we catch the train?"

Rupert and Tilda helped clear the table in silence. Billy and I were left sitting there. I pulled his hand from under the table, raised it, and brushed my lips along his knuckles. I looked into his eyes. I saw that Billy, too, was thinking of that time, twenty years ago, when we were children who recognized each other as lost.

Chapter Eighteen

"You coming for a walk?" Malcolm, Geoffrey, and Rupert were at the door. Rose was struggling into a coat and Tilda, in front of Lily, held her jacket down so the child could point her arms like a windmill to get her arms into it.

"You go ahead," I called. "We'll catch up."

Billy and I sat unmoving at the dining table and watched the front door close. I heard him take a deep breath. He put his hand on my chin and gently pivoted my head toward him.

"You ran away. You left me hanging. Why?"

"In September? After our one-night stand?" I could hear my voice clang.

"It didn't have to be. I thought you'd come back that evening. But you left, leaving your stuff at my house. No explanation. No call, no e-mail. How do you think that felt?" He dropped his hand to the table so hard the cloth squirmed.

"I thought you were two-timing me. Not that I had any right to expect anything else. I thought perhaps you just wanted reunion sex."

"You bet I did. With you."

"Where did you think it would lead?"

"I don't know. I hadn't got that far. I saw you again and it all came back."

Yes, it had. But obviously not as strongly for him

as it had for me. I stared at the smeared tablecloth. Then I looked up and saw his face soften. His hand relaxed. He said, "You're beautiful, you know."

"That girl I saw you with, in the restaurant—"

"What girl? What restaurant?"

"That day. The day after. I was at the Royal Academy with Lucy and then she left, and I was walking around, aimlessly, in Mayfair. I looked in a café window and saw a girl. I don't know why I stopped and then she looked at me and you turned halfway, and I recognized you."

"So, why didn't you come in and introduce yourself?"

"Oh, Billy. Don't. I just assumed, stupidly, that this was your lover. I know now why I assumed that. My husband, Vincent, he dumped me for another woman so I guess it was just an instinctive reaction."

"The girl was Rachel."

"Rachel?"

"My sister. Half-sister. None of you asked her name, by the way, this afternoon."

"Rachel," I said the name slowly, letting the "l" roll on my tongue.

"She'd only just got in touch with me. She could only go looking on her own once she turned eighteen. Somehow she found me."

My fingers curled. I couldn't seem to get it right, my dealings with men. I'd missed their signals, misunderstood their intentions and their actions. What Billy had been dealing with for months, he'd been unable to share with me, the person who used to be his best friend. The idea that his mother had had a baby without his even knowing! I pushed a clenched fist to my forehead.

"I'm so sorry. I should have talked to you, shouldn't have jumped to conclusions. What you've had to go through."

"Pretty incredible. To find I have an actual sister, a half-sister, anyway."

"Didn't you realize your mother was pregnant? That was pretty unobservant of you."

"Yeah. Well, she told me she had cancer, and I thought her swollen belly was the tumor. Actually, she had breast cancer."

"Oh. I shouldn't have said that, Billy. It was thoughtless of me."

"Mum was so pretty." He took a strand of my hair and stroked it between his fingers, drawing it downward. "She had blue eyes and brown hair like you do, come to think of it. Maybe a bit more red, in the color." He put his hand on my cheek and rubbed his thumb gently down my face. "It was just me and her together against the world she used to say. She always said she came to England because she wanted me to get an education, get a scholarship to one of the good schools so I could go to university. Of course, that didn't happen. I was disappointed too, I suppose, but probably not as much as Mum was. I thought we could just go on as we were."

I kissed his thumb, then put his hand gently back on the table. The three little green pots of jasmine that Tilda had so carefully arranged looked abandoned now that all the silverware and plates had been removed. "Then you came to us," I said.

"The first night was awkward when your father said I should stay. I hoped he would. Mum told me that was the plan, but I had to wait for him to suggest it to the family. I could see that you were not quite surprised. Kind of resigned. Geoffrey and Tilda were not pleased." He smoothed the tablecloth with his palm.

"I wanted the attic for myself! To do my painting. But Daddy said it was too hot up there and the paints might explode and the fumes would give us all cancer. So he made the attic into a bedroom. That other girl, Katerina took it. When she came to live with us, she upset the balance of everything. I couldn't understand why we couldn't just live with our own family."

"You told me your dad made a habit of bringing needy kids into the house. It must have been difficult. At the time, I just thought Tilda was snotty. Not that she was there much."

"I think Geoffo might have been a bit jealous of another male in the house."

"Probably. These sibling relations were pretty complicated for me to understand. I felt I walked on eggshells."

I laughed. "Having more than one sibling certainly prepares you for life! It's a jungle out there. As you know."

"Geoffrey was younger, so I didn't get it at first. But later I realized there was something different about him—I wasn't really surprised when he came out as gay. I always liked him."

"You and Geoffrey were alike, in a way. Calm. I used to feel Tilda and I were hysterical compared to you two."

Billy laughed. "Estrogen. Teenage girls." He looked at me, both of us remembering.

Hormones ran rampant in our house at the time, as

in any house with teenagers. So our relationship was inevitable. It must have been at the dining room table that it started. We were doing homework, a few months after Billy arrived. It was spring, and a soft breeze came through the dining room windows so the curtains fluttered.

His eyes changed color with the sky, his hair flopped forward a bit, revealing a fair streak in the brown. I stole glances at him from under my eyelashes. I could see that he was looking at me too, now and then, from behind his book. I had more homework than Billy did, but he seemed to be having some difficulties.

"What does 'pertubation' mean?" he'd said.

"Dunno. Can you look it up?" I shoved the dictionary across the table to him and it spun on its side and flopped, its pages falling open.

"We have to read all these pages and answer questions on them," Billy said. "I prefer algebra. It's either right or wrong."

"Why do you have to know that word?"

He grinned. "I don't. I just thought of it. That's what you're doing." He pushed his books in front of him and leaned over them, looking directly at me. "You're pertubating me."

"Perturbed is a word. Pertubating isn't."

"It does sound a bit obscene, doesn't it?"

We giggled.

Something broke that day, some sense of formality between us. Billy and I, almost the same age, subtly allied against Tilda, three years older, and Geoffrey, still a boy at three years younger. Tilda was not home much, in fact hardly at all. That helped.

"You were the one I could talk to. We talked about

everything, didn't we?" I lifted his hand from the tablecloth to run my finger down his palm. He still had those clean square nails on long fingers with a tinge of ginger hair across the knuckles.

What did we talk about in those days, and where? Down in the bottom of the garden mostly, or walking by the river, or sometimes, we met after school and went to the movies, holding hands in the dark. Billy didn't say much about his mother because it made him sad, but as teenagers, we considered the big questions. The big one. Why did his mother get sick? There was no answer, he told me, to be found in religion. His mother's illness had exposed the hollowness of heavenly hope, he said, and I had to agree.

"How does Daddy explain it?" I'd asked. "Don't people see the contradiction in God allowing terrible suffering if He could intervene at any time?"

"People pray for all sorts of stupid things, such as being able to pass their exams. Then they pray for something important. It doesn't seem to make a difference."

Billy had looked morose then, and I tried to cheer him up. I said, "We pray to strengthen the Queen so that she may vanquish and overcome all her enemies. I used to imagine the Queen doing push-ups and weight-lifting to increase her strength." He'd laughed at that.

"If we'd just left it at talking, everything would have been all right." I squeezed his fingers, hard, and the tablecloth rippled.

He gave me a quizzical look as if to say that was beyond imagining. I thought, not for the first time, that my parents must have been blind not to realize what would happen when they put two adolescents together in the same house with little supervision.

One day in the narrow passage to the hall he'd bumped into me as I was coming out of the bathroom. It was not deliberate, I could tell. But his body brushed against my breasts and I tingled through my sweater as though everything were electrified. He didn't say he was sorry. He didn't leer lewdly at me either. We looked at each other for a long time, and I put out my hand and took his. Our breaths sharpened.

We moved away from each other then. But it was a signal, and the next day we both seemed to be at the bottom of the garden at the same time. Billy made a show of putting the bags of rubbish in the bins, and I was about to cut a sprig of parsley for dinner. There was a woodshed at the bottom of the garden, and we both moved toward it, without consciously thinking. Ivy entwined the old wooden building, spiders had cobwebbed the window and the door creaked as it opened. Inside, he pulled me toward him, and we kissed.

What a kiss. So different from the greedy kisses of the few boys I had gone out with. Billy's kiss was gentle, soft, exploring, and I felt myself warming, a new sense of connecting to another, a sense of who I was, who he was, stirred from mouth to groin. When we pulled away, I saw that he understood that if we were to begin, we had to finish it. Not in the sense that we had to have sex then and there, we were teenage virgins after all, but that if we were to have what the adults called a relationship, it would not be frivolous. It would not be conquest on his part or the desire for experience on mine. It would be about becoming adults together. I would call it being in love, I suppose, except that was a silly phrase that my friends sometimes used. I'd have to say that what I felt was more of a deep understanding of this other human being.

It didn't happen for a while. Months, in fact. In retrospect, we were so good. Kids today would be into it in no time. But we were innocents for the longest while, considering we lived in the same house. Regretting, not what we did, but that we didn't do more of it, I now gave the dining table a little kick. Look what had happened, and here we were, twenty years on.

"You saw Geoffrey! You've been friends all this while, and I never knew. But you never even tried to get in touch with *me*!" I banged my hand on the table as a sharp pain of sibling jealousy tore through me. "You didn't write me a note or anything after you left. I would have met you somewhere, anywhere!"

"What would have happened if I'd tried to see you? Your father couldn't do anything more to me, but he could have made life even more difficult for you."

I picked at the hem of the tablecloth. I caught his eye and saw his determination to be honest.

"I think the main reason you're so angry at him is that you didn't protest hard enough. It's yourself you're really angry with. You could have taken a stand. At the time I wanted you to run away with me and you never stood up to your father." His voice sounded hoarse.

My throat ached. That was true. I was as much to blame as he was. I'd known I had too much to lose by chasing after Billy. I might have romanticized our relationship as Romeo and Juliet but I had not been nearly so brave as Juliet. I'd been too frightened, or too comfortable, to contemplate running, and while I had been depressed for months, I'd never once thought of suicide.

"I did want to. But I had no idea where you'd gone. Mummy said she didn't know and Daddy refused to discuss it."

"I'm sure. But anyway, what was the point? We were kids. Your parents made it quite clear I wasn't good enough for you. Good enough to be taken in like a lost puppy but not good enough for their daughter."

"How could you forgive me for that?" Tears wet my eyelashes.

"How could I ever ask you to give up your family?" Billy ran his thumb beneath my eye. "Anyway, we couldn't support ourselves, we were too young and had nowhere to go."

I hung my head.

"It was quite a while before Geoffrey tracked me down. We used to see each other in London from time to time. Never mentioned it to your parents, it seems."

"Among other things he never mentioned to them. Good old Geoffo."

My siblings had been in touch with Billy but hadn't let me know! I banged a fisted hand on the table. "But if he found you, why didn't he tell me, why didn't you?"

"He guessed about me and you and didn't tell anyone. Didn't want to upset you, I suppose."

"Used to keeping his own secrets." I raised my eyes to his. "But how could you forgive me later?"

"You mean, how could I forgive you after I realized that you'd given up your family after all, by marrying that bloke and moving to America?" He turned away as his voice grew hoarse. "It was hard. I never approached you. Didn't even come near you at your mother's funeral."

I got up from the table, went into the kitchen and brought back two glasses of water. I placed one in front of him and took a long draught from my own.

"You know, after that fiasco in London, I thought maybe you'd just wanted to have a one-night stand to get revenge for what my father did to you," I said. "It was so terrible. You can't throw someone out on the street like that."

"Yeah." He swallowed visibly.

"What happened after you left us? You won't talk about that."

He didn't answer. I felt the house's quiet through my skin. From outside I heard a distant train whistle. Billy pinged a little green vase with his pinkie. Finally, he said, "I went to a group home, modern name for an orphanage. For a while, till a friend at school told his parents, and they took me in. Stayed there till I turned eighteen. Worked part-time. Got a job as soon as I left school. Saved up and started taking classes in coding. I got loans and grants to help pay for my education. Without family means, I was entitled to some support from the government."

I could not imagine how hard it had been for him. My palm opened over the tabletop. The satin cloth smoothed under my hand, offering threads of comfort, as when a child, I had stroked my blanket.

Billy circled his arms around me, and drew me close, kissing my hair. He whispered, "Thinking of you kept me going. I held onto it, for years, you know, after I left."

"Me, too." I nuzzled his neck. "But now, you've got us back, and you've found a real sister."

"Would you like to meet her?"

I stiffened and drew back. No. The truth was, I didn't want to meet this stranger at all. What if Billy had had a sister all along? Would they both have come to live with us? If there had been an older sister, my relationship with Billy would have been entirely different. Billy's aloneness had made him what he was.

I wished this Rachel had not searched for her birth mother. I wanted my Billy all to myself. And Billy in his present form, sexy and grown up now, free, free for me, for both of us to explore a relationship. I didn't want to share it with a sister. But what was I thinking? This half-sister had nothing to do with my intimate relationship with Billy, our past, and our possible present. But, of course, there could be no present. I could not reclaim Billy. My life was in the United States now—I'd made that decision seven years ago and must return. I slipped from his embrace.

"We need to get outside into the fresh air," I said, "before it gets dark."

Chapter Nineteen

After Billy, Geoffrey, and Malcolm had left, and I'd made custard for the children's supper and sat politely through a boring television program with my sister and brother-in-law, I lay on my back in the guest bed on the top floor. I pulled the counterpane up to my chin and twisted it round and round.

Billy had a sister. Orphan Billy had a sister he'd just discovered. Or rather, she'd found him. It was like a Victorian novel. It seemed to change everything, but I couldn't figure out why. It should have been a relief to learn that the girl I believed Billy was two-timing me with was merely his sister. Half-sister. I should have been pleased. But I wasn't.

Rachel wasn't the only thing I'd learned about today! When Billy and I sat alone at the dining room table today and talked about what happened when we were young and then last September, I heard, for the very first time, about how Billy felt after he'd been banished.

What had hurt beyond anything was that after he had left our house, I never heard from him again. I knew now I was complicit in that. I had not fought hard enough for him. I'd not been able to stand up to my father, who was supposed to show compassion but displayed, instead, a flinty hardness.

My shame, when I asked Billy about what had

happened to him after he had left the Fetherwell home, made me want to hide. I rolled over on the bed and pulled the coverlet over my head. Then I pulled it off in a sudden rage. How blind had my parents been? How could they bring a teenage boy into their home without anticipating something like this? They had two daughters, after all. Had Tilda too, been attracted to Billy when he was a boy? Awful thought! But no, I didn't think so. Tilda didn't see much of him, or any of us, for that matter, at the time. She was away at university. And it was Tilda's absence that opened up the space within the household for me, a nubile young girl, and Billy, changing from boy to man, to turn to each other.

And now Billy had come back into my life. The ache of wanting him shocked me. The truth was, Billy was more attractive now than he ever was as a boy. He'd grown into himself as it were. He'd asked me to come up to London to see him in the next few days. Maybe I would. Then again, maybe I shouldn't.

At least he'd been honest. He'd wanted reunion sex. So did I. With him, with my particular, sweet, gorgeous Billy. No strings attached. To get him out of my system. Then the relationship could die a natural death.

But it didn't seem to be dying at all. The longing just got a whole lot worse. It was all such a tangle, that's what it was. A thicket of confused feelings.

The fact of the matter was that I lived on the other side of an ocean. And by being involved with Billy I would break his heart all over again, and mine.

I pushed the bedspread away with my legs, and it fell to puddle on the floor. I went to the bathroom and washed my face, splashing it with cold water after the warm so it stung. The sharp cold woke me up from my reverie.

The package Geoffrey gave me today, I should look at it. Just to check that it concealed no clues as to Daddy's—what? Just what he was getting up to, I suppose.

Tiptoeing downstairs, I edged my way into the study. I had to put my hands in front of me not to knock into furniture and fingered my way to the antique desk. My hands felt papers, and I was relieved I was able to reach to my right, where I remembered a lamp sat, to turn its low light on. The envelope lay on the desk, unopened. I slipped my finger into the flap and slit it.

As Geoffrey had said, the envelope contained notes, some with figures, some with writings, the beginnings of what looked like a paper on some medical discovery. Boring. Then, from the bottom of the pile I had laid out on the desk, I retrieved a printout of a photograph. It was of horrible quality. On the photo's pixilated surface, I discerned an image of my father. It seemed to be a photo of a ribbon cutting ceremony. The person cutting the ribbon looked familiar, too. I wracked my brain to remember the man who stood smiling next to my father. Then I recalled him. Dr. Petrovsky, Katerina's father. Well, that was no surprise. The two were friends; that's how Katerina had come to invade our house all those years ago. I peered again. Just behind the image of Dr. Petrovsky was that of a woman. The photo was black and white, but I could have sworn that her hair was distinctive, familiar. It fell in waves to her shoulders in varying shades of darkness. She was very pretty and smiled directly at my father.

Something roiled in my gut. I moved the photo from the pile of papers, folded these and slipped them back in the envelope. Clutching the photo-copied picture in my hand, I switched off the lamp and tiptoed my way out of the study. Trying not to creak on the stairs, I climbed back to my room on the third floor. I crossed to the bureau and pulled out the color print from under the lining. In the sharper light of my private room I studied both photographs. It was not quite clear, but I thought I could tell. The same woman peered out at the camera in both photos. N.B.

All right. I was overreacting. Two photos of the same woman and one was a picture of a public meeting, not a secret tryst. But the point was, they'd been hidden. I lay on the bed and stared at the ceiling. Outside the window an owl hooted, and the lights that had winked on in the neighbor's windows early in the winter dark went out one by one.

Chapter Twenty

The kettle whistled in Tilda's sunny kitchen, and though on Monday morning no one else was home to be disturbed by its shriek, I quickly silenced it. I was taking a late breakfast because of lingering jetlag, and besides, I'd had no desire to come downstairs to greet a grumpy Rupert gulping his tea and toast before hurrying to the train. I'd waited till the house was quiet and Tilda had driven Rose and Lily to school, before coming downstairs. I had just skipped over an article about suicide bombings and was searching for the comfort of the crossword puzzle when I heard the front door open, footsteps in the foyer, and a clatter as my sister flung her keys on the hall table. Tilda strode into the kitchen and glanced impatiently at me still in my robe and furry slippers.

"I do need to go back again," I said.

"Yes. Good. We've only done the ground floor." Tilda swished the breakfast dishes under the faucet and laid them on the rack.

"I mean I need to go back to the US. I can't spend too much more time on this, Tilda. My people in Boston are frantic."

"It's William, isn't it? Every time you see him you seem to be the one to get frantic."

"What do you mean?" Tilda's busyness made my toast stick in my throat. I bolted my tea, put the cup in the sink, and grabbed a sponge.

"I mean, inside, Camilla. All jiggly and nervous, like a deer."

I paused, about to wipe crumbs off the breakfast table. I slammed my hand down, and if it had not been protected by the sponge, I would have smashed my fingers.

Tilda emptied the sink, and its gurgle sounded like a strangled voice as she said, "You know, William's turned out so well, after losing both his parents so young and then, just leaving us so abruptly—I imagine you know all about that, of course."

"I'd say so, yes." I picked up the blue, sunflower-patterned tablecloth—a gift from Provence I'd given Tilda years ago—shook it into a trash can and laid it back on the table, all the while avoiding Tilda's eyes.

"It's clear that William's very fond of you, too. Lately, he's been asking about you, wondering if he could go over for a visit, try to get a job in America and so on."

"What?" I straightened with the salt and pepper shakers in my hands and stared at Tilda.

"Hasn't he discussed any of this with you?"

"No. Not at all. I wasn't in touch with him at all after we saw each other in September, after Daddy's funeral. I was a bit annoyed with him, in fact."

"Why?"

"It doesn't matter." None of your business, I wanted to say. "Anyway, none of that has anything to do with me. He can come to America to visit, who am I to stop him?"

"Well, that's all right then. I thought he was talking about going over for work."

"Getting a work visa is going to be difficult."

"Really? Maybe he does have grand career plans, I have no idea. Don't know what he can do there that can't be done here, after all."

"True enough." Why hadn't Billy talked about any of this with me? Of course, I hadn't given him much of a chance. I put the salt and pepper shakers carefully on the table and looked at Tilda out of the corner of my eye.

"I can never keep enough clean tea towels." Tilda produced one from a drawer. "But I suppose, really," she said, "Rupert and I were hoping you might want to come home."

"You mean you actually care?"

"What do you mean, silly sister?"

"You mean, you and Rupert care enough about me to suggest that I give up my life in America to come home to England—to start all over again? Build up a business, try to have a social life—spend the rest of my life here in this quiet little village, an hour's train ride from London?"

"Don't sound so snotty! You make it sound like a fate worse than death."

"I'm sorry. Of course, I didn't mean that. I'm just rattled, that's all."

"I can tell." Tilda gave the cups and saucers a swipe with the towel and stacked them, her back to me.

"Billy has just dropped this bombshell about his mother having a baby while she was dying, and so now he has a sister!" I pushed the salt next to the pepper with a little ping, then lifted the ladder-back chairs one by one and shoved them into their places at the table.

Tilda winced at the scraping sound. "So? Aren't

you glad for William? He's found some real family."

"He wants us to meet her."

"Why not? I'm curious. Aren't you?" Tilda swung around to face me. "You're jealous!"

"Am I? How could I be? This girl is Billy's sister. Nothing to do with me. It's just that I need to get back to my employees. They depend on me."

Good thing I hadn't actually made an arrangement to see Billy again, not a confirmed plan anyway. A vague promise.

Tilda was silent for a minute, then said, "It's so important then, this cooking business of yours?"

"I've made such an effort to make it a success. Had to, after Vincent and I divorced."

"Do you really like it there, in Boston? America? You're English. How can you adjust so easily?"

"People learn to adapt. My business has really taken off. I'm not sure I have it in me to start over again."

Tilda sighed. "All right then. Let's see what we can finish at the old house. Give it a couple more days. Then we can call the agent to take it from there." She took off her apron, hung it on a nail by the stove, and smoothed the front of her jeans. She hooked her thumbs over her belt as she leaned against the counter and faced me. "You still haven't put together your boxes of things you want to send over."

I folded my arms. "I think you don't really want me to. You want to keep everything here."

"Reminds us of our parents, of our childhood. Yes. To be truthful, I do."

"Well, you can have it all then! It's just too difficult for me to send furniture over the ocean. You

170

and Geoffrey divide it up, take the books to Oxfam—we've already discussed all that. It's all so old fashioned."

"You're so dismissive. Can't imagine what's got into you. Such negativity about our family. It's hurtful, you know." Tilda stalked into the front hall. "By the way, you might want to get dressed. We have lots to do. Please."

I didn't bother to shower, put on my dirtiest clothes, and grabbed a parka from the front hall closet as Tilda tooted from the car. I dived into the passenger seat, shivering.

Frost lay on the doormat of the old house. I picked the mat up and flicked it back and forth, shaking little crumbs of ice onto the ground. Outside, cold numbed the extremities, but everything inside me seemed to be on the boil. I attacked the house with a vengeance. Was I irritated at missing my work, not to speak of my income? I swept cobwebs out of the corners with a brisk broom. Was I frustrated at Tilda's inability to understand my situation? I ran an unnecessary amount of water into a bucket. Was I confused about Billy? I marched from room to room on the lower story and wielded the dust rag savagely at any available surface. Finally, the ground floor was as clean as it was ever going to be. With trepidation, with a sense of defeat, I suggested finally that we go up to the attic, and then finish up on the second floor.

Today I'd have to tackle, with Tilda, the bedrooms of the old house. Too many memories lay there, but Billy's presence yesterday set the stage to relive what had happened back then. I had not gone up to my old bedroom yet. I wondered if the window still opened with a creak, if the bedspread still had the pattern of faded roses. I imagined it would; Mother never changed a thing.

****

That bedroom. It had happened on a quiet Friday night, our first time, in my bed. I was reading. It still felt strange without Tilda snoring lightly across the hall. Tilda had changed now she was at university. Too busy to come home, she said. I didn't really miss Tilda. But Geoffrey, I missed him now that he was away at school too. It felt very weird, actually, to have my darling brother gone to boarding school. I wondered how he was coping. I felt the odd one out, the only Fetherwell child left in the house. But Billy was there, too. His mother had died just before we'd both turned sixteen. I suppose my parents felt sorry for him since he seemed to have nowhere else to go. Every night I eyed Billy across the dining room table, played footsies with him, and often enough we sneaked away for kisses—and more—at the bottom of the garden.

Tonight my father, the vicar/doctor, was at a conference. My mother was home. She was downstairs in her study, writing. Mummy was always studying, teaching, or writing a book. She kept the study door closed and worked with classical music playing softly on the new CD player we children had clubbed together to buy her last Christmas. The CDs held much more music than the old tapes could, and Helen could write and write without having to get up to change the music so often. It kept her so absorbed.

I froze at a sound in the hall. I heard the toilet flush and footsteps. Those footsteps I recognized, and they stopped outside the door. The door opened, and Billy

172

crept in, finger to mouth in warning, eyes sparkling with daring and desire. I opened the covers and let him in. We coupled quietly. The need for silence added to the urgency yet slowed down our inexpert stroking and exploring. I thought I would explode, my body thrummed while my ears listened for my mother's step upon the stairs. I'd never thought of a condom, never thought of it because this was unexpected, but now he helped me slip on the awkward balloon-like thing, and I guided him. The whole thing surprised me, that first time; it was both natural and new, so full of curiosity and wonder was I that I failed to enjoy it fully. But I soon learned to.

After that, the secrecy and the excitement, or perhaps it was the excitement of the secrecy, fueled us. Always wondering if anyone realized. We were teenagers. And we were having sex any chance we got.

It was amazing we got any work done at all. I studied at an independent girls' school, Billy attended a local comprehensive school. What we learned and how we learned it was supposed to be similar, but what we learned and how we learned was different. Fatherless Billy, whose mother had died, did quite well on his exams. I, from a privileged academic family, did not. I struggled, I had always struggled with mathematics, science, and languages. I was not so bad in subjects that had "people in them." I loved art, the history of it, and the art studio at school. Still, my eyes hurt with so many hours reading. School was an endurance test till I could be home with Billy.

It was my mother who had found us in bed together. I'd heard her calling, faintly, in the distance, and ignored her, engrossed with Billy in his attic bedroom. Not that we were having sex, exactly, at that moment, on that particular Saturday afternoon. But we were fooling around, giggling in bed, only partially clothed. I heard her voice, then no sound at all, until all at once, the door squeaked open, and Helen Fetherwell stood there, her mouth agape.

She'd just stared, standing there in her business suit. She was wearing her sensible brown shoes with the low heel. I focused on them, unable to lift my eyes to my mother's face. Then Helen said quietly, "I think you'd better come downstairs, young lady. You too, Billy."

Mummy averted her eyes as we slowly pushed away the covers and pulled trousers and leggings on, dragged shirts over our heads. Billy took such a long time putting on his socks. I touched his hand as he reached for his shoes and felt it tremble.

When Helen marched us into my father's study and told him, or rather struggled to tell him, swallowing the words as she sought a euphemism that described the situation rather than naming it outright, I saw his face change color. It went white, then mottled pink.

"Is this how you repay this family for our generosity?" he shouted at Billy. The curtains on the windows shook and the desk rattled against his fist. Papers scattered to the floor.

My mother looked helpless, running her hands up and down her skirt as if they were sweaty. "I have to go," she said. "I'm supposed to be chairing a meeting at two o'clock."

My father ignored her for a heartbeat, two, or three, then he swung round and said between clenched teeth, "For God's sake, Helen, it's a weekend. And this is your family. We have a crisis here!"

I was so frightened I almost wet my pants. "And is he," he flung his hand out in Billy's direction, "is this what you want to throw yourself away on?"

Billy's faced paled as Frederick said, "You. You pack your things. I am going to call Social Services. A place will be found for you, but it's not here."

My heart almost stopped.

"Really Frederick, surely a talking-to would be sufficient. There is absolutely no need to be so dramatic!" My mother stamped her brown-heeled foot.

Frederick's face registered surprise at his wife's resistance. For a moment I thought he would relent. But he shooed her out of his study, leaving Billy, his face ashen, standing on the floral carpet looking at his shoes.

The door slammed behind Mummy, and I could hear no more. Despite the uncomfortable quiet in the room, I put my hands over my ears. Then I ran. I ran down to the bottom of the garden, into the woodshed. I crumpled onto the dirt floor and cried.

The sound of my self-absorbed weeping obscured the silence for a while. I half-expected Billy to come out of the house, to come to the shed, and tell me it was all a misunderstanding, and that Frederick had calmed down. But no one came. And when hunger took me back to the house my father had locked himself in his study, and Billy's attic room was empty.

I'd tried to find him, I really did. I'd hung about the gates of his school for a week until finally one of his friends recognized me and told me he'd gone. Gone. Just disappeared.

In retrospect, it was amazing we'd been able to get away with it for so long.

But get away with what, exactly? I had friends at school whose boyfriends would stay overnight. Even if they were technically in separate rooms at the beginning of the evening, even if their parents found them in one bed in the morning, it was not so terrible. The kids might have been embarrassed, but no one was shamed in the way I had been. No one had been thrown out of the house.

After he'd sent Billy away, Frederick Fetherwell sent me to Coventry, as the saying goes. He spoke to me only when necessary. When Tilda came home from university she asked about Billy in a desultory sort of way but seemed so caught up in her own life that she accepted our parents' explanation that his sojourn with us was always meant to be temporary. Geoffrey bought that story, too, but looked as if he did not quite believe it. As for me, guilt haunted my days.

And shame seemed to shadow my mother as well.

I sensed that she felt relief after Billy had gone. But her outward distress seemed directed at me. After the hideous afternoon when Billy had been banished I was in disgrace—and treated with disdain.

"It's your deceit that's the worst of it, sneaking behind our backs," she'd said.

That was it. Deceit was the worst crime. Tension hovered in the household for months after the incident. You could cut the air with a knife, as they say, and I thought it was all about me.

****

"You do the bathroom? Would that be all right?" I called to Tilda. "I'll tackle the attic myself." I began the climb to the top floor, holding the unwieldy broom in one hand, bashing it against the stairwell, struggling

176

with a sloshing bucket and rags in the other.

I arrived at the top of the stairs and stepped into the room. I knew it was not the weight of the bucket and mop that had me breathing heavily. The attic opened before me; sloping ceilings, wooden floor, a skylight and a window at the end of the room. The winter sunlight shone brightly today, revealing the dancing dust motes. I remembered them from years before. How there is life even in the air, even when people are not breathing. Life that was visible only when you looked at it a certain way, life that went on without you. It used to make me wonder about existence, one person's insignificance. I put the bucket of water on the floor carefully, so it would not slop. There was not much to clean. There was no bed, no pine chest of drawers and no desk. All traces of Billy's life here had been removed. Boxes stood in a corner. The attic was simply a storeroom now.

A whooshing feeling went through me from top to bottom. I took a deep breath to steady myself. The attic's air tasted dusty-dry and had lost the scent of humans. Could Billy and I have ever lain here together, squashed up in his single bed? I dipped my mop and washed the walls and floors, rubbing till my arms ached.

"That's it then. One more floor to go!" My breath came short as I put down the mop. I could hear water running in the second-floor bathroom as I started to clamber down the stairs. I met Tilda coming out and pushed past her with the pail. "I just cleaned in there."

"I know. But I need to empty the bucket." It was a relief to watch the attic's dust dissolve in the toilet bowl. I dried my hands, and leaving the broom and rags in a corner, tiptoed into the landing and headed for my childhood bedroom. If I could just get there before Tilda, I could gather all the memories and then maybe, hopefully, let them go.

But Tilda was already there. She looked pleased, as if showing off a present. She opened the door of my old room and motioned me to enter.

"My gracious. My bedroom has been changed into a guest room!" I gasped.

The flowered bedspread was gone, replaced by an ecru-colored duvet. The bed had morphed from single to double sized, a pine chest of drawers had been replaced by one of mahogany, and a comfortable chair covered in a soft rose velvet sat in front of a floor lamp, tempting a guest to sit and read.

"They were trying to lure you home, I suppose." Tilda looked at me from under her eyelashes. "Didn't need a guest room for me, of course. Geoffo's room is the same, though he made it look attractive. He used to come and visit Mummy and Daddy from time to time."

I knew she was trying to make me feel guilty. I was not going to fall for that. My reasons for not coming home were all in this house. I forced myself to open the door of the master bedroom.

Our father had slept here alone, presumably, since Mother died four years before. I sensed rather than smelled him in it. Still, upon entering, I tiptoed across the pale green carpet and raised the window. Cold air rushed in. As I turned and faced the room, I almost knocked my knees on a double bed. It had a low wooden headboard and an artichoke-colored eiderdown patterned with large pale flowers. It must be at least thirty years old. Two bureaus, in dark burled wood, flanked the walls. They were the only things in the room that could be called lovely. "I hope Geoffrey will take these, if you don't want them." I swept a hand along a bureau top, smearing a gap in the dust.

"Geoffo and I could have one each, I suppose," my sister said, and for a moment I felt my position as the middle child again.

I was being unreasonable. I'd told Tilda I didn't want the furniture. My duster flicked over my mother's dressing table, with its scalloped edges and tall mirror. "This on the other hand, is hideous," I said.

"Those things are not in fashion now." Tilda looked around the room, scanning it from top to bottom. She shivered. "Do close the window, please, it's freezing." I flourished the feathers. "Can I just knock off a few cobwebs first?" I made a circuit around the room, thrusting the duster up to the moldings, over the furniture and along the skirting boards. I shook it out the window and then pulled the sash down so hard little bits of sill paint scattered to the floor.

Suddenly I paused. "Doesn't it strike you that this bedroom seems frozen in time?"

Tilda frowned. "What are you getting at?"

I waved the duster at the old-fashioned bedroom. "Daddy seemed most at home in his downstairs study, where he had everything at hand, just as he wanted it."

"Yes, I suppose so."

"He took what he wanted from home."

"You're right. Everyone revolved around him. I never thought of that before."

"How could Mother stand it? Do you think they were happy, Mummy and Daddy?"

Tilda's back bent as she stripped the bed. "What?"

She turned, annoyance on her face. "Give me a hand here, would you?" She threw two pillows at me. "I'll keep the pillowcases, if you don't mind."

The pillows, uncased, looked lumpy and slightly grubby. "Happy," I said. "Our parents?"

"They were married forty years. That counts for something doesn't it?"

"They hardly seemed to notice each other! Do you think, Tilda, do you think—I'm just suggesting, mind you, just the possibility—that Daddy might have had some sort of extra-curricular activity?"

"Extra-curricular?" Tilda straightened with the sheets crumpled in her arms and looked at me as if I were Rosie misbehaving. "He was too busy for golf if that's what you mean."

"No. I mean, Mummy was so bound up in her books and her research. Not giving him any time or attention."

Tilda averted her eyes and picked up a trash bag. "You mean he sought comfort and understanding elsewhere."

I looked down at the floor.

Tilda stuffed the hideous bedcovering into the bag and said, "I'm afraid your thoughts may be colored by your experience with your husband. Not every man is unfaithful, if that's what you're getting at."

"Not at all. I'm sorry you even drew that conclusion." I swept my hair off my forehead. Tilda was refusing to take the hint. I shivered, suddenly cold. I crossed the hall and opened another door.

A golden light filled the room, flooding its corners, and making the wooden floorboards gleam. Tilda's room had been made into an upstairs study. Our mother's workplace. History books lined the shelves along one wall, breaking up the warm buttercup yellow that suffused the room. A wide desk stood in front of the window, opening to a view of the college's playing fields across the way. A ditch separated the edge of the field from the road, probably an ancient ha-ha cut to keep cattle in when the pasture stretched over where the street now lay. It still lay choked with gorse. I remembered walking with Billy along that ditch, when the plant was in its golden bloom, smelling its incongruous scent of coconut and vanilla.

When her children were younger, Mother made do with a dark downstairs study, a former storage room near the kitchen. Our father took the official den of the house and there he wrote his sermons and read his medical journals. Helen, who actually wrote books, had to do it in a plain room with a single window. She didn't seem to need a visual distraction, so absorbed in her work did she become. Now I saw that after the children left, Helen took her own room. A room with a view of a field and flowers. An opening out of her vision, a sense of freedom. I sensed this as I sat down at Mother's desk and ran my fingers along its edge. My mother, a woman who did appreciate beauty when it was offered to her. It seemed a revelation.

A couple of botanical prints hung on the wall. I picked them up. "I can fit these in my suitcase. They're of local flowers. I'll take them as mementos of home, if you don't mind."

"Of course."

Someone had cleared Helen's desk of her books and the old jug that held her pens, her yellow markers. I opened the desk drawer. It was empty, except for some rubber bands that had lost their stretch, and an embroidered handkerchief. How typical of my mother to keep such a useful, old-fashioned object close to hand.

Tilda stood at the door, watching.

"I'd like to take this, as well," I said.

"Of course. It's not much. Take whatever you like."

I put the handkerchief to my nose and sniffed it. It smelled of cotton underlain with old wood. The embroidery was of a gorse bush. Perhaps our mother had looked out at the ditch and had bought herself a piece of cloth to remind herself of it. Perhaps it inspired her to seek out the pleasure of color.

There was an old phrase, *When gorse is out of blossom, kissing's out of fashion.* Maybe the invasive golden plant had inspired my trysts with Billy. Mother should have known better, Daddy should have known better than to thrust us together. Now, forced apart, Billy and I seemed stuck somehow in our adolescent selves. Or at least I was. Today, I understood something. Everybody else in the family had moved on—especially my mother. Yes, my mother had moved on, and I'd been so wrapped up in my own life I had not noticed.

Chapter Twenty-One

Tilda had a doctor's appointment the next day and asked if I would watch the girls after school. I was happy to. We made paper dolls out of cardboard and glitter and glue, and then I made them a chocolate pudding as a special treat before tackling dinner for Tilda and Rupert. To my surprise, the couple came in the door together and both looked tired. Their daughters, bathed and in their Snow White pajamas, ran to their parents and were hugged in return and released to watch television.

"What is it?" I gazed at my sister and brother-in-law's drawn faces.

"Just some blood tests I have to do." Tilda hung up her coat and slipped off her shoes.

"Are you ill? I thought it was a check-up only."

"I'll be fine. Anemic is all, probably."

"Red meat. That will help. I made lamb tonight—it was on sale today."

"My favorite." Rupert rubbed his hands. "We could get used to you living here." He patted my shoulder. "Sherry?"

"Wouldn't mind. You've been very hospitable, Rupert. I appreciate it."

"I'm taking you to lunch tomorrow," Tilda said.

I sat down on a chair with a thump and the glass of sherry jiggled. "Oh? That's a nice surprise. I'll go up to

London to see Lucy Thursday if you don't mind."

"All right. Now, I think after dinner, I'll just go right to bed."

"It has been exhausting tackling the old house. Emotional, too. I'm with you on that."

"Yes, I'm sure." Rupert downed his drink. "Let me do the honors serving the dinner tonight. You girls sit down."

I stared at him in amazement. Maybe I had underestimated Rupert.

****

Wednesday dawned cold and the chill did not let up as Tilda threaded the car to the crowded downtown parking garage. A light snow had fallen in the night and made walking difficult as people slid on ice. Wind whistled through the garage's concrete pillars and after making our way from its elevator to the street, I had to hold onto my sister's hand to negotiate the crowded slippery pavement.

Tilda pushed me toward the restaurant. Its foyer, insulated from the cold outside and the noise of patrons, offered a moment's respite. Then my sister pushed open the brass bars on the glass doors and we faced a pretty girl holding menus. Tilda mentioned a name to the hostess and said there would be four of us. Four? Had she invited friends, a little farewell party? That was nice of her.

Toward the back of the room we went, shedding coats in the warmth. The restaurant's walls of polished wood were interrupted at intervals with floor to ceiling mirrors. The hostess seated us. We waited.

"Who are the others? Kind of you to think of this."

Tilda was looking, eyes shining, beyond my head

to the reflection in a mirror. "It's Wi—ah, here they are."

I turned. Billy. And a young woman I recognized. Slender. Hair the color of warm ale with a tinge of red, blue eyes. My stomach tightened. This was the girl I'd seen with Billy after the night we'd spent together in September. His half-sister. I rose, my shin hitting the chair. "Ouch! Really, Tilda, I…Billy?"

Billy smiled and reached out to pat my arm, and I sat down again, calmed slightly by his touch.

"Camilla, I'd like to introduce Rachel."

"Rachel?" My voice rose.

Rachel put forward a hand. I kept mine under the table.

Rachel stood there, looking confused, and then Billy pulled out a chair for her and she sat down.

Tilda was staring at Rachel. Her lips had parted in a smile, but her eyes pleaded somehow. She seemed about to say something but halted just before she spoke.

"It's so windy out, my umbrella got turned inside out!" Rachel broke the ice, showing a pathetic broken thing like crows' feathers stuck together.

"I can see. Happens to mine, too. We can get you another," Tilda said. "Will, it's so good of you to take the time in the middle of the week to introduce us to Rachel."

"My work's flexible. And I wanted to introduce Rachel to Camilla before she goes back."

Why? Why would I want to meet this interloper? I picked up my napkin, pulled off its ring forcefully, and shoved the cloth onto my lap.

"This weather's nothing to what you're going back to, is it Camilla? What is it, the day after tomorrow you're returning to Boston?" Billy's eyes lingered on mine.

I twisted the napkin under the table.

What was he doing? Pretending to be back in the bosom of his foster family, he and I pretending to be just good friends. What was I doing? What was wrong with me, that I couldn't get over a teenage crush? And why couldn't he acknowledge us, openly? If I could just have some uninterrupted time with Billy now, some sort of normal—what? Dating time? Friendship time? But then, what would that achieve? How could I reclaim him when I lived in another country now?

"I'd love to come to America. My dad has relatives there, actually. Maybe I will go over, one day," Rachel said. Her teeth shone. An orthodontist had been paid handsomely to work on them, no doubt. Her mouth was a perfect rosebud and her unlined skin the color of rich cream.

"What do you do, Rachel?" I could feel the tightness in my own smile.

"I'm at university," Rachel said. "I do have a part-time job, though, in digital marketing."

"How impressive." Tilda raised her empty water glass in acknowledgement. "Figuring out what you want to do before you really have to."

"You mean tweeting and all that stuff?" I said. "I know I should do it myself, for my company, but I find word of mouth really is best in the catering business."

"Should we order?" Tilda beckoned over a waiter. "Let's have a bottle, shall we?"

Billy smiled and took the wine list from her. "White all right for lunch?"

We agreed. We ordered.

I was growing impatient. I'd believed that Tilda had invited me for a last sisterly lunch. I did not know when I would next be in England, and it was good that the gulf between us seemed to be closing, at least tentatively. I'd wanted to drink to that.

But here was Rachel. I puzzled as I fingered a piece of bread—why did I feel so miffed at meeting this girl?

Everyone chatted inconsequentially as their fish and salads were served and Rachel looked slightly disappointed at her "vegetarian option." I ate little.

Tilda addressed Rachel. "We're so pleased to meet you. William told us about you the other day at lunch. We're almost family, you know." Her tone sounded formal, almost forced.

"How did you find Billy—Will?" I lowered my fork. The lemon I'd squeezed onto my sole seemed to stick in my mouth, tart and sour.

"It was after I found who my birth mother was, of course. One of those genealogical websites that gives the offspring of whomever you're looking for."

I stabbed a spear of fried potato, squirting some of the sole's sauce as I did so. I wiped my mouth with the napkin. "But you have to have the parents' names first," I said.

"Yes. I can understand why it must be difficult for family members to have their peace invaded by a stranger who claims to be related." Rachel looked doubtful, her eyes scanning the faces around her.

"But we're not related, are we? Just old friends of Will's. So do go on. We're all ears," Tilda said. Her voice rang like a tin can banged with a fork.

"Thank you. I always knew I was adopted. Mum

and Dad must have let me know when I was very little because I can't remember the first time they told me. Special, they said, chosen." She took a drink of water. "My sister Jessica is adopted too. She looks very different from me. She's got dark hair, olive skin. I'm fairer and burn easily in the sun."

I looked at the three of them, sweeping my eyes across them all. Tilda, Rachel, Billy. I looked at their reflections in the long mirror opposite the table. The reversed image emphasized the same tea-colored hair and blue eyes. The perky nose Tilda and I shared. But maybe I was imagining that. Something started to rumble in my lower guts. I clutched my stomach.

"Camilla?" Tilda looked sharply at me. "Are you all right?"

"I'm fine. I might be getting a cold or something. I'm a bit chilled is all."

"I was always curious of course." Rachel looked around the table. "I loved my parents, but I wanted to find my real mother. When I turned eighteen, I decided to look for her. I told Mum and Dad and they were a bit reluctant, but there was nothing they could do. Not that I'm not grateful to them of course. They'll always be my parents."

"It's complicated," Billy said.

Rachel smiled at him.

That's about all you're going to get from him. I forked a piece of fish. He won't talk much about his feelings—unless to me—and even then, not much. I slammed the knife and fork together across the plate, signaling I'd finished my lunch.

"So who was my father? I don't think I'll ever know. It's not on the birth record."

"All I can say is," Tilda broke a sudden silence that settled on the table, "we're glad you found William. It's so wonderful for him to have a sister."

I smiled weakly. "I think we should order coffee," I said. I raised my eyes to Billy's. He leaned toward me and put his arm around my shoulder. I turned toward his whisper.

"Come to London. Please." His breath warmed my cheek.

I had to stop my fingers caressing his Adam's apple to feel his voice-box throb.

When we got in the car half an hour later, I pulled my seatbelt on aggressively. It caught against my middle, a momentary stabbing pain.

"I think I'll go up to London tomorrow," I said. "Lucy and I want to get together, and then, I'm going to stay the night." I turned to observe Tilda's profile as my sister started the car. "Billy's asked me to stay."

Tilda stared ahead, concentrating on the steep curves of the parking garage's exit.

"Billy asked me to." There. It was out. Something had just burst. Why pretend any longer? Billy and I were thirty-four years old. Tilda, at lunch, implying we were like family to Billy, when I had been his lover all those years ago and still was. Possibly was, anyway. Billy had asked me, he'd murmured in my ear and later repeated the invitation as we were about to say goodbye.

Tilda moved the car adroitly into the street, avoiding hitting anything. "Well, you've finally admitted it! I know you thought we didn't realize. But Rupert and I, well, we're not as foolish as you seem to think we are."

"You've noticed?"

"Camilla, you really are silly. I'm not so blind." Tilda braked as a pedestrian darted across the street. "I knew you were becoming fond of William. I have to tell you, Rupert and I, well, we were hoping that perhaps…well, we saw that you and he hit it off after Daddy's funeral."

God, was it that obvious?

"I could see you've been distressed about something. And it's clearly not just grief about Daddy's death. You and Daddy—well anyone could see you and he did not get along."

I relaxed in the car seat and put my head back on the headrest, stretching my neck. "You're right there. You don't understand why, do you?"

"No. Not really. Just personality, I suppose. It happens in families. But tell me about Billy. Why is it difficult with him?"

"Because I live in another country and I have to go back. There's never going to be time for us to get sick of each other, get annoyed about someone leaving the cap off the toothpaste. Whatever people fight about. So there's no point in it."

"Yes. I see."

I looked at my sister, who moved forward on green. She drove so sedately as if it were a normal day. Tilda! Understanding, or trying to. Just amazing.

Tilda turned the corner. "I think you'd better go up to London tomorrow then. Or tonight, for that matter. You could text Billy—he and Rachel will still be on the train on the way there now, I expect."

"Oh, Tilda. Thank you," I managed. My head started to spin. Tilda and Rupert, actually encouraging me to see Billy? "But first, before we pick up the girls from school, can we go to the toy shop on the way home? I need to get those presents I promised. I saw just the thing the other day, but I didn't buy it because we needed the car."

"Oh? Goodness, you're not thinking of a bike or one of those electronic toys Rupert and I don't approve of, I hope."

"Not at all. It's a dollhouse, Tilda. A beautiful, old-fashioned wooden dollhouse. I thought the girls would enjoy playing happy families with it." I looked out the window at the river we were driving past. Snowdrops clustered on the banks. A harbinger of the coming thaw. I touched Tilda's arm.

"Like you and I used to do," I said. "When we were little."

Chapter Twenty-Two

We lay in bed. Billy toyed with my hair, while I rubbed my hand lazily up and down his arm.

"I'm glad you came. You had me worried for a while." His mouth glided over mine.

"Hmm." I punched his arm lightly, unable to answer him. Tilda had given me permission, and this had freed me. How ridiculous was that? Childish. She'd let me go, and I had caught the very next train, not giving myself time for second thoughts.

Billy lay on his side, facing me. He said, "I didn't think Tilda looked very well yesterday."

"What do you mean?"

"She looked pale. Thin."

"Yes, she is too thin." I pressed my fingers against my waist. "But I'm always so focused on being annoyed with her to notice things like that. Selfish me."

"Silly you. Tilda is fond of you, you know."

"Is she? I always feel obliged to her somehow. Like coming back here to go through our parents' house." I sat up and pushed a pillow behind my back. "She could have done that with Geoffrey. Or alone. She's not working, and the kids are in school, at least Rosie is. Lily goes mornings."

"Maybe it's her way of trying to mend your relationship, trying to rebuild the family, so to speak." He stroked my arm. "Calm down."

"I guess that's why you and she collaborated on yesterday's lunch, to bring Rachel."

"Maybe." Billy now raised himself on his elbow, eyes alert.

"All these surprises, Billy. I'm reeling! All these changes! Daddy's death, then rediscovering you, and now finding you have a sister."

"It's a lot to process." He sat up, flinging off the coverlet.

"Rachel's so unsettling. Suddenly appearing like that, claiming she's related."

He was out of bed now, facing me. His body was trim and tall, towering over mine. It surprised me once again to see how the skinny adolescent he was had grown into a man, rising from sculpted thighs to muscled chest. Just looking at him made me feel warm all over.

"I think we have to move on from this, Mille," he said.

"I suppose." I struggled to move my eyes above his waist.

"I'm getting something to drink. You want something?"

"Maybe some water. Thanks."

Looking at his naked back as he went into the kitchen, I imagined him doing the same thing in my little apartment in Boston. It would be nice to wake up to that every morning, the tapered spine that ended in two sculpted cheeks, the strong legs, the long feet. I loved the soft hollow between his ankle and his heel, the arch of his foot, the way his second toe pushed out beyond the thick big toe. But how could I live with him? We were separated by an ocean.

A few minutes later he came back with a tray. On it sat two green squat bottles of sparkling water, a knife, a plate, and an apple. "Hope you like fizzy. All I could find."

"Thank you." I eyed the apple. A Granny Smith. I hated their bitter taste.

He got back into bed and settled the tray between us. "So. You want to talk about Rachel. What did you think?"

He would want to know. I'd have to choose my words carefully. The girl obviously meant more to him than he could really articulate.

"It's so strange, don't you think?" Billy didn't wait for an answer. "It's just that—perhaps you don't see it because you can't look at yourself unless you're in front of a mirror, but when I look at Rachel I see you at about the same age."

"Really? That's a funny thing to say."

I had noticed a resemblance—now he saw it too? Queasiness rose in my throat.

"How do you feel about your mother having a baby and you not even knowing about it? Aren't you the slightest bit angry?" I said.

"She did nothing wrong."

"Maybe not. But kids feel abandoned when their parents die. It's normal. So I've been told. And now you've found out something about her that's a bit shocking, isn't it?"

"Don't judge. Whatever she did, it's no worse than what we're doing, is it?"

"I mean—" I was about to say that if we had a kid at least I'd know who the father was but stopped. There was no need to insult Billy's mother. That was a question for Billy to pursue if he cared to. He must have known with whom his mother consorted.

But he was on his own train of thought. His hand gripped the bottle, fingers splayed around it. "Rachel told me she was relieved to learn that her mother died. Because it meant she didn't just give her up. Rachel said that would have been hard to take. Understandable. For her, it was a relief to know that Mum had died and hadn't abandoned her."

"If she hadn't died you would have had a real sister." I felt my chest squeeze. "And then, of course, you would never have come to us. We'd never have met, probably."

Billy smiled, looking at me sideways. "It feels weird to know about the kid. I'm glad too, I guess. It's good to have a real member of my family. But it's strange, isn't it, that Mum never told me?"

"I suppose she knew she'd have to give it up because she wouldn't live long afterward and telling you would just unsettle you further. You'd feel responsible for it, knowing you."

"Knowing me?"

"Yes. You're so kind and loving."

"Hmm. Glad you think so." He grinned. "How loving?" He pushed me gently down on the bed and stroked my breast.

He had that delicious Billy smell, that particular lingering of perspiration that aroused me. I tried to ignore his hand. "I imagine her adoptive parents will want her to keep her distance from you."

I sat up again, tipped up a bottle and felt the water slide down my throat. "I probably would, if I were them. Want you to stay away. They did all the work to raise her after all."

"Yes, she loves her parents and her sister. She was curious, that's all."

"And Tilda was curious, so she planned that little surprise lunch. She's so devious."

Billy smiled. "It's done. No need to repeat. We're almost a generation older, so she probably isn't all that interested, to be honest."

"Good." I put the bottle on the floor and lay down again.

Billy, resting on his elbow, pushed back my hair from my forehead with the other hand. He murmured, "I know you have to go back. I know you do. But my job, I'm a software developer. They're in demand. I could get a job in Boston. Be near you."

"You mean, see how it goes with us when we are not so far apart?"

"Something like that." Billy nosed my shoulder. I felt his breath on my skin.

"Well, yeah, that would be nice. It would be lovely. But how would you get a job over there?"

"Dunno." He twirled a lock of my hair in his fingers. "Maybe just come and look for one."

"You can't just do that, Billy. There are visas and so on. You're not allowed to work in the US just because you want to live there for a while. If you had a job in advance, I guess, a company could get you a working visa, but I don't really think that's very likely."

"Why not?"

"It's not that easy. Without a job, they'd just give you a ninety-day tourist visa and if you overstayed, you'd be deported." I hated this kind of conversation. It reminded me of the difficulties I'd had to negotiate when I married Vincent and look where that had gotten me.

"Well, what about you? You work there, don't you?" He sat up, twisted to face me. He gripped my upper arm as it lay on the sheet.

"Yes, but that's different. I married an American citizen."

"Are you American now?"

"I'm both. I took out my citizenship after the waiting period when I got my green card from marrying Vincent, but I'm still British." I could hear the flatness in my voice.

Billy said nothing. I could sense his mind spinning down the corridor of my past as he imagined it, my failed marriage, my strangeness, the distance from what he and I had together as kids.

"You mightn't like my American self." My voice was muffled.

"What are you talking about?"

"I've changed. Everybody's changed by moving away."

"Yeah. Like I had to."

"It's different, going to a new country. I'm a slightly different person there."

Billy turned over. "Are you? How?"

"I spell things differently, for one thing."

He laughed. "What else?"

"I'm a hard-driving businesswoman. I run a tight ship. I'm so busy I don't have time to cut my hair!" I sat up again, pushing the sheets and blankets in a tangle before me. "So how can I give you anything, if you come over and you're dependent on me to show you everything, introduce you about?"

197

"For God's sake, I'm not a child. If anybody can take care of himself, it's me."

That was true. Maybe he could make a go of it. Maybe he would get the urge to succeed that I experienced in the United States. That was what I really liked about it. That it was perfectly acceptable to go for—what did they call it—the brass ring. That it didn't matter where you came from or who your parents were, you could try. I could tell Billy all this of course, but until he'd felt it himself he might not understand.

I gathered the bedclothes and folded them around me, hugging them to my chest, separating myself from him as I lay down. The room throbbed; it must have been the beat of my pulse I heard because only the alarm clock ticked. A lone light from the kitchen softly illuminated my clothes crumpled on the floor, his neatly slung over the back of a chair.

We lay silently, not touching.

There had to be a way. It would be good to spend a few months together. Then if our relationship died a natural death, I could settle.

The quiet puddled around us, rippling to the edges of the room. Finally, I spoke. "All right. Come over for a visit." I poked a finger at his chest, smoothed my hand across the light fuzz. I could feel his heart beating. "You said your work was flexible. On the web you can work anywhere, can't you? So you wouldn't be taking time away from it. Just come for a visit in the spring— you wouldn't want to come now. Too icy."

He took my hand away. He raised himself up again so he sat, not looking at me. He cut the apple in quarters, took out the core, and handed me a piece without turning to face me. He said, "You could come back to me, too. Stay here, work here." His voice sounded like he had a frog in it.

"It's so complicated, Billy. I can't just readjust myself like that."

"Life's a constant state of readjustment."

"I know. I've already done it myself several times. As you have, of course. You moved from Ireland when you were little, then you lost your mother, then us."

"Everyone does it in some form or other. People are like limpets, cling to a bit of rock for a while, then get knocked off by the waves, only to float by, trying to get another foothold." He picked up the tray with one hand and lowered it to the floor, the apple uneaten.

Was I just a foothold? "It's too early, Billy. We've only just got to know each other. You really know nothing about my life now, and I know very little about yours."

"Oh, I don't know," he said. "We've waited years." He stroked my arm. "But if you want, we could talk about something else."

"Of course. What do you want to talk about?"

"I don't want to talk about anything. You're leaving tomorrow. Let's not talk at all."

Billy's skin was warm, his breath close, and his mouth on mine. The moment took over. But my mind drifted as we made love.

Later, as he slept my mind twisted about. This Rachel had really put a spanner in it. Not just because she reminded Billy of me when I was young. But that was it, really.

Rachel looked like I did when I was young. Even I could see that. Now I looked at Billy sleeping, his face relaxed, his brown hair tousled—he'd been growing it since I'd seen him in September so the color was more pronounced. I saw his masculinity softened into nocturnal vulnerability and his resemblance to someone else. The woman in the photographs. He'd said that Rachel was his mother's daughter. Was that mother the woman in the photos? The woman in one glossy, one photocopy. I didn't have them with me to ask him. I didn't think to bring them. But I didn't really need to. My father had hidden both these photographs of a woman smiling happily at him.

I banged his arm, gripped his bicep. He woke, grumbled.

"Billy, what was your mother's name?"

"Wha? My mother? Didn't you know her name, even?" He took my hand away. "Mille, I need to sleep. But if you want to know, Mum was Nora. Nora Elizabeth actually. Now, stop talking. Please."

Nora. Nora Blanchard. The photograph bore the initials N.B.

I sat straight up in bed. Certainty hit me like a thump on the head. Rachel, Nora Blanchard's daughter, looked just like me.

Of course. My father had hidden Billy's mother's photo. Like she was his guilty secret.

I should go. I. Should. Just. Go.

But, of course, I would wait till morning. I could tell him why we had to end it, but he would not welcome the information. Maybe it was best just to slip away and let distance itself take care of the romance. Our love affair could not continue. Rachel tied us up in too close a knot.

Chapter Twenty-Three

Once again, a six-hour flight took me back to Boston. Could this be my future life? My sister and I were becoming closer, if not exactly friends. I could manage the flight back and forth once a year. The distance between us had been psychological rather than physical. Of course, an ocean and a way of life separated us. But even in the British Isles that could happen. Why, if I lived in Scotland, it would take five hours by train to get to Tilda's house.

My sister's home now had another house within it. The large dollhouse Tilda and I had struggled to put in the back seat of the car now dominated the playroom. Rose and Lily delighted in it. I wanted to start buying furniture for the dollhouse, and Tilda said that would be a nice birthday present for them. I made her promise to send photos of the girls opening each gift. I saw a series of birthdays ahead, each memorialized with an old-fashioned wooden miniature piece, a settee, a table, a bed.

A bed. Billy. In the end, my courage failed me, and I couldn't break it off with him. In the clear light of the morning, I saw that Rachel's likeness to me proved nothing. From what I could remember of the photo and Rachel—and they were getting muddled in my mind now—I could discern no clear resemblance between those two except that they both had unusually lovely coppery hair. So in the end, I'd told Billy I'd welcome him if he came for a visit in the spring. See me as I was in my new life. He'd have to accept me as I really was now, not as a fantasy girl who'd haunted his imagination for years. But really it was all so foolish. It was impossible to maintain a long distance relationship. I should stop this—somehow—before I got in any deeper. Maybe now that we were older and not so fancy-struck, time and distance would do the trick.

The plane landed with the usual thump, the passengers cheered and immediately the plane's interior rang with the ping of cell phones being activated. Mine, however, remained silent. I had no one in particular to call.

I breezed through passport control, retrieved my suitcase from the carousel, and whipped through the green, nothing-to-declare line at customs. It hit me suddenly, the moment I got through and could stop concentrating on what I had to do next. I was back. I exited the sliding doors at Terminal E and leaned for a moment on the luggage cart. I took several deep breaths. What now? All I had to do was to take a cab to my apartment. How unspeakably lonely.

I looked up. Someone was waving. I registered shock, and at the same time, pleasure swept through me. Jake pushed his way through the crowd and took the baggage cart handle.

"Good heavens! What are you doing here? How did you know I was coming on this flight?"

"Um—" he blushed. "Mindy told me you were returning this evening, and I guessed—there are not that many British Air flights a day…"

"Mindy?"

"Yeah. You hired me to do bartending, remember? There have been one or two parties your team has catered in your absence. I'm getting to know them. Your people."

"Oh. Of course. I mean, I wasn't expecting you, but how kind of you to come!"

"Mindy said—" He looked away, stroked his stubbly cheek. "Actually I really came just to make sure you were all right. Coming back."

"Coming back? What do you mean?"

He smiled. "Of course, I didn't come to the airport to whisk you back to work. But I don't live far away. As you know. I just hopped over on the T. I thought we could have dinner in the North End tonight."

"Oh, Jake!" Suddenly my jet lag melted.

He picked up my bag, and we walked out into the evening. The cold took my breath away, but the sky was clear and above the lights of the city it sparkled with stars. As we waited in line for the cab, I glanced at his face and he smiled, his brown eyes friendly. Despite the cold, he wore only a sleeveless down vest.

"You New Englanders. Amazing how you put up with this cold."

"You could warm anyone up."

I giggled. Inside the taxi, he put his arm around my shoulders and pressed me gently toward him. I didn't know what to do. I felt flattered but wary. What would Billy think? A small tug of guilt pulled at my diaphragm. I took a deep breath, then allowed Jake to snuggle. His body was firm; I fit perfectly under his arm.

Jake helped me and the luggage out of the taxi in front of an unpretentious restaurant. We slipped out of the cold and into the embrace of warmth and noise, tables adorned with red and white checked cloths, Italian music playing in the background, badly drawn murals of Italian villages on the wall. In normal circumstances, I'd be fighting sleepiness but the novelty of the situation, Jake before me, attractive and apparently interested in being more than a client/employee, roused me. A waiter handed me a menu.

"This is such a wonderful surprise. I feel like the biggest and most decadent lasagna! Comfort food."

Jake agreed. "And a nice bottle of wine. Yes. Let's do that. Was it difficult, going back and sorting through your parents' house?"

"You don't know the half of it." I picked up a glass of water, avoiding his eyes. "Your mother, she's no longer with us, is she?"

"My mother passed away some years ago, and it's just my dad now. I don't have siblings."

"I suppose some would say you were lucky in that."

"How so?"

"Oh, I don't mean that, really. Actually my sister and I—we never used to have anything in common at all, and we still don't. But she was kind to me, and I think I've been judging her too harshly. She and her husband, yes, they were welcoming to me. In fact, they were plotting to find a way to get me to return to England to live."

He leaned back, his hands pushing at the table in front of him. "Will you, do you think?"

I ran my finger over the rim of the water glass. "Hmm. It would seem like the end of an adventure if I did that. And I'm enjoying it, my adventure."

"Good." He thumped his chair forward again, clinked his glass against mine.

"Even if I am getting a bit old to be having adventures. Actually, I was settled once, married, you know, but that ended. I'm still finding my feet, having to support myself, and trying not to think that I might end up an old lady with cats."

"Why on earth would you think that?"

"Dunno. It was a silly thing to say. Tell me, what did you do before you became a painter? Or, should I say, what made you become a painter?"

"I was in the war."

"What?"

"Iraq, then Afghanistan. When I got out I had to do something completely different. You know, something that would have no impact whatsoever on society."

"Excuse me? I thought art did have an impact on society."

"Yes, hopefully it has an impact. Not on *society*." He waggled his fingers in quote signs. "On individuals. People who allow imagination to be the best part of the brain."

"Personally, I always feel my imagination gets the best of my reality." I frowned. Maybe that was my problem.

"Going to work in a nine-to-five job, making money, getting the mortgage, all of it, seemed pointless. They said we'd gone to war to protect democracy. Bullshit. What's that got to do with making money, working for the man? All that. Working to put enough money away for your retirement, then getting sick before you can enjoy it." He paused as a waiter deposited two huge plates of pasta before us.

"Gosh. American portions are so enormous. One forgets that." I took a forkful. "But art. It's important to do what you love. I get that."

"Most people can't do what they want, though. Or think they can't."

"You don't strike me as a typical soldier."

"I'm not, exactly. I mean, I didn't anticipate an actual war. I joined the National Guard when I finished high school. Wanted help with paying for college. They made it seem easy. Then 9/11 came, then the war in Iraq, and before you know it I was deployed three times."

"That must have been difficult. Scary. You survived."

"I survived. Lots of good people I knew didn't. Or came back injured."

"And that's what made you want to pursue art?"

"Only got one life, babe."

"Is that why you got annoyed when Mindy said she didn't like art to be about politics? I wasn't sure I understood that." I smiled tentatively. "Lots of art is political."

"It is. But sometimes the people who go on and on against war—in their art anyway—have never served and are just being holier than thou, kind of. I mean they don't know what it's like."

"War must be terrible."

Jake dipped bread into his pasta. I stared as the torn pale sheets of lasagna and the red sauce turned into an image of mangled flesh and blood.

He ate, saying nothing for a bit, then raised his eyes to mine.

"Yep. Mixture of boredom and terror. Sometimes necessary. Not black and white."

"Really?"

"Politics, war. It's all about dominance, one group or individual over another. Might as well be animals. I thought that can't be all there is. I'm not religious. But it seems to me that trying to understand what the world is about is what makes us not animals."

I frowned.

"Painting makes me hopeful." He pushed his plate forward a little.

"Are you? Hopeful?"

"It's on a different plane. Subject to any interpretation you like, but art never hurts anyone. There aren't many jobs out there that don't impact the world in a physical way. Painting though, couldn't be more physical. But it's all mental."

My head started to spin. "What do you mean?"

"The eye sees certain things, but the mind interprets it. Painters like Picasso made a point of that, putting an eye or a hand where you don't expect it to be. Now, in the twenty-first century, people are trying to break down barriers of time as well as space. An artist can put an installation up, or create something on the internet, and other people can get physically involved, move around in it or alter it."

"Why would someone want to alter another person's work?"

He grinned. "I guess those artists are pushing for a more intimate connection with the viewer. Painting's a communication like anything else. The artist is trying to get you to see the world a certain way. That velvet dress, that whitecap on a wave, it's all just flecks of paint. An illusion. It's all we can ever see."

"Like putting lipstick on a strawberry to make it look pretty in a photo."

"You got it. Things aren't what they seem at first glance."

"Philosopher. Don't know why you think that's hopeful."

"Pushing the boundaries, trying to understand more, you realize the bad things of the world are not all there is."

"Well." I put down my fork. I could feel my brain buzzing as if little electrodes had been strapped to my skull.

He scrunched his napkin. "You want dessert? You look a bit tired. I've been talking too much."

"No. Thank you for this. It's been just delicious, such a surprise, and so nice to get to know you a little. Would you mind—jet lag is making my mind all fuzzy—could you get me a cab? I need go home now. It's been wonderful, but I need to sleep."

"Sure. It must be three in the morning your time."

We paid—I insisted on paying my share—and we got into another cab. When we reached my apartment building, he got out of the taxi and walked around to open my door. He leaned down to the cabbie's window and told him to wait a few minutes. Taking my arm, and holding my suitcase in the other hand, he walked me up the steps and stood behind me as I put the key in the lock.

"Maybe we can repeat this," he said. He turned my face to his. His eyes were so dark.

I hesitated, then gave him a soft, short kiss, missing his mouth by a fraction, deliberately. "I'd like that," I said. I pushed my bag inside the front door, turned, and waved goodbye.

Chapter Twenty-Four

Sunday morning. Darkness. I reached over to snuggle against Billy and found the empty sheets warmed only by my own body's heat. I'd been dreaming about him; the two nights we'd spent together melded into a long continuity. I opened my eyes and remembered I was back in Boston, and Jake had picked me up from the airport and said goodbye at my door.

Well, that was all right. It felt good at the time, anyway. Though perhaps it was not fair to Billy. But then, I couldn't have just sent Jake on his way, could I? He'd made the effort to come to the airport. I needed a bit of time to sort out my thoughts, and here was the gift of a Sunday.

A quick shower, the pulling on of the warmest clothes in my closet, and I was out in the early morning street. Very cold, but the sun was gaining strength, shining on the dirty snowbanks separating the icy footpath from the road. My neighborhood had been passed by in the spate of renovation that had transformed the city from the waterfront to its central highrise business district. Where I lived, brick and wooden apartment buildings rose directly from the pavement. Some of the quainter cobbled streets were now slowly being gentrified and their handsome brick houses reminded me of England. This was one of the oldest parts of Boston. My wooden apartment building was in a less affluent neighborhood, but I'd rented there because it was close to the station and the shops, and now the scent of coffee drew me down the street. Sit down, I decided, it's a Sunday. Sit down and eat a leisurely breakfast rather than grab the quick cup I usually ordered on my way to work.

I was one of only a few customers at the little café at this early hour of eight o'clock. Of course I was. My contemporaries were spooned up against their beloveds, up with crying infants, or putting pancakes on the table for their older children before heading out to the snowy hill to sled.

I took a sip of coffee. Too hot. I poured in more cream to sooth my burning tongue. What was Jake doing this early on a Sunday morning? Should I call him? No. That could be embarrassing. What if a woman answered the phone? Even though he'd dropped me off chastely last night, he could have had a later date, couldn't he? Not very likely but possible. I knew nothing about him really. I wished Lucy were here. It would be so good to giggle and gossip and analyze relationships with men, the things women talk about. Gosh, those eggs were good. I didn't regret eating them for a second, sunny side up the English way with two slices of toast, and I even crunched the bacon.

"Could I have another coffee, please, Sam?" I asked as the waitress hovered.

I wondered if Mindy would be awake yet. I'd ring her, just get a quick overview of what happened while I was away.

Mindy's answering message said she would call back later.

Good. Okay then. When I got back to my

apartment, I'd find my old address book, call those old acquaintances who were not on my phone contact list and make arrangements to see them. I'd clean the apartment from top to bottom, restock the empty fridge, and maybe even go to the Fine Arts Museum to catch the latest exhibition. I would not on any account spend this Sunday attending to business. This would be a new Camilla.

****

When I arrived at the catering kitchen the next morning, I noticed it was surprisingly orderly. Quiet.

"Mindy?" I called, blowing on my paper cup of coffee as I walked into the large work area with its industrial charcoal-colored cabinets, its steel appliances, its double sink under the large unadorned window. The room was empty. Silent. No one was cutting, chopping, stirring or frying.

"Manuela? Hannah? Paige?"

The deserted kitchen looked, at first glance, the same as when I'd left it, but when I inhaled I smelled stale air, and something stronger. I opened the trash receptacle and saw a black plastic bag straining at its ties, misshapen, rubbish beginning to stink. Disgusting. That should have been thrown out by the last person in the kitchen.

Where was everyone? Mindy had not returned my phone call yesterday, but since it was a Sunday without a catering function, maybe Mindy had taken a day off. A much needed day off, for sure. We'd all been working pretty hard over the holidays.

But today was a Monday. I ran a hand over the steel front of the range. It was cold. My hand recoiled. The stove was not only cold. It was greasy.

I pulled a paper towel and stared at the brown smear my fingers had made. Could I not trust my staff to stick by one of my most stringent rules—cleanliness—while I was away for a mere week?

A week. I'd only taken a week off, for goodness sake. It was true that I had not been in touch with Mindy as often as when I'd gone to England for my father's funeral. That was because I got the distinct impression Mindy resented my daily calls then, taking them as a sign of my mistrust in her management skills.

Mistrust surfaced in my throat like a dirty rag. I knew I'd e-mailed everyone to say I was looking forward to seeing them. Jake had learned from Mindy about the flight from London, so the staff must know I had returned.

I picked up the phone and began calling.

"Yeah?" a sleepy Hannah answered. "Camilla? I thought you'd left the country."

"I did—on family business for a week, but I'm back. Are you planning to come in to work today?"

"Huh? Do you have anything specific today, Camilla? I have an exam tomorrow."

"Oh." I began to tap my fingers on the top of the desk.

"Mindy didn't say there would be anything on today."

"Mindy." The sick feeling started to resurface.

"I thought Mindy was the boss while you were away."

"Hmm. Yes, I did leave her in charge. Did you work at all this week?"

"A couple jobs last weekend. Then she said things were slow. I have a big project due at the end of the week for school, I was happy about that."

"Well, okay," I sighed. "Good luck with the test and all. I'll be in touch about the schedule when I have a chance to look at it properly."

I pushed at the papers piled on my desk. Bills probably. I'd look at them later. Hannah at least had a legitimate excuse not to come in. But the others? We needed to get working for an event next Saturday. I scrolled my phone—what was it? An elegant sit-down dinner party for twelve for a hedge fund manager. That would be fun to do, no expense spared. But Camilla's Creative Catering needed to get on with it. Where was everyone?

I could hear the relief in Manuela's voice when she answered the phone. Then a burst of anger.

"That Mindy. She say it dangerous to work while pregnant. She fire me! But I need money, Miss Camilla."

"What do you mean, she fired you? Manuela, Mindy had no right to tell you that! You can't be fired just because you're pregnant. How are you feeling now? Does your doctor want you to continue working long hours, at night, carrying things and so on?"

"I need job, Miss Camilla."

"All right. I'm going to set you up in the kitchen so you can sit as much as possible, how about that? Take a break every hour or so. Come in and we'll make a plan for the length of the pregnancy and then afterward—maybe you'll take some time off then."

"I not fired?"

"No! Of course not. When can you come in so we can have a chat?"

"I come in later today. Maybe early afternoon?"

214

"Good. I'll see you then."

I tried Paige next. In her small girl's voice, Paige said, her voice quivering, "Mindy said you'd left Boston for good. She said she was the boss now."

"Oh, Paige. Yes, Mindy was in charge but just for the week! Did she give you a contract like I did? Does she have a name for her new catering business?"

"Excuse me?"

"No one can just take over my business and all my clients and use my business name without telling me, let alone compensating me."

Paige was silent as if trying to follow.

"Do you understand, Paige? I'm back. Mindy is not the boss. In fact, I don't know where Mindy is. Do you?" I was shouting into the phone.

"No!" Paige started to cry.

"Where were you planning to cook out of? What does Mindy have in mind?"

"I don't know! She just said you weren't coming back." I could hear her blow her nose.

"Calm down, Paige. Why don't you come in this afternoon with Manuela, and we'll see what's up."

I rang Mindy again. It went to message mode. I checked my own phone and saw I'd called the sous chef several times already. Something was seriously wrong. Clearly, Mindy did not want to talk.

Money. I lifted the papers on the desk. No checks. No credit card receipts. Where was the payment from the parties on the books for last week? There had been a fortieth birthday party, a diplomatic reception, and a bridal shower. It had been a slow month, but January was always slow. The biggest event had been an affair at one of the consulates. They'd needed bartenders and a full array of hors d'oeuvres.

I had relied on Mindy. I searched the desk, first calmly and methodically, then more anxiously, scrabbling through the papers. Some fell and settled on the floor.

I checked the bank accounts online. The automatic withdrawals had made their usual depletions, but I recognized no peculiar checks, no forged signatures. On the other hand, nothing had been deposited in January. I'd given Mindy the power to deposit, and Mindy had not paid in the final payments for the last events. Most of the clients paid by check or credit card. There was no way Mindy could cash those checks, made to Camilla's Creative Catering. Maybe the payments were on their way.

No. I shouldn't fool myself. Mindy seemed to have cheated me.

Still, I could not quite believe it. Maybe the absent girl had had some kind of accident, or had just taken a few days unauthorized leave?

I wondered if I could call Mindy's parents. No, I could not. Because I had refused Mindy's invitation for Christmas, I had no idea where they lived. I cursed and kicked the legs of the desk. I should have been more open with Mindy. I'd worked around the younger woman rather than with her in the past, knew she had a temper and could be jealous. I should have been friendlier with the staff. It wasn't that I hadn't been friendly—after all, I'd invited Mindy and Jake to my house on New Year's Day, but to be honest now, that was to get to know Jake, not Mindy. Of course, Mindy had picked up on that, loud and clear.

As I called Mindy's number again, it was both

intimate and off-putting to hear my assistant's purr. "I'm not able to take your call right now. But I will call you back if you leave a message. Have a great day."

Saccharine. Utterly unimaginative. Stealing from her employer. What a cliché.

I would not call Jake. This was a private matter between Mindy and me. I'd work it out with the regular staff. Paige and Manuela were just confused, that was all. Hannah did not seem to be aware that Mindy had tried to close up the shop. That was all good. I would move on. As for the money, perhaps I could retrieve it from the clients. I started down the list of last week's jobs. I'd have to call them all.

"Good morning," I said in my plummiest English voice. The accent always helped when I called one of the consulates. A cocktail party for a visiting dignitary had been the gig. I'd had plenty of these in the past and did not want to lose this contact. "This is Camilla Fetherwell, and I'm just following up on the event we did for you last week. Was everything satisfactory?"

"Yes, it was very good. Thank you."

"That's good to hear. I'm wondering if you could put me through to the accounting department."

A busy-sounding bookkeeper crisply answered my questions.

"Your employee, I think her name started with an M, did give us a bill at the end of the evening." I heard irritation in the tone. "I wasn't there, of course, since it was after hours, but our events manager said that your assistant asked to be paid in cash, said that she needed to settle up with her staff on the spot. Our staff person was surprised, I must say."

"Oh. That's not usually how we do things. I do

apologize." I stifled a splutter. "You see, I was away on business myself at the time. I should have left clearer instructions."

"Yes. Well, not a problem. Our manager just told your employee she didn't have checkbook authority. Send me the invoice, please, and we'll take care of it."

So it went with the second party of the week. But at the third—the bridal shower—the hostess had been so tipsy she just handed over the balance in cash.

Mindy had bolted. She'd tried to get the money from the last week's gigs but had only partially succeeded. Had tried to capture Paige, had fired Manuela, and had ignored Hannah. She'd told Paige and Manuela Camilla's Creative Catering was on the skids and that they should not return to work. It had been so easy to do. If I had not come back when I did, who knows what would have happened to my business, to my credit, to my reputation.

The phone rang. Relief made my voice rise enthusiastically as I heard his voice.

"Jake?"

"Just wondering how you're feeling, Camilla. Jet lag over? I was wondering, are you working tonight? If not, would you like to grab a drink or something?"

Like a teenager, I suddenly felt giddy. Then the thought of Mindy, who'd worked last week with Jake, made me take a sharp breath.

"I'd like that. But Jake…what happened when I was gone? Did you do any gigs?"

"Huh? I told you. There were one or two I worked. Mindy was in charge of them. There were some others, she said, but she told me she could handle them on her own."

"How did you know exactly when I was coming back?"

"What do you mean?"

"Well, you knew when to pick me up from the airport. Only Mindy knew that, my plane schedule and all."

"You're not mad about that, are you, Camilla?"

"No. No, of course not. It's just that…Mindy's done a bunk."

"Excuse me?"

"Ah, sorry, English expression. She's gone. Bolted. Tried to close up my shop."

"You're kidding."

"Nope. Certainly looks like it. I was just wondering—"

"If it was anything I said."

"Not in so many words, maybe. But—oh, let's talk tonight. I'll have a drink with you, whatever." As I spoke, I realized my mistake with Mindy. The girl was jealous. Jake had shown he was interested in me. And she was ten years younger than I was. That must have stung.

I said, "I just have to straighten out my staff and get them to understand that Mindy misspoke. Camilla's Creative Catering is alive and well. A bit short of cash but alive and well."

"Good. I have to do something this afternoon. But can you meet me at Sullivan's Bar at eight o'clock?"

"Deal."

Before the staff arrived I threw out the trash and scrubbed and polished the kitchen. Even if Mindy had not instructed Manuela, Hannah, and Paige to do that, they should have known better. I'd speak to them about it but wanted to lead by example. Speak gently. Maybe that way I'd learn something about what had happened.

However, sitting Manuela and Paige before me in the cramped office, I could not get any coherent answer except that Mindy had blown up at them a few days before. She'd fired Manuela and told Paige that she was the boss now and that I was never coming back from England.

As if. As if? The thought that Billy and Tilda had more or less suggested the same thing flew across my mind like a banner.

"Do you think she told Hannah the company was closing?"

The employees sat dolefully in the blue office chairs. Paige swung her feet in front of her, back and forth. "I don't know. I think maybe Mindy's a bit afraid of Hannah."

"Why?"

"Because she's so smart! Hannah just organizes everything so pretty and she can cook fast too. She takes photographs, makes it all look so great."

Hannah could be the key to the business. Maybe I should offer her more money and a full-time permanent job whenever she wanted it. I exhaled, and the tension eased.

"Manuela, Paige, you are absolutely not fired. You'll work for me for as long as you want. I'll go through the orders and see what's been booked. Hannah can help when she's finished with her exams. We should be able to get through the winter with just the four of us. Then," I looked at Manuela, "we might have to hire some more people to help. But please let's just forget what's happened with Mindy. She's left, but I'm back, and we'll carry on as before. All right?"

Manuela grinned. Paige's pinched pale face betrayed her doubt, though she gave a small smile.

"When you talk to Mindy—and I think you will—just tell her we've moved on. Okay?" I stood up and patted Paige's thin shoulder. "Stay here a while."

In the refrigerator, I'd seen a large cake iced with roses. I laid it on the table and said, "Let's have a treat, shall we?"

"Hannah made the cake. Mindy said it was for a party last week. Forgot to set it out, I guess." Paige bit her lip.

Mindy. I sliced the cake. "Here, Paige, Manuela, I want you to have the biggest pieces. Tell me how it tastes."

Manuela's eyes grew wide. I noticed that she, too, was thin, except for her expanding middle. I turned again to the fridge and opened the freezer. I pulled out a tub of vanilla ice-cream and spooned it over the cake on all their plates.

The kettle whistled. I made us all tea, and we sat together, as the kitchen warmed and the afternoon darkened outside. Snow started to fall silently, its icy coldness needling the window pane so that steam rose on the inside from our mingling breaths.

Chapter Twenty-Five

About five o'clock, I sent Paige and Manuela home. As the snow swirled outside, I called a taxi and told the driver to drop Paige first, then Manuela, and gave Manuela the money to pay the higher than usual fare.

I locked up the commissary and made my way through a blizzard to the subway station. There was no way I could walk the few blocks in this weather! In the fug of a hundred breaths, stamping boots, and crushed coats, the platform turned alternately hot as a train hurtled to the stop and freezing as it left me standing on the station waiting for the next one. Battered by the icy wind, I finally made it home, took a bath, and started to dress. I slathered lotion over my body, put on the perfume I'd bought at the duty-free store on my last trip from England. I thought of Billy. I thought of the five-hour time difference, of his life in London where it rarely snowed. I paused, spritzing the perfume. It seemed all very far away and long ago.

Out the window, I saw how fast the snow was falling. It was not really a good idea to go out.

I called Jake. No answer. He must be out shoveling snow or slogging home through the blizzard. Something.

An hour later, I still hadn't heard from him. So I texted.

See you at Sullivan's at eight.

He was probably on his way. Not able to text or call. No problem. I pulled on my snow boots, tugged my black beret tight over my hair, and put on a scarf and my quilted winter coat with the hood. I glanced at myself in the hall mirror and did a double take. I looked like an Eskimo. I grabbed an umbrella from the hall stand and ventured outside.

Taking a breath as I stepped out the front door, ice crystals fell into my throat, numbing my tonsils. I pulled the scarf tighter and pushed my way forward. It was only a few streets to Sullivan's Bar, but the snow was falling so fast now it took half an hour to get there. Or seemed to. My phone was buried deep in my pocket, and I couldn't stop to check.

I pushed open the door of the bar and the heat, after the cold, shocked me further. The bar clamored. People drank, under the delusion that the snow would stop soon and they could wait out the storm. Eyes were trained on a television screen showing a golf tournament in a far-off, sunny state, a warm outside world inside another indoor world within an outside world of snow and ice. It made me blink. I wondered what the weather was doing in England and knew that whatever it was it could not be as bad as this.

"Hey, Camilla, what's up?" Joe, the bartender, greeted me cheerily. Camilla's Creative Catering had run a couple of private parties in the back rooms of Sullivan's. I'd enjoyed those events, smoke-filled bachelor parties, their billiards and music, redolent with the scent of masculinity.

"Here for a drink with Jake. He's not here, yet, is he?"

"The painter guy?"

"Yes, Jake. That's the one."

"Look around. I haven't seen him. Not yet, anyway. What can I get you?"

At the bar, the patrons downed their warming whiskies. I wished I was brave enough to order one. But with the weather as it was, I needed to keep my wits about me. "I'll have a glass of pinot noir. Thanks."

"You got it."

I wrapped my hands around the tulip bowl of the glass, warming the wine before sipping it slowly. I waited. I chatted every now and again to Joe and started to worry. One by one the other patrons put their glasses on the polished bar, pushed themselves off their stools, grabbed coats, and forced themselves out into the driving wind. Eventually, there were only a few drinkers left. I looked around at the regulars, and self-pity ran down my insides. Jake hadn't shown. I'd been stood up.

"Looks like the storm was too much for Jake. I'll go. Tell him no problem if he comes, but I have to get out of here before I turn into an icicle." I reached for my coat.

"Yeah, it's bad out there. Terrible traffic tie-ups. You're better off at home. I'll tell him if I see him."

I checked my phone for texts and phone messages but there was nothing. I thrust my way, one step at a time, through the storm to my apartment. This time the wind was at my back, pushing me on. Upstairs, warm and snug, I let my sopping coat drip out on the back of a chair, shook out my hair, sat down on the sofa to pull off my water-logged boots, and sagged back into the lumpy cushions. Central heating. One of God's great gifts. Or some engineer's. I must get a new sofa. I comforted myself imagining its color, maybe a raspberry red. And I must paint the apartment. I liked the sunny yellow of Mother's study. That's what I'd do, paint and redecorate.

Some part of me knew I was doing what I always did when I did not want to face something unpleasant. I would make a plan, distract myself with irrelevancy. Anything was better than facing the truth. Jake had not kept his promise to meet me.

I took off my pretty clothes, put on my rattiest old nightgown, and settled in bed. My ears filled with fluid and my sinuses clogged. Perhaps it was the cold, or perhaps merely tears of self-pity. I must have misheard him. Obviously, I didn't understand the conventions nowadays. Maybe Jake just wanted to talk about work. After all, I was his employer; it would not do to get too friendly. It could make things awkward.

My throat started to hurt. I got out of bed, heated water to boiling, mixed it with a lemon slice and cloves, brown sugar, and a good thimbleful of whiskey. It tasted very good. I drank the hot toddy down quickly, had another, and then fell asleep.

Was it morning? My eyes peered groggily at the clock radio beside the bed, confused by the gray weak light in the bedroom. The snow had thrust a thick woolen scarf over the day. I switched on the light. My throat felt like someone was scratching it with a stick. The thing about traveling by air was that every bug on the planet had a free ride too. Sitting too close to strangers for six hours, I'd picked up a nasty one. Going out last night hadn't helped, either.

Maybe Jake was sick. Maybe he'd had an accident.

With this weather, anything could have happened. Now my chest began to ache and my nose streamed. Not an attractive sight. How could I get to work today? I hadn't even really gone through the books yesterday—I was so upset at finding that Mindy had tried to cheat me, and I'd had to meet with Manuela and Paige. Fortunately, there was no work tonight—the day would have been spent in prep.

I turned on the radio and heard the voice of the Governor. Schools and airports were closed, he repeated. The storm was dumping at least thirty inches of snow on the state. That never happened in England! I tingled a little with glee and fear when he instructed the residents of Massachusetts. "We strongly advise business owners to let all non-essential personnel stay home, so the snowplows can do their job unimpeded."

Well, it was official. I'd have to tell my workers not to come to work, and I could indulge my cold.

Manuela, for one, was delighted to have the day off. "Even if I need the money, Ms. Camilla, I don't come out in this," she said. "My husband says too much risk of falling."

Hannah was pleased to have another day to study, and Paige sounded like she'd been woken from a deep sleep.

"You hibernating, Paige?"

"What?"

"Sorry. I meant, are you just hunkering down till the snow stops? I hope so. I'm sick, actually, may have the flu. Just take the day off, and we'll talk tomorrow."

The storm raged.

By a miracle, the power did not go off in my building. With my hot toddies, my warm blankets, and the internet, I holed up. I dozed, tried to read, and worried.

Jake didn't call. Good thing, really. I would not be very good company in my present state of stuffed head and runny nose. So I kept my hands from the phone. Its silence weighed on me. I turned on the radio again, and the sound of music or the news bulletins echoed through the rooms. The chairs sat unoccupied, the table cleared, the kitchen cool and clean. The snow fell outside, faintly audible, a very soft rustling sound, on and on.

The almost silent fall of snow can make a person feel very isolated. The white blanket blocks out the sounds of the city. I was left alone with my thoughts, and I didn't like them.

What had happened to Jake? Had he hightailed it with Mindy? Fled to the Caribbean? Was she his dupe? Had Mindy manipulated him to keep me guessing, lulling me, on that night of my return, to think that I could just walk into the business and find it all humming along smoothly? Maybe he was a partner in crime. An abettor.

How ridiculous. The hot toddies must have turned my head. Jake had come to pick me up at the airport, had hinted that maybe Mindy was jealous. Then he had asked me out. He really had.

I flung my quilt on the floor, sat up, and stretched. Took several deep breaths, or tried to. It felt like a car muffler had buried itself in my chest. I coughed into a tissue.

No matter the reason, Mindy had cheated me. Mindy had tried to get the money for the week's gigs in cash. But all she'd got was the fee from the bridal shower and the tip money, which she'd kept to herself.

Well, too bad. It happened in this business.

I padded the few steps to my tiny bathroom and throwing my nightgown into the hamper, stepped into a steaming hot shower. Toweled off, dressed in my warmest sweater and thick socks, I paced the apartment, holding a tissue to my face and blowing my nose every so often. I turned up the radio, then turned it off, and stared out the window to the whiteness outside.

A gift of a snow day was just what I needed to sit down and rethink the business. It would have been nice to have a trusted colleague. Mindy could have been that colleague, but Mindy had left. I pulled a yellow lined pad from a drawer and sat on the sofa, pen poised to make a list. I liked lists. Not only for shopping but to organize my thoughts.

Hannah would make a fine production assistant. Still a student, she could not work full time yet. But she could learn some of the more mundane business aspects, like taking calls and taking deposits, e-mailing the menu lists, and possibly sourcing vendors.

Hannah's photos made weddings look dreamy and her youth and wide contact base could be exploited, too. Soon her friends would start marrying, and she'd be a whole new source of business. With Manuela about to take maternity leave, we needed an additional person for prep work and dishwashing. Paige couldn't handle it on her own.

Suddenly, a thought forced me to my feet, to the window. Snow plows rounded the corner noisily, scraping the road, making a path forward.

Meghan Blainey, at the Elm Street Shelter, had dismissed my offer to create a cookie-making business with the homeless. Perhaps I'd have better luck and more reliable workers if I took another tack. Didn't the state offer tax credits for businesses to hire intellectually challenged people? It would require more effort on my part if I hired a person who needed so much help. But the new employee would be trained and my business would have another set of hands. I could look into this, call around when offices reopened.

I made some tea and sipped it slowly, feeling the ginger and honey warm my throat. How must it feel to have everything that others take for granted just beyond your grasp? To struggle to make change, to find one's way on the bus, to follow instructions?

Oh, I could sympathize with that. I'd struggled at school, had found it hard to live up to my parents' academic expectations. But they were so ludicrously high. My father's congregation, if one could call it that, consisted of brilliant young people, who, though they might have crises of the heart, were students at one of the most famous universities in the world. In the cocoon in which my family lived, I had never actually met a truly disabled person.

A huge headache settled behind my eyes.

I filled the kettle again and let it come to a boil. The steam cleared my chest a little bit more, and my head felt lighter. I nibbled on a cracker and sat down again to make my lists and plans. I looked at the pad of paper. Under "employ disadvantaged" I'd listed several steps to take. Then, I saw, I'd doodled loops and bubbles with ears on them, petaled flowers with smiley faces. I hadn't been aware I'd daydreamed my way to the bottom of the page, where I had scrawled the name, *Billy.*

Billy, who said he wanted to come to America. He'd give up his newfound sister, to come to live in America with me. But that was complete fantasy. He had no idea what such a move would mean. The disruption to the psyche. The act of immigration really challenged a person's sense of identity. Billy was damaged enough as it was. He had done well. But the injury was like broken glass inside him, bleeding unseen.

The issue of Billy had to be dealt with. I must try to dissuade him. The link with Rachel meant something disastrous, I just knew it. We looked alike. And she was Nora's daughter. The connection was there to be made. There was no way I could prove she and I shared a father—but I could not put it out of my mind. I coughed and spluttered into a paper towel, scrunched it up, and threw it in the trash. Billy needed to understand. I should take the bull by the horns. Talk it out with him.

I sent Billy an e-mail and arranged to ring him in a couple of hours. At five o'clock on the snowy Boston afternoon, the dull light of the day was already faded, and my funky fringed lamps cast shadows on the floor.

My lungs squeezed like an accordion, so I put on a loose-fitting nightgown and my quilted robe and fitted my feet into thick bed-socks. I snuggled into the cushions of the old sofa, pulled a blanket around my shoulders, set the box of tissues next to me, a cup of steaming broth beside the tissues, cradled the phone close to my body, and called my sometime lover. It was ten o'clock at night in London.

I wheezed. "Billy, I hope you're not sick, too. I think there is something wrong with me."

"You don't sound too great, Camilla. Maybe a bad

case of jet lag?"

"No—well, actually I think I have the flu, bronchitis or something." I coughed. "But I'm not calling about that."

"Sounds like you need some warming up." His voice was low and sexy.

I laughed. "I do. Wanna come over?"

"If you only knew." It sounded like he was drinking something.

"Bit far to come for a cuddle." I giggled. It made me splutter into the phone. "It's not snowing there, is it?"

"Nope. But a nice cold evening. Good to be home. I'm doing some work here tonight, I've a bit of a deadline actually."

"Ah. Oh, I am sorry. I really didn't mean to disturb you."

"Always good to hear your voice. You had such a quick trip again. Wish you stayed longer. You're not coming back to England again are you?"

"Not planning on it." I shifted the phone to the other ear. His voice, his lilting accent, its familiar timbre warmed me and made me want to tell him everything.

"Oh, Billy, you won't believe what's happened here. When I came back I discovered my assistant had stolen from me! Disappeared with some of the takings from last week's work."

"Nasty. Is that all she took?"

"From what I can see. She had deposit authority in the bank account, but couldn't withdraw, you know. She told the staff I was closing the business and she was taking over. She tried to persuade the clients to pay her in cash. She took the workers' tips, too."

"Hey, that's terrible. Sorry, Camilla. Happens. People embezzling, cheating, and so on."

"I'm trying not to make a big deal of it. It could have been a lot worse. I've told my employees that it's business as usual—as soon as this storm lets up."

"Will it last long do you think? The news said the whole of your Northeast was affected by the big snow."

"Yes, we get one or two really bad storms a winter. They can last up to thirty-six hours. It's actually beautiful then, all pristine and white. You should see it."

"I'd like to." His voice gentled.

"Yes." I could hear myself purr.

"What are you wearing?"

"At this very moment? As we speak—we could be on webcam so you can see, but on second thought, let's not—I am wearing my old nightie with embroidered flowers at the top. It has a very high neck by the way. It's flannel. Your basic grandmother's garment."

"Sounds like that needs to come off immediately."

I almost knocked the cup off its perch on the side table. What on earth was I doing? I took a sip and all of a sudden its warmth and aroma so close to my lips made Billy's reality immediate. That warm, urgent ache started between my thighs. "Well, with you here it would. Of course."

"Mille. I do want. That is—I'd really like to come over."

"It's a bit far. As we said." I breathed, my congested chest making the words hard to say. "Oh, Billy, do. In the spring or the summer when the weather's better, when I don't have this ridiculous flu thing, then I would love to see you. With nightie on or not."

"I'll go to bed here and think on that."

As I hung up I realized that the phone call had not conveyed the message I'd intended. In fact, it was the complete opposite. I'd meant to tell Billy it would be best if we just cooled our relationship; it was too difficult long distance. And there was something distinctly weird about being wooed by someone you'd shared a bathroom with when you were a teenager. Like a wormhole in time. Not my real life at all. Or so I felt the moment I set foot on this side of the Atlantic.

But I'd ended up practically having phone sex with him and inviting him over. What was wrong with me?

I had to admit it. Billy aroused me like no other man had ever done. His kindness and good humor never seemed to fail. But he was now—even though he didn't know it—forbidden fruit.

Chapter Twenty-Six

All I could think of to prevent myself dwelling on this inconvenient truth was to make an enormous hot toddy. I was quite tipsy by the time I curled on my side and went to sleep.

When I opened my eyes a clear light streamed in through the window, reflecting the snow outside. The sky, I could see from my bed, shone blue. I stretched. I sniffed. My nose had cleared. I sat up, threw off the covers, and stood. I felt amazingly refreshed. I stretched, and my old flannel nightgown tightened across my chest. I stripped it off. I showered, dressed, and strode the few steps to the galley kitchen, pulled out the refrigerator drawers, finding leeks, onions, and carrots, celery, and parsley. I defrosted a chicken and stir-fried everything in olive oil in a big pot, then poured a kettle of water over it all and watched it come to a simmer. I hadn't even had coffee yet, but I was not about to let another snow day go to waste. Just the smell of chicken soup made me feel better.

Coffee cup at hand, I sat on the sofa and reviewed the week's upcoming jobs. It was slow as always in January, but apart from the hedge fund dinner, we had several events that would keep the wolf from the door. I wrote a couple of quick blog posts and e-mailed them to Hannah to update the web page.

My notes from the night before seemed to make

sense. Thankfully, the hot toddies had not entirely addled my brain. I searched "government assistance for hiring homeless people and the developmentally disabled," and saw that there were also tax credits to encourage companies to hire veterans. This made me think of Jake.

I gave in and texted him.

To my surprise, he replied in a few minutes.

My dad in hospital. Fell. Get back when he's settled.

I took another sip of coffee. It warmed my throat at first, and then I felt a jagged stab. Jake's father was hospitalized. Once more I had jumped to the conclusion that it was all about me. And of course, it wasn't.

Let me know what I can do to help. I texted back. *Maybe I could visit later.*

An hour later I got an answer.

That wld B gr8 sometime. Home from hospital this p.m. Has to stay w. me for safety. Temporary.

****

Some careless person had left the street entrance unlocked, so I entered Jake's building without having to press the bell. I bounded up the stairs to his door, or rather, felt like bounding, but was hampered by an enormous hot pot of chicken soup.

I knocked softly and heard shuffling, a chain being slowly pulled out of its catch, and a wavering voice asking, "Who is it?"

"Me, Camilla."

"Don't need any today, thank you. No caramels."

"Could I speak to Jake?"

"Who are you, you selling something?"

"No, I'm a friend."

"All right, then." The door opened. A disheveled old man barred the entrance. He wore an old gray cardigan over a stained green shirt. Two of the cardigan buttons were fastened and the other flapped against the shirt, emphasizing the elderly man's thin frailness. The fly of his pants was unzipped under the buckle and a faint smell of urine floated in the doorway.

The pot made my arms sag. "Can I come in?" I said.

"Jake? Jake?" The man called back into the room. He held a mottled hand to his back as he did so and winced when he turned.

No answer. Apparently remembering his manners, the old man beckoned me in. "I'm Jake's father. Tom's my name. Jake will be here in a minute."

"Pleased to meet you, Tom."

"Had a devil of a time getting up those stairs. Jake practically had to carry me up. Says I can't live at my own house anymore."

"What's he doing?"

"He said he was looking at an apartment for the two of us."

"Oh."

Did Jake want that? I couldn't imagine it. If he moved in with his father, Jake would not be able to invite me there. I pursed my lips. I should be ashamed of thinking such a thing.

Tom put his hands out to take my burden from me. "Let me take that."

"It's fine. Thank you." Still holding the pot, I looked through to the studio, even more crowded with crates, paintings, and random pieces of furniture than when I'd seen it before. Jake's paintings stood against the walls. He must be a prodigious worker. How did he find time, between the bartending and looking after his dad?

"It's only a couple of months since his gallery opening, and I don't recognize this series," I said.

"He'll be back soon. I'll make you a cup of tea." Tom shuffled toward a galley kitchen in the corner of the studio. I followed.

"Thanks. Could I put this down?" I hoisted the pot onto a small round metal table next to the kitchen's counter. I pulled off my coat and hat and hung them on the back of a chair.

The urine smell became stronger as the old man stood in front of me. He seemed to have forgotten his offer of tea. Perhaps he had wet his pants. I opened the narrow refrigerator and nestled the soup pot between a loaf of sliced bread and a carton of milk. I could feel Tom's eyes following my every move.

"What's in that? Not poison is it?"

"Poison? Of course not. It's soup. For such a cold day, and you've just come home from the hospital."

"They try to poison you there. Get rid of old people. Put them in a home." The old man slumped at the table, a pale hand grasped around a salt shaker as if it were a weapon.

"Surely not. Could I?" I picked up a kettle and filled it with water, then turned on the electric stove. "Teabags?"

The old man pointed to a canister. He looked helplessly around the kitchen as if trying to remember what to do next.

"Here, let me help you get these cups down." I pointed. "That shelf is very high."

"I'd do it if I hadn't hurt my back. Used to be able to do things. Jake'll be here soon. He can get them."

"No problem." I pulled a chair over and stood on it, then pulled two chipped china mugs from the shelf. I stepped down. "Wish I had brought some cupcakes or cookies. You like cookies? What are your favorites?"

"Are you Jake's girlfriend?" Tom stared at me.

"Oh." I could feel myself blush. "No. Does Jake have a girlfriend?"

"Should have. That boy should be married by now. Give me grandchildren. He's close to forty. Still living like this…" The old man swept his hand toward the paintings in the studio.

My knees went soft. So no girlfriend. Not that the father would know everything about a grown son's private life. I sat down on the chair. "My knees. I've just had the flu I think. A bit winded by the walk upstairs. That tea would be great." I smiled and tried to explain. "Jake was a client of my catering company, for his exhibition. Now he does some occasional bartending for us. He's strong, it's an easy job for him, and he earns a little extra cash. I think he enjoys it."

Why was I telling the old man all this? I should shut up. It was Jake's business what he was doing with Camilla's Creative Catering.

"You're pretty, is all. I was wondering." He sat down at the table opposite me.

"Thank you. Jake's a big help at my parties. But he's a wonderful artist. Tell me about Jake when he was a boy. Was he always interested in painting?"

"He was always drawing planes and cars. But he was more interested in taking things apart and putting them together. Clocks and stuff. Once I caught him

238

with a radio, one of those portable ones. Before those big boom boxes came in. He had the front off and was trying to pull it apart. It was expensive, that radio, I got mad at him. He said he was trying to find where the sound came from."

"Trying to understand things. Get at the truth of everything. That's what he told me he was always wanting to do."

"I thought he might be a mechanic."

"Oh?"

"Said he wanted to go to college. I told him we can't afford it. That's when he found out that if he joined the service, he could get help to pay for it."

"Then 9/11 came."

"That's right. Got more college money for serving in Iraq. But he didn't want to go to work like the rest of us after that. Look at that!" He pointed to a canvas on an easel. "Does that look like anything you've ever seen? Like a child's painting if you ask me."

"People seem to like his work. I think it's beautiful." I rose at the kettle's whistle and turned off the burner. Tom made no move to help me get the tea, so I poured steaming water over the teabags in the mugs. I said, "Would you mind if I put milk in mine? I'm English, you know."

"Well, you would." He looked at me thoughtfully.

I wasn't sure if he was referring to my liking milk in my tea or Jake's painting, so I said nothing as I opened the refrigerator. My hair fell around my face as I splashed the liquid into my mug.

"Did I say you're pretty?" Tom's tone turned flirtatious.

"Did Jake say he would be coming back soon?"

"Any minute. Wish I could go home."

"Home?"

"Yes. I own my house. Had it forty years. Jake grew up in it. Wife died in it. Know the neighbors. Did. They're mostly moved on now, younger families coming in. The yard, can't do that anymore."

"Who helps you?"

"Jake tries. But he says he has to work. He does this painting, and he does other work to earn cash. Oh, are you the lady he works for?"

He must have forgotten. "He lends a hand, yes. A big help."

Footsteps clapped up the stairs, coming closer, and I held my breath. The door opened. Jake stood there, staring at my hand on the fridge door as I returned the carton of milk. His chocolate eyes held my gaze. He looked, not exactly pleased, not unpleased either, but a shadow annoyed as if he had been caught at something he'd rather have kept hidden.

"When you texted that your dad had had an accident, I thought I'd bring over some soup," I said.

"Thanks. Sorry I wasn't here. I've been busy. Didn't expect you so soon."

"Was that the wrong thing to do?"

"My dad's not one of your people projects. Like at the homeless shelter."

My hand went to my throat. "It's the kind of thing friends do for one another. We're friends, yes?"

"Excuse me. I've been distracted." Jake bowed his head, then approaching his father, sniffed the air and pursed his lips. "Dad…" he said. He lifted his arms, then let them fall.

"I'd better go." I reached for my coat. "Nice to

240

meet you, Tom," I said to the old man. His hand was fiddling with his fly. "I'll see you, Jake. I'll e-mail if there are any more gigs you might be interested in."

"Right." His expression was unreadable. "I'll walk you down. Back in a minute, Dad."

He opened the door, ushered me to the stairs, and followed me silently for a few seconds till we were on the landing. As we reached it, he pulled at my hand, halting my progress. The small octagonal window on the stairwell held the view of the harbor, sunken now into darkness, surrounded by the dense sparkling lights of the city. I focused on the lit-up dark outside the window, embarrassed to face him, conscious of the warmth of his fingers on my wrist. I felt his grip intensify as he turned my face toward him with his other hand. I drew closer to him, aware of every inch of his body from thigh to face. I saw his brown eyes go still, then lost sight of everything as we kissed.

He smelled as if he had been up all night. His stubble scratched, but his lips were soft and urgent. His hands pressed into my back. If it had not been a public stairwell, I supposed we might—well who knows what we might have done.

He said, when we pulled apart, "Guess you understand I can't come to work with you for a bit."

My heartbeat resumed its rhythm. "How long has your father been like this?"

"A while. He fell on the ice yesterday. Into a snowbank, he hurt his shoulder, his back is bruised. The X-rays showed he didn't break anything, luckily."

"I saw he was walking gingerly. The confusion is a bigger problem I guess."

"Yeah. I was meeting with a social worker at the

hospital when you came. Trying to figure out some options for him."

"Assisted living?"

"Probably."

I held on to the sleeve of his jacket so he wouldn't pull away. "But your dad, he seems to think you're going to share an apartment."

Jake opened his mouth, then stopped, as the sound of something smashing to the floor reached our ears.

"I have to go back upstairs. I'll call you." Turning, he took the stairs two at a time, leaving me standing on the landing.

Chapter Twenty-Seven

After that, I didn't hear from him. I imagined his frustration at trying to work around his father's constant interruptions. How could Jake support himself if he had full-time care of an old man with dementia?

I picked up the phone and called him.

"Things are going forward. It's taking a while." Jake's voice was warm, though his words were quick as if he sensed his father was standing behind him. "Dad's on the waiting list for an assisted living place. Right now he has to stay here."

A muffled voice interrupted and Jake said, not into the phone, "That's right, Dad. We're finding you a new house." He resumed his conversation to me, speaking softly. "I've hired a woman to come in to help with the household chores. She takes him out to do the shopping too. Gets him outside. Keeps an eye on him."

"That's a relief. I'm glad. You'll be able to get back to work."

"Yes. Trying to make up for lost time. Painting like crazy. Sorry, Camilla, I won't have time for bartending. Maybe later?"

"Of course. Don't worry about that. Plenty of students want bartending jobs. It would be nice to see you, though."

How ridiculous to feel jealous of his painting! The kiss on the stairs. Did he even remember it?

"Okay. A couple weeks. I might be able to get my head above water then. We could have a meal or something."

It sounded very cool.

I finished the call, put my hands behind my head, and raised my eyes to the office window. A winter gray blanketed the city. Jake was here and preoccupied. Billy was there and seemed to have me on his mind.

I worried about Billy. I obsessed. I didn't know what to do.

He had been sending e-mails and texts. He was coming, he said, getting ready to book his flight for May. Yes, he wanted to come in the spring—one of our busiest times.

I drummed my fingers on my desk as I struggled to compose a calm e-mail to him. I restrained from putting him off or encouraging him and tried to find a neutral tone. I did not want to hurt him again. But maybe it was myself I wanted to protect. I longed for him, for his beautiful body, for his ability to take what life handed him. Perhaps—here I banged my fingers so hard so that the nail on my index finger snapped off—my concern about the unseemliness of our connection if we shared a sibling was just an excuse. Perhaps, if we lived together as adults with all our grown-up faults he might be the one to find me unsatisfactory. As Vincent had done. The truth was, I was afraid.

What a confused and ridiculous creature I was! I heard my mother's voice in my ear and closed the lid of the laptop with a little slam. I must get back to business.

Ah, the business. I hated to admit it, but I missed Mindy. Not Mindy herself, that little traitor! But a colleague. Someone who could share the load. Manuela would soon have to go on maternity leave, and so I went into the kitchen to find Hannah.

I could see her raise her eyebrows at the others as I asked her to come with me. But I'm sure her delighted whoop could be heard through the office door when I asked her to work full time after her exams were over.

"OMG!" she exalted. "To get a full-time, paying job by early February—none of my classmates have that! Thank you, thank you, Camilla!"

****

Hannah celebrated by getting another tattoo. She waltzed around the catering kitchen, charming Manuela with her concern for her coming baby, intriguing Paige by her clanking bracelets and her ever-changing hair color. Her camera was busy, capturing colorful images of cakes glistening with shaving cream to simulate frosting, grapes spritzed with deodorant to make them shine, drinks bubbling with added dish soap. She planned the placement of the food on the plate for color and balance, light and dark, even sketched a shoot before she took it.

Hannah brought energy and joy to the kitchen. How had everyone put up with Mindy's moodiness? Still, Hannah, more artistic, was less focused on the bottom line. Wonderful as that creativity was, it meant more administrative work for me. But in the meantime, I had more help in the kitchen, so Manuela did not have to labor so hard. Even as Bethany got in the way and needed lots of reminders, she was a help.

Bethany had started in the business learning to scrape dishes and load the dishwasher and had moved on to chopping and grating. The sweet short girl with Down syndrome had fine hair the color of oatmeal, and it fell around her face, obscuring her eyes. She liked it when I gently pulled the hair into a ponytail and pinned it under a cap.

"Now I am a baker!" she said and her voice sang as she asked, "When can I bake cookies? When?"

That will be the day, I thought, though I knew I had to teach her. Sometimes I wondered if I had done the right thing by hiring someone who needed so much supervision, even though the girl was sweet and willing. Not only that, but Paige seemed to resent Bethany. Paige, whose own learning disabilities were not so physically evident as Bethany's, perhaps disliked the special treatment the other girl received. I sensed this but knew it would offend Paige if the subject was raised.

So we bumbled along. Orders had resumed after the January lull and it was almost Valentine's Day.

I was just sending off a proposal when rising voices in the kitchen roused me, the door opened and Bethany stood there, her slanted eyes questioning, broad face smiling.

"Can I use these to cut the shapes?" The girl waved a handful of tree-shaped cookie cutters.

"It's not Christmas, is it?"

Being allowed to shape cookie dough was a goal that Bethany had set herself. Or, in truth, it was a goal the job coach had set for Bethany. I took a deep breath. This training really was slowing the business down. Normally Manuela could make and rest the dough, then cut it into squares, rounds or other shapes or simply scoop it onto cookie sheets almost without thinking. But here was Bethany, eager if slow.

"Has Manuela prepared the dough?" I forced a

smile. "What kind of cookies will we make? It's February, so let's find some other shapes to make."

"Sugar cookies, Man-ella said. The dough's in the fridge."

I stood up, relieved to stretch, and walked Bethany back into the kitchen. "All right then. What day is coming up? Valentine's, that's right." I took the cookie cutters from Bethany's hand. I pulled some heart-shaped cutters and a rolling pin from a drawer underneath a marble counter in the baking area. "Let's use these cutters, shall we?"

"Can I make heart cookies for my boyfriend?"

"You have a boyfriend? That's nice. We can talk about that later. But Bethany, you're at work now. We're making these for a party, aren't we?"

A frown crinkled Bethany's broad brow. She rolled a cookie cutter across the marble surface. I caught it just before it dropped to the floor.

"What happens next, Bethany?"

"Roll dough?"

"Yes, but first, shouldn't we make sure the cutting surface is really, really clean?"

"I guess."

"Okay." I handed Bethany a clean rag. "Rinse this and squeeze it out and wipe it over the counter. Cold water! We want to keep the dough cold, so it will roll better."

"Oh."

"Good. Now let's wipe it dry with paper towels. Great. Now what? I think some sugar would be good on the cookies, wouldn't it?"

"Yum!" Bethany grinned.

"What kind of sugar?"

Bethany looked blank. I glanced at the clock on the wall. How could I speed this up? "Let's use powdered sugar. Here, sprinkle some on the counter. Good. Now on the rolling pin. Excellent. Now we're ready. Ta-da! Can you pull out the dough from the refrigerator, please? One package at a time."

Bethany tugged at the door of the big refrigerator, carried a wax-covered roll of dough to the counter, and unwrapped it very carefully. Slowly. I bit my lip. It was crucial in making sugar cookies to keep the dough cold. As I watched Bethany slide the rolling pin over the dough, turning it around every so often with stubby fingers, I reached into a slot underneath the counter and brought out a cookie sheet, which I whipped into the freezer. Just in case the cookie dough became too warm, I could place the cookie sheet over it for a few minutes to chill it.

Bethany struggled. The dough was warming and her shapes were becoming less distinct and little bits of dough clung to the cutters. I quickly brought out the freezing tray, dumped ice cubes on top of it and placed the tray on top of the dough. I really had to think how I could keep this girl on. How could I spend all this time on a few cookies for Valentine's Day?

The girl was looking at me, waiting for direction.

"Put the cookies you've made onto the parchment on the cookie sheet. There you are! We'll put the rest of the dough back into the fridge for a minute. We have to keep the dough cold."

"Did I do it wrong?"

"Not at all. But cookie making's not as easy as it looks. You're doing a great job. I always think it's best to chill the dough one more time after it's shaped. Then you can bake several sheets at once. When we've used up all the dough, shaped all the cookies, we'll rest it all again, then bake it for nine minutes. Okay?"

"Can we put sprinkles on them after?"

"Better than that. You can sprinkle them before we put them in the oven."

Bethany laughed and her green eyes lit up.

"Look in that canister over there and choose the right color," I said. "Red would be nice, wouldn't it? A Valentine's Day heart, that's what we're making today."

Bethany almost danced over to the glass jars, in which the little sugar dots were displayed, red for Valentine's, green for St. Patrick's Day, a mix of white, red and blue for Fourth of July.

I quickly brushed the cookie tops with a little milk to help the hundreds and thousands stick. I much preferred the descriptive English name for the tiny confection.

We'd made little cards, around this time of year, at school. The teacher, perhaps thinking of children like Bethany, had made the students give one to everyone in the class. Valentine's love could be indiscriminate. Who should be my Valentine this year, Jake or Billy? How immature was that! I smiled as I watched Bethany choose the correct jar and carry it slowly, carefully, across the room to the marble counter. Maybe they could both be my Valentine. In the meantime, I could give a bit of my heart to Bethany.

Chapter Twenty-Eight

"Smells good in here."

My hands stopped over the keyboard, startled at the male voice. As I walked into the kitchen the door slammed and the high-pitched chatter of the staff fell suddenly silent.

Jake stood there, grinning, lips blue, and cheeks chapped red with cold. On the doormat, he stamped the remains of dirty snow off his boots. He carried a big bunch of pink roses. They were wrapped in white paper, and as he waited, several petals dropped to the floor.

"It's windy out there," he said.

Automatically, I brushed a few crumbs off my sweater, and pushed my hair behind my ears, wishing it was cleaner. I saw Jake's grin and felt a bit weak in the knees. "Oh, Jake, what a lovely surprise!" I moved forward for a hug.

"Happy Birthday." Jake thrust the roses at me and bent to peck my cheek.

As if on cue, Manuela opened the refrigerator and produced from its inner recesses a plate of cupcakes, iced in pink and yellow. She gestured silently Bethany, and after a few seconds' hesitation, the girl lifted one white plate after another carefully from a shelf, until there were five lined up on the counter in the center of the room.

I leaned back against the sink for support. My heart filled. "How did you know it was my birthday?"

"Can't keep many secrets in the age of social media."

"You're sweet." I smiled, then looked at the floor. The whole world seemed to know I'd hit the milestone year of thirty-five. Still, to have Jake remember this birthday seemed nothing short of astonishing.

"I did the frosting!" Bethany beamed.

I reached out to give Bethany a hug. "It's so pretty, too. I wish Hannah were here to photograph it."

"She's at school." Paige had been hanging in the background, and now came forward with cups and saucers, having put on the kettle. "Should we have tea?"

"Wonderful, Paige. You're the best."

Jake leaned over and reached into a canvas bag. "I can do better," he said and produced a bottle of champagne.

"Goodness, this is very special!" I began to feel warm and flustered.

"Everyone needs a party now and again." He turned to Paige. "Do we have any glasses?"

Then his eyes sought mine. He said, "I just sold another painting so it's my celebration, too. And I hope you don't have plans tonight because I'm taking you to dinner."

I smiled back at him. The day was shaping up to be really exceptional. Something more than my birthday and selling a painting must have lifted his mood. I'd never seen him look so lighthearted. Jake and I had spent the last weeks' texting after we'd talked on the phone but had never actually connected since that exciting goodbye on his stairs. My heart quickened.

"That would be fantastic, Jake! As it happens there are no gigs tonight. In fact, after we have our little party here, why don't you all"—I waved a hand at my staff—"take the rest of the day off?"

"What about my ride home?" Bethany wailed at the breaking of her routine.

"Don't worry. Stay here with me," Manuela patted her arm. "We lock up. You go, Camilla. Enjoy."

Jake grinned. "Pick you up, Camilla, say seven?"

I mentally inventoried my meager wardrobe, which generally consisted of various shades of black for catering events. I'd fix it up with scarves and earrings and necklaces. Not that I could ever look glamorous, but with freshly washed hair and a few baubles I passed for pretty.

None of that seemed to matter a couple of hours later. Jake, as he collected me, wore a happy smile. He chose a very good restaurant. I supposed that he, like most people, might be intimidated to take a caterer to dinner. But Jake forestalled any feeling of guilt about the meal's expense by telling me again, as soon as we sat down, about the sale of his painting.

"I seem to be on a bit of a roll," he said.

"That's amazing. I mean, I think your work is wonderful. It's just that hasn't it been difficult to paint while your father's been living in the studio with you?"

"It has. But because he needed room in the studio it forced me to clear out some space and I found some canvases I'd abandoned. I looked at them again, made some changes, took them to the gallery, and bingo. Sold."

"Maybe you should do some more clearing out."

"Yep. Actually, I have. I'm sorry I haven't been available, Camilla. It's been six months since we met, and we really haven't been able to get this off the ground." He reached for my hand across the table, and as he did so, squeezed the candle flame between his thumb and forefinger, snuffing it.

I became acutely aware of the thick plush chair underneath me. The tablecloth had shimmered white under the candlelight, illuminating a small vase of dark blue hyacinths. Suddenly, they lost their vibrant color. I'd been at another table, staring at another small pot of winter flowers when Billy had thrown me off-kilter by mentioning Rachel. That girl undermined our whole relationship. It would have to end. Well, that was a worry for another day. I wouldn't let a simmering concern ruin a perfectly promising evening.

Nevertheless, I gently flattened my hand against the table. Jake released his hold on my fingers.

A waiter came over to take our orders and as he did so, relit the flame.

"Don't do that," Jake said.

The waiter didn't comment, snuffed the candle, and took our orders.

"Do you prefer to see me in the dark?" I joked. I rubbed my hand over my face. "A sign of age, when you look better when the lights are low. I'm thirty-five today, Jake."

"Beautiful as ever," he said. "But I just don't like open flame."

"You're a painter, you work among flammable materials all the time. I'm surprised."

"Yeah, but I'm careful not to put a flame near them. Don't smoke, have an electric stove." He looked uncomfortable. Then he blurted, "Reminds me of Iraq."

"That must have been a hard time," I said. "You can tell me about it if you want."

"I'd rather talk about something else."

He looked at me steadily, trying to read my face, I guessed, then changed the topic. We chatted. Our meals were served, and they were delicious.

"I'm making mental notes," I told him. "Want to know how to make these sautéed sweetbreads. Lovely with capers."

"You need a notebook. I usually walk around with a sketchbook and pencil. Not that there's much promise here in this dark restaurant." He peered around, pausing to look at a group seated behind me. "Except maybe over there. An older couple and a young woman. They look like they're having a good time. I'm thinking a scene, happy people in shadow. A sense of comfort about to be shattered by danger. Dark pinks and purples, slash of cream."

I laughed. "Do you imagine stuff like that all the time?" I twisted in my seat to see, but the angle defeated my gaze. The restaurant was not crowded on this Tuesday evening. Diners conversed quietly, and the thick white tablecloths and fabric chairs muffled sound, a delightful contrast to the raw brick walls and noisy floorboards of my usual hang-out, Sullivan's Bar.

"It's romantic, though," I said. The evening held a promise. Jake and I, finally getting to know one another.

"That was the idea." His eyes held mine. "The other reason I'm celebrating, apart from your birthday"—he raised his glass—"is that I've found a placement for my dad."

"That's great!" I clinked my glass against his and then took a deep sip.

His relief washed across the table and seemed to catch the sparkle in the wineglasses so they glowed.

"In more ways than one," he said. "Not only will I be able to work without putting on earphones to block out the noise of the damned television he has on all day, but I can go out at night whenever I want." His smile crinkled his eyes, and they looked directly into mine. "I haven't been able to leave him overnight all this time."

"Ah." I took his meaning instantly. I considered my napkin in my lap for a long moment. Enough of this babyish guilt about Billy. I raised my eyes to Jake's and saw him grin.

"I showed him the new place today. Just to see if he would like it. Test run. He protested at first, but then he caught sight of a pretty nurse and told me to leave and get on with my day."

I laughed. "Is it very expensive, this new place?"

"They all are. But Dad has more assets than I realized. Never spent much, I guess. I had to go through guardianship application so I could be his power of attorney and now I've put his house on the market. The agent said the beginning of March is the best time."

"Isn't it a bit cold, still?"

"Sure, but this is when the sales season starts, apparently. It will warm up soon. Spring in Boston lasts about two weeks, as you know. Anyway, I've been over there clearing out the place. What a mess!"

"I understand. I had to do exactly the same thing to my father's place. With my sister. You wouldn't believe the stuff we found." Like that photo in Daddy's desk. I pinched my fingers into my napkin. Let that go.

Focus on the now.

"Should have just hired a dumpster. A thousand trips to the Goodwill. It's almost done." Jake raised his glass and clinked it against mine. "That's another reason I haven't been around," he said. "I promise to make it up to you. Soon as Dad's settled. He'll move into the nursing home next week. Just doing the paperwork now."

I lifted my glass and downed the wine. A warm glow started its way up from where I was sitting to my face, and I felt it flush.

"You seem awfully nice for a painter. Normal. Kind." I smiled at him.

"Normal?"

"Artists have a reputation for being egotistical."

"Really?" He seemed amused. "The bad-boy artist. That's a cliché. I try to avoid clichés. Maybe I'm difficult, I don't know. I think I am pretty focused on the work, though. Haven't I apologized enough for not being very available lately?"

Once again he reached across the table for my hand, which was grasped around my glass. He unlocked my fingers one by one and ran his own index finger over the back of my hand. I tingled all over.

From the corner of my eye, I saw a movement in the direction of the Ladies' Room. A person, coming toward us. The swish of a skirt, the toss of a coppery mane, an outstretched hand.

Rachel.

"Ah, goodness, Rachel, what a surprise!" I rocked back in my seat as I struggled to take it in. Rachel on my turf, in Boston.

"Yes! How amazing to see you here!" Her voice

chirped. "I'm with my aunt and uncle." She gestured toward a shadowed corner where a middle-aged couple were drinking from coffee cups. I turned and realized they were the people Jake had talked about earlier.

"I told you when we met, that my dad has American relatives. I'm here on my Easter holidays visiting his family. We're on a history tour. Seeing where the Revolution started, all that."

Jake was staring at us, and I remembered my manners. "Excuse me. Jake, this is Rachel, an...er...acquaintance of my family in England." Rachel raised her eyebrows at this description. "And Rachel, this is Jake, a good friend. He's kindly taken me to dinner for my birthday." I knew I shouldn't have to explain this and certainly didn't want to bring attention to my age but guilt about Billy was socking my solar plexus.

"Oh yes, Easter. I forgot. Happy Easter, Rachel." Jake was staring at her. "We were just about to leave. Nice to meet you."

"Won't Will be surprised when I tell him I saw you here!" Rachel was all smiles at the coincidence.

Jake looked confused. My hands tightened beneath my napkin.

"I'm adopted. Will's my biological half-brother. I just met his foster family recently. Will introduced us. I only just discovered my brother a few months before. He's really nice and the Fetherwell family—they seem really, really fond of him. Especially you, Camilla." Rachel turned her gaze to me. "Imagine running into you here, in Boston. Just amazing. When we met that day you said you lived in America but it's a big place."

Not big enough, evidently. A smile froze on my

face.

"Are you enjoying your trip?" Jake asked, all politeness.

"Of course! Done a bit of shopping. Clothes are much less expensive than at home. Where do you shop, Camilla? Got any tips for me?"

I fingered my black cardigan, which was my go-to outfit. "I'm sure you have much better taste than I do. How lovely to be on such a wonderful trip."

My mind raced, trying to signal her wordlessly. You're so lucky to have been adopted into a financially comfortable situation. Much more fortunate than Billy was. My Billy. Just leave him alone, Rachel.

Rachel grinned. "Yes! Nice to meet you." She smiled at Jake and strode off in her purposeful, confident way toward her dinner hosts. I stared after her.

"That was a mouthful," Jake said, looking at her receding figure. "You and I have a lot of catching up to do. I never asked about your family in England. Remiss of me. Who is Will?"

"He was a boy my parents took in when his mother—Rachel's mother—was dying of cancer. We're the same age, grew up together."

"Oh. That girl. I'd like to paint her. She reminds me of that Botticelli painting—you know, The Birth of Venus."

"You mean her hair. Yes, it is a pretty color."

"It's funny. You could be sisters. You look so much alike."

"Oh. You think so?" The evening suddenly spoiled.

He looked at me strangely. "I was giving you a compliment," he said.

"Thanks. Anyway, it's been great, this birthday dinner," I replied in a stiff voice. How lame. I fell silent. I felt limp, all of a sudden depleted of energy. I twisted my head toward the other side of the room. Rachel and her hosts were hauling themselves to their feet, fussing with coats.

A thought flashed into my mind. I could get her DNA from her water glass. No. How ridiculous. I could not. I was not a television detective, but all of a sudden I leapt to my feet and muttered to Jake, "Just going to say goodbye to Rachel," and dashed to their table. They'd already stepped through the door, so I pirouetted, made an instant decision. I could not take Rachel's water glass, it would be too obvious. I dropped my purse to the floor and bent over to pick it up, pulling Rachel's napkin, which lay scrunched on the table, down to the floor. I stuffed it into my bag, rose, and walked, trying to look dignified, back to where Jake sat staring at me, bemused.

"You were a bit late, there, to say goodbye to them."

"Yes. Sorry, I was rude earlier. I should have asked her to join us for a minute." I fussed with the catch on my purse, trying to push the white napkin under the latch. It seemed to taunt me, a white corner poking up. Rachel's genetic imprint was on the lipstick smearing the cloth and I itched to match it to my own. I'd find one of those DNA matching services and send the samples off.

Jake raised his eyebrows. "Yeah. I guess. But she seems to have given you the twitches. Come on, the evening's ours."

We refused dessert, left the rest of the bottle, Jake

paid the bill, and we stepped outside into the street.

The cold shocked me through my coat. The early spring light, which had gradually extended itself as the month edged to equinox, had been vanquished by the tenacious winter, the night made worse by vicious winds. Jake grasped my hand, and we both bent our heads against the wind as we headed to the parking lot. It ripped through our clothing and carried with it a scent. Strange, it was March, and the air smelled like a bonfire.

Suddenly, wails of sirens hit the air, one screech after the other, then a continuous, rising scream, and passers-by stopped, stared, shouted. Down the street a building was aflame. The wind had been so strong and so loud that it had directed us away from it as we exited the restaurant. At first, we had not heard the roar of the fire. Police cars joined the fire trucks, and uniformed men leapt out, stopping traffic, shouting, directing people to move. I saw in the burning building the outlines of people at windows. Terror rose, gripping my throat.

Jake dropped my hand. He stood frozen beside me. I looked at his face and his eyes were staring but not at me. They seemed stuck in some scene in his imagination, or his memory. His neck tendons stretched like ropes and sweat dripped off his face despite the cold. All of a sudden he ducked behind a car and crouched low.

Fire trucks crowded the sidewalk as well as the road. I saw the fiery building lurch and there was a sickening thud as part of the burning structure collapsed. I couldn't look anymore, but the smell and the sound engulfed me. Bile filled my throat. I leaned against a parked car, holding my stomach, and slowly lowered myself to my knees. After a minute the feeling of sickness subsided. I bent my head to the ground, peering under the car, trying to see Jake's feet, but it was too dark. I could feel the damp gritty asphalt beneath my knees, the cold rising up my body. As I rose, the wet hem of my coat slapped the back of my legs. I shouted Jake's name, and the noise of the wind and the fire trucks and shouting nearby drowned it out. I turned into the violent wind, my hands feeling along the side of the car in the dark, searching for him, stumbling amongst the cars in the lot, calling him. I found what I thought was his car, though I was not sure, I had never been very good at identifying the various brands of cars. Did he have a Japanese car or an American car? I had no idea, and I wouldn't recognize it anyway except that it had a dent near the rear bumper and was certainly not the latest model. Every part of me felt frozen and afraid for him. The candle in the restaurant. He'd snuffed it. Veterans had flashbacks, didn't they? Did he imagine he was back in the battlefield?

He seemed to have simply vanished.

I had no idea if it was ten minutes later or an hour, but finally, I gave up searching and pushed my way through the gawkers and the now diminishing wind to the subway station. I took the train to my stop and scurried down the two blocks to my apartment building. Dirty mounds of ice lined the street, partially obscuring the fire hydrants, so I panicked for a second about the possibility of fire in my neighborhood and wondered how quickly firefighters could knock off the ice to open the flow of water. I stumbled and nearly fell as a rocky mound impeded my way, ruining my dress shoes as I clambered over it. Trembling as I fitted the key in the lock, I slammed the door behind me and leaned against it, breathing heavily. In a few seconds, my hands and feet began to sting as the blood vessels expanded in the warmth of the foyer. Pain needled my extremities, then seemed to extend into my brain. Tears sprang into my eyes, and I knew I would just have to endure the agony until it passed.

Chapter Twenty-Nine

Rachel. Had she engineered a trip to Boston with her aunt and uncle to check me out? Of course not. It was sheer coincidence. She could have no real interest in me or anyone in our family. She was Billy's half-sister, and I was, what? As far as she was concerned, our family and Billy had a close friendship, that was all.

Then Jake had pointed out the resemblance.

Somehow I had to solve this. I felt like a puppy with a rag toy, shaking it and pulling it apart, trying to get to the heart of it until all that was left was a shredded mess. When I'd warmed up in my apartment after the dreadful end to the evening with Jake, I fished out the crushed stolen napkin from my purse. There was lipstick on it all right, lipstick blotted in one corner in the shape of Rachel's bow-like lips. But the cloth was no longer clean—my mess of keys, comb, makeup, money and old bus tickets had probably contaminated the residue left by Rachel beyond all recognition. Still, it was all I had to go on. I put the napkin in a plastic baggie. I'd have to research those companies that find your ancestors through your spit. If my DNA and Rachel's matched, then I'd have an answer. An answer which would solve a question and create a problem.

In the meantime, I felt mortified that my date with Jake had fallen flat. Not flat, worse than that. It had started out so well but turned out disastrously. It was not my fault. It was not that my guilt about Billy made me on edge. It was not even Rachel's interference in our intimate evening. Jake seemed to see demons invisible to anyone else. Post-traumatic stress disorder, they called it. His symptoms fit that diagnosis. How awful for him.

I texted him the next day, left a message saying I hoped he was all right. I said I'd like to see him anytime he wanted to call.

As had happened during the snowstorm, I heard nothing from him. I wondered if he had checked himself into a hospital. I looked in the newspaper for an account of the fire and its casualties and was glad he was not counted in them. Irrational, I knew, but I feared Jake might have rushed into the building to rescue the poor people stranded as the flames approached.

I tried to waylay him. A few days after the fire I gave Bethany a lift home, and at the last moment, put together a package of baguettes, half a ham, a couple of rounds of cheese, some ratatouille I had left over from a dinner party I'd catered, and bundled it in a paper shopping bag with a ribbon and a note on top. Bethany and I stopped at Jake's building and went upstairs together. I knew I was using Bethany as a kind of a shield. I didn't want to embarrass Jake, yet wanted to signal support. As it was, Jake was not home, his father inquired if Bethany was my daughter, and I'd left the studio wondering if I looked so old as to have a child of twenty-two. Of course, not! Though I had to peer at my face in the car's mirror just to be sure. Tom had no idea of anyone's age and Bethany looked like a child anyway.

Then Jake called. Without preamble, he said, "That

was really bad. Ruining your birthday like that."

"It's all right. I knew something must have happened to you." I waited for him to go on.

"That fire. Sent me right back to Iraq. Scenes like that. It was the noise, mostly. It's like an explosion in my head."

I could hear the embarrassment in his voice as he apologized. I could not imagine living with such guilt and such fear. He had never told me, and would not, if he'd seen buddies go down in flames or if his unit had fire-balled a house with civilians in it, by mistake. Maybe all those things had happened. Now I understood why he had chosen to work as an artist. Standing in front of a huge canvas, working silently, slashing on energetic layers of paint served a therapeutic as well as a creative purpose.

"Oh, Jake. How terrible for you. How are you now? Do you feel better?"

"It's just...unpredictable. I can't say. I'm sorry."

I held the phone, hearing my inadequate response, my heart aching as I sat helpless and sad. Could he ever recover from his tendencies given the terrors he battled? I supposed I would find out. But only if he made the first move. Still, I said, "Come over, any time, Jake. I'll make us a nice quiet dinner, no need to go out at all."

"That would be great," he said. "I'll look forward to that."

"Me, too."

Neither of us spoke for a minute. Then I said, "Well, how about next week? Wednesday? I don't think we have a gig that night. Come over, and I'll make us something simple."

"Really?" He sounded relieved, though I could

sense doubt in his answer.

I ended the call. My back hurt and I stretched. My legs felt strangely wooden. Perhaps it was disappointment. Jake had so much to offer the world, so much talent. I could not help but be fascinated by him. But his war experiences left him moody and perhaps unstable. With all that was going on in my life right now, I didn't know if I could deal with his demons. And I wasn't sure he wanted me to, either. He was preoccupied with his own worries of making a living in an uncertain profession and coping with a demented parent. If I were my father, I could have given him medical and spiritual help. But I had no such skills. All I could give him was food and friendship. More than that? I'd have to work that out. My own romantic feelings were a tangle. I had to push Billy away, though he held my heart. The least—but perhaps the most—I could do for Jake was to listen.

I sat down and turned on the laptop. Among the e-mails was one from Tilda. All right. I'd get to my sister after I'd gone through the business e-mails and poured myself a cup of tea. Sitting down with it, inhaling its aromatic steam, I felt a sense of comfort. It was good to know that my sister now sent the occasional chatty missive. Tilda, alive and well on the other side of the Atlantic, would probably natter on about the daffodils and how cold a March it had been. It was always a cold March. Her letters, a reminder that somewhere in the world was stability and safety, boredom even. But still, home.

I opened the e-mail and read:

Dear Camilla,

The house has been sold. It got a very good price

too. Rupert says everything is final now. When the death duties are paid, there will be quite a nice sum for each of us.

Actually, Camilla, I would like to send some of my share to you. I know you are extremely busy, but could you contemplate coming over here once more—in the spring?

The fact is, dear sister, my doctor says I have to have a hysterectomy. I have been diagnosed with endometriosis and this seems the best way to stop the pain. I will be a few days in the hospital and need to rest afterwards. I know it is a real burden to you, but could you come for the time I am in hospital to help with the children and for a few days afterwards? I won't be able to drive or lift anything for a few weeks. I'd like to send you the money for the airfare as I know you have had to travel twice to us in the last few months.

There is nothing like family at a time like this.

Love,

Tilda

I kicked the legs of my desk. I let out a little scream. Tilda sick? How awful for her to realize she needed this surgery at such a young age. I must go to her. But first, Tilda must understand that it was not so easy for me to dump my own responsibilities once more. And I wouldn't dream of taking her money! It would only make me even more indebted to her like I'd always felt as the younger sister. I wrote:

Dear Tilda,

What a shock it was to read your letter. I am so sorry to hear your news.

I will, of course, do my very best to come over, but

it may again be only for a very short time. If you can give me the date of your operation, I could make arrangements to scale back for a week. I wish we lived closer but even if I lived in England I am afraid I would not be able to be terribly much help.

Thinking of you and sending love,

Camilla

I hit send. And wrote another e-mail.

Billy,

Not sure if you've heard the news. Tilda needs an operation and wants me to come over in April. We do need to talk.

xxx C.

I hit send again and found my hands were trembling. Sadness for Jake, distress about Tilda, confusion about Billy—all jumbled up in my brain. I needed to go home, at least for a little while. Tilda had offered to pay my fare. And she'd mentioned my inheritance. I could use some of that to give my staff an extra paid vacation. It would give me time to sort out the muddle of my life.

Chapter Thirty

I signed off on the e-mail to Tilda feeling a sense of inevitability. I'd go to her in April. And this time, I could use the visit to forestall Billy. Though that was not the word I was seeking. The whole relationship was peculiar, and it was not just the difficulties of long distance.

Jake had interfered. He had cast his beautiful, driven personhood into my life.

The week after our ill-fated dinner, he came to my door with another armful of flowers. They were lilies this time. I'm sure he had no idea that lilies signified death. Men don't think of these things. The last time I'd seen so many lilies was at my father's funeral. On the other hand, I'd read that the Greeks associated lilies with eroticism because of the shape of the pistil. Maybe that's what Jake had in mind.

Sex and death. The two were doing somersaults in my mind as I handed Jake the corkscrew and two glasses. I'd made dinner simple and manly, roast beef and potatoes and a salad. I'd thought of a filet mignon, pink and bloody, but remembered that open flame freaked him out. Instead of candles on the dining table, I'd lit the low lamps beside the couch and dimmed the overheads. The apartment was suffused with a rosy glow this evening, and the wine was red and plentiful. I wanted him to talk, to tell me what set off his demons. I doubted I could help, but often talking relieved tension. Not that I was good at talking through my own troubles.

It took several glasses of wine before he broached the subject. I wanted him to start, because if he couldn't, there was no way I would bring up what happened the night of the fire. But if he didn't, I would not be able to move our relationship forward at all. Finally, he downed his glass.

"Those flashbacks. I know why I get them but not when they're going to happen." He slid his hands out across the table as if fending off danger. "Not going to talk about the war," he said. "It's just that—I owe you an apology. I find it difficult. I can't get close to anyone. I push them away, or I pull back."

"I know," I said. "I get irritable, too, sometimes."

"Yeah, but not like me."

"Maybe not. I don't know." I started to fold my napkin.

"I don't want to push you away." He came over to my side of the table and put his finger under my chin. I rose, and we stood nose to nose. He looked into my eyes.

"No," was all I could say.

We stood there for a couple of seconds. I wrapped my arms around him, buried my nose in his shoulder, waiting for one of us to make the first move. I could feel his heart banging. I should tell him about Billy. I should have told Billy about Jake. I stiffened in his arms ever so slightly. Jake tensed, too, then his body loosened as if he'd made a decision.

"It wasn't just Iraq," he said. "I had a fiancée."

I opened my mouth to say I, too, had lost a life partner, but he wasn't listening. He murmured close to my ear as if he could not bear to say the words aloud.

"A month before we were to get married I killed her."

"What?" I jumped back, almost knocking over the wine.

He put his arms out to steady me, held me at arm's length in front of him. "Knew you'd do that. It's bad. I was driving too fast, we skidded, hit a pole on the passenger side and rolled over. She was killed instantly."

"I'm so sorry, Jake," I said. My gaze locked on his. He'd gone far away again. "How long ago was this?"

"Three years. It was three years last month."

"How awful!" My breath caught. I was about to say I'd lost my mother in a car accident, but he looked too agitated to be interrupted. He gripped my arm.

"That's why—it's more than PTSD."

"I can imagine. Are you talking about trust? Trusting the universe to ever let you be happy?"

"Something like that. Maybe in time. I can't get my groove back, can't—I'll make it up to you. You're the first one I've been really interested in since—"

He started kissing me then, silencing the rest of his sentence. He pushed me gently up against the wall. My head almost knocked off my mother's botanical prints behind me, not that I cared. Jake was running his hands up and down my skirt, then opening my blouse. I let him.

The buzzer sounded.

"Shit. Ignore it," Jake said.

I kissed him again. The bell buzzed more urgently than ever. I could not help it. I eased myself from Jake's arms and went to the speaker. "Who's there?"

"It's me, Billy."

I froze.

"Let me in, would you, Camilla? It's cold out here." His voice was insistent.

Jake stood still. His body tensed. I smoothed my skirt, buttoned my blouse. I stood between Jake and the security door speakerphone, paralyzed.

"I think you'd better open the door," Jake said.

I kept my eyes on him as I pushed the button and heard the *sprrr* of the opening entry door, and then the sound of footsteps climbing the flight of stairs. My God, Billy! What would I say? I started breathing hard.

The door to my apartment cracked and a small suitcase pushed through. Billy followed, arms open to embrace me.

He took in the scene. Jake looking annoyed and guilt plastered on my features I'm sure. The smile on his face disappeared, his mouth opened, and his arms fell.

I tried to explain. "Billy, this is Jake. Jake, Billy is my foster brother. That girl, Rachel, the other night, is his sister. I don't know what this is about, but—"

Billy stood there, his face white. Then he said, "You don't know what this is about!" His eyes flared. "You sent an e-mail about Tilda being sick. Rachel said she saw you. Said you looked upset. I just booked a last-minute fare, thought I needed to get here immediately."

"You could have told me."

"Yeah. Obviously, this is a bad time." He turned toward the door. "I'll find a hotel."

Jake made the first move. "No. I'll go." He strode to the coat closet by the door and in one quick gesture un-shouldered his windbreaker from a wooden hanger. For a second, he stood there with the hanger raised in his hand. He held it like a bow. All he needed was an arrow. Then he was gone. He closed the door quietly.

"Looks like I interrupted something," Billy said.

"I'll make you something to eat," I started.

"No. You won't. I'll go to a hotel. Rachel rang when she got back from her trip and told me she'd seen you getting all cosy with a man. Him! Am I correct? Then she said you seemed out of sorts when you introduced him. So, I'm not stupid, Camilla. We live too far apart. I came, so I could see for myself how you live. What's happening with you?"

"I have to go back again to England, to care for Tilda. We could have talked then."

"Talked? Talked? You mean we just talk?" He was shouting, his face flushed.

"Yes, talk. I've been trying to tell you. I need to find out if Rachel is my half-sister as well as yours. If that's true, then I don't know how we can be together."

"What are you talking about?" He kicked his suitcase. It skidded toward a chair.

"I figured it out when I saw Rachel. I'm frightened, Billy. I don't see how we be—I think we're sort of step-siblings. At least."

"You're nuts. Bonkers. This is complete and utter insanity. I don't know why you're doing this."

"Because I think my father was your mother's lover."

"That's ridiculous. You can't prove that."

"No. But I could at least eliminate the possibility if you and Rachel and I all took a DNA test."

"I'm not going to do that. And I'm not going to ask

her to, either. It would be like demanding she prove she's related to me." His eyes held mine in a hard glare. "I don't want her to feel unwanted. It must be bad enough being adopted. I should know. Foster brother! You told that wanker Jake I was a foster brother!"

I had no answer.

"You're sick. Really sick. I'm leaving. If you feel you have anything to say to me, text or e-mail."

He turned toward the door, but I grabbed his arm. "Billy, please. Stay. You can't go out on the street like that—it's late, it's cold. Please. Have a glass of wine. If you want to call a hotel from here, all right. Inside, at least it's warm."

I backed toward the table, my gaze never leaving his face. He hesitated.

The wine bottle was still a third full. I poured a glass and handed it to him. Without a word, he downed it.

I poured another. "What would you like? There's more beef, or I can put together an omelet."

Billy didn't smile, but he nodded. "All right, thank you. But put away that bloke's leftovers."

I opened another bottle and went to the kitchen to hunt down eggs.

He ate ravenously. Drank several glasses of wine. And of course, he stayed. He offered to sleep on the couch. I insisted he stop that.

Exhausted after his flight and the five-hour time difference, he staggered into the bedroom. I told him I would follow. He didn't see me put his wineglass and fork into a plastic baggie and zip it shut. I crept in beside him. He breathed gently in and out. His body was so warm and familiar. We fit perfectly together, like a nut within its shell. But because I knew what we'd do when we woke, I made myself get up and get a spare blanket and a pillow. I curled up on the lumpy couch. I could not get warm, and though I brought my knees to my chest, all I could hear was my hollow heart. It thumped and thumped so hard I thought it might shatter.

Chapter Thirty-One

In the morning, Billy regained his sense of umbrage. He told me he would change his flight to London, packed up and left. He hadn't even allowed me to show him around my adopted town.

I didn't hear from Jake, either. A seeping sorrow drenched me when I thought of the grief he'd had to bear and the damage his war experiences had caused. I'd hoped to have been able to help him, but I'd messed everything up. What must he have thought when Billy showed up so unexpectedly? Then again, I had no right to be with Jake when the situation with Billy was so unsettled. It all came down to Rachel. I had to solve the mystery of who she really was.

So, in a way, it was a relief to find myself on British Air once again, flying east. I'd been assigned a task, to help Tilda, and it would distract me from myself. It seemed almost routine this time, the descent through the clouds to Heathrow, the customs check, the collection of luggage, the train rides first to King's Cross Station, then a long wait and a much-needed coffee and roll at the station before the hour's journey to Cambridge.

Rupert did insist on picking me up at the station this time, fussing cheerfully. Under the bluster, I detected an undercurrent of worry for his wife, who would go into the hospital the next morning.

****

In the recovery room, Tilda opened her eyes to my smile, and Rupert reported that the doctors said she should feel better soon. We left Tilda to the care of the nurses and went back to the house. I tended the girls. Rupert was solicitous and helpful, so helpful in fact that I began to wonder if the family could have managed perfectly well without me. After a couple of days, Tilda came home, walking gingerly.

With the children off at school, and Rupert disappeared to work, I took breakfast upstairs. Tilda lay buried under the covers, so I set the tray on a bedside table and retreated to the kitchen to sip my coffee and look out at the greening garden. I thought again about Jake. Such an interesting guy, a really good and attractive man, but I could not help him withstand the demons that attacked him from time to time. I, safe and privileged, could not imagine the dangers he'd had to face nor the shocking death of a partner.

It was my fault, all of it. I owed both Jake and Billy an apology but I hadn't been able to pick up the phone.

I held my coffee cup over the sink and let it fall. It clattered but did not break. Up the stairs I climbed and opened the door to the master bedroom.

Tears leaked from Tilda's eyes. She lay there, averting her head from my gaze.

On her tray her boiled egg and toast lay half eaten.

"Do you need another pain pill?" I picked up the tray and stood near the bed. "I think it's time."

"I'm not going to be able to hold another baby in my arms." A sob escaped Tilda's chest.

I stiffened. Would I ever hold my own baby? "I know the feeling," I said.

"It would have been nice to give Rupert a son. We never achieved that in the five years since Lily was born."

"Two children. Fine in this day and age." I set my lips in a line.

"Oh, don't start with that middle child complaint, please! It's so tiresome."

I stepped toward the door. Tilda was only feeling sorry for herself because she'd had her insides cut up, and ouch, that must hurt! "I'm sorry," I said. "It must be hard to know one doesn't have a choice about whether or not to have a baby."

Didn't I know it.

Tilda patted the coverlet. "Sit," she said.

Cautiously, I moved closer, still holding the tray.

"That was tactless of me." Tilda smoothed her hands on the bedcover. "I know, with your divorce, you're in that position, too. No babies in sight. I wish we could find you a nice, suitable man."

I let that comment settle in the room. The curtains flapped in a spring breeze and sitting on the bed, I felt a chill.

Tilda's tone brightened. "But really, it's such a relief," she said.

"Relief?"

"Yes, you see I thought I had cancer or something, I was in such pain. And I could not conceive again. It was just endometriosis, though. Undiagnosed for a long time."

"Tilda, if you were worried about cancer, why didn't you get it checked out earlier? You have a family you're responsible for."

"Yes, but we were taught not to complain,

remember?"

"Can I get you something else? You don't seem to like eggs."

"I'm not much of one for eating," said Tilda. "As long as it is food, I don't care much. We could buy prepackaged stuff all the time for all I care."

"Maybe you'll feel better once you recover from this surgery, have more energy, and the pain is gone."

"I hope so."

I stood up again and began walking to the door. I couldn't spend all morning up here. Tilda's lassitude depleted me. We had so little in common. Every time I came to England I felt this strange wall against pleasure. Tilda, hating food all her life. Tilda's abstemiousness had much in common with Mother's, come to think of it. Helen, engaged in a life of the mind, still had a house and children to manage. She did it by ignoring what she would call the small stuff. The sensual pleasures of good food, the garden, trinkets and treasures. My mother the historian studied the Puritans partly because she didn't have to travel far to do so. Oliver Cromwell, Lord Protector of England in the 1650s, founder of England's only attempt at a republic, had grown up near where we lived in East Anglia. I knew all this because my mother talked about it to us as children, and somehow, though she was a woman of the twentieth century, her own values became puritanical, at least as seen through a lens of feminism. I wonder how Daddy coped with that. What yearning in his heart had caused Frederick Fetherwell, a successful general practitioner, to seek another career in the church? Did he feel the need to express his urge for thanksgiving to something ineffable, since he could not get much purchase on it at home, his own hearth and bed?

The tray sagged, heavy in my hands. A wave of sympathy washed over me. My father was distant, busy, yet I remembered, dimly, climbing on his back as he crawled around the room pretending to be a horse. I must have been younger than Lily, then. What had happened to that lightheartedness? Did he search for it elsewhere in a more tangible form than religion? That photo I'd found in our father's desk. Of a woman, laughing. He'd made someone happy. And he'd deliberately kept that from his wife.

Tilda was staring at me. I offered, "Before I pick up the children from school I'll run some errands."

"All right. Would you mind picking up the dry cleaning? I'll make a shopping list. Thank you, Camilla. You are a help." She sighed, and I could see her legs relax under the covers.

"It's a pleasure, Tilda."

"Will you go up to London to see William?"

"I don't know. I probably should." I shifted the tray to one hip as I moved to the doorway. "But maybe I should not, Tilda. It is confusing. He did visit me in Boston. It didn't go so well."

"Maybe it's run its course. Whatever you like, dear. Now, could I rest, please?"

"All right. By the way, thank you for the advance on the airfare. I'll pay you back when the bequest is actually doled out."

"Oh, yes, Rupert is seeing to that. There is one thing I forgot to mention—the three of us, you, Geoffrey and I, inherit everything equally, of course, but there's one document Rupert found that shows that Daddy was rather fond of William."

"What?"

"It seems Daddy took shares in a company—bought them years ago when the company was in its infancy. Daddy made Will the beneficiary, for some reason."

"Really." I grasped the doorknob in shock. "Do you know the name of the company?"

"Oh dear, I'm not good at that sort of thing. Rupert will know."

"How amazing."

"It seems that the business was started by one of Daddy's colleagues at the university years ago."

"I had no idea our father was interested in that kind of thing."

"Cambridge has always had its share of scientist-entrepreneurs, I suppose."

"What are you getting at?"

"The little company grew and grew. Those shares might be worth quite a bit now."

My knees weakened. The shares could be worth thousands of pounds for all I cared. The point was that our father had given them to Billy, not his own children. Why had he done that?

Tilda's hands smoothed the coverlet. "I always thought all that nonsense you went on with about Daddy not really caring for William was overblown. Of course, he liked him. He wouldn't have taken him in otherwise, would he?"

"I don't think we really know the answer to that question, do we?"

"Oh, Camilla," Tilda sighed. "He was a clergyman. He was supposed to do good deeds. He saw young people who needed a temporary home, and we could give it to them—so we did. You make too much of these things."

"He gave to each according to his needs."

"Something like that. Now would you mind—please close the door so I won't hear you banging in the kitchen."

I withdrew. Downstairs I took a long time gathering the dishes, running the soap in the sink. The sloshing of the water and the rinsing of the plates always settled me.

Chapter Thirty-Two

Our father had remembered Billy in his will. The boy he had thrown out of the house. That made no sense at all. I'd always known Frederick Fetherwell's behavior toward Billy was over the top, but now his apparent repentance raised more questions than it answered. Or rather, it seemed to confirm my suspicion that Billy was, to my father, more than the son of an acquaintance.

When I called Rupert at the office, he answered with a laugh. "About time, sister-in-law. Of course, you must see the will. You are very nicely set up with what Frederick left you. We'd just completed everything and then Tilda got sick, but now you're here, why don't you come in, and I'll give you a copy. We can arrange transfers into your bank account."

"Thank you, Rupert. Tilda told me that William is the beneficiary of some shares as well. Does that strike you as strange?"

"Not for me to judge. You'd be surprised at some of the bequests I've seen. I don't find it odd, really. After all, William lived with your family for some time, didn't he? Anyway, these are for shares in a medical devices company—let me find the name."

I could hear papers rustling.

"Yes, here it is. A company called Inoculese. A local company, I believe, which is always good to hear.

Went public a few years ago."

"Oh. Thank you. Could you bring the will home with you this evening? It's hard for me to come to your office, what with looking after Tilda and picking up the girls and doing the shopping and everything."

"Of course. Yes, that would be easiest. Now do take a day off, Camilla. Tilda is on the mend, thanks to your good care. I hope you can spend a little time enjoying the spring weather. Sit outside and rest for a bit."

If Rupert only knew. Tilda was running me off my feet, and I had to look after Rose and Lily because he wouldn't take more than a few days off! I repressed all this as I said a sweet goodbye to my brother-in-law and hung up the phone.

I did need to see Geoffrey anyway, I could not neglect my own brother, and Lucy, too, was my oldest friend. Tomorrow, I'd hit all the birds with the one stone, see Billy, have dinner with Geoffrey and Malcolm, and stay with Lucy.

Of course, Billy had every reason not to see me at all.

He answered on the first ring. He must have been waiting for my call.

"I do need to talk to you, Billy. I'm very sorry for what happened in Boston. Could I come and see you in the next day or so?" I said.

"You're full of surprises."

"Yes. And I've got a big one, now. Can I see you?" I knew I sounded cool and business-like.

"Of course. Talking is what you want." Disappointment edged his voice.

****

Green fields furled over low hills as if rolling away from the moving train. Spring had arrived in England. Blossoms candied the copses white and pink, lambs nosed their mothers, and I could see, but not hear for the rattling of the train, the scores of birds perched along the telephone wires. As the train drew nearer King's Cross, houses huddled together under skies that grew grayer. The train sped past modest back yards with laundry flapping in the brisk wind, then closer in, whipped past apartment buildings and the football stadium and finally nosed into King's Cross. Alighting, I had the sense of being hemmed in by millions of people in the throbbing city. I always felt squashed in England. The low sky exaggerated the effect. I could not decide if it was just that the little green island which was my former home was simply too small for all the people who flocked here, or whether my web of connection made me feel trapped.

I wanted to know, I needed to know, why my father had remembered Billy in his will if he also seemed to hate him. In my handbag I had stuffed the manila envelope with the photo from the diskette and the faded instant photo. I hoped this time to convince Billy to take me seriously. Was his mother my father's lover? And if so, for how long?

Billy greeted me warily. He held his hands on my shoulders and looked at me. I said nothing, sensed that the restaurant's greeter was hovering, menus in hand, and moved away from him.

"We'd better sit down," Billy murmured and put his hand at the back of my waist, propelling me to a seat. He took one opposite and said, "What's going on? Why do I always have the feeling I have no idea what you'll do next?"

"Congratulations," I said. "It seems our father has made it all up to you."

"What are you talking about?" Billy's eyes widened and two red splotches appeared on his cheeks.

"He's left you some shares. Quite valuable, I think. Lucky you."

"What?"

"In a company called Inoculese. They make medical instruments."

"Really? How amazing." Billy sat back, staring at me.

"Rupert's settling everything now. He says you're the sole beneficiary of these shares."

"Can't imagine why your father would do that. How weird."

"The thing is, those shares are worth a lot. Maybe more than all the rest of the money my father left."

"Oh. Fantastic! I mean, embarrassing." Billy's face contorted as if he were trying to control his facial muscles. "For God's sake. You're not going to challenge the bequest, are you?"

"No. No. Not at all. But the question is, Billy, why? Why did Daddy take you in, get so very upset when he found out about us, and then throw you out so abruptly? And after all that, leave you some valuable shares? Why?"

"We know why he threw me out. Having it on with your host's daughter is against the rules. Maybe he just felt sorry for me, later. Or perhaps he bought the shares earlier, when I was part of the family, so to speak, and just forgot about them. Why are you so angry about this?"

"I'm not angry."

"Could have fooled me."

"Have you decided?" A waitress appeared beside us, pen poised over a pad. Billy waved her away. "A few minutes, please."

My hand held my napkin upright. I let it fall, and a knife and fork rattled to the table. "Tilda found a bunch of floppies. She said they were in a shoebox in Daddy's wardrobe behind his suits."

"People put stuff in surprising places."

"Yes. But it looked to me like he was hiding them. Can you guess why?"

Billy ignored this, and said, "Do you have them here by any chance?"

"No. Not the disks. Tilda asked Geoffrey to scan them. He didn't find much of interest on the documents but he made paper copies. Here's something, though—a photograph from that trove."

"Let me see."

Last night I'd searched Rupert and Tilda's study for the manila folder I'd last seen in January. It was still there in the mahogany desk with the hideous ornate handles. Now, I reached into my bag and retrieved the folder. I extracted the photograph which Geoffrey had printed on white copy paper. It was very grainy, hard to make out, but Billy's eyes lit up as he seized it.

"Also amazing." He turned to the waitress, who had come back. "We can order now, I think. Bangers and mash for me, a salad for you, Camilla?"

"A very small one, please. Some bread, thanks."

Billy stared at me, a frown on his face. "You all right?"

My stomach twisted. "Feeling a bit off. That's all."

"This photo is a coincidence, you know." He held the paper toward the light.

"How, exactly?"

"That's my mother. With her boss, Dr. Petrovsky."

My chest started to thud. "That was Katerina's name! She stayed with us for a while—before you did. Dr. Petrovsky was a friend of our family."

"Really? Cambridge is a small place." He held the piece of paper reverently. "Look at the photo. It's faded, but Mum looks as I remember her just before she got sick."

"She is pretty, isn't she? What did Dr. Petrovsky do?"

"I think he made medical instruments or something."

"His company wouldn't be Inoculese, would it?"

"Just a minute." He put down the photo and from a pocket, retrieved his smartphone.

"Inoculese is a medical devices company whose most successful product is the disposable needle," he read. "Seems to have been started here in Cambridge and has since taken off. A public company now." He grinned. "Aren't I lucky?" He rocked back and forth in his chair, clicked his knuckles, and then turned his attention once more to the phone.

"Good to know something like that started here," I said.

"It says here the business was started by a man named Petrovsky."

"Really? That proves the connection then. I can see why Daddy would be interested in anything that would make immunizations easier. When Dr. Petrovsky returned to Russia—maybe for the business—Katerina was left behind. Actually, we resented her living with us." I smiled at him, suddenly coy. "Not like you."

Billy grinned. His shoulders relaxed. "When I saw Petrovsky in the photo I remembered him. Mum was his secretary—actually more than that I think, his chief admin assistant." He smiled up at the waitress, who placed our meals in front of us. "Thank you."

Relief made my hunger return. I poked a fork into my salad, retrieving a piece of radish. "Well, that's one puzzle solved. Dr. Petrovsky persuaded Daddy to invest in the company. That's how he met your mother. How you came to inherit the shares."

"Explains the publicity photo. End of story."

I put my fork down. The riddle remained. Daddy was an academic type, a clergyman and a practicing physician. The word "investor" did not apply to him. Yet the shares had come from Frederick, not Nora.

The radish tasted bitter. I swallowed and the harsh taste made my eyes smart. "One would think he would have bequeathed them to his own children, not a friend's child."

"You do have a problem with jealousy, Mille. You know that, don't you?" Billy looked at me from under his eyelashes.

"You're missing the point."

"Which is?"

"Your mother was more than a friend."

"She was his patient. He did everything he could to save her life."

"Doctors don't usually socialize with their patients."

"Not usually."

"No." I studied my water glass for what seemed a

long time. "How long do you think they knew each other?"

"Who? Petrovsky and your father? Petrovsky and Mum? I don't know. Why?"

"There's another thing. I found this photo."

"You already told me."

"Another photo." I could hear the agitation in my voice. "I found it in Daddy's desk back in September, and it seemed he wanted to hide it. It was stuck in the back of a drawer, and there were no more photos of anyone, anywhere, in the house and I thought, well, I suspected, maybe he had some kind of secret."

"Maybe he didn't want your mother to know he had invested in a risky venture. Will you let this rest? Please! I don't want to hear it."

"I don't think it was just that." I reached down again to the bag nestled next to my feet. "Who is this?"

He had his hand out, anticipating, before I fished the faded picture from its envelope. I looked at it one more time before handing it to him. The edges were creased and the colors were waning. But still there was the image of a woman in a blue shirt against a green field, bronze hair peeking out from under a scarf.

He reached for the photo. "That's Mum!"

My stomach tumbled, over and over.

Billy had turned over the photo. "N.B! That's Mum's initials. Nora Blanchard. It's my mother all right. How long have you had this?"

"Since September."

"You've been sitting on this for six months! You could have shared it!"

"I had no idea who it was."

"I think you guessed."

"Well, yes. I guessed." My voice sounded smothered as I forced the words out. "I tried to tell you then, and you wouldn't listen. Won't listen. Oh, Billy, don't be so obtuse!"

"We've been through this before. I know what you're saying, but I don't have to believe it."

"All I'm trying to do is to learn about you. I don't know your background or anything before you came to us. And you say you want to live with me."

"Don't be so insulting! I was born in Belfast, Ireland. I have my birth certificate. Had to get it to get a passport."

"You got a passport?"

"Yes, to come and see you! We decided on that, remember? And I did come over—to find you with someone else!" His face was pale, his lips tight.

"Why didn't your family in Ireland take care of you when you were a kid? Before your Mum died, I mean, or afterward? Don't you find that strange? Who was your father? You never mention him. Ever. Clammed up when we asked."

He brought his hands to the table, fiddled with his knife and fork, scraping the plate. Just to delay his answer, probably. Finally, he brought the utensils together with a bang. His eyes were blue as ice.

"Because that's what Mum always said to do. She did tell me, before she died, not to seek him out. My father was violent, she said. He would have killed her if he'd known she came to England. He hated England. See, Mum was a Protestant and he was a Catholic. When they met in Belfast their families were against their marriage."

"What happened?"

"After I was born, Mum's family refused to help. My dad became radicalized then, Mum told me. I was born just before Bobby Sands starved himself to death in an English prison."

"Bobby Sands? I never heard of him."

"No? Look it up on online, then! I'm not going to give you a history lesson." He slammed a fist on the table. "A lot of Irish people became activists, both on the side of the Unionists who were the Protestants, and the Irish Nationalists. My father joined the IRA."

"He became a terrorist?"

"A patriot, he would have called himself. Anyway, he's dead too. Killed after he got out of prison and went back to it all. Never reformed. I found that out later."

"This all sounds so far-fetched Billy."

"You say so. But it happened. It's why I never talked about my father. Who wants to know the son of a killer? What you're suggesting seems much more unlikely to me."

"What I'm suggesting?"

Billy would not look at me. The din of the diners around us rose like a bee swarm, made worse by Billy's silence so that the buzz seemed to sharpen and invade my head. Why couldn't he think through the next step, take responsibility for it? Why did I have to spell it out?

"When Rachel appeared…" I looked at my plate.

"What?" He spoke through clenched teeth.

"She looks like I did when I was young. You said so yourself. Hair color the same. Eye color the same. Even Jake said so."

"Jake! Him again. Giving you ideas. Who in bloody hell is he? You've got something going on with him, haven't you? That's why you're making all this up about my mother and your father. You want to end this."

I felt sick. "Jake has nothing to do with this. He just pointed out what you did—that Rachel looks like me."

"That means nothing. Just a coincidence."

"I don't think so." My throat ached. If he only knew how I longed for him. "Billy, I do think maybe we shouldn't see each other till I work this out."

He looked at me uncertainly and that curtain came down over his eyes. Then he slammed his hand on the table. His bread plate jumped. "You're doing a pretty good job of acting like I have no right to these shares. Now you're casting all kinds of aspersions on my mother as well as your father. Implying they were lovers. At the very least."

"Yes. Because Daddy went so insane when he found out about us. Like it was breaking some taboo only he knew about. He meant we could never ever be together. And now we find out he's remembered you in his will like you were his child, or at least, a kind of stepchild."

He looked at me from under his brows. "You're not suggesting—you can't seriously think that your father was generous to me because he and my mother had an affair."

Finally. "Exactly! I've been trying to tell you." I could feel the tears pooling in my eyes. "Can't you understand why that's distressing? She was free to love my father, but he wasn't free to love her. And she got pregnant. And Rachel was that baby. She is a sister to both of us. Half-sister."

He sat back in his chair, fury in his eyes. "You

can't prove any of this."

"Not yet. But it's ruining us. It's—it's dislodging everything I was taught about Daddy. I always thought we were to blame for what happened when you left us. And now, Daddy, and what your mother did—seems vile. He was a doctor, Billy. And a priest. This goes against all the values he taught us. And I hate it. I'm not sure I can bear this anymore."

I rose and swept out of the restaurant, not looking back.

Chapter Thirty-Three

Later that afternoon it poured. I'd arranged to meet Geoffrey after work and walked through the drizzle to greet him. Leaning on his arm for comfort, I suppose, I took the Tube with him to the nest he shared with Malcolm. The Tube, crowded and smelly, didn't allow for much talk; I was jammed up against a pole by wet gabardine, inhaling the early evening smell of people who'd toiled all day and felt out of sorts.

But as soon as Geoffrey keyed the lock and opened the door, the aroma of roasting chicken aroused my appetite and lifted my mood. Turning on lamps as he called out a greeting, my brother pushed me toward the kitchen. In the narrow galley, crammed with whisks and spoons in pottery jars, a mortar and pestle squashed next to a food processor, condiments perched precariously on a shelf above the stove, steam wafted from a pot, and there stood Malcolm, huge, sweaty, and in an apron. All this I noted with a professional eye, and grinned approvingly. Malcolm put down a tasting spoon and enveloped me in a hug so that the two of us rocked for a second or two, knocking against the counters.

"Welcome!" Malcolm boomed. "I'm no chef like you, but I hope you'll put up with my meager effort." A smile lit his face, and he winked at Geoffrey.

"Malcolm's actually a pretty fantastic cook," Geoffrey filled in the expected response to this familial repartee. "We'll leave you to it, Malc, while I show Camilla around."

Geoffrey had made the two-bedroom flat purr with comfort; sofas were thick and firm, oil paintings adorned the walls, and his attention to detail had produced a dining room in which tomato-red walls made framed paintings glow and the walnut table gleam. He'd set candles and silver out, and fragrant white freesias in the center of the table gave off a spicy, soapy scent.

"Oh, how lovely!" I clapped my hands.

What a contrast Geoffrey's small and cosy home offered to Tilda's stuffy, old-fashioned house, where the temperature was set at sixty-eight degrees, or to my own flea-market jumble of furniture. I ran water in Geoffrey's small bathroom, soaping my hands, rinsing my face, and reaching under my shirt to wash under my arms. The filth of the great city of London always seeped into my nooks and crannies, but today I wondered if it was the situation, not the place, which made me feel grubby. I wanted stability so desperately, and the way things were going, it seemed as far away as ever. Vincent had dumped me, Jake was fettered with unpredictable mood swings and hardly had time for me anyway, and Billy, well, Billy's own link to me made our relationship crumble before it ever reached a state of equilibrium. Malcolm, I hoped, might be able to unlock it all for me. Wasn't he a geneticist or something like that?

Over the spatchcock and roasted potatoes, making sure I praised the rosemary and lemon that infused the chicken meat, I asked Malcolm questions about his work.

He believed in the future of genomics. "It's not so far off at all. In the not so distant future scanning a person's DNA will be routine." He handed me the bowl of potatoes.

"But why?" I said, holding up my hand against another serving of carbohydrates. "What would be the point of that?" I had an idea but wanted it to sound like it came from him.

"Oh, there are many diseases that have a genetic basis. One might want to know, for example, if one had the gene for a certain type of cancer."

"Testing can't prevent cancer, can it? It seems to me we hear more about these diseases than we ever did before."

"There's more publicity, certainly. People talk more openly about these things than they used to. But DNA testing does more than just find the potential for disease. Right now they're testing individualized treatments for disease that are based on matching the patient's DNA with the cure." Malcolm pushed his seat back and regarded me carefully. "Of course, there are other issues with DNA. You're what, Camilla, thirty-five?"

"Just."

"Well then, you'll be thinking about the biological clock."

Geoffrey put his hand on Malcolm's arm. "Malc. Let's drop it, shall we? Camilla's business, that. I'm sure she'll have options when she wants them."

My face grew hot. Let Malcolm go down this path. It would lead me where I wanted to go. "Oh? What do you mean, Malcolm? Are you suggesting I freeze my eggs?"

"That's a good idea, yes!" Malcolm beamed. "But of course genetics will give people other options. Soon, doctors might be able to sample just a few cells from fetal blood to detect any number of abnormalities."

"I thought they could already do that."

"Yes, in the case of Down syndrome and a few other disorders."

"You might call them disorders. Others might just call them differences. You, of all people, should be sensitive to that." I heard my voice grow indignant as I saw in my mind Bethany's eager face. Her sweet willingness to help and be of use in the world.

Malcolm looked uncomfortable. Geoffrey said, "Good point, Mille. Anyway, didn't mean to interrupt. Go on, Malc."

Malcolm took a long sip of wine, leaned forward, about to resume his pomposity. I noted the equable give and take between my brother and his partner. Very different, they seemed well-matched. My body heat lowered under my shirt.

"You talk, I'll get the pudding." Geoffrey rose. "Raspberry fool, people?"

"Sounds delicious." I should not be indulging in a dessert made with sugar-infused whipped cream, but I wanted Malcolm to go on talking. He did not need much encouragement.

"Besides medicine, DNA testing is used, of course," he said, "in criminal investigations and in paternity testing."

Ah. At last. Malcolm had walked into my labyrinth of questions.

"Paternity testing. So if someone wanted to look for his or her father, how would they go about it?"

"They'd have to have a potential candidate. Are you thinking of anyone in particular?"

"Oh, I'm just making conversation, Malcolm, but remember Rachel—the sister Billy—I mean William—found? She wanted to find her father. William said there was nothing on her original birth certificate about that."

Geoffrey came back into the room carrying three tall glasses filled with peaked cream striped with red swathes of raspberry and little flecks of orange peel.

Malcolm beamed appreciatively. I could see he was going to eat the whole thing.

Geoffrey was looking at me steadily. His eyes told me he wondered what I was getting up to. I bent my head and sampled the dessert.

"Scrumptious! Wonderful, wonderful dinner." I trained my attention on Malcolm. "What if she found a potential sister, or brother—couldn't a test uncover that they shared some genes?"

"I'll get the coffee," said Geoffrey. "You've got to go across town, and I'll ring you a taxi."

"Thank you, darling. But I'm just asking Malcolm—"

Malcolm was in full flow. His florid face was fully engaged, and his wiry head leaned toward me. "Females have two X chromosomes, one from their mother and one from their father. Males have one X, one Y. Sisters can be matched if the true father is sought because the man passes on his one X chromosome to his daughters. If we're looking to confirm which mother matches a child it might be difficult, since an X could come from the father or the mother. But, in the case of sisters, there are two X chromosomes, and if we know there are different mothers, but there is a match on the other X chromosome, we have to assume that they have the same father."

I felt my head spin, trying to follow. "How can that be tested?"

"From a cheek swab."

"Is it expensive?"

"Used to be. Now a test kit can be bought and sent off to the lab and the results come back in a few days. It costs a bit. Not as much as it used to, however."

"Sounds like half-sisters are easier to identify than a half-brother and sister?"

Geoffrey said in a low voice. "Why do you want to know, Mille?"

"Oh, Geoffo." Geoffrey, whose life has been full of secrets, would understand. "Don't you notice how Rachel looks a bit like our family?"

"I've never met her."

"Oh."

"When did you meet her?" Geoffrey stood at the table, plates gathered in his hand.

"Tilda arranged a lunch for me with Billy and Rachel. Last time I was here. I suppose Billy might have pestered Tilda to do it. He seems very proud of Rachel as if he had something to do with her sudden appearance."

Geoffrey looked uncomfortable. "Will just wants a family, don't you think? A real family."

"Yep. I know." That was thoughtless of me to snark on Billy. I dug my fingernails into my hand.

"I'm not sure I like where you're going with this." The plates jiggled in my brother's hand. "For your sake,

Mille."

"I just have a thought, that's all. But I think you can guess, Geoffo."

"I'm several leaps ahead on that. But why do this? Aren't you opening a can of worms?"

I looked at him, at his liquid, gray, empathic eyes. Misunderstanding everything.

"Thanks so much, both of you," I said. "Don't need the coffee, sweetie." I stood.

Malcolm's eyes flicked between us, confused. I smiled at him, that dear, kind, tactless person, now entrenched in our quirky family, and I said to Geoffrey, "I have to get Billy to understand the implications. For now."

"Can I have a word, Mille?" Geoffrey, plates in hand, flicked his eyes toward the kitchen. I gathered glasses and followed him. I could sense Malcolm staring at us as we left him sitting at the table.

"I think you're barking up the wrong tree, sister." Geoffrey laid the plates on the stone counter.

"Oh?"

"I know you're fond of Will. I know what went on when you were kids. I know why Will got thrown out of the house."

"You do?"

"I think so. I saw Dad once. With this woman. It was years ago, but you don't forget something like that. Then I recognized her from the photo on the floppy disk."

My hands started to shake. I gripped my handful of glasses tightly. "That was Billy's mother. But that was a publicity photo for the company that she worked for. The company Daddy invested in when it started."

"Yes. But you see, I saw her and Dad holding hands. In a park. He didn't see me. Looked like it was a budding relationship. Eyes only for each other and so on. So then, when Will told us at lunch that day that he had a half-sister, I had a suspicion."

"Tell me." The raspberry fool threatened to come up in my throat.

"I don't think I have to, Mille. I think you know. Nora's child might have been our father's too. Of course, it might not be. But I thought, if our father found out what you and Will were up to, then he would have lost it."

"As he did." My voice quivered.

"Can you imagine, knowing his daughter and his lover's son had a mutual half-sibling! All the while you were risking having a kid yourselves."

The glasses clattered into the sink, one after the other, shattering. "You mean you've suspected this all along? That Daddy and Billy's mother had an affair?"

"Well, nothing that could be proved of course. Not now he's dead. Mother never challenged him, obviously, and I wasn't about to break the peace in the family." Geoffrey put his hand on my arm, steadying me as I shook.

Billy and I, sharing a half-sister. Geoffrey's words confirmed my fears. I had to break it off with Billy, once and for all. I'd tried to, but I was not sure he understood how final it must be.

"I don't want you to get hurt again, Mille. And not just you. If you try to prove this thing with DNA testing, Rachel will have to be a willing participant. She'd have to know the reason you wanted to know. She'd have to know all the seedy secrets in this family."

"Why does she have to know?"

"Because in this country you can't just pinch someone's DNA from a used cigarette or a fork from a half-eaten meal." He looked at me sideways. "You've got something of hers, haven't you? Something you stole to test this theory of yours."

I must have looked guilty because he went on. "It's illegal in England to test body tissues or DNA without a person's consent. Thank God," he added.

"So without involving Rachel, upsetting her whole life, upsetting the whole family when they learn about Daddy and Nora, there's nothing I can do? Nothing I can do to let Billy and I...?" I could not go on. I clutched my brother, feeling I was about to fall, and he enveloped me in a hug, kissing the top of my head, patting my shoulder.

"I'm so sorry, Mille." Geoffrey rubbed my back. "I think it's best—for you and Will—just to drop it. Try and get over him, move on. Live your life."

"Could you call me a taxi, please?" I managed to say. My fingers had now gone numb.

I taxied back to Lucy's. My friend's comfortable, carpeted house welcomed me, yet made me feel off-keel. Lucy was waiting up for me, we had a small glass of wine together, I said little about the evening, and we hugged and went to bed.

I could not sleep. The thick mattress, the neatly arranged pictures on Lucy's guestroom walls, the polished bureau, and the walk-in closet all seemed to mock me. Where was my home? Where was the home that Vincent and I had imagined together? A fantasy, now completely dead. Why were all my relationships with eligible men so fraught? I was running out of time.

A future as an old lady with a pet parrot beckoned. How pathetic was that? My heart tugged a little for child-like Bethany. Was the sweet, slow girl a substitute recipient for my maternal feelings? What Malcolm had said about the biological clock ticking made me feel old and already barren. Tilda had two children and greedily wanted more. I had tried with Vincent, had failed, I'd tried to move on and engage Jake in a relationship too, when all I ever really wanted, truth be told, was Billy. But the idea of us being together, having children together, seemed tainted by the fact that our parents had together made love, had borne a child.

My stomach hurt thinking of it. I put a hand on my belly to calm it. After a while, its fluttering abated. I needed to talk to Lucy about it. Dear Lucy. In the morning, we'd talk and talk and maybe the pain would dissipate.

****

"Oh, my dear friend," Lucy hugged me. I had hardly been able to keep in my anxiety as I waited for Hugo to go to work and the children to leave for school. At Lucy's long wooden kitchen table, coffee wafted from my cup, untouched.

Lucy pushed a plate toward me and sipped her own coffee. "What a pickle. What a complete and utter nightmare to have all these terrible insinuations about your father. And about this girl, Rachel."

"Geoffrey seems to feel I should put it all away, try to forget it. Proving Rachel's related will be too difficult, he says, she'd have to know and then everyone would know and there'd be a scandal. I mean Daddy's memory would really be tarnished."

Lucy put her cup down, slowly, carefully, and

looked me in the eye.

"You know," she said, "Your brother had to live his life till recently with a curtain over it. Do you think, darling, do you think it's possible that Geoffrey might be the teeniest weeniest bit jealous of what you and Billy had together?"

"Why would he be?"

"Think, sweetheart."

"You mean because Geoffrey's gay and he was sweet on Billy himself?"

"Maybe."

I put the coffee cup back onto its saucer, leaned back, and looked at my friend. My head felt like it was going to explode with all these secrets, all these possibilities. "You mean all that time Billy lived with us, my poor brother was making moon eyes at him?"

"Maybe without really understanding that he was. Geoffrey was only about twelve at the time. Kids get obsessed with sex at that age."

I swallowed. "Yes, I suppose. Anyway, Billy's definitely hetero, I can tell you that!" I laughed.

"Not suggesting he isn't. But unrequited love is the hardest to bear, and maybe Geoffrey's jumped to an entirely wrong conclusion. I bet he has, actually. He's still jealous and wants Billy for himself."

"Malcolm's a pretty nice consolation prize. He's a keeper."

Lucy put a hand on my arm. "And Billy's yours to keep, if you want that. My impression of Billy is that he's thoughtful and protective. You and he—you deserve to be together."

"You are kind."

Lucy smiled, her eyes sympathetic. "Sweetie, you

have had the most awful year, haven't you? First, your father dying—that must be hard, to know you're completely on your own now, with both parents dead— then you've been struggling to keep your business going without much money after that bastard of a husband left you, and it sounds like you've had employee troubles. And now Billy…" She patted my arm.

"Could I have another piece of toast? I feel a bit faint," I said.

Lucy forked a slice out of the toaster and handed it to me. "Here, put some jam on it. You need the glucose. But none of this is the real problem, I think."

"Remind me what is."

"You're stuck. You have to get to the root of all this so you can heal. Understand why your father acted as he did. Then you can decide whether to let Billy in, or whether you can move on from him."

"Oh." How true. The relationship with Billy had derailed me. Perhaps its urgency and its abrupt ending, which magnified the loss, ruined me, not only for the kind of career my parents might have had in mind for me but for marriage. Perhaps Vincent was a victim of my unintentional coldness rather than a perpetrator of the distance between us. I'd never been able to make headway with Jake and now Billy was suffering from my indecision.

Lucy waved a hand. "Let's list the practical issues. You think Billy's half-sister looks like you, and you have a strong suspicion of why that would be so. You think that photo you've told me about is a clue. First, because it is of Nora and second, because your father hid it. You think that the legacy your father left Billy is a clue. If he was so angry with Billy, why did he look after him financially? You think there is a link there. So does your brother. You need confirmation to settle your mind. Now go where your logic takes you!"

"Oh, you dear friend." Tears burned my eyes. "There is no one else I can talk to about all this. Mummy's dead, Tilda's been in a daze since Daddy died and it turns out it's because she's been preoccupied with her health, and Geoffrey's comments have not helped, as you say. It's been so hard to find anything out about my father because he was so emotionally removed."

"Who might be able to shed some light on him, his way of working, his way of thinking?"

I clapped my hands, rattling the cups. "Barbara. Barbara came to Daddy's funeral. She was his nursing assistant at the practice. She asked me to come and have tea with her one day. I did, and we had a nice talk, and she asked me to come again."

"I think it's time, don't you? Why don't you call her right now?"

"Her number's back in that chest of drawers at Tilda's. But yes, I'll just get my things and head back on the train and ring her this afternoon." My eyes swam. "I'm so grateful to you, Lucy. You're the only sensible person in this whole messy business."

"Friends for life." Lucy crossed her right index finger over mine in the gesture we'd invented when we were eight years old. "Friends for life."

Chapter Thirty-Four

A leaky spring sun, in and out of the clouds, cast a dewy glitter on the flower gardens I glimpsed from the bus window as I rode to Cherry Hinton. April in England could be beautiful, but I could not help thinking of T.S. Eliot's poem. It was the cruelest month.

I didn't bring flowers to Barbara this time, knowing that her garden would already be abloom. Instead, I'd baked a cake, perching it in its domed cover on my knee as I rode the bus.

Barbara greeted me happily and said that coffee walnut cake was her very favorite and should we have tea, or would I prefer a sherry. I opted for the tea. I needed a clear head. Although, as soon as the cup and teapot were placed in front of me, I wished I'd asked for the alcoholic drink to give me courage for the questions I'd come to ask.

"It seems that my father had an interest in a medical instruments company," I began. "Inoculese. Do you know it?"

"They made all kinds of things. But I remember they made a stir when they came out with the disposable injection needles. A huge time saver and of course at the time AIDS was such a scourge. I think people believed that single-use needles could halt it, especially among drug addicts."

"Really?"

"Medications have helped, of course, but possibly these needles made a difference. They were certainly easier to use. Why do you ask?"

"Apparently, Daddy had shares in the company."

"Oh. I wouldn't know anything about that. I have no idea about his financial affairs."

Affairs. Here was an opening. This was what I had come for.

"Were there any patients my father took a particular interest in?" I let out a breath.

A shadow crossed Barbara's face, and I could see her compose an answer.

"What do you mean?"

Did I imagine it, or did Barbara give Petunia a gentle push toward me so that the cat took a sudden leap onto my chair? I buried my fingers in the feline's silken furred back. The cat purred. "I'm still trying to understand him," I said. "Why he acted so uptight. Like no one could question him."

"Is that how he was at home? Goodness me." Barbara looked away.

"A doctor, too. A doctor should be accepting of human frailty. Especially one who is also a priest. I mean forgiveness is their trade, isn't it?"

"Forgiveness? I don't know, my dear. I'm not religious at all. Haven't set foot in church for years. Never understood the idea of original sin, I must say."

"Well, that's a relief. Nor did I." I smiled.

A sudden squall of rain lashed the windows, sending petals flying in the garden.

"I'll have to get out there and deadhead the flowers when it stops," Barbara said. She added, when I looked blank, "The flowers will bloom again if you do that."

"Oh. I'd like to learn how to garden. All I know about it is that you can eat certain flowers." I'd have to try another tack. I took a tiny bite of cake, swallowed, and said, "Barbara, I want to talk to you about Rachel."

"Who's Rachel?"

"Rachel…actually she's the reason I contacted you. Not that I don't enjoy your company, of course." I lowered my eyes, suddenly embarrassed. "You see, Billy tells me that after Daddy's funeral he was contacted by a young woman."

"Billy? You mean Billy Blanchard? I thought you said you hadn't kept in touch." Barbara's face was expressionless.

"He's been friends with Geoffrey all that time, and then he came to Daddy's funeral."

"Yes, of course. Of course, he did." Barbara looked directly at me. "This young woman—is she Billy's girlfriend? High time he settled down, surely."

I almost spat the cake into the napkin. "Um, no." I recovered. "This girl, Rachel. What can you tell me?"

Barbara took a sip of tea. "What is she to Billy?"

"She told him she'd looked up her mother on her birth certificate, and from that she found her mother's age, then she found a death certificate for someone that age with the same name, then she found her mother's birth and marriage certificate, and eventually, she followed the trail to Billy."

"Oh." Barbara looked confused for a moment, then her face twitched to calm. It was like watching a camera click to take a photo, the subject smiling only for a second.

"Would you know if that's true?" I put down my

cup very carefully on the saucer. My fingers trembled. "I just wanted to confirm that. For Billy of course."

Barbara reached out and touched my hand. The cat poured itself out of my lap and returned to Barbara's feet. She said, "Is this girl…does this girl pose a threat to you, Camilla, in some way?"

"Nuh, I mean, not directly." I clenched my nails against my palm, stopping myself from telling Barbara about my relationship with Billy then and now. I said, turning my gaze to the tea leaves in my cup, "Well, you know Billy lived with us and now we've all reconnected. I just thought you might know how Rachel came to be born since Nora was a patient."

"Yes, she was a patient. A very sick one indeed, in the end. As you know. So sad. She was only thirty-nine."

"I suppose Billy finds it all fascinating. He claims Rachel as his sister. He's so proud of her." My voice caught. "I don't know why I should be jealous of that, Barbara. Why would it matter if he had a sister? I don't understand."

"His sister?" A baffled look crossed her face as Barbara reached for the teapot, held its lid with hands that shook slightly, and held it over my cup.

"Rachel says she is Nora's daughter. Nora Blanchard, that is, Billy's mother."

Why did I have to repeat myself? I waved the pot away. "No thanks. Nothing more for me."

Barbara put the teapot back on its tray and started to stack the cups and saucers.

I took it as a signal that she wanted to end the conversation. But she sighed and went on, "You know why Billy had to go to you—he had nowhere else when

311

his mother fell so sick." She stood, moved over to a side table, and began to rearrange some daffodils in a vase. "You see, it was too dangerous for him to stay with relatives in Belfast. The Protestant vigilantes and the Catholic IRA were targeting the children of mixed marriages."

I brought my hand to my mouth. "I had no idea. Poor Billy. Poor Nora, to be in that situation to know she was dying and to have her child at risk."

Barbara's hand gripped the vase. "And of course…" She stopped. She pulled out a dead flower and stood there for a second, water dripping on the floor. It soaked into the Oriental rug.

I felt a tremendous urge to mop it up but sat motionless. "Go on," I said.

"Well, Nora was pregnant and in some kinds of breast cancer the pregnancy makes the cancer cells proliferate. The hormones of pregnancy cause the cancer to rampage through the body. Perhaps if she had terminated the pregnancy when she found out, she might have lived. But she wouldn't."

"Did my father recommend that?"

"Oh, Camilla," said Barbara breaking the stalk in two, then reaching for a paper napkin to wrap it in, "this kind of talk really violates patient confidentiality, and I am still bound by that, you understand. I'm talking in general terms. This could apply to anyone in her situation."

"I don't mean to pry." I gripped my hands together between my knees. "But it is odd, my father being simultaneously a chaplain and a doctor. Sometimes his roles might conflict. What's the moral choice in a case like this?"

Barbara crossed the room to the kitchen, pulled a small door under the sink open, and thrust the dead daffodil into the trash. "In medicine, the morality gets muddled sometimes. Particularly in the area of reproduction, churches can't keep up with it all. The new technology brings new choices. Difficult, sometimes." Her gray eyes looked troubled.

"Is there something you want to tell me, Barbara?"

"Oh for goodness sake!" Barbara ran water in the sink. "Could you bring the tray over, please?"

I did so. Barbara washed the cups and plates and kept the water running.

"I did ask before. Was there anyone, as a patient, I mean," I stood, steeling myself, "Who meant something special to my father?" I stopped to see Barbara's reaction, but she was turning off the water. She put the cups on the draining rack.

I said, "You see, when Tilda and I were cleaning out the old house, I found a photograph of a young woman. It had been hidden at the back of a drawer. It had the initials N.B. on the back. I thought that these initials were just a reminder to my father about something, but now I realize Billy's mother's initials were the same."

"Ah."

"I showed the photo to Billy. He said it is a photo of his mother, the only one he has. So I gave it to him."

"That was good of you. Must have meant a lot to him."

"Yes, it was selfish of me to hold on to it. But actually, I didn't really want to know. I think I realized who it was the day Billy told us about Rachel. I hadn't really remembered his mother's name before." I put a hand on my chest. "But why did my father keep her photo so long and so secretly?"

"Oh." Barbara slammed her fist on the counter. The cups trembled. "Let's not beat around the bush! Now you're here, and you're what, thirty-five years old or something? You deserve the truth."

"What?"

"Forget patient confidentiality. This has nothing to do with that!" Barbara's voice rose to a tinny laugh. "They tried to hide it, but I knew. Oh, I knew. The way Frederick looked at Nora, the way her eyes lifted up from her magazine in joy when I announced the doctor was ready for her. Nora was in love with your father."

"And he with her?"

"I think so. I am so sorry, but I think so."

"Was my father Rachel's father too?"

"My dear." Barbara twirled to face me. "You don't think that, do you?"

"Isn't that what you've been telling me?"

"Good Lord. This is such a muddle." Barbara pushed one hand against the counter, holding her other arm across her stomach as if in pain. She limped to a chair by the kitchen table and sat down with a thud. She looked me in the eyes and said, "No."

"No?"

"Nora was so very sick. She was pregnant, but the baby died. It was stillborn. Nora died soon after."

"What?" I rocked back on my heels and held onto the table for support.

"Yes. You see, your father tried to get Nora to agree to chemotherapy. It can often be safely used in the second and third trimesters. That's what I meant about difficult choices with medicine. She refused the chemo, not wanting to hurt the child. But it died anyway. Tragic. Just tragic, the whole thing."

"So how come Rachel believes Nora was her mother?"

"My dear girl, I don't know."

Her hand scrabbled over the table and reached for a paper napkin poking up from a ceramic holder. "I admired your father so greatly, you know." She wiped her eyes. "Our conversation this afternoon, I was finding it hard to follow, all this supposition about this young woman being Nora's daughter. I wanted to see what you knew."

"What I knew? I know nothing! I came to you for confirmation."

"Yes, well. If this Rachel believes Nora was her mother, the birth certificate must have been falsified."

"How could that be?"

"My goodness, I don't know. I don't think it necessarily means that Frederick had anything to do with it. The parents of the child are the ones who register the birth, not the doctor."

"Who would do that, though? If the mother is too indisposed to do that, who else would do it?"

"The father, usually. Though in the case of an unmarried couple, the mother may choose not to put the father's name on the certificate."

"All right. So if the mother is still in the hospital, and the father is not listed, who else could certify as to the facts of birth?"

Barbara looked at me, her eyes brimming now. "I suppose your father, as a doctor, could state that a child was born and name the mother."

"Why would he do that? Was he trying to protect

someone?"

My mind skidded. My fingers bit into my palm. I already knew.

Chapter Thirty-Five

The rain spat on the bus windows, forming a mosaic of muddy streaks and glittery glass. My mind sank and soared in a confusion of feelings.

In the hour that had passed since I'd arrived at Barbara's tidy home with my cake, my world had utterly changed. And I suspect it had changed for Barbara, too. Barbara, my father's practice nurse for many years, admired him greatly. Perhaps there was more than admiration in there, too. Perhaps that's why she'd burst out that Daddy and Nora were in love in a voice full of simmering frustration. She'd probably been dying to tell someone for years.

Standing there by Barbara's sink, shock had rocked me as I took in what she said.

Nora's baby had died, and someone had falsified the birth certificate for another woman, to hide the fact she'd given birth. It had hit me with the force of a stone to the head. There was only one person for whom my father would walk to the ends of the earth.

My sister.

Tilda had to be Rachel's mother.

Tilda, the perfect daughter. Frederick's shining jewel of a child. His open favorite. Geoffrey had missed the mark. My brother was bright and personable, but different in a way Frederick's religion found unacceptable, while I was the untidy underachiever, the daughter who preferred the company of the college housekeeping department to the discourse of the academy. While I was learning to cook for a crowd, running the Sunday Soup Kitchen in the church basement, Tilda was away at university.

My stomach hurt. The bus jolted and I lurched forward. A leather seam on the seatback in front of me had started to unravel, and I picked at it compulsively. Tilda, a teenaged, unmarried mother, who gave her baby away. It was still all supposition, but the timing was right. I'd never asked Rachel her birthdate, but it must have been about the time Nora died and a few months before Billy left our house. Tilda was away the whole time.

I tried to remember the summer Billy's mother died. By early June, she was extremely ill. My father told Billy it would be too upsetting to visit her. To distract himself, and to earn his way, Billy offered to do all kinds of odd jobs, at home and in the neighborhood. He mowed lawns. He fed cats when neighbors were away. I, on the other hand, was sent away to be an au pair in France. Possibly my parents suspected I was getting too close to Billy, or maybe they just wanted me to improve my French. I hated it. Tilda, too, spent the summer away. Another au pair job, my mother told me, in the north of England. When I returned, it was to a sad home. Billy's mother had died. He was still living in the house, for it seemed that Frederick and Helen hadn't the heart to send him to foster care, which would have been the only alternative living arrangement for him. Summer ended, and Geoffrey went off to boarding school and Tilda back to university. Billy and I, left alone after school most afternoons and often on weekends, intensified our relationship. Until it was discovered and ended, we were so wrapped up in each other we did not notice the silence in the house, the fact that my parents barely spoke to one another, and that Tilda, if she came home at all, said little and spent a lot of time staring into space.

Poor Tilda. If she'd had a child, she must have been persuaded to give it up. Was that my father's doing? Had he made a false affidavit, to pretend Tilda's teenaged motherhood had never happened?

My father, so high and holy. If Barbara was right, and he and Nora were lovers, he could have fathered the baby who died. That was a violation of his code of ethics as a doctor—and as a priest. Then he'd made it worse, much worse. To protect his daughter, he'd lied for her. It seemed unbelievable. But it made sense.

The dark green leather seam ripped open at my pulling, and bits of stuffing, none too clean, bulged from the opening, spilling out. I picked at those, too. Maybe I'd be arrested for vandalism, but I couldn't stop.

My father—not only a hypocrite but a liar and fraud. Had he committed an actual crime by making a false declaration on a birth certificate? I wasn't sure. I'd have to ask Rupert. Ah, poor Rupert. If what I now believed was true, his world would come apart. I recalled the day Billy told the family about Rachel. Rupert obviously hadn't an inkling she was related to Tilda.

Tilda! What a burden she'd carried all these years. Poor Rachel, too, to have met her mother and not realize who she was.

Particles of fluff floated downward. My foot

scuffed the white bits into the gray grit of the floor. If it was true that Tilda gave birth to Rachel, it didn't alter the fact of my father's betrayal of our own mother. And it didn't alter the fact that he'd compounded this failing by flouting goodness knows how many codes of conduct. That was not good. But it made Rachel much less of a threat.

The seatback looked frightful now. I dabbed at it several times with moistened fingers, trying to insert the stuffing back, and the grubby leather left a sour taste on my tongue.

Lucy was right. This family kept far too many secrets. Not just deeds. Feelings kept under wraps. Geoffrey's for example. My dear brother allied with me when we were little, against Tilda, our bossy older sister. But once Geoffrey had gone to boarding school, I'd lost touch with him emotionally, and when I went to America, literally. He hardly ever wrote or e-mailed or called. I took his silence for disapproval. I'd hoped that the mobile phone and the laptop would help us keep in touch. It didn't. I'd become busy, involved with my own life, and Geoffrey and his discontents, even his newfound love with Malcolm, had simply slipped my mind. And Lucy was probably correct—Geoffrey had always harbored feelings for Billy that were not returned, and his imagination got the better of him.

The bus came to a halt and I stumbled off the step and into a puddle, soaking my boots. When I picked up Lily from her friend's house, the child came to the door wearing a pink tutu and a wide hat adorned with ribbons. She tottered on a pair of sparkly high heels.

"I'm going to a wedding," she said.

"Are you? Whose wedding?"

"Your wedding!" Lily pirouetted, her arms wide.

"Oh? How lovely. I've already had one of those," I smiled at Lily's little friend's mother. "Perhaps another would be nice."

"You can come over another day, Lily," said the woman, smoothly removing the hat and helping Lily step out of the shoes, then the tutu. Lily allowed all this without protest because it was someone else's mother doing the ordering about. I watched in wonderment at the woman's warm competence, inhaled the delicious smell of dinner, some kind of stew, I guessed, that wafted from the kitchen.

Lily and I faced a damp walk home. I bundled her into her rain slicker and her miniature gumboots, patterned with ducks.

"Goodness," I said, "I had no idea it was so late. We must rush to pick up Rosie now and run home. Mummy will be wondering where we are!"

I wondered how I would be able to face her.

In fact, when the three of us got home, mud-splattered and weary, Tilda was sitting on the sofa, engrossed in a book. She looked up at us with a slightly guilty smile. "I forgot the time! I got carried away. I'm starting my reading for the course. My master's in literature," she added when I must have looked blank.

"You already have a degree. In literature." Of all the useless things. I bit my lip to resist saying it.

"Yes. I'd like to start the M. Phil next year."

"What on earth is that?"

"A master's degree in contemporary and modern literature. Then I could continue with the Ph.D."

"You want to teach, like Mummy?"

"Probably, yes. I'll have to broach the idea with

Rupert of course. He's quite a traditionalist, as you know."

Tilda, wanting to be an academic like our mother. She always did have her head in a book. If Tilda turned into our mother, I wondered if she'd have the same uncanny ability to shut her mind to what she didn't want to see. Of course, that is just what I suspected her to have done, to my cost. I must raise the issue of Rachel with her. I just had to find the right time.

I nodded curtly at her and holding each child by the hand to warm my own numbed fingers, took them into the kitchen.

I pulled the legs off the chicken we'd had last night, fixed carrots and beans and then sat with the children at the table. Tilda remained in the sitting room with her books.

As I watched the girls eat, a wave of tenderness washed over me. Rose kept up a stream of conversation about her day at school while Lily ate in silent concentration. Chicken grease adorned her lip and she stabbed at the carrots inaccurately, so they slithered around the plate. A bean shot out and landed on the table and with another slide of the fork a piece of chicken also became dislodged and dangled on the plate's edge. Rose laughed and Lily looked up at me tentatively, and as if given permission by my smile, laughed as well.

"Ruby has a bunny. I'm going to ask Mummy if we can get a bunny too," she said.

"Some people eat rabbits." Rose grinned cruelly.

Lily let out a wail, and I put my arm around her, giving Rose a disapproving look.

I couldn't deny the fact to Lily. How did grown-ups impart unpleasant facts to children without hurting their feelings? They had to learn. "We can read *Peter Rabbit* tonight," I said and hugged Lily closer. She gave me a doubtful look and returned to her dinner.

The room stilled. Suddenly I knew. I wanted to be present with these little girls always, to see them grow up. That snowy day in Boston, thinking about the financial constraints that kept Paige living with her parents, Hannah in a run-down shared house, and Manuela and her husband crammed in with her large extended family, I'd felt sorry for them, guilty about the privilege I'd been born with, a privilege that enabled me to rent an apartment, however small, of my own. But what was the point? Why was that even worth having? Why not live surrounded by family? How would I cope in Boston if I stayed there, met someone with whom I could have a child? I was an entrepreneur there, a manager. I didn't want to be anyone's boss anymore. I just wanted to be enmeshed.

And besides, I was needed here. How would my nieces navigate the world with a mother whose mind seemed always elsewhere? I hoped they'd do a better job of navigation than I had.

This parenting business was a mystery. I wondered if I would be any good at it at all. How must Tilda have felt, to have a baby, then to give it up, knowing that she would never even see it smile? She was cool as a long drink of water, never letting on.

I put an arm around each little girl, crushing them to my chest. Rosie turned her big blue eyes to mine, questioning, and Lily protested.

"Aunt Camilla, you're squashing me!" Lily's brow felt damp with grease and exertion, her lingering baby smell mixed now with a miasma of anxiety. I kissed each girl's forehead and relinquished my hugs.

I tried to imagine how Tilda must have felt, cradling each little bundle, knowing there was one she'd lost forever. And now, what reservoirs of self-control was she drawing on, that she could actually meet Rachel and not break down? If Tilda didn't have a stone heart, it must be close to breaking apart like peanut brittle.

While Tilda resumed her reading, Rupert did a cursory clean-up of the kitchen. I had to pinch my fingers into my hand to resist taking up a broom to complete the job. After I had bathed and put the children to bed and did a very quick run-through of *The Tale of Peter Rabbit,* I retreated to my nest on the top floor. I needed to talk to Billy.

Of course, I owed Billy the biggest apology. In my mind, I'd concocted several dreadful ideas, all of them wrong. But that was not the only thing I needed to tell him.

When Barbara had walked me to the door this afternoon, she'd grabbed my arm. "Camilla," she said urgently, "I can see that all this has upset you. As well it would. But why is it so important to prove Rachel's parentage? Why trouble yourself over this, all these years later?" She paused, looking me in the eyes. "You don't want it to affect your own happiness, dear," she said. "The main point is, Nora's son had so many disadvantages, and yet he has turned out so well. From what I hear he has chosen his mother's path of peace and love rather than violence."

I'd held onto the doorframe, suddenly weak.

Barbara put out her hand to steady me. "This has

been a lot to take in," she said. "When you came to see me after Frederick died, I thought something must have sprung up between you and Billy recently. But of course it is not recent, is it? The thing is, I think you love Billy, and you always have." Barbara squeezed my wrist. "You must tell him. The time for all that hurt is over."

But for Billy there would be more hurt to come. Unless Tilda took it upon herself, and so far she showed no sign of doing so, it would be me who would pull the rug from under him and tell him he no longer had a sister.

I sat by my phone for a few minutes, fingers itching, and then heart thumping, called Billy.

"I'd like to push the reset button," I said when he answered.

"What? Why do you think I'd want to do that, after the other day?" His voice was cool.

"Oh, Billy, I am sorry. There was so much bursting in my head then. I need to sit down and talk to you."

"If we do that, don't run away. You have a tendency to bolt just as things are getting interesting."

"I have to be here for Rose and Lily while Tilda recuperates. I can't come up to London."

"How is Tilda?"

"Getting better every day. Now she's studying. Apparently, she's going back to university this autumn."

"Well, good for her. I suppose you'll be going back soon, to your work."

"Yes, I imagine I will." I heard the doubt in my voice. "When can you come?"

"To Cambridge? I'll have to take time off."

"I need to breathe. Can you come to the Botanic Garden?"

"Tomorrow afternoon? I'll make arrangements."

I went downstairs slowly and put on the kettle.

Rupert sounded a trifle annoyed when I asked him if he could come home early the next day but caught himself just in time. I saw Tilda nudge him and whisper, heard her soothing tone. I saw my brother-in-law's look of chagrin.

I filled the cups and laid on a plate several Shrewsbury biscuits I'd made the day before. I handed Rupert a cup of chamomile tea, and he placed it gently on the little table next to the sofa where Tilda sat and kissed her head tenderly. Seeing them together, I knew I could not bring myself to ask Tilda if she'd had a secret baby while away at university. At least not today.

I said to Rupert, "I'll be back a little late tomorrow, but I'll pick up things for dinner. If you could get one of the other mothers to pick up Lily at school at lunchtime, would it be all right if you picked up Rose later?"

"You know their schedules better than I do," Rupert grumbled. He pronounced the word, "shedule" and I stopped feeling guilty that instant. The girls' own father should know his daughters' routines better than their aunt who lived in a foreign country.

I took a bite of the biscuit. The round butter cookie flecked with lemon zest, named for a town in Shropshire, was popular in England but unknown in Boston. Perhaps I should add it to my repertoire. Familiarity and foreignness. The foreign could become familiar over time. And the familiar could become estranged. It was all a matter of perspective.

I'd pushed Billy away, and it wasn't just that I lived across an ocean. I'd turned the anger inward. My entire adult life had been based on the idea that I was the one at fault. I'd told myself that I was the one who deserved to be betrayed. I'd let Vincent do that to me and for a while believed Billy had, too. All because of my father's sins and my sister's mistake. I wasn't going to let her get away with it.

As I rose I gave the bottom of the sofa a surreptitious kick and left Rupert and Tilda to the television.

Chapter Thirty-Six

I walked to meet Billy at the station. The day sparkled after a receding shower, the stones of the buildings gleamed wet, and puddles gathered at corners. Though I'd brought an umbrella, as I walked along Trumpington Street I kept my eye out for a café or pub we could dart into if the pause in the rain refused to hold. A high window caught my attention. It was centered in a narrow stone building, and looking up to the second floor, I saw the sun glint off a large pane. That room, whatever it housed, would be full of light. Below, I peered into a little shop. A bakery, there were few offerings in the smudged window at this hour of the afternoon. The cases displayed a dozen or so muffins, some cupcakes. Passers-by ignored the sad little shop. The caterer in me felt sorry for my fellow kitchen laborer, whoever he or she was. I guessed the rent might be late this month. My sympathies.

At the station, I saw Billy push through the gates and look about. He wore his leather jacket, and it emphasized his slim build. I noticed little slivers of gray in his brown hair. He smiled and the skin wrinkled at the edges of his eyes. I wanted nothing more than to kiss him but held back and just rocked on my heels while I took both his hands in mine.

"I thought we'd walk," I said, and we strolled to the Botanic Garden and meandered along its paths, not speaking. I was acutely aware of him next to me, shoulders held stiffly, expecting me to make the first move.

After a while, he said, "Your turn. You didn't bring me here to admire the flowers."

Where to begin? I took his hand. He pulled it away a little roughly. He had reason to be angry, but I needed to get this out. I said, "Let's sit, please."

We found a bench and I wiped it dry with a tissue. As we sat with the width of the seat between us, I avoided Billy's eyes, focusing on the path, which shone slightly with the remains of the shower. Swathes of blue scilla adorned a flower-bed across the way, mixed with white and yellow daffodils. They'd started to shrivel and I wanted to pick them so others could take their place. But that would happen naturally. Which gave me courage.

I began. "You suffered so much when your mother died, and then you had to leave us, and I haven't been sympathetic enough. I have just been so freaked out by Rachel—"

"You keep bringing her up. Stop it, please. She has nothing to do with us." He shoved his elbows into the back of the seat, staring stubbornly ahead. "I told you I don't believe your theory."

My theory had been blown out of the water, thank goodness. But I'd get to that. Right now I had some questions for Billy. Perhaps to relieve my own conscience. To forgive myself for not fighting hard enough for him when we were sixteen. If Tilda could have persuaded Daddy to do something illegal, surely I could have kicked and screamed till he relented about Billy. But I hadn't. I was a wimp and a coward. On the other hand, here was Billy, competent, in no way neurotic, and apparently happy enough. Doing well. He had inner strength I'd like to emulate myself.

"I still don't understand exactly how you survived when you left us. Emotionally, I mean. I had such a hard time, and you were all alone. With no one."

"Yeah, I was. Alone. Had to go to a new school. Kept in touch with some of my old mates, though. Luckily, a friend's parents got me out of that group home."

"What was that like?"

"You just have to go into yourself, you know, and make a vow you're going to survive. It's hard to trust anyone. You can get a bitter edge. Without parents to protect you, the wind comes through." He pulled his jacket around him, wrapping his arms around himself so his hands nestled under his armpits.

"Must have been awful." I put my hands between my legs, moved a little closer to him. "You're like a rock, to have got through it."

"Mum gave me that. Never acted sorry for herself. After what she had to go through when she got married. Kicked out by her own parents." He turned to me, a defensive look on his face. "Why do you care about this?"

"Geoffrey said he didn't want me to get hurt. But why would I? With you I mean." My eyes sought his. "You're the last person to do that."

Billy shot to his feet and stood away from me as if I'd touched him with a burning stick. "He said what?"

I looked at the ground. "He said I should just move on. Try and forget you. Us."

"Yeah? Well, I am disappointed in Geoff, I must

say," he said.

"He might have been jealous, maybe."

"Why? Oh." Understanding softened his face. "You mean Geoff wished I was gay too?" He took a few strides toward me. "Well, sorry. Can't help him there."

"But really, this has nothing to do with my brother. It has to do with Rachel."

"Her again. Just stop this! You're so angry about Rachel. Jealous."

"Yes, I suppose I am." I splayed my hands out in a gesture of helplessness. "It was just you and me, years ago. Then, we meet eighteen years later, and I had this fantasy we could start again. And then—immediately—the very same day, Rachel interferes."

"You think she's a rival?"

"Not in the same way, of course. Not *that* way. But your sister. Taking some of your love. Not that I have any right to ask for that, after what my family did to you."

"Hey, Camilla. You weren't responsible for what happened to me."

"You don't seem to be able to acknowledge our relationship in public."

"Nor do you! You keep putting me off. Blowing hot and cold. Taking up with this Jake character."

"No longer."

"Right. Should I believe that?" He turned away, picked up a pebble, and then threw it forcefully. It landed next to a daffodil, making a dent in the earth.

"There's nothing to tell." I looked at the ground. "That fizzled before it started. But us. I know I have been horrible to you. I'm trying to apologize."

"Are you?"

I broke out in a smile, stood, flung my arms out, and did a little dance around the bench.

He stared, bemused.

I said, "It's just that…I think I was inventing reasons why we can't be together because I was so worried that there's a connection between us that's sort of tainted."

"Are you still on about that thing you mentioned the other day? That idea that my sister is your sister, too?" Billy sat down again on the park bench, looking fed up.

I stood behind him, my hands on the bench back. "I went to see Barbara."

"Who's Barbara?"

"You remember, I told you. Daddy's nursing assistant."

"And?"

"Barbara said—she thought, anyway—that my father and your mother had an affair! My father was so sure he was doing the right thing. Such a paragon." My voice turned sarcastic. I hated my tone, but I couldn't stop. "Here he was, a doctor, ministering to the sick, and also a priest of the church, even if part-time, administering the sacraments, trying to teach people the better path. All the while he was carrying on with a patient!"

Billy clenched his fists. "Mille! That's enough."

He leaned back against the bench, so his head faced the sky. I couldn't see his expression. He said, "You're not only being judgmental, you're making a huge leap of logic. This still sounds like bullshit. You know, you can't even prove your father cared for my mother. That photograph of Mum—I could have just dropped it when I left the house. When I was thrown out."

That possibility had not occurred to me. I felt disoriented for a minute.

Billy's voice grew more determined. "Just because Rachel looks a bit like you doesn't mean she's related. There's no proof she was Frederick's child. Anyway, he's dead so I don't see how you could test for that." His fist balled in his hand.

I took a deep breath. Time to put us both out of our misery. "She looks like me because she is related to me. But not to you. And she's not my father's kid either."

"What? What on earth are you talking about?" His head shot up, and he stared at me.

"Barbara said she believed my father and your mother were in love. She also confirmed that Nora was pregnant while she had breast cancer. Her baby, though, was stillborn. So Rachel could not be her daughter."

"Huh?" His face contorted. "The baby died? You mean, I don't have a half-sister after all?"

"Yes. I mean, no."

"How is she related to you, then?"

"Rachel is not my father's child. I think Daddy falsified the birth certificate to protect someone else."

"What? You're going too fast for me here." He stood quickly, paced a few steps, and whirled around to face me.

"Daddy was a doctor. But he was also a clergyman. Afraid of scandal. So is it just possible that he covered up Rachel's birth to protect someone else who'd had a baby?"

"Excuse me?" He sounded confused. "There is no

way Rachel could say Mum was her mother unless she really was. You can't fake a birth certificate. The physician who attends the birth has to certify who the mother is."

"That could have been Daddy. He'd need identification for the mother, but not the child's father if the mother was not married. In fact, I think the father must be asked if he wishes to have his name on the certificate."

"How do you know all this?"

"The requirements for registering a birth are online. I looked them up."

Billy regarded me with skepticism.

"My father was your mother's doctor, wasn't he?" I paced three steps forward, three steps back.

"Yes."

"And, if she was about to die, no one would be able to question her afterward."

Billy stared, silent.

"And if Daddy was her lover, wouldn't he have had access to your mother's house? He could have taken her passport, her utility bills, as proof of her ID."

"Don't tell me. He pretended they belonged to Tilda?"

All of a sudden I needed to sit down. I curled up at the edge of the bench. I said, "Tilda was away at university nineteen years ago. She was gone for months and we didn't see her. She could have had a baby that year. She could have persuaded Daddy to lie on the birth certificate when she put the baby up for adoption."

"Good God. You do have an imagination!" He paused, then said, "I suppose it's possible." His voice sounded reluctant.

My words slowed. "I'm trying to understand it. Daddy was a GP, not an obstetrician. I don't think it's likely he would have actually delivered the child. He could have been there, of course. He had the perfect excuse, being a doctor."

"Tilda having a baby. Not a crime. Why lie about it?"

"I don't know. That's what doesn't make sense."

Billy picked up a stick that had fallen from a nearby tree. He pushed out his foot on the gravel path and traced it. "Lying about who the mother was. That would involve your father's breaking his oath as a physician as well as a clergyman. Think about that."

"It's hard to take in, isn't it?"

"Doesn't make sense. If Tilda had the baby adopted, she wouldn't humiliate the family by being an unmarried mother, if that was what Frederick worried about."

"It does seem ridiculous. From our perspective."

I sensed Billy's alertness at the suggestion we had a mutual point of view. "But Tilda and Daddy shared that trait. Always wanting to appear over-the-top respectable. It's like they wanted to bury the truth completely. It wouldn't be that hard to do, either!" I hit my foot on the bench's curved metal leg. It hurt.

"Makes me sick. All those lies. Literally over my mother's dead body."

Billy sat down again, next to me. All the air seemed to have gone out of him, a deflated balloon. I put my arms around him and buried my face in his chest. I could feel his heart beating.

He banged his fist on the seat, pushed me away, and said, "None of this explains Tilda's reaction to

Rachel. I mean, when I said I had a sister, Tilda hardly batted an eyelid. She acted like you all did—surprised, and supportive, really. Then she asked me to arrange for all of us to meet Rachel. If she were Rachel's true mother, don't you think she'd behave differently? Wouldn't she want to meet Rachel on her own without having me tag along?"

"Maybe she was using you as a shield? Not letting on to you or Rachel who she really was?"

"You really think so?" He kicked a pebble and it dribbled into the middle of the path.

"I don't know. Maybe. Probably."

"Tilda's kept it all from Rupert."

"I just cannot imagine having to do that. Giving up a child. It must be so painful."

"Painful to keep hiding the secret, too."

"Yes." I hugged my arms around myself. Perhaps that was one reason Tilda was so distressed at her failure to give Rupert a son. It brought back that memory of loss.

"So much at once." Billy stretched his legs. His heels kicked up a little cloud of dust. "You know, this is a huge relief in a way. You've been shoving me away because you couldn't face the fact that your father had an adulterous relationship."

"Probably. But really, thinking we had a sister in common. That was what made me so sick."

He reached for my hand, pulled it away from my chest, but still didn't look at me. "Think of it this way. Your father must have loved her, then. My mother. That explains why he took me in. Felt responsible for me."

"I suppose. He made us suffer for his sins, though." I let out a long breath. "That's why Daddy got so upset.

He knew, if your mother's child had lived, you and I would share a half-sister."

"Sounds a bit Shakespearean. Convoluted relationship like that."

"But now we know it's not true, the fact that you and Rachel aren't siblings makes it worse for you—and her."

"And Tilda, of course. But then, she's known all along." Billy pulled me back toward him. He put his hand under my chin, turning it to face him. "I lost my only real family member today. That hurts. It really hurts. But maybe I could get another?"

"Umm?"

"If Rachel's not our half-sister, then there is no suggestion of any untoward relationship between you and me."

I felt my fingers relax. We sat like that for a minute. A pool of relief seemed to spread between us, rippling gently. I nestled in his arms, and we rested. His leather jacket pressed against my chest, and the warmth of his body seeped through.

"We'll have to speak to Tilda. She has to come forward with the truth."

He became as still as a mummy. "No. Rachel doesn't have to know. No one has to know. No one has to get a DNA test. Don't upset Rupert. It's completely unnecessary and cruel."

"Cruel?"

"I think so. Why make things harder for Tilda when she's going through a difficult time?"

"Because it's the truth. Shouldn't everyone be truthful in life?"

"Ideally. But what is done is done. That secret is

hers to keep. Confronting Tilda now would mean Rupert would feel betrayed. And it doesn't make any difference to us, does it?"

He held me a little too tightly. My ribs hurt. "She's involved you in this deceit! And you want to protect Tilda? I don't understand." I pulled away from him.

"It's the least I can do for Rachel. Don't you think it's best to let sleeping dogs lie? She's found her mother." He made quote signs with his fingers. "She thinks she's dead. And she doesn't know who her father was. Doesn't ever have to know. And we don't know who he was either, do we? That's much, much easier to handle for her, and for her adoptive parents, don't you think, than to find out that her real mother is alive and well and doesn't want to acknowledge her?" Billy's gaze turned away, toward the lawn. "There's so much wrong in all this. Let's not make it worse."

"I guess you're right."

No. He wasn't right. All these lies and cover-ups. The cost of deception.

We sat silently, taking it in.

"Your poor mother," I said, finally. "And mine. Doubly betrayed."

"Poor Helen."

I sat straight up, spread my hands, raised them palm upward as if in offering. "Mother. For all your suffering. For all your gentleness. You never judged."

"Your mother may or may not have guessed. Maybe their marriage suited her the way it was. You can't know that. No one knows what goes on in someone else's bedroom. Look at us! We kept it under wraps for over a year."

"Yeah. We did. Can you believe it?" I moved

sideways on the bench so I nestled under his armpit. "Kept it under wraps far too long." I raised my face toward his. "I loved you all this time, Billy."

"Yes, you did. Me too. You were always the only one."

I was? My eyes sought his in wonderment. The past few months flashed before me, all the misunderstandings and mistrust. And Billy loved me still. Always had.

His kiss was warm and soft. A gentle breeze carried the sweet scent of grass as the air warmed around us. Across the green lawn, a cherry tree spread its arms wide, clothed in a crinoline of the palest pink blossoms. Renewal. It could happen. Did.

But reconciliation couldn't happen without facing the truth. As painful as it would be for Rachel, she had to know her real origin. And Tilda had to be the one to tell her.

Chapter Thirty-Seven

Billy went back to London, saying he would come up next weekend, and Tilda and I went through our usual routine of her telling me what to do and me obeying like a little puppy. Except now I didn't mind it one bit. An enormous burden had dropped off my shoulders.

On Saturday, Billy came up again, and I met him at the station.

"I've been thinking," I said. "Let's walk to town. I want to show you something." I hauled him along by the hand to the little shop, the sad little bakery no one visited. Not to my great surprise, it was closed. In fact, there was a sign across the dirty window advertising it for rent.

Billy and I stood outside. "Are you thinking what I'm thinking?" he asked.

"It's a bakery—all the equipment must be in there. Needs cleaning and painting. But I'm thinking of something more elegant, a patisserie. Make use of my French pastry training."

"Upstairs?" he turned his gaze upward. The huge windows shone in the morning sun. "Living quarters?" He pulled me toward him.

"Art studio," I said.

"Office."

"Office? Yours?"

"Yes. I can move here, no problem. Rent has to be cheaper than London. If you want to come back here and live with me, that is?" He crushed me closer.

I said, in a muffled voice, "What about my work, my employees, Bethany?"

"Bethany?"

"She's a girl with Down syndrome. I'm teaching her to cook. Mentoring her. It's part of a program to help the disabled get jobs."

"That doesn't sound like the efficient, bottom-line oriented Camilla you've been telling me you've become."

"It's not, is it?" I laughed, disengaging from his arms. "Yes, it is a different focus. I guess I'm not Daddy's daughter for nothing. It's something he taught me, to help other people even if it's hard."

"Yeah. He taught me that, too. I teach football to the kids at the group home. Not that it's a hardship. It's fun. Anyway, it's good you're worried about Bethany. But she's not going to stay forever, and as for the others, all your people can get other jobs, can't they? Your outfit, it has a great reputation. You could give them good references."

"Mmm."

"You can do a lot of good here, you know. There are plenty of needy people."

"I know."

"We can take it slowly, you and me," he said, his hand caressing my hair. "Let's not make a decision about where to live yet. No need for you to abandon your business and America right now. Maybe we can make a go of it there, together. Seems like we have a lot to learn about each other. We just assumed we knew everything because we knew each other when we were kids. But we don't, obviously. So let's pretend we're starting again."

I groaned. "I don't, I really don't want to go back to being a teenager. All that acne and anxiety."

He laughed. "You know, Rachel seems to have disrupted everything. But it doesn't have to be that way. She has her family. She's your niece but not my sister. It shouldn't stop us making our own family. Think of it…you and me…a proper family, with kids. That's the family I want."

He kissed me then, the longest, deepest kiss, there in the middle of the street.

When we came up for air, we heard the passers-by applauding. We grinned back, and Billy hurried me into a nearby pub, where we sat in a dark corner for a few minutes, nibbling at each other's ears.

"Come on," I said, finally, "they'll be waiting."

We needed to get back to Tilda's and Rupert's. Anxiety nagged me, about what I wanted to find out. During the week, between ferrying the girls here and there, doing the shopping, tending to Tilda's endless demands, my sister and I hadn't had time to have The Talk.

That's where I disagreed with Billy. For me, it had been such a relief to find out the truth. I couldn't believe that Tilda, too, would not feel unburdened if she could speak of her inward agony about Rachel—it had to be agony—out loud. After all, Barbara knew now. As for Nora, Lucy, Geoffrey—everybody close to Frederick Fetherwell now suspected what he had concealed all these years.

Our talk had to be private, between us sisters,

alone. So that Saturday afternoon, I suggested that Billy accompany Rupert and the girls to gymnastics. Rupert grumbled—for God's sake, he was the kids' father, he should be used to this!—but I mollified him with the promise of a delicious dinner for the grown-ups in the evening.

Tilda breathed in relief to have the chattering children away from the house for a couple of hours. "While you're cooking, I'll just get some reading done, Camilla," she said. She started to walk off, but I stood in the doorway blocking her way.

"Tilda, I'd like to ask you something, and I know it is going to be difficult. But Billy and I…well, we've decided to see each other more and probably will start to live together soon."

"Goodness, you're coming back? I'm glad. I know you two have been fond of each other."

"Come into the kitchen," I said. "Let's get comfortable."

"All right." She frowned. "You're not going to try to teach me to cook, are you? It's really not my forte. Truly, Rupert and the children are happy with the simple things I make."

"Sit down." I gestured toward the table. "I need to talk about me and Billy. It's become difficult for us. Or rather Rachel has made it difficult for us."

Tilda tottered and collapsed onto a chair. "Rachel?" She brought her hand to her mouth. "Why on earth is that?"

"Let's have a cup of tea, shall we?" I walked to the sink with the kettle, filled it, and placed it on the gas ring. "Well, Rachel says she is Nora Blanchard's daughter, and she doesn't know who her father is."

"True. Well, that's all right, isn't it?"

"No."

"No? Why would that inhibit you and William in any way?"

"Because 'father unknown' doesn't mean she had no father."

"You're talking in riddles."

"Well, you see, I believed that Nora Blanchard's daughter was also the daughter of our father."

"What?" Tilda's eyes went wide and her face white. She held onto the table's edge.

"I believe that Nora and our father were lovers. And if Billy and I were to share a half-sister, I think we can't be together."

"I'm so sorry, Camilla." Tilda's face contorted. She seemed to fight to compose it. The kettle started to shriek.

"Well?"

"What do you mean, 'well'?" Tilda's voice rose like the kettle.

Rage started a slow burn from my toes to my head. Even if it cost me and Billy our future happiness, she wasn't going to admit her part in this. I turned off the flame and turned, my back to the stove, to face her. "Tilda, I think you know what I'm saying."

Tilda looked at me helplessly. "Why on earth do you think Daddy and Nora…? Oh, Camilla, Nora was Daddy's patient. He wouldn't."

"Wouldn't he? You know perfectly well he wasn't as saintly as he purported to be."

Tilda's eyes turned hard. "I don't know where you're getting all this from, Camilla."

"I found a photo of Nora in Daddy's drawer.

Hidden. Geoffrey saw Daddy and Nora holding hands. Nora worked for Dr. Petrovsky. So she may not have been Daddy's patient when they met or maybe she was, but they had a connection outside the consulting room from the very beginning. He was close to her, Tilda. I think he loved her."

"What about poor Mummy?"

"Who knows if she knew? She was so focused on her work. Maybe she didn't pay Daddy much attention. Oh, I don't know!" I gave the tea caddy a sharp shake, remembering all the times I'd let Vincent manage on his own at home while I was catering an event.

"You're not saying that Daddy is Rachel's father?"

"That's the premise I've been laboring under."

Tilda looked at her hands. Silence filled the room as I stood there with the spoon poised over the tea caddy, and Tilda sat glued to the chair.

"Aren't you going to put me out of my misery, Tilda? Your misery, too?"

Tilda looked as if she would faint. She gripped the side of her chair so hard her knuckles whitened. Finally, she whispered, "Nora's child was stillborn. Rachel is not her daughter and not our father's daughter, either."

I let out a long breath. "Yes. I know that."

Tilda would not look at me.

"Are you going to tell me whose daughter she is?" I spoke slowly, trying to keep my voice down. Fury at her obfuscation made me clench my teeth.

"It must have been a clerical error," Tilda said.

"Yes!" I breathed in deep. Then the humor of it hit me. I burst out laughing. "You could say that! Double entendre, Tilda. Someone—a cleric—made a deliberate 'clerical error' to put the wrong name of the mother on

Rachel's birth certificate. Who would that be, do you think?"

Silence.

Tilda and I stared at each other. Neither wanted to make the first move. Finally, she said in a small voice, "Daddy?"

"You tell me."

"I don't want to."

"But if you don't, Billy and I can't have any peace. Rachel has to know her true parentage, at least who her real mother is!"

"Why?" A sniffle.

"Because you owe it to her! For genetic reasons, for one thing. Everyone deserves to know the medical history of their family."

"Oh."

"Tilda." I scooted over to her now and put my arm over her shoulder. I pushed the smooth hair from her brow and settled it behind her ear. "It's the twenty-first century. Rachel needs to know this, and there's really no shame in admitting you had a baby when you were in your first year at university."

"How do you know this?"

"I don't know it. I'm waiting for you to tell me. It matters, Tilda."

Tilda put her face in her hands. Her shoulders shook as small mewling sounds came out. I rubbed her back as the sobs grew louder. Great heaving cries, then, on an on, as I held my arm around her till she stopped.

"I'm going to make us some tea," I said gently. "Then you can tell me how it all happened."

Instead of just sitting there, Tilda stood up and threw her arms around me. My aloof and proper sister actually hugged me! We both cried, then. Her body, thin as a scarecrow's, was frail. She shook as she clasped me. She did not take her eyes off me as I reheated the kettle. The scent of tea exploded from the pot as I poured boiling water into it. I arranged chocolate biscuits in a circle on a plate and set the milk jug on the table.

"I do understand how Daddy would want to protect you," I said. I did not need to point out that Tilda was the golden girl in our father's eyes, the favorite, first-born child.

"I didn't know what to do," Tilda said. "I did some stupid things, my first year away from home. Drunken parties, things like that. After some wild rave, I found myself pregnant. I have no idea who did the deed."

"You don't know who impregnated you? Tilda! That's not like you!" I nearly spilled the tea as I poured her a cup.

"I know. I was such a goody-goody at home. Had to be, I suppose. We all did. Had to hold up the side for Mummy, who was such a role model for all the girls she taught, and for Daddy, of course."

I paused, a teacup in the air. All of us, except perhaps for our mother, concealed our deepest yearnings. Tilda, hiding a baby. Geoffrey hiding that he wanted men, not women, and I—well I had been so shamed for loving Billy that afterward I'd hidden my own feelings even from myself. The pressure to be good spilled over and ended in tears.

"Of course." I laid my cup gently on its saucer. "You can tell me, Tilda."

"I just felt so free when I went away to university. I went wild. Lots of boyfriends, several at the same time, as a matter of fact." Tilda looked at the floor, but a slight smile played about her mouth.

"Oh," I said. This was a side of Tilda I never knew. "In the US we call those hook-ups."

"That's a graphic description. But yes, they were casual encounters."

"Which led to a grave result. I'm so sorry." I bent my head to my sister's, so our cheeks touched.

"I told Mummy, and she wanted me to get an abortion," Tilda said. She pushed the cookie away.

"Why didn't you?"

"Oh, Camilla!" Tilda shook off my hand, which had nestled over hers. "Mummy told Daddy and there was a tremendous ruckus. He didn't approve of that idea, which is natural."

"Since he was a priest."

"I think he was very disappointed in our mother for suggesting it. Not that it was at all unusual. Anyway, Daddy arranged for me to go away for the last trimester to a home run by Anglican nuns who took in girls like me."

"Oh, dear. How was that? Were they mean to you? One hears such awful things."

"That was in earlier times." Tilda turned her face up and smiled. "They were nice, actually, very kind. Unconventional. They were a little loopy. Sort of counter-cultural. They ran a farm. I helped. It made me never want to live on a farm again, mind you, but I did enjoy the hens."

"Hens?"

"Collecting eggs."

I laughed. That's another double entendre. Think about it."

For the first time that afternoon, Tilda laughed too. We slurped our tea, giggling, and made a mess on the plate when we both reached for the cookies at the same time. They crumbled between us and the crumbs spilled onto the tablecloth.

"Go on." I had to know all of it.

"What happened was, Daddy was visiting one afternoon when I went into labor. He took me to the hospital and stayed till after the delivery. I'd already decided on adoption. Daddy asked me if I wanted the child to contact me when she turned eighteen, and I said no. Just no. Very definite I was about that."

Her face fell again. I reached out and patted her arm.

"How painful," I said. "I just cannot imagine."

"I felt so ashamed, you see. I didn't know who the baby's father was, and you can imagine how Daddy reacted to that. He just wanted to block the whole thing out, pretend it never happened."

"Oh. Yes, I see."

"I wasn't in my right head at the time, of course. No inkling that I would miss that baby every day of my life. Forever." She paused and clasped her hand to her breast. Little keening sounds erupted and were stifled, then long, slowing breaths. "When Billy said Rachel had found him, it was all I could do to control myself."

"You never told Rupert?"

"Do you think I should, now?"

"Probably. I know it will be hard, after all this time."

"I want to do the right thing. Now you've uncovered me." She put her hand out toward me, then withdrew it, uncertainty widening her eyes.

"What about the birth certificate? How did it happen that someone else was named as the mother?"

"Daddy came to see me often while I was with the nuns. He told me Nora had given birth and the baby girl had died, and that Nora had died too. He was so sad, Camilla, you have no idea. He actually cried in the visitors' room at the convent. I thought it was just because he lost a patient, but I guess, well, your theory may be right. He and Mummy certainly weren't getting along at that stage."

"And?"

"Well, of course with Daddy being a clergyman, the nuns trusted him completely. Anyway, he told me not to worry, he would put Nora's name on the birth certificate and no one would put two and two together. I was up in Nottingham and Nora died in Cambridge. The baby would be a kind of memorial to her, he said. Some life to come out of so much death. Or words to that effect."

"How sad for him—and for you."

"I never realized you and William would suffer for it."

"We certainly did suffer for it. Daddy was so edgy. I suppose he was remorseful, too. He'd committed fraud, after all, and could lose his license."

"No one found out."

"Luckily."

"Yes. But, of course, there are consequences. It's all my fault. Rachel has been lied to. How will she feel if she learns that her mother never, ever wanted to be found?"

"Oh, Tilda."

"And you." She put her hand over mine and

squeezed it. "You lost William—Billy as he was. I knew Daddy was angry and the fact that no one was ever allowed to mention Billy's name again—it was so extreme. I suppose he was so afraid. I managed to get myself pregnant by being stupid, and I suppose he was terrified you would, too. And the father of that baby would be his lover's son. You can see why that would make him crazed."

Tears flowed down our cheeks, unchecked. Pity, for Rachel, for our father Frederick, for Nora, for our mother Helen, and for ourselves, dribbled into the teacups.

Eventually, Tilda whispered, "It's been good to let it out, finally. But I'm not quite ready to tell Rupert yet, nor Rachel. Would you mind if I wait a while?"

"Rupert and Billy and the girls will be back soon," I said. "Let's start dinner. I'll peel the potatoes. Can you top and tail the beans?"

Tilda looked up, her eyes alight with a shy smile. "She turned out all right, though, didn't she? Rachel, I mean. She's bright and happy. No thanks to me, but I'm proud of her, actually."

I could see she wanted my approval. I did feel sympathetic, but something jiggled, our sisterly roles had turned topsy-turvy.

I could not resist.

"Right." I turned to go into the pantry. I said, "By the way, I think I'd like that pine dresser that was in our old kitchen. It would mean a lot to me."

"It's in the garage. I'll tell Rupert and we'll have it delivered. Whenever you want it and wherever you are."

Perhaps it was this tiny gesture of magnanimity

that gave me pause. Tilda sat there looking so bereft. My moral certainty left me. Why tell Rupert? Why deprive Rachel of the delusion that her mother would have kept her if she could? Was I still looking for revenge? As I retrieved the potatoes from the pantry, my hands shook.

Later, when we'd had dinner, and the girls had been tucked in bed, and Billy and I sat there holding hands, Rupert and Tilda saw he was not going home, he was going to spend the night in the attic room with me.

"As long as you're here," Rupert said, "we may as well read through Frederick's will."

"Shouldn't Geoffrey be here?" I said.

"Ideally. But he and Tilda already have the gist. You've been away, of course."

He took the will from his briefcase and read it aloud. All the Inoculese shares went to Billy, none to us, though we siblings were perfectly well provided for.

Tilda and Rupert smiled at Billy, happy for him. I looked at the floor. The faded Persian carpet poked out from under the table, its uneven seams and worn-thin weave proving its authenticity. Reality. Not pretty. How guilty our father must have felt, to have betrayed our mother—with a patient no less. This was one means of reparation, I supposed.

But then, Rupert produced an envelope, addressed to Billy. Billy looked up with astonishment as Rupert handed it to him, together with a knife from the table.

Billy sliced the seal. Inside a letter. Not to him from Frederick, but a letter from Nora to Frederick. Billy's voice became firmer as he read it aloud.

"Please take these shares, dearest Frederick, in deepest gratitude for the care you have taken of my beloved son. They may be worth something—or nothing—but they're all I have to give. Your friendship has meant a great deal to me, especially over these past months of illness. I have always admired your devotion to your patients, to your family, your kindness, and your integrity. I give you this, with dare I say it, love. Nora."

Billy looked at me for a long time. I stared back, in shock. A blush rose from my breast to my cheeks, and I bowed my head. Shame flooded me, for the months of speculation about Frederick and Nora, about Rachel, about the ruin of my parents' marriage, about my own unworthiness for love. Perhaps Nora and Frederick did love each other but had never actually been lovers. Or perhaps they were lovers, but would not break up our family. Perhaps they'd actually sacrificed their happiness for the sake of others.

All that suffering, hidden. Lies and betrayal and grief. Love caused it all.

Out of the corner of my eye, I saw Tilda rise from her chair. She came over and hugged me, rocking me close.

"Come back to us," she whispered. She reached behind her and pulled Billy into the huddle of our arms. We breathed. I heard Rupert rustling the papers in the background, then the clink of glasses on the silver tray on the sideboard, the tinkle of liquid.

"Brandy," he said. "Don't know what happened just now, but I think we need to drink to it."

Tilda tilted her face to me, her eyes full of trepidation.

"I'm here, it will be all right," I said and kissed her on the cheek. My sister, my lover, and I broke our circle. We turned to hug Rupert, all at once, in the sweet soft glow of the lamplight.

Camilla's Recipes

Camilla's Cullen Skink

Adapted from an old recipe from the Scottish fishing town of Cullen.

Ingredients:

1 ½ pints whole rich milk

1 oz. butter

1 bayleaf

1 lb. undyed smoked haddock (or any smoked white fish)

1 large onion, diced finely

1 leek, washed and thinly sliced

2 large potatoes, diced into quarter inch by half inch cubes.

Method:

Poach the fish and bayleaf in milk, very gently, until fish is cooked through, about five to ten minutes. Turn off the heat and remove fish with slotted spoon and reserve.

In a pan, melt the knob of butter and cook the onions and leeks gently until translucent, add potatoes and sauté until they are golden all over. Then add the potatoes and onion to the milky fish stock. Poach the liquid mixture until potatoes are tender—this could take up to 40 minutes, because the milk should never boil.

In the meantime, as soon as the fish is cool, skin it (skin should lift right off), flake the fish meat, and chill in refrigerator until the rest of the soup is ready.

When potatoes and onions are tender, remove the bay leaf, replace fish into the soup, bring gently to a simmer, and pour into bowls, garnishing with parsley or chives.

Traditional cooks will mash the potatoes to make the soup thick. Camilla finds chunks of potato poking out of the soup with the fish to be more interesting. An option is to mash half the potato to thicken the soup and chunk the rest. This is the most delicious chowder with a wonderful smoky flavor. Serve with crusty bread and a salad for a complete meal.

Camilla's Cornish Fairings

Adapted from a traditional English recipe.
Note: This recipe has no eggs. British golden syrup is available in the USA, most often in stores selling imported foods. Camilla uses an organic ginger syrup from California.

Ingredients:

4 oz. butter
4 oz. light brown cane sugar. Could even use a little less sugar if you like.
3 tbsp. ginger syrup or golden syrup (see note about ginger quantities)
8 oz. plus a little bit more of all-purpose flour
2 tsp. baking soda
2 tsp. baking powder
1 tsp. mixed spice or pumpkin pie spice
1 tsp. cinnamon
½ tsp. salt
1 tsp. ground ginger if using ginger syrup. The traditional recipes call for 3 tsp. if using golden syrup. That's a bit too gingery. Try 2 tsp. Experiment to taste.

Method:

Heat oven to 350 degrees.
Mix up the dry ingredients in a big bowl. Sieve or whisk to bring up the air in the bowl. Meanwhile, heat the stick of butter, the sugar and the syrup in a saucepan until melted.
Pour into the dry ingredients and mix. Then, working quickly with floured hands, shape dough into balls about the size of a walnut. Place on parchment sheets or baking paper on cookie pans. Leave quite

a bit of space between each biscuit as they flatten and spread.

Press the back of a fork into the dough as it rests on the cookie sheet.

Bake for 8 minutes, then if it needs a tad more, move to lower shelf of oven and cook for 2 more minutes.

Remove from oven, carefully bang the pan on the counter—this causes the cookie to crack attractively. (It is not really necessary to do this but the recipe says to.)

Let cool and harden on the parchment in the pan before removing to a parchment paper lined plate to cool completely. These cookies are huge, round and scrumptious. Easy to make, too!

Camilla's Golden Custard

A classic English recipe. It's often poured over fruit pies, or served in little ramekins. Also considered nutritious for children and nursing mothers.

Ingredients:

4 eggs
1 tbsp. cornstarch (cornflour in the UK)
1/4 cup sugar
2 ½ cups milk
1 tsp. vanilla

Method:

In a bowl, mix the cornstarch with the sugar.

Separate the eggs. Save the whites for another use (egg white scrambled eggs, or meringue).

Mix the egg yolks and the cornstarch and sugar mix in a stainless steel bowl and whisk until combined.

In a steel-bottomed saucepan, bring the milk and vanilla to a boil, then remove from the heat, and slowly pour the liquid over the egg mixture, whisking constantly. Pour this mixture back into the saucepan and cook very slowly over low heat. You will need to stir it constantly with a wooden spoon so it thickens but does not turn into scrambled eggs. This is tricky. If you have more time and need to leave the mixture to itself for a few minutes at a time, heat the mixture in the top of a double boiler over a saucepan of simmering water.

To test if it is ready, take up the spoon, which will be covered with custard. Draw a line through the custard on the back of the spoon. If it puddles the custard is not ready, but if there is a clear line, it is done.

Camilla's Chicken Citrus Soup

Chicken soup is good for the flu, and citrus contains vitamin C, which also helps healing. The addition of the zest and juice of a lemon and an orange really adds zing to this soup.

Ingredients:

2 tbsp. olive oil

3 leeks, white parts only, diced

2 white onions, peeled and diced

3 sticks celery, chopped

2 spring onions, diced

1 one lb. package of carrots, peeled and chopped

2 cloves garlic, squeezed

½ a butternut squash, peeled and chopped

1 whole chicken

1 lemon, 1 orange

Rosemary sprigs, parsley, thyme, a bay leaf

2 kettles of water—or 1 gallon

Salt and pepper

Method:

Make the Stock:

In a big Dutch oven, sauté 1 onion, 1 leek, celery, and two cut-up carrots in 1 tsp. oil. Lower the chicken onto the bed of now translucent vegetables.

Add the water and the bay leaf, and bring to a boil. Skim the scum that arises from the chicken fat. Lower the heat and cook gently until the chicken is no longer pink. Turn off the heat, remove the chicken and cool.

When the chicken is cool, take it off the bones. Reserve the best bits of breast for another use within 24 hours, such as a chicken pot pie, or chicken with asparagus in a pasta sauce, or chicken with mushrooms and Marsala. What you want is to keep the less prime bits of the chicken for incorporation into your soup. When removed from the bones, set this meat aside and refrigerate.

Now put the bones back into the stock and heat it again, to infuse the stock with more flavor. Cook for half an hour.

While it is simmering, cut up the rest of the carrots, peel the squash and cut it up into half inch pieces, peel and dice another onion, chop the 2 remaining leeks and green onions, squeeze the garlic, grate the zest of one lemon and one orange. Squeeze the fruits and remove the seeds from the juice. Set all aside in separate containers and refrigerate.

Strain the stock and refrigerate. You want to make it cold enough so that the fat rises to the top and can be skimmed off. This is most important for best flavor. Camilla usually rests it overnight in the fridge. When it has cooled and you have removed the fat from the top, what remains will be a gelled stock, with bits of onion, celery and carrot in it.

Make the Soup:

Now get another Dutch oven or stock pot, and pour in another 1 tbsp. olive oil. Sauté the additional onion, leeks, carrots, and squash. Pour over all the strained stock. Put back into the liquid your chicken pieces, diced. Add the garlic. Add the citrus zest and the juice of the orange and the lemon. Add the rosemary sprig, the thyme, salt and pepper.

Cook gently for 20 minutes. Add a bit of parsley and save more for garnish.

Camilla's Coffee Walnut Cake

This is a classic British cake. You might think the walnuts in the batter would give this cake the texture of a torte, but the addition of buttermilk lightens it, while the rich but low-sugar frosting renders it a truly special cake.

Ingredients:

The Cake:

1 cup shelled walnuts

1 cup sugar, using half cup pale brown sugar (organic cane sugar) and half cup regular white granulated sugar. Mix the sugars together and take out 1 tbsp. and put in another little cup or ramekin and set aside.

1 tbsp. good quality instant espresso coffee.

1 1/3 cups all-purpose flour

2 tsp. baking powder

¼ tsp. baking soda

¼ tsp. salt

½ tsp. ground cinnamon

1 1/4 sticks unsalted butter, (10 oz.) room temperature

4 eggs, room temperature

½ tsp. vanilla extract

1/2 cup buttermilk or substitute 1 tsp. vinegar in the milk and leave for 10 minutes while you organize the rest of your ingredients. (You need the acid to react with the baking soda to create a lift in this recipe.)

The Frosting:

There are many variations on the frosting for coffee-walnut cakes. Many recipes call for a butter-cream icing. Now that is delicious—but the idea of mixing a ratio of 1 cup butter to 4 cups powdered sugar together sets Camilla's teeth on edge. Healthy, not!

Here the fats (butter and cream cheese) are equally balanced by the sugar. Whipping heavy cream will give an almost butter consistency but is easy to spread.

The recipe below calls for cream cheese, a slash or two of sour cream (or yogurt) to soften it, butter, all mixed with coffee granules dissolved in water, vanilla, and heavy cream, then stirred with confectioner's sugar. The big difference between this and most buttercream recipes is that the confectioner's sugar is reduced to a cup. The result is a tangy, coffee flavored frosting to cover our beautiful coffee cake.

4 ½ tsp. instant espresso

1 tbsp. hot water

12 oz. chilled heavy whipping cream

4 oz. cream cheese mixed with 3 tbsp. sour cream or whole milk yogurt (to provide additional tang and to make the cream cheese easier to process)

½ stick (4 oz.) butter, softened

1 cup powdered sugar

½ tsp. vanilla extract

About 16 walnut halves

The Pans:

This cake is a layer cake, so use two or three layers depending on preference.

Butter and flour three 8 ½ pans (the cheap aluminum pans from the supermarket do just fine) or use two 9 inch pans with sides that are 1 ½ inches high.

Method:

Make the Cake:

In the blender or food processor, grate the cup of
walnuts, the kept-aside tablespoon of sugar, and
espresso powder until the nuts are finely ground.

Whisk the flour, baking powder, baking soda, cinnamon
and salt in a medium bowl to blend. Whisking the
flour mixture is important as it aerates it, creating a
lighter crumb.

Now heat your oven to 350 degrees F. while you
prepare the wet ingredients.

In a large bowl, beat the butter until it is smooth.
Gradually add the remaining 3/4 cup sugar and
beat until fluffy. Beat in the eggs, one at a time.

Add the walnut mixture and vanilla and blend gently.

Fold in the flour and the buttermilk alternately, starting
and ending with the flour.

Divide equally among the pans and place in the oven.
Cook for 25-26 minutes or until a skewer comes
out clean.

Remove the cakes from the oven, let cool in the pans
for five minutes, then turn onto racks and cool
completely.

Make the Frosting:

When the cakes are cool, stir the espresso powder into
the hot water in a large bowl. Add the cream
cheese/sour cream mix, butter, sugar, vanilla and
cream. Beat until the filling is thick and forms
swirls. This will only take a minute or two. As
soon as it is thick and creamy, stop beating! Cream
will form butter very quickly, so you want to stop
before that point is reached.

Place the first cake layer, flat side up on a plate. Spread
filling over the cake. Place the second layer, also

upside down, on top, and again spread the filling over it. Place the last layer top side up, and frost. If you use 12 oz. heavy cream you will have enough left over to ice the entire cake around the sides as well.

Place four walnut halves around the top of the cake, then another four and so on, till you have walnuts circling the rim of the cake.

Cover with a cake dome and chill for at least an hour or overnight.

A word about the author...

Margaret Ann Spence, admonished as a child for always having her head in a book, now indulges freely, though she's as likely to read a recipe as a novel.

Born in Australia, she has made the United States home from the age of twenty-three. After living for many years in Boston, she now lives in Phoenix, Arizona, with her husband, tends an unruly garden, cooks, writes, and enjoys her family.

http://www.margaretannspence.com

Thank you for purchasing
this publication of The Wild Rose Press, Inc.

If you enjoyed the story, we would appreciate your
letting others know by leaving a review.

For other wonderful stories,
please visit our on-line bookstore at
www.thewildrosepress.com.

For questions or more information
contact us at
info@thewildrosepress.com.

The Wild Rose Press, Inc.
www.thewildrosepress.com

Stay current with The Wild Rose Press, Inc.

Like us on Facebook

https://www.facebook.com/TheWildRosePress

And Follow us on Twitter
https://twitter.com/WildRosePress